RUNAWAY HALEY

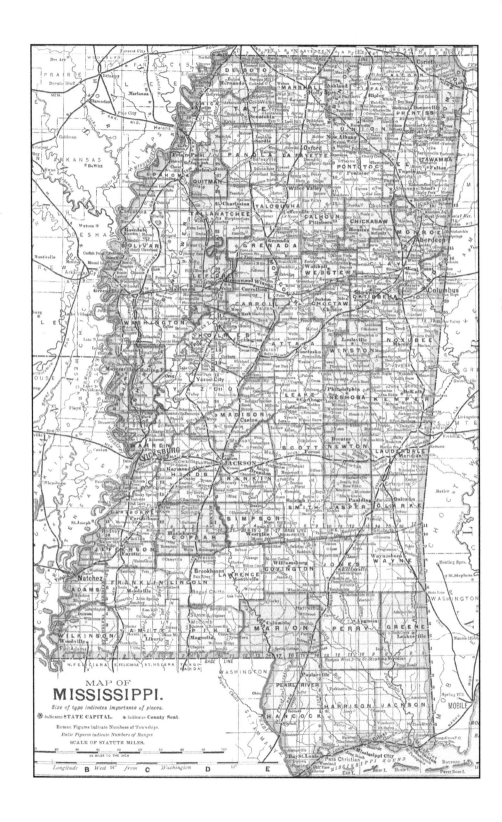

MAP OF
MISSISSIPPI.

Size of type indicates importance of places.

⊕ indicates **STATE CAPITAL.** ⚬ indicates **County Seat.**

Roman Figures indicate Numbers of Townships.
Italic Figures indicate Numbers of Ranges.

SCALE OF STATUTE MILES.

25 MILES TO THE INCH.

Longitude B West 14° from C Washington D

RUNAWAY HALEY

An Imagined Family Saga

WILLIAM A. THOMAS JR.

GREEN ALTAR BOOKS
SHOTWELL PUBLISHING

Published by Green Altar Books, an imprint of

Shotwell Publishing LLC

Post Office Box 2592

Columbia, South Carolina 29202

Cover Photo: Robert L. Haley Family, Carroll County, Mississippi, about 1910. Courtesy of Mrs. Terry R. Jones of Grenada, Mississippi

Cover Design: William Thomas

Frontispiece: Mississippi, The Library Atlas of Modern Geography, Appleton & Co., Buffalo, New York, 1892. Courtesy of David Rumsey Map Collection, www.davidrumsey.com.

ISBN: 978-1-947660-38-0

10 9 8 7 6 5 4 3 2

An Imagined Family Saga

For My Family

Contents

Author's Note

What follows is a work of fiction—my imagined account of the events in the life of Michael Haley, my wife's great-great-grandfather, and his family. During my genealogy research, I collected several interesting primary source documents, but they left me with more questions. A letter written in 1958 finally compelled me to write a story to fill in the gaps.

Thanks to transcripts of documents, newspaper citations, and place names, I was able to accurately establish various times and locations. I also pulled some contemporaries into the story by accessing census reports. Where actual documents are cited, I have included a reference and bound them with flourishes (✦✦✦✦✦); however, with the exception of the aforementioned 1958 letter, I have imagined the correspondence.

Mississippi (detail), The Library Atlas of Modern Geography,
Appleton & Co., Buffalo, New York, 1892.
Courtesy of David Rumsey Map Collection, www.davidrumsey.com.

Prologue

Saturday, January 11, 1958

Jefferson Community, Carroll County, Mississippi

Ruby Lott hurried back from the mailbox in the rain, stepping around muddy puddles on the path to the house. She wiped her shoes on the mat at the back porch and entered to sit at the small kitchen table. After flipping through several pieces of mail, she found the letter she had been hoping for. The unfamiliar handwriting gave her a moment's pause, but the postmark told her this was the reply from her uncle. Ruby had written to him just after Christmas with some questions about her father Robert and his sister Aunt Fannie.

In a couple of weeks, it would be twenty-four years since her father had died. She missed him even more around Christmas, and she recalled with admiration how hard he had worked while taking care of his family over the years. Quiet and strong. Early mornings to the barns, and long hours in the fields with no complaints. She missed him.

Ruby had last seen Aunt Fannie when she had come to visit them in Carrollton in 1927. In Ruby's mind, her aunt never changed. She was the same small size as her father and wore a loose-fitting, simple dress with an apron. And always, those spectacles. She was plucky and quick-witted and fun to be around.

Her father and Fannie clearly enjoyed being together despite their different personalities, but they seemed to share a sadness. They would spend long periods huddled together on the porch, alternatively talking in subdued tones—punctuated by an occasional smile or chuckle—or just sitting, silently. What had they talked about so intently? Whenever anyone tried to engage them in conversation with probing questions, they deftly evaded, always managing to change the topic to recent news from town. Ruby recalled that one of her older sisters had said their grandfather had come from Ireland—named Michael, she thought. They had lived up near Memphis, but Robert and Fannie never talked about their childhood or their parents.

Ruby sliced open the envelope with a table knife and unfolded the single sheet of paper, which revealed the irregular, tremulous handwriting of someone very old.

Perkinston, Miss Route 10

Jan 8, 1958

Dear Ruby

I received your letter and was glad to hear from you. I will try to answer your request about your Dad + Fannie. I don't know to much I think they was borned in Memphis Tennessee . . .

Part I
Michael and Sophronia

Georgia (detail), Map of the United States, Calvin Smith, 1852.
Courtesy of David Rumsey Map Collection, www.davidrumsey.com.

Chapter 1

Tuesday, February 10, 1852

The Federal Union (Milledgeville, Georgia)

A BEAUTIFUL SENTIMENT

John G. Whittier, the Quaker poet, in writing about Irish emigrants among us says: "For myself, I confess I feel sympathy for the Irishman . . . Amid all his apparent gaiety, and natural drollery, the poor emigrant has sad thoughts of the "ould mother of him"—sitting lonely in her solitary cabin by the bog side . . . the new world is forgotten for the moment, blue Killarney and the Liffy sparkle before him—Glandelogue stretches beneath him its dark still mirror—he sees the same evening sunshine rest upon and hallow with nature's blessing the ruins of the seven churches of Ireland's apostolic age—the broken mound of the Druids—and the round towers of the Phoenician sun worshipers, beautiful and mournful recollections of home awakens with him—and the rough and seemingly careless and lighthearted laborer melts into tears.

Tuesday, February 10, 1852

DeKalb County, Georgia

Michael Haley realized that his decision to run off had been a bad one. Hunger gnawed at his gut—something he hadn't noticed until he'd stopped to rest. The baby wasn't crying so much now, but only because she was growing weaker.

In his growing desperation, Michael had no idea what to do. He crept into the back of the cowshed and laid the baby on a pile of straw inside the only empty stall. Despite the smell, the warmth from the cows and the opportunity to lie down for a bit provided relief. The chickens announced their displeasure from the coop at the far end of the barn.

Reaching across the rail of a stall, he squeezed some milk from one of the cow's teats onto a corner of a cloth and let the baby suck on it. It calmed her a little. After several rounds of this, she quieted down some, and he tucked her into the hay between him and the wall for warmth. She finally fell asleep just before dawn. He dozed off, too.

"What you doin' here? Hey! Who's there? You get on outta here now!"

Michael startled awake to hear the surprised voice of a black woman near the door. The light from her lantern illuminated the aisle where his legs and boots stuck out toward the middle of the room. The cows became restless.

"I'm gonna go tell Mista' White if you don' go on now."

"Aye," Michael said, trying to contain his panic. "We'll do ye no harm. We had to rest. 'Tis too cold to stay out. We'll move on in a minute."

His thick Irish accent surely made her more suspicious of him, a stranger in her master's barn, but she took another tentative step forward. "You got sumoddy else in here? Y'all caint stay. Mista' White won't like it. I gotta get eggs for cookin', an' Jesse comin' out soon to milk."

The baby whimpered and stirred.

"You got a baby in here?" Surprise registered in the woman's voice, and she peeked around the end of the stall, tightening her shawl around her shoulders. She lifted the lantern, casting light on the sad, motherless nativity scene. "Oh Lawd, lookee there. Where dat baby's mama? So little."

Michael sat up and hugged the infant to his chest, tightening the thin cloths around the tiny little girl. Again, she started to cry in earnest.

Too exhausted to make for the door, and no longer feeling threatened by the woman he could now see, he slumped against the wall. "She died. Two weeks ago." He started to cry, too, suddenly feeling overwhelmed by all that had happened since then.

The slave woman hung the lamp on a nail inside the stall and set down her basket. She came into full view, her breath visible by the lamplight in the chilly morning air, and took another step forward. "Dat's turrible bad. Where you from? You goin' to your family now?"

"Don't know," he said. "I haven't family here. Been working construction wi' the railroad, but I can't work wi' this baby, can't pay the rent wi' no work." He sniffed and wiped his face with the sleeve of his coat.

She pursed her lips and shook her head slightly. "Turrible bad, Lawd."

Michael's hunger overcame his pride. "I haven't eaten for two days now. I don't suppose you've anything you could share? We'll move on then."

The baby's fussing escalated, and he bounced her gently in a weak attempt at consolation.

"You hol' on right there. I can get you somethin'. We got some meat an' cornbread from last night, but then you gotta go on. Jesse comin' to milk, an' I gotta start the kitchen." She took the lantern and turned to go, leaving the basket. The dancing light faded as she walked toward the door.

As his head cleared, he remembered where he was and how he'd gotten there. The events of the past two weeks seemed like so long ago. It was a dream that had turned into a nightmare: the anticipation and excitement as the baby's arrival neared, a full day of pacing and worry as his wife labored in pain, the relief of finally seeing his first child, the rising panic of the midwife as the bleeding continued unabated, and the warmth draining away from his young wife's body.

He'd borrowed some money from his friend Eamon McGinn to have his wife buried. There was no money for a grave marker, but he promised himself he would get her one, eventually. Mary Tierney, the neighbor upstairs, wet-nursed the baby. When he showed up to work four days later, he'd been let go. A week after that, with no money to pay the rent, he was evicted from their room in the cold, dilapidated two-story tenement that housed the Irish immigrants building the railroads in Atlanta. The landlord had shown no sympathy. He just wanted the rent paid. There was no shortage of men ready to take Michael's job—or of families who needed a place to stay. Eamon lived in a dormitory with twenty other men where children weren't allowed. The five Tierneys' tiny room couldn't possibly hold two more, and Michael couldn't pay them anyway.

After he found his things piled in the street and a padlock on the door to their room, he took a few belongings and started walking—with a baby in his arms, no money, nowhere to go, and no idea what to do. That had been two days ago.

Michael heard the door close at the kitchen up the hill. The spot of light wagged back and forth, getting larger and brighter as the woman returned. He didn't want to, but he knew he had no choice. He wrapped the baby tightly and put some straw in the bottom of the basket.

"I'll come back for you," he whispered, "I promise. *Bí láidir.*" He kissed his baby girl on the forehead before tucking her into the basket. After peering out to make sure the woman was on her way back to the barn, he picked up his sack and disappeared into the night, running back the way he'd come.

～

Near dusk, Michael rounded the corner and approached the door to the bunkhouse in Blackhall.

Eamon sat on the steps eating slices of apple as he cut them with his pocketknife. "What's this now? Where's the baby?"

"I left her with a family till later. Just for a while. I'll go back and get her, to be sure. I just need some money first, and I need to get me job back."

"Our team's going to need a new hand. Charles Mulligan got killed today when some powder blew. Took his arm clean off. Couldn't stop the bleeding."

"Jæsus, Mary, and Joseph!" Michael said.

"I don't know how it happened, but you can have his bed and his things, too, as far as I can see."

Eamon stood to greet Michael and handed him the rest of the apple as they walked into the unlit and unheated dorm. It was nothing more than a big shed with a dirt floor, with rows of beds and a fireplace on either end. It stunk of unwashed laborers. Other men trickled in, only some of whom Michael recognized. Like Michael and Eamon, most of them had left Ireland to find work in America. A low crowd that took work where they could find it, they cleared the land and laid the track to build the rail lines coming into Atlanta. That meant riding out on a railcar with supplies for several days and camping along the way as the construction moved forward. The work was hard, but it paid every week, and they got fed every day. It wasn't the place for family men and wasn't the kind of work folks usually stayed in for the long term.

The rope slings creaked as Michael collapsed onto the bunk across from Eamon's. "Och, I left her with a family by the name of White. They'll keep her until I'm back on my feet. We'll be a family again. I just have to figure out how."

Michael had been through adversity before, but nothing had left him as worried and as sad as this. He thought about his mother and wondered if she'd ever know that she now had a granddaughter here in America.

Sunday, April 18, 1852

Atlanta, Georgia

Michael stood beneath a shade tree, from where he watched the small, square Methodist church on the other side of Peachtree Street. It was a neatly painted wooden structure with plain rectangular windows. A small cupola on the roof over the door bore a painted cross, serving as the only indication that this was a house of worship.

At half past twelve, he saw the family file out of the church. The man, dressed in a suit, donned his hat as soon as they exited. He shook the minister's hand, and the two spoke briefly. Behind him, a woman who appeared to be his wife held a toddler. A younger woman—perhaps his oldest daughter—stepped into the spring sunshine holding a baby. Five other children in stair-step ages—two boys and three girls—ran out to play in the yard.

The family moved to the shade of a large tree beyond the bell tower and approached their wagon, where an elderly black man and a short, heavy black woman waited. The older woman put down the little girl she was holding, and the girl wobbled on her feet, clutching the matron's skirts. The oldest daughter, tall and gangly with brown hair tucked beneath her bonnet, followed. Plain, but not unattractive, she handed the baby in her arms to the slave.

Michael recognized the black woman.

~

Michael told Eamon about the family after they returned to the bunkhouse the next evening. "I think it was his daughter tha' was holding her. She's gotten so big."

Eamon scoffed. "Och! There's lots of babies. How do you know it's her?"

"You'd know your own, don't you think? I can see that she'll look much like her mother, to be sure. There's a resemblance to my little sister, as well. Besides, I saw that slave woman again. 'Twas her, to be certain." Michael was already making plans. "'Twas her. I've got to get her back, but I need some money."

"And what in heaven's name are you going to do then? You can't just take the baby back." Eamon laughed. "We live in a bunkhouse. Gonna bring a baby to work with you swinging a sledgehammer?"

"I need a different job. This work's not for a family man. Never home. Too dangerous. Had two near misses this month, I have. Last week a load of timbers rolled down and nearly killed me, it did. Before that, I could have been crushed between while they coupled the railcars."

"Aye, your head's not been right, and I see you daydreamin' about. You need to put your mind on the work or you'll be fired—if you don't get killed first."

"'Tis only for my baby daughter I been worryin'," Michael said and sat down on the side of his bed. "Thinkin' about her all the time, I am. You just don't know. It's like a part of you is missin'. I've got to get us back together." He removed from under his shirt the leather pouch that hung around his neck and, before untying the lace, surveyed the bunkhouse to see who might be listening or watching. He then pulled out a wad of railroad notes to count. He lowered his voice and whispered, "I got nearly two hundred dollars saved. I'm goin' to figure out how to meet that family next week."

Eamon shook his head. "And then what?"

"I don't know," Michael said. "We'll see." He was determined to get her back. He just had to figure out how.

As he lay in his bunk that night, he had difficulty falling asleep, and when he finally did, he dreamt about both of the families he'd lost: his mother, brothers, and sisters, followed by his wife—God rest her soul—and now their child. He didn't even know his baby's name.

~

On Sunday morning, Michael washed in the bunkhouse basin with cold water, shaved, and put on his cleanest clothes. He ran a comb through his curly hair and inspected himself in the small, broken mirror hanging on the wall. Outdoor work and hard labor had conspired to make him look older than his twenty-nine years, but he was lean, strong, and handsome. *Well now, Michael Haley,* he thought, *ye don't look half-bad.*

Upon arriving at the church on Peachtree Street just as the bell rang the eleven-o'clock hour, he searched for the family from the week before. Worshippers made their way into the building while the drivers and other slaves collected the wagons under the shade of the trees. Michael entered the back of the church and came down the aisle on the far left side. This didn't resemble any church he'd seen before. It looked more like a courtroom and felt practically empty. The ceiling was plain and flat and painted white. No pictures hung from the walls, and no colored panes decorated the windows. The congregation sat on simple, plain benches with a single rail for a back. Hymnbooks hung from racks attached to the back of each pew.

He made his way down a couple of rows and found a seat near the back with a good view. From there he spotted the man and his wife with the whole family, including the children and the two babies, sitting on the other side and toward the front of the church.

Before he took his seat, he genuflected and made the sign of the cross. An old couple sitting at the other end of the pew stared at him, clearly perplexed. Michael didn't know what to do, so he just mimicked the others in the congregation. When they stood to sing, he picked up a hymnbook, too, and pretended to read. Later, the old man at the end of the pew dropped a coin into the collection and handed the basket to his wife, who passed it on to Michael. With no money to spare, Michael held on to the basket for a moment before the usher standing in the aisle leaned over and took it from him.

Eventually, the minister stood at the pulpit to speak. "The scripture for today's sermon is from the book of Exodus, chapter two. Listen to the word of God, and then consider the depths of love a mother has for her child, and even so, how much more the Lord must love us." He picked up his worn black Bible and turned to the passage.

While the minister read the story of baby Moses and the Pharaoh's daughter, Michael kept his eyes glued on the young woman and his baby. After the final hymn, he fell in after the White family as they filed out of the church.

The young woman—apparently the oldest of the family's children—held the baby and shepherded the smaller girls while the bigger boys laughed and punched at each other behind her. She turned around to shush her brothers. "Francis! Luther! Stop that! Father will be cross. Don't fidget. Greet the minister politely. You can play when you're outside." She was tall and rather skinny. Her brown calico dress hung loosely from her shoulders, exaggerating her plain look. No color, bows, lace, or jewelry. She looked rather like a tree.

The baby in her arms—*his* baby—grabbed at the unruly brown hair sticking out from under the young woman's bonnet, and a surge of emotion ran through him.

He smiled brightly and waved his fingers at his little girl. She was close enough to touch. "Well, hello there," he said to his daughter.

The young woman turned and, after making eye contact with Michael, blushed. She smiled as she repositioned the infant on her hip and then turned away to catch up with her parents.

As he stepped outside, Michael squinted in the bright sunlight.

The minister appeared directly in front of him. He was an elderly man wearing a plain white alb over his shirt and pants. He had a blue stole around his neck, which, with the exception of an embroidered cross on one end, was unadorned. "Good morning," he said as he shook Michael's hand with both of his, refusing to let go. "We're glad to see new friends here today. Please tell me your name."

"Michael," he said, glancing over his shoulder at the family, now making their way to the wagon.

"And are you new in Atlanta?"

"Uh, not new, sir," he said, surprised at being detained. "I work for the Macon and Western Railroad. Two years now."

"Well, then, that's very good." The minister smiled and freed one of his hands to adjust the spectacles on the bridge of his nose.

With the children loaded into the back of the wagon, the driver untied the horses from the rail.

"Say, who's that man there in the wagon with all the children?"

"Yes, that would be Mr. James White," the minister replied. "A fine Christian man. Very nice family. He's a farmer and merchant and has a beautiful home south of here."

"And the young woman? The one with the tiny babe?"

"Ah, Sophronia. Lovely girl. Nineteen this year, I believe. Her father's pride and joy, she is."

Michael looked back at the minister. "So her husband wasna wi' her today?"

"Oh, she's not married." The minister shook his head. "Her father hasn't allowed any suitors to call on her." He leaned in toward Michael as if to share a secret. "Much to her dismay."

"So that's not her baby, then?"

The minister scoffed. "Oh, heavens, no. They've so many children I can't be sure, but their youngest daughter is baby Camilla, I believe. Mrs. White took that smaller one in as a ward earlier in the year. Someone left her in their barn. Please tell me your name again."

"Michael Haley."

"Well, Michael, please do come back next week."

"I will, sir. Thank you."

~

A week later, Michael waited until the family entered the church and then approached their driver, who had parked the horse and wagon in the shade. The old black man sat leaning against the tree, and the woman from the barn sat in the back of the wagon. Neither appeared to notice his approach.

"Hello," he said to the driver.

The man looked up, surprised, and then leaned forward to stand.

"Do you work for Mr. White?"

"Yassuh," he said, making it to his feet.

"I understand he has quite a large place. Does he hire any workers?"

The black woman turned to look at Michael. Their eyes met. She studied him and then turned around without speaking.

"Yassuh," the black man said. "He hire some."

The sounds of the congregation singing the first hymn inside the church floated on the mild breeze.

"Thank you," Michael said, backing away a step before turning toward the church.

Once inside, he took a seat unnoticed behind the White family, who filled a whole pew themselves. Mr. White and his wife sat on the end near the center aisle, and Sophronia occupied the outside aisle seat, with the younger children sandwiched in the middle. The youngest two fussed more than they had on the previous Sunday. While Mrs. White waved a rag doll at the toddler as a distraction, Sophronia rested the baby against her shoulder to pat her on the back. Michael's daughter peered out toward him, and he smiled and gave a tiny wave. She looked back inquisitively, stopped crying, and extended an arm past Sophronia's shoulder, making grabbing motions with her hand.

He almost reached back to offer her a finger to hold, but he thought better of it. As he stared into her eyes, he saw the resemblance to her mother and felt his heart ache. He spent the sermon watching his daughter and thinking about his wife. The service was exactly the same as the previous week, as far as Michael could tell.

Sophronia again looked his way and met his eye as they left the church. "Good morning."

"Aye, 'tis a lovely day, indeed," Michael said, smiling at the baby.

When the minister greeted him at the door and called him by name this time, Sophronia appeared to take note.

As the White family climbed into the wagon, Michael took off his hat and approached the head of the family. "G'day, Mr. White, sir."

"Hello, I'm James White," he said from his seat in the wagon, but not offering his hand.

Suddenly keenly aware that he was out of place here at the Methodist church with his accent and appearance, Michael felt his ears burn and his mouth go dry. He glanced at Sophronia and the baby in the back of the wagon and stirred up the courage needed. *Bí láidir. Be strong.* "I'm Michael Haley, I am. I build for the Macon and Western Railroad. I live in the bunkhouse at Blackhall, and I'm lookin' to make a change. If you have a position, I would certainly be most grateful for the opportunity for work. I came from a little farm in Ireland, and I can do most anything that you need."

Mr. White gave him a blank stare. "The slaves have already planted the crop and will be working the fields, so we're adequate through the summer. I do hire some for ginning and getting to market. Picking commences in October if the cotton is ready. Please ask again then." He turned to the black man holding the horses. "Jesse, let's go on now."

At the old slave's encouragement, the horses took a step forward, jostling the family in the back.

Michael followed and added more urgently, "I'm properly handy with construction and repairs, and I'm strong and fit, sir."

Mr. White seemed taken aback by Michael's persistence. He put his hand on Jesse's arm to stop the wagon.

Sophronia, who had been watching from the back, joined the conversation. "Father, didn't you and Nathan discuss bringing on another foreman last week? This just might be the man you're looking for." She glanced at Michael and offered a tight-lipped smile.

Mrs. White leaned over to her and whispered loud enough for Michael to hear, "Sophronia, do comport yourself as a young lady! Business dealings are none of our affair."

Mr. White looked over his shoulder at his daughter, who gazed back at him innocently. "Well, come to the house tomorrow and ask for Nathan, my foreman. If there's something to be done, he'll let you know."

"I will, sir. Thank you."

Jesse clicked his tongue at the horses and snapped the reins. The mares shook their heads and began to pull again. From her bench in the rear of the wagon, Sophronia looked back at Michael as they rolled away.

He gave a small wave and lifted his eyebrows hopefully.

She smiled in return.

The black woman sitting beside her with the small baby in her lap stared at him, stone-faced.

Wednesday, August 25, 1852

Weekly Chronicle & Sentinel (Augusta, Georgia)

A correspondent of the News, who has been traveling through the State, says that the crop of corn is immense, and the cotton crop never gave better promise at this season of the year. He does not think the amount of land planted in cotton is as large as it was last year. All the other crops look well and give promise of an abundant harvest.

Tuesday, October 19, 1852

The Southern Recorder (Milledgeville, Georgia)

COMMERCIAL COTTON—*during the month of September, there were shipped from the Depot in this place 426 bales of the new crop. Within the present month, up to Saturday evening last, 865 more bales have been received—making 1,291 in all. This is exclusive of what has been sent off from Woolsey's Depot, a few miles below this on our road.*

Cotton has commanded as full a price here as at any other point in the up-country. There are several buyers and a plenty of loads. Present prices 9 to 9 ¼.

Cotton.—300 bales sold on Saturday last in Charleston at from 9 ¾ to 10 ⅝.

In Savannah, same day 612 bales were sold. Prices from 9 ¼ to 10 ¼ cents. Largest sales at 9 ¾ cents. In Augusta, prices ranged from 9 ¼ to 9 ¾ cents. In Macon from 8 ½ to 9 ⅛.

SWEET POTATO PIE

Peel your potatoes, wash them clean, slice and stew them in a very little water till quite soft, and nearly dry; then mash them fine, season them with butter, sugar, cream, nutmeg and cinnamon, and when cold, add four beaten eggs and press the pulp through a sieve. Roll out plain or standing paste as for other pies, put a sheet of it over a large buttered patty-pan, and bake it in a moderate oven. Grate loaf sugar over it when done, and send it to table warm or cold, with cream sauce or boiled custard.

Thursday, November 4, 1852

The White Plantation, DeKalb County, Georgia

Jesse guided the two mules around and around in a wide circle, as they pulled the rails to turn an upright pole capped by a large gear. A series of other gears eventually turned a giant wheel running a long leather belt in and out of the side of the small building to power the cotton gin. A dozen slaves brought large baskets of cotton in from the wagons and tossed the bolls into a box on top of the hopper, where whirring reels of combs reached up through slots in the bottom, pulled the cotton fibers below, and left the seeds trapped on top. On the backside of the gin, another slave kept the cotton moving as he pulled the seedless white fluff back into the baskets with a curved stick. The afternoon sun streamed in through the northwest windows to the gin house, glinting off the sweat on the backs and brows of the workers. Cotton fibers and dust hung thick in the air.

Nathan managed the ginning operations, which had the advantage of being done inside, away from potentially bad weather, while Michael directed the work at the baler. There the cotton was pressed by a plank under a giant wooden screw, turned by several other slaves, squeezed into big blocks, wrapped in burlap, and tied with ropes. Finally, four men sunk hooked handles into the sides and pulled the bales out onto waiting wagons.

Michael had been working for Mr. White six days a week now for more than two months. He shared a cabin with Nathan, and they ate the same meal as the White family, taking their supper at a small table in the kitchen house each evening. In addition, he was paid five dollars a week. The work wasn't nearly as hard as swinging hammers and laying the railroad, but he got paid a lot less. He continued to attend the Methodist church on Sunday since it was his only chance each week to see the baby. To make the trek on foot, he left the plantation much earlier than the White family. He didn't want them to pass him on the road.

This week the plantation was busy with ginning the harvest from the third and final picking of the fields. Once the job was finished, Michael wasn't sure if he'd get to stay on with Mr. White.

As it neared lunchtime, he heard a wagon approaching on the road. Mr. White pulled up in the springboard buggy that he used around the farm. He had the shade pulled up to keep the sun off Sophronia, who sat on the bench seat with him, holding the baby. The slave woman sat behind them on the tailgate.

Michael jumped down from the baler platform. "Good morning, sir." He turned to Sophronia. "Good morning, miss."

"Good morning, Michael," Mr. White said. "You've been such a tremendous help with the crop. I came to commend you on the fine job you've done for us over the past two months and to let you know how pleased we are. Nathan said you were a hard worker, and Jesse spoke well of you too."

"Thank you, sir," Michael said. "I have truly appreciated the opportunity, and I have enjoyed the work."

"I'd like you to stay on through the winter with us. We'll have hogs to butcher and get to market in a month or so, and Jesse will need the help. In the spring you can help organize the planting. Would you like that?"

"Oh, indeed, sir, I would be happy to stay. Thank you." Michael restrained himself from jumping with joy, but he was unable to wipe away the big grin on his face.

Mr. White stepped down from the buggy and then turned to assist his daughter.

"Ruth, please hold Katherine," Sophronia said, turning around to hand over the baby. She took her father's hand and lifted the edge of her skirt to step down. As she did, she flashed a smile at Michael, but no one else seemed to notice. "Father, will you show me the cotton gin and tell me about how it works again?" She walked toward the gin house, and her father followed.

Michael could hear them talking with Nathan inside as he watched the black woman bouncing the baby on her lap. She neither met his eye nor spoke.

"How old is the baby?"

"Hmm, Christmas time be 'bout a year now, I 'spect," she said, smoothing the baby's pink smock.

"And her name is Katherine?" Michael asked.

"Yassuh," the woman said. "Das what Miss Sophrony wan' to call her. She pick out de name."

"What's this now? The young lass named her?"

"Yassuh, dis baby foun' in de barn. Mista White say she could stay, so Miss Sophrony keepin' her like it was her own baby."

"Found, you say?"

"Yassuh," she said, finally looking Michael in the eye, unblinking. "You knows that."

So there it is, he thought. *You do remember.* Michael recalled the night in the barn when Ruth's sympathy and kindness had given him this chance to regain his life. *Who has she told?* he wondered. He looked away when he heard Mr. White, Sophronia, and Nathan coming down the steps from the gin house.

"Yes, sir, that will be good," Nathan said. "Michael's a good hand, and we get along just fine."

Michael grinned at him and gave a nod of appreciation.

"Well, then, that settles it," Mr. White said to the men. "There's plenty of work before we have to plant again in the spring. Now that the crop is all in, we'd like both of you to come to dinner on Sunday after church services."

"Yes," Sophronia said, "Ruth is going to make her sweet potato pies, and they are just so delicious!"

"To be sure," Michael said, "that will be very nice. Thank you, sir. Thank you, ma'am."

Sophronia turned to Michael and offered him her gloved hand as she took the step up into the carriage. "Yes, that will be lovely, and we are so looking forward to having you."

Ruth remained expressionless.

~

Sunday couldn't arrive fast enough for Michael. He washed, shaved, and donned his cleanest clothes to attend church, and, as usual, he left early to get there before the family. About a half mile from the church, he heard their wagon behind him. They pulled alongside, and Mr. White had Jesse slow to a stop.

"Good morning, Mr. Haley. Please join us for the rest of the ride." He slid over toward Jesse to sit in the middle of the front bench and make room.

Michael smiled. "I will, sir. I greatly appreciate it." He stepped up to take his seat and looked back at the ladies and the children to greet them. "Good morning, Mrs. White, Miss White," he said, nodding at each of them.

Mrs. White had baby Camilla in her lap, and Ruth held Katherine.

"Good morning, Michael," Sophronia said.

Her mother frowned and said in a hushed voice, "That should be Mr. Haley to you. Remember yourself." To Michael, she said, "Good morning, Mr. Haley."

"Ruth made those sweet potato pies for this afternoon like I told you," Sophronia said. "I know they'll be the most delicious thing you've ever had."

"Well, I've been looking forward to it," he said as the wagon lurched forward, "and I'll enjoy them, to be sure."

When they arrived at church, Ruth held the babies while Michael offered his hand—first to Mrs. White, then to Sophronia— to help them down from the wagon. He'd noticed that Sophronia was always so good with the baby and the other children, and her mischievousness appealed to him. As he watched her with the children this morning, he realized that she was actually pretty in an unpretentious way.

Michael followed the children into the church and again sat in the row behind Mr. White and the family. As in weeks prior, Sophronia sat on the end of the row with Katherine, but when she looked back over her shoulder at Michael, she made an odd face. Then, with no apparent care for how it might seem to anyone else, she got up from her pew and moved back one row to sit beside him. Mr. White turned and gave her a disapproving look, and Mrs. White, going one step further, appeared too shocked to speak. Even Michael stared at her in wide-eyed confusion.

"Well, if you're coming to our house for dinner after church," she explained matter-of-factly, "we can't just have you sitting by yourself during the service." She put the baby in Michael's lap and reached forward to take a hymnal from the rack.

He froze in surprise. It was the first time he'd held his daughter in nearly eleven months. He put her on his knee and bounced her gently, and she smiled up at him. He was thrilled—so thrilled he swallowed hard to keep from crying. He didn't hurry to give Katherine back, but Sophronia retrieved the baby after she found the page for the first song.

After the service, Mr. White insisted that Michael ride back with the family, and they came straight to the house, pulling up to the large two-story plantation home. It was painted white and adorned with green shutters on the front porch windows that matched those on doors of the second-floor balcony. Two black girls came out of the back door to take the babies and the youngest children. Mr. White followed the family into the house and gave his coat and hat to one of the servants, who took Michael's coat, too, before disappearing.

Mr. White motioned for Michael to follow him through the house and out to the chairs on the sunny front porch. The grand home sat on a slight hill and afforded a view down across the fields. The kitchen stood apart from the main house on the left, with the barns farther below. Nathan was there and stood when Mr. White came through the door.

"Good afternoon, Nathan," Mr. White said.

"Good afternoon, sir," he said as a slave girl appeared with pitchers of water and lemonade.

"How was the service?" Mr. White inquired of Nathan.

Nathan went to a different church on Sunday—closer to the plantation and in the opposite direction from the Methodist church. There was a young lady there whose parents he knew—and in whom he was interested.

"Very inspirational."

"And did you get to see the lovely Miss Paula?"

"Yes, also very inspirational," Nathan said.

They chuckled.

In a few minutes, Mrs. White came out to the back porch, and the men all stood.

"Gentlemen, time for dinner."

Following the others, Michael found himself in a large dining room with a side door to an adjoining small pantry, through which he could see the door leading outside to the kitchen.

"Mr. Haley, please come in and take this seat here," Sophronia said, smiling as she indicated a chair next to hers.

Mr. White pulled out the chair and seated his wife, who was glaring at her daughter, and then stood behind his chair at the head of the table while the children took their seats. Sophronia cleared her throat and cut her eyes downward toward her chair, and Michael realized she was directing him to seat her. He did as instructed and, after Mr. White nodded to him, took his own seat.

With everyone in place, Mr. White gave thanks for the food. The children bowed their heads and clasped their hands together, and the four servants stood reverently inside the dining room, heads bowed. After everyone said "Amen," Mr. White sat down in his ladder-backed chair and began passing the serving plates.

Michael had never seen so much food at any one time: four roasted chickens, a large ham, corn, squash, black-eyed peas, sliced tomatoes, cornbread, and a big pile of biscuits to slather with butter and honey. For dessert, Ruth served beautifully browned slices of sweet potato pie topped with freshly whipped cream.

"Mmm," Sophronia said, taking her first bite of the pie. "Didn't I tell you? It just melts in your mouth. Ruth makes the best pies anywhere!"

Michael was shocked to feel Sophronia's foot and lower leg press against his. He could only hope no one had noticed the look of surprise flash across his face. "To be sure, I don't think I've ever had anything so lovely," he said, glancing across the room at Ruth, who gave a hint of a satisfied smile.

After dinner, the children ran off to play while the adults sat at the table and chatted about the cotton crop, the market prices, and the plans for hog butchering next month.

"Mr. Haley," Sophronia said, clearly bored by the business talk and eager to join the conversation, "I've been reading the most interesting novel: *Bleak House*. It's the newest book by Mr. Charles Dickens. He's from England. The story comes in a few chapters at a time, and Father brings me the new issue when he finds it in Atlanta. I've read the first two magazines, up to chapter seven. It does have some mystery. It begins that Miss Esther is being raised in the home of Miss Barbary, who's really her aunt, but Esther doesn't know this and thinks she's her mother . . ."

As he took the last bite of his pie, Michael suddenly became aware of what Sophronia had said. His mouth went dry. He took a swallow of water. *What? Does she know?*

". . . Then after Miss Barbary dies, she later finds out who her real mother is—"

"Oh, Sophronia, don't prattle on about scandalous things, dear," Mrs. White said with a terse tone. "It's just not ladylike. Honestly, I wish you'd never even started that book." She turned to her husband. "James, do look more carefully at what you're bringing home. Surely there are some nicer things for young ladies to read?"

"Well, most everything else seems to have too much in the way of politics." Mr. White eyed his daughter. "None of that is any good either."

"But Daddy, it's the most popular thing now, and I find it so very engaging. I think Mr. Haley might like to read it." She turned to Michael. "Does that sound like something you'd be interested in, Mr. Haley?"

Michael hesitated. "Uh, yes, that would be nice, I think."

"Well, gentlemen," Mr. White said, turning back to Michael and Nathan, "enough of that." He stood. "It's been a good harvest. Thank you for all your hard work. I do hope next year is just as fortunate."

"Indeed," Nathan said as they headed toward the back porch. He shook Mr. White's hand.

"Thank you so much for dinner," Michael said to the ladies. "Truly delicious, indeed."

Sophronia put her hand on Michael's arm as he turned to go. "It's just so lovely to have you visit, Mr. Haley. Do please come again."

Mrs. White's eyebrows shot up for the third time that day.

"Yes," Michael stammered, "thank you. I had a very nice time."

~

After the men left, Mr. White sat at the table, drumming his fingers. Sophronia pressed her hands in her lap, doing her best to look unconcerned and innocent. She saw her mother in the front room peeking out the windows from behind the curtains, watching Nathan and Michael as they departed. When they were out of hearing range, she picked up the front of her skirt and hurried back to the dining room with a stern look on her face. Sophronia's father gave an eye to Ruth, who promptly took the two kitchen girls out the back, shutting the door behind them. He nodded to Sophronia's mother.

"Outrageous behavior!" her mother said in a sharp tone. "Shameful! Proper ladies listen and learn, and they keep their own counsel. They do not speak in such a familiar way to single men—hired help!—much less call them by their first name. Or touch them! I nearly fainted!"

"Mother—"

"Not another word! Such forward talk and behavior do not cast you—or our family—in a good light. I am very disappointed. Don't think for one minute that the help did not notice or that this afternoon will not become the talk out in town within the week. You are to spend the remainder of today and every Sunday for the next month reading your Bible in your room."

Sophronia looked to her father for some defense, but none came. "Yes, ma'am," she said, downcast.

"And no more of those salacious novels!" her mother added with a sniff. "Go. Now."

~

Sophronia slammed the door to her room and threw herself on her bed, burying her face in her pillow. *Mother and Father must never have been young,* she thought. *Things are different now. It's a new time. They have to realize I'm not a baby anymore!*

She moved to her dressing table and stared into the mirror. She was no beauty like some of the others. Her curly hair was unruly at times, and she wasn't buxom, which only exaggerated her skinny frame. She pulled her hair back with a pair of tortoise-shell combs and pinched her cheeks to give them some color.

I have a nice smile, she thought defiantly. *I'm smart and quick-witted, and people do like me. Ladies can do so much more these days. Maybe I don't want just to read and sew and gossip. There's more to see in the world than this silly town!* She imagined all the things she knew she could do if she wanted to—if she had the nerve to try. She thought about Michael and smiled to herself. He was handsome and hardworking—never mind the fact that her parents would never approve of him. *I'm old enough to make decisions for myself. I want to get acquainted with Mr. Michael Haley—and I will!*

～

That evening, Michael lay in his small bed staring at the ceiling, not satisfied with merely seeing his daughter on Sundays. To get his daughter back, not only would he have to provide for her, she'd also need a mother. Before him, it seemed, was the readymade situation he longed for, but he knew he could never be a suitor for Miss White.

Thursday, December 1, 1852

The White Plantation, DeKalb County, Georgia

Sophronia made any excuse for an excursion with the baby and Ruth when she thought it might allow her to run into Michael. She was never permitted to go out unchaperoned, which she hadn't minded before, but now that she was determined to get to know Michael better, the limitation was maddening. She was aware, however, that the lingering glances and quick little smiles that she exchanged with Michael when no one was watching could alert her parents and might cause trouble. She wondered, too, if Ruth had become suspicious. After toiling for a week over the embroidery on a handkerchief, Sophronia had asked Ruth to give it to Michael as a present.

This evening, though, Sophronia had a plan. Mr. White was away in town on business and wouldn't be back until late, so, on the premise that she was still hungry, Sophronia went out to the kitchen to see Ruth while her mother and sisters sat in the parlor after dinner.

"Miss Sophrony, what you need?" Ruth asked with a hint of suspicion. She must have known Sophronia was up to something—Sophronia never came to the kitchen.

"Ruth, is there any more cornbread? Perhaps some more milk before I go to bed?"

"Yas'm. I'll bring some up directly. I'm fixin' supper for Mr. Nathan an' Mr. Michael."

Sophronia feigned innocence. "Oh, are they here?"

A lantern bobbed toward the kitchen as someone came up from the barn in the darkening dusk.

"Yas'm, they come anytime now."

The lantern grew closer.

"Ruth, would you please get some more well water before it gets too dark?"

Ruth turned with a confused look. "I jus' filled all the pitchers in th' house an' don' need no more in th' kitchen." Her eyes narrowed, and she put a hand on her hip.

Sophronia knew she'd been found out.

"Miss Sophrony, I don't think yo' daddy will like all this." The corners of her mouth turned down.

"Oh, Ruthie! You know Father is always just so unreasonable! I am nearly twenty, and all the other girls my age have suitors. Some are even married now! I think he's nice, and I just want to talk to a nice young man without Mother and Father around. You know I've always been a good girl. Ruthie, please?" she pouted.

Ruth took the bucket from the hearth and opened the door, letting in the brisk evening air. She shook her head. "Don't like this, not one bit. I knowed you since you was a baby. Kep' you just like you keepin' little Miss Katherine. You an' me both gon' be in bad trouble." She headed toward the well, in the opposite direction from the barn. When she reached it, she looked back over her shoulder at Sophronia.

Meanwhile, a lone figure crested the last hill just as a second lantern made its appearance below at the barn.

When he arrived, Michael seemed surprised to see Sophronia at the kitchen door. "Well, good evening, Miss White." He looked around.

"Hello, Michael." For the first time ever, they were alone together. "Ruth is up at the well, and I came to get something to eat before bed," she said, explaining the unusual circumstance before he had a chance to ask.

"Oh. Well, then, I'm glad to see you."

"Yes, it's a pleasure to see you, too. I always enjoy seeing you." She smiled and backed into the kitchen, out of sight of both the big house and the well.

Michael looked uncertain, but she motioned to him, and he followed her inside, stopping to stand awkwardly just inside the door.

Smells of the outdoors, of soil and hay—along with tobacco and hard work and the lye soap on his hands—made her want to take a step closer. She moved forward and put her hand on his arm as she looked at his face.

Ruth called to Sophronia, interrupting the moment. She was hurrying toward the door with the water bucket in hand.

Sophronia stepped outside and then glanced back at Michael, who had scrambled to take his place at the table.

Ruth filled the kitchen door and turned her stout body into a formidable barrier between them. She glared at Michael. "I'll get yo' supper in a minute."

Sophronia turned to leave after Ruth gave her the milk and the cornbread.

Ruth followed. "Miss Sophrony, lemme come on back up to th' house with you."

When they reached the porch, Ruth put her hand on Sophronia's arm. They stopped on the lawn.

Sophronia could sense her concern. "Ruth? What's wrong?"

"Miss Sophrony, I got to tell ya."

"What?"

Ruth pursed her lips, and her mouth twisted sideways as she looked back over her shoulder. "R'member we found baby Katherine in the barn las' year?" Ruth hesitated.

"Yes." Sophronia felt a sudden pang of alarm. "Tell me what's wrong." She put a hand on Ruth's elbow and shook it gently.

"Miss Sophrony, dat Michael Haley—he the one lef' her there. I the only one knows dat, 'cept him. An' now you."

Sunday, December 4, 1852

Peachtree Street Methodist Church, Atlanta, Georgia

Sophronia was relieved when they didn't pass Michael on the road on the way to church. She'd been dreading this day. She wanted to see him—she thought about him all the time—but since Ruth had told her about Katherine, she'd felt anger toward him too. She wanted to know more, to talk to him about it, but the farm had been busy with hog butchering the past two days. She didn't want to witness any of that. In the evenings, when she'd considered creating a rendezvous at the kitchen again, waves of anxiety had flooded over her and she'd lost her nerve. She'd paced the floors, hidden in her room, and been short-tempered toward her family.

Sophronia snapped at her younger brothers, who were fidgeting next to her on the bench in the back of the wagon. "Luther! Francis! For goodness sake, stop that!"

Her mother put a hand on her knee and gave her a look of admonishment. "Sophronia dear, patience, please. They're not misbehaving. They're just little boys."

When the family arrived at the church, Ruth held the babies as Jesse and Mr. White helped the ladies down from the wagon.

"Come here for a moment." Sophronia's mother took her by the hand and led her a few feet away from the others. She lowered her voice. "What is wrong with you? You've been acting so cross for the past several days. Your father commented on the stomping around and slamming of doors. It has been very unpleasant for everyone." She leaned in and whispered, "It's not uncommon to feel badly before you have your monthly time, but you mustn't be so disagreeable."

Sophronia yanked her hand from her mother's grasp. "It's not that," she said curtly, and in exasperation turned to go. "Honestly, Mother!"

She took Katherine from Ruth and marched across the lawn, up the steps, and into the church. She glanced at the row where the family usually sat, halfway down the aisle on the right-hand side. When she spotted Michael sitting at the far-right end of the pew behind and gazing out the window, her mouth went dry. She ducked back into the vestibule and waited on her family. Then, as they came down the center aisle together, she sidestepped her father to position herself between him and her mother in the pew, with Katherine nearer the center aisle.

Michael caught her eye, apparently confused and expecting her to sit nearer, but she gave no acknowledgment and spent the entire service staring forward. She held Katherine in her lap, and the baby eventually fell asleep.

Sophronia recalled the panic and excitement when Ruth had arrived in the house on that cold, dark February morning, hollering for the family to come see. She had been the first to pick up the bawling baby from the basket, warming her against her chest and wrapping them both in a blanket to sit by the fire. She'd fed her and held her the whole day. During the year that she'd spent mothering the baby girl, Sophronia had grown to love her, as had the rest of the family.

This is my baby, she thought. A wave of uncertainty washed over her again. *But what about Michael?* She couldn't tell what she felt. The uncomfortable mix of emotions was overwhelming. When they stood to sing the final hymn, she looked back over her right shoulder—but he had gone.

As the family left the church, her father stopped to speak to the minister. Sophronia ducked behind him with the baby in her arms and searched the yard for Michael as she descended the steps. He wasn't there, but she did spot her friend, Anna Hawkins.

"Sophronia!" Anna waved to her with what seemed to be some urgency.

Sophronia came to where her friend was standing and followed her beyond the wagons. "What is it, Anna?"

"You know my brother, Charles?" Anna asked, glancing over her shoulder as they walked.

"Of course. He's so very nice. How is he? Is something wrong?"

"Well, not really, but perhaps you could talk to your father about him."

"Whatever for?"

"He spoke to your father last week when they were at the cotton exchange." Anna stole another glance over her shoulder. "He wants you to accompany him to a Christmas party, and he asked your father first, but Charles says that your father was very short with him. Says he barely got the question out—you know how bashful Charles is—before your father said, 'Most certainly not!' Sophronia, Charles is hopeful that you two can develop a friendship."

"Oh, Anna, I'm so sorry. I hope his feelings weren't too hurt."

"Well, he was upset. He doesn't know what to do. He really would like to take you to the party. I thought that if you mentioned him to your father, and then if Charles asked again next week, that perhaps your father would allow it."

Sophronia heard her father call to her from the wagon, now loaded with the family and ready to depart. She waved to him and then turned back to Anna. "Do tell Charles that I'm so sorry about Father. Tell him that."

"Should he ask again then? Next week?"

Sophronia hugged her friend. "I'll tell you next week," she said and hurried back with Katherine on her hip to where the family was waiting.

She handed the baby to Ruth and then, fuming, glared at her father as he helped her into the wagon. *He might have at least talked to me about it!* She made up her mind during the ride home to take control of her life. *I'm nearly twenty years old! I'm old enough to decide some things for myself!* Over the last five years, she'd been so envious of her friends as the boys started to take an interest in them, but seemingly didn't notice her at all. Other girls her age had been out at debutante balls, and some were even married already. The one thing she worried about— that she'd never shared with another soul—was that she'd be a spinster, like old Miss Weathersby at church. Unattractive. Frequently sitting by herself, painful to have to talk to as she smothered you with questions and boring reminiscences. Such a busybody.

During the next weeks she contrived numerous brief meetings with Michael at various places on the farm. A quick passing on a side porch, out of view, allowed her to hold his hand, unseen for a minute. At church, she sat by him again, just a tiny bit closer than before, and slid her ankle behind his. She made repeat evening visits to the kitchen, with Michael returning a bit early from the barn, and she continued to pressure Ruth to fetch water that wasn't needed.

Wednesday, January 5, 1853

The White Plantation, DeKalb County, Georgia

After he and Sophronia had secretly been meeting for more than a month, Michael decided it was time. He knew he had to tell her the truth if there was to be any hope of a relationship between them. A common laborer who couldn't read courting a daughter of a wealthy planter? Mr. White apparently liked him well enough, but Michael surely wasn't son-in-law material.

Still, he knew he had to tell her. He'd played the conversation over and over in his head, wondering how she'd react, and had finally resigned himself to the fact that he'd have to leave the plantation and his daughter for good.

He waited for Sophronia behind the kitchen. When she arrived, she had the baby on her hip. The happy child had a fist stuck in her mouth and clutched a rag doll with the other hand. She had beautiful gray-blue eyes and curly hair, just like her father.

Sophronia glanced around furtively and then turned and smiled. Michael, however, looked at Katherine sadly before turning toward the barn below.

Sophronia's face fell. She put the baby on the grass. "What's wrong, Michael?"

"Sophronia, there's something I must tell you," he said, turning back to her. "About Katherine."

She didn't seem troubled about what he might say. Katherine took a few wide-legged, wobbly steps on the lawn and then plopped down on her bottom, looking up at Sophronia for reassurance.

"There's something you have to know." Michael looked at his feet, thinking. "I was married before. We met in Macon. Married for nearly two years, we were. She died when the baby was born, and I couldn't work. After a bit, I had no money, then no place to live." He felt tears well up in his eyes as his voice caught in his throat. "And I couldn't feed the baby, and . . . I'm sorry." He looked at Sophronia. She didn't seem angry—in fact, the look on her face showed sympathy.

"Michael, I know it was you who left Katherine in the barn. Ruth told me after that time you came to dinner. I worked out the rest myself."

Michael felt relieved, then embarrassed. "Do your parents know?"

"I don't think so. Surely they would have said something to me if they did."

"Maybe I should tell your father. He likes Katherine. Then I could tell him about us."

"Oh, no. Father thinks I'm far too young to have any gentleman callers, and I don't think that would be good at all. Mother will have him turn you out—and perhaps Katherine too." Sophronia took his rough hands in hers and stared down at them.

Michael suddenly felt self-conscious. He couldn't help noticing how his hands—calloused and cut, unwashed, leathered from work outdoors—contrasted so sharply against the milk-white smoothness of her skin. He was reluctant to suggest the only other possible option.

"I love you," she said, shocking him, "and I want for us three to be a family. We could run off together and get married."

And just like that, she'd made the leap for him. Her confidence cast aside his doubts. He could feel his face brighten. "Oh, and I do so, too. I can make a home for us. I can."

She leaned forward and kissed him on the cheek, and suddenly he was filled with relief and joy at the prospect of a new beginning for him and for Katherine. In a moment though, a new sense of worry and unease crept back in as Michael started trying to figure out how he was going to make this really happen.

Monday, February 28, 1853

The White Plantation, DeKalb County, Georgia

The little lady in the gold-framed cameo brought such fond memories. Carved in relief on the pink shell no bigger than a walnut, her tiny features were rendered in careful detail—even her eyebrows and the waves in her hair. On special occasions, Sophronia wore it around her neck on a matching pink ribbon or pinned it on her dress as a brooch. She fingered the details and remembered the look on her father's face when he had given it to her for her fifteenth birthday. It had been his mother's piece, and Sophronia often thought of how she would give this to her own child someday. Along with this prized possession, she packed a few other pieces of jewelry, seven sets of clothes for herself, then baby things and diapers for Katherine. The ornately colored, oversized bag made from an Oriental rug was full, but she saw her Bible sitting on the table near the window. As bad as it was going to be for her mother when they found out she was gone, if Sophronia left her Bible behind, she couldn't imagine what people would think, so she stuffed it into the bag too. She added even more baby things and diapers, overstuffing the carpet bag, which she then hid between her bed and the wall.

She counted all the money she had and came up with seventeen dollars, mostly in coins, which she had saved over the years in the back of a drawer in her dressing table. She'd never really needed any money, for she'd never actually purchased anything herself. She didn't know how little a sum this was, but she knew they'd need it. Michael had told her he had nearly five hundred dollars saved and seemed certain he could get railroad work out West.

She dozed throughout the night, excited and nervous. Although tempted to tell her parents, she knew they would never approve. Michael was a laborer. He was older than she was. They knew nothing of his family. He was Irish. She could just hear her mother's snooty protests: *"He's not our kind, dear!"*

It was still dark when the tapping of tiny pebbles against the second-story window woke her, but she couldn't see anyone down below. The sash made more noise than she'd anticipated when she lifted it, and she paused momentarily, listening for any sign that she'd awakened someone. She heaved the big bag out the window with some difficulty and was relieved to see Michael step from behind a tree. He waved and then grabbed the bag and hurried it back to the barn.

At breakfast, Sophronia engaged her father with questions to which she already knew the answers. "Father, what will you be doing today?"

"Don't you remember? I'm going to take the train to Milledgeville. Jesse will take me after breakfast. I have business at the Capitol."

"Oh, that's lovely. Will you have time to look for some new books for me while you're there?"

"Yes, I'll do that before the return train in the morning."

"So you'll be staying there tonight?"

"Yes, Jesse and Nathan can manage things here. I should be home for dinner tomorrow evening."

Sophronia thought again about what she was preparing to do. She took in each moment with fondness, cementing the memories of her home and her family in her mind, knowing that it was unlikely that she'd ever be back there again. Waves of nervousness washed over her periodically, but she reassured herself by recalling her anger over the dismissed suitor. *I'm twenty years old, and I should be able to make my own decisions!*

The teacher, Miss Tilghman, arrived just after breakfast and took the older children to the big room upstairs for their lessons. At midday, Ruth fed the little ones in the pantry while the family ate their noon meal in the dining room. In the afternoon, everyone lay down to rest, and most of them slept.

"Mother, I'll help Ruth put the babies down," Sophronia said, rising from the table. "Then I think I'll read in the parlor."

Her mother didn't object.

In the kitchen, Ruth washed the babies' faces and hands and gave little Katherine to Sophronia to hold.

"Ruth," Sophronia said, "put Camilla down upstairs. I'm going to keep Katherine with me and let her sleep in the parlor while I read this afternoon."

Ruth didn't seem to take particular notice of the departure from the usual routine, which she probably chalked up to another of her mistress' whims. Sophronia hadn't dared tell even Ruth about her plans for fear of being found out by her parents—or getting Ruth into trouble.

As soon as she heard Ruth upstairs with Camilla, Sophronia grabbed her hat and a heavy cape for herself, as well as a wrap for the baby, and then quietly sneaked out the front door. Turning right, she kept close to the house to stay out of sight of her mother's window above, and at the corner, she scurried away from the main house to hide behind the kitchen. She paused to calm herself. Then she repositioned Katherine on her hip and set out toward the barn. The long dash was in full sight of the house, and she was worried that she might be seen. She surveyed the barn, searching for a signal, and then raced down the hill. *Where is he?*

Suddenly, she saw Michael peek out from a side door, looking for her. He opened it wider, and she ducked into the dark room, relieved to be out of sight, breathless from running.

Michael took the baby and led her to sit down. "Did anyone see you?"

"I don't think so, but I can't be sure. We need to go on as soon as we can. How will we get to town?"

"My friend Eamon will take us."

She saw their escape waiting for them there: a small wagon already loaded with her large bag and what little Michael owned.

Eamon sat in the driver's seat. "Pleased to meet you, miss. I waited on the road until your da' and his man passed so I wouldn't be seen comin' in. We need to hurry on now before he returns."

She smiled at Eamon. "Pleased to meet you." She turned back to Michael. "Did you get the marriage registration?"

"Aye, Eamon and I went for it earlier in the week. Ready to go then?"

Sophronia hesitated slightly.

"Have you any doubts, love? Are you sure you want to do this?" he said.

She realized that he was giving her a chance to change her mind. A moment of panic gripped her, thinking of her sisters and brothers, of her parents and of Ruth. What would she be giving up? What was there to gain? She became aware of the pause as Katherine squirmed in her arms, and she offered the child over to Michael, who seemed to be holding his breath. She steadied herself internally, thinking of her frustration with her father's maddening control over her social life. *This is my decision. I'm not going to be an old spinster lady.*

"I've never been more certain of anything in my life," she said.

Michael helped Sophronia into the back of the wagon, then passed the baby to her, climbed in, and covered them all with an old quilt. "I can't believe this is happening."

A half-hour later, she heard Eamon call out to a passing wagon on the road. "Well hello again! Lovely day, no?"

Still hidden with Michael under the quilt, with Katherine asleep in the hay, she heard Jesse's familiar voice.

"Yassuh, nice day, shurly is."

After a few more minutes, Eamon called over his shoulder to them. "Looks clear now. You can come out from there."

Sophronia and Michael pulled the quilt from over their heads, and sat with their backs against the side of the wagon.

"Well, Eamon, pleased to meet you again." Sophronia pulled out her hat and shook it off as Michael picked stray bits of straw from her hair. Then she donned the hat and tucked her hair beneath it.

"Pleased to meet you, to be sure," Eamon said. "Happy to have a bit of adventure today."

"Michael hasn't mentioned you before."

"Och, but I've heard much about you, so I have." Eamon smiled over his shoulder at the couple. "You're every bit as lovely as he said, that Michael."

Sophronia turned to Michael, who held Katherine, still asleep, in his lap. "You've never told me about Eamon. How do you know each other?"

"Oh, that's something now. We met in Ireland. Came over together."

"Tell me about that," Sophronia said. "Tell me about your home in Ireland and how you got here. That must have been some adventure."

"Oh, to be sure," Eamon said.

Ireland (detail), Carey's School Atlas, Carey and Lea, Philadelphia, 1825.
Courtesy of David Rumsey Map Collection, www.davidrumsey.com.

Chapter 2

Friday, December 9, 1842

Rural Ireland

The tiny, cold, stone house on the meager strip of land near the river was barely large enough to hold the widow Haley and her six children. The single room had been built with stacked stones, mud-and-manure chinking, and a thatched roof. The lack of windows and a small single door helped the pitiful fire in the corner keep the room warmer but also made the long, dark winters that much worse. The family farmed as subtenants on less than an acre of rocky land, producing just enough to pay the rent. They counted themselves fortunate at the end of each summer if they had even a few extra cabbages and potatoes to sell or trade for a pig to slaughter, but every winter was a challenge to find enough to eat. Their survival depended too much on the weather and the success of their crop, over which they had little control. There was never a way to make enough to get ahead or to buy some land of their own. The past two winters had been especially cold, and they'd gone hungry often. Michael's mother and younger sisters took in mending and laundry to make enough for the family to get by.

After the children had gone to bed, huddled together in the corner under thin bedding, nineteen-year-old Michael watched his mother take a stick from the hearth to light the lamp—a woolen wick sitting in a pool of tallow that filled a carved-out potato. His mother wasn't well. Her back and hands were crippled from arthritis and hard work, and her vision was beginning to fail her. She leaned forward, holding her fingers nearer to the light, and squinted as she tried to thread the needle to start her evening's work.

Michael pulled up the wooden stool to sit next to her and leaned back against the wall. He'd thought it through for weeks now, rehearsing in his head what he was going to say, but he still wasn't sure how his mother would react. For the four years since his father had died, he'd taken on all of the work on their land, including teaching his younger brothers how to plant, keep the animals, and mend the fences. Other than fetching water from the river and collecting fuel for the fire, it was all they'd need to keep the family's tiny enterprise going. Michael had nothing to look forward to here, no hope of breaking free from the cycle of poverty.

"Ma, the boys are big enough now for the chores and the farming here." He hesitated. "I want to look for work. 'Twill be one less mouth to feed here this winter."

His mother put the sewing down in her lap and was quiet for a minute. The shadows and the dim light exaggerated the wear and hardship that fifty years of work and worry had carved into her face. Michael wondered if she'd become angry or cry.

She looked over at him and reached out to put her hand on his. "So restless now, you are. I knew this day would come. You want better from life, and I know you surely willna find it here."

Reassured by her reaction, he let loose his words in a flood. "I could get work at the dock in New Ross. If I worked there, perhaps I could make enough money for us to go to America. A man can make something of himself there. I could learn a trade or maybe even start a business. There's many a ship headed west."

"I know ye have a longing for better," she said. "It wouldna be right for me to keep ye from it. Ye been so strong for us. *Coimeádann an teaghlach tú láidir.*" She repeated the admonition that he'd heard his father say so often before his death, linking family and togetherness as a source strength. "But ye can do more, and ye should."

"Aye, Ma, a strong family keeps you strong, to be sure. You've been strong since Da' passed. The boys wi' be strong, too."

"Ye ha' my blessing. I know ye must go. If we can join ye some day, oh, that wi' be lovely—if not, then 'tis God's will. Whatever happens, God wi' keep ye." The old woman wiped a tear from her cheek. "If your father were here, he'd tell you so the same."

"I'll be strong when I get to America, Ma, and when I've made my way, I'll surely send for you all to come as well."

"When ye go, don't look back. The boys here can help me wi' the garden and the chores, and the girls wi' learn to keep house and surely be good wives someday. Ye needn't worry when ye go, but if ever ye do send for us, we'll come."

As he put his arm around her, she put her head on his shoulder and then wiped the tears from her cheeks. He felt an odd combination of relief, joy, and guilt. Then sadness.

Two days later, while it was still dark outside, he embarked on his new life. After turning his spare pair of pants into a sack by tying the legs together at the bottom and cinching the waist with a cord, he tucked his other clothes inside. He took just one potato, a small knife, and a few coins, leaving everything else in the house for his family. He kissed his two sisters as they slept and ran his hands through his three little brothers' hair and then took off before dawn to make the twenty miles to the city. He wondered if his mother would cry again. If she did, he feared he would lose his nerve to go, so he didn't wake her to say goodbye.

Monday, December 12, 1842

New Ross, Ireland

Finding work wasn't quite so easy as he'd imagined it would be. He was just one of hundreds of other young men who had the same plan to work and save for a trip to America. It seemed that they all looked for work at the dock. Laborers clustered in small groups as ships came in, hoping for a foreman to call for additional hands, and queued in front of warehouses looking at the posted notices that Michael couldn't read. The cold wind bit even harder here near the coast, especially at night, forcing him to wear both of his shirts and both of his pants at the same time under his thin coat.

With barely enough money for food and no place to stay, Michael climbed the hill from the river, looking for a place to bed down for the night. He passed through the graveyard at the ancient church, making his way through a forest of stone crosses—some taller than he was. Beyond the town wall, he crossed a pasture and sneaked into a woodshed behind a house. Someone else already had the same idea.

"Och, come on then," the man tucked into the corner said. "There's room enough. Another body will keep it warmer."

Michael rearranged the split wood to make a place for himself. "Aye, thankful, I am."

Seated against the wall, he rested his arms and head on his knees. His stomach growled, the potato long gone. *I can do this,* he thought. *I just need one bit of good luck.*

~

Michael watched from a short distance as the merchant argued with a ship's captain over a large delivery.

"I'll surely need more men and another two hours if you won't move them any farther," he said with obvious irritation and a tone that approached disdain. The well-dressed elderly man had arrived to find his pile of goods stacked haphazardly on the quay, while all of the day laborers had gone to look for other opportunities after the crewmen had headed to the pub. The load of hardware, housewares, and bolts of cloth needed to get into storage before he transported them for resale to shopkeepers in smaller towns further inland. "My warehouse crew just took their passage, and I haven't replaced them yet." He spoke with an accent that confirmed his education and status.

"That's not for me to worry about," the captain said, "is it then? I just deliver dockside. Sign here for the goods." He set some papers on top of one of the crates, dipped the tip of a quill into a small inkpot, and then held the quill out to the businessman.

The man didn't take the pen. Instead, he picked up the bill of lading and looked back and forth between it and the stack of goods, comparing the list to what he saw in the pile. Finally, he put down the document and signed the page with a scribble.

Michael stepped forward and addressed the man. "Sir, if you please, I've just come to the city and am in need of a position. I'll be happy to assist you if you're hiring," he said, bravely injecting himself into their conversation.

"I can as well," said another young man from behind Michael said. "Strong and able, I am." It seemed he had overheard the conversation, too.

Michael had gray eyes and wavy brown hair. He wasn't very tall, but he was confident in his robust appearance and strong hands, having spent years working outdoors, farming and helping the neighbors. His pants and shirt were well-mended and clean. He tried his best to look earnest and trustworthy, hoping that the man would hire him.

The new man was taller, with red hair and lighter, freckled skin to match. He was lanky and didn't seem as muscular as Michael but appeared healthy, nonetheless. He looked like he could use a bath and a new shirt.

The mariner rolled up the papers and collected the other items from the impromptu desk. "Well, there you have your new crew. I'm sure there's a pint and some hot food waiting for me somewhere now." He strode off, leaving the merchant with his pile of wares.

The merchant studied Michael and this new man. "Well then, I'll need the two of you to mind this shipment. My son is bringing a wagon and a wheelbarrow. The three of you will have to take this load to the warehouse. What are your names?"

"Michael Haley."

"Eamon McGinn," the new man said.

They shook hands with the merchant.

"I'm Robert Cousins. I trade in mercantile goods. My son, William, manages the warehouse. He'll let me know how it goes today. If he approves, then you can hire on and help us move cargo. Can you drive a wagon?"

"Aye, I can," Michael said.

"We have a place in the warehouse where you'll stay, but you have to be in at night to mind the place. I only pay ten shillings a week, and I won't tolerate drink. If we find you drunk, you'll be out. If you steal from me, the police won't be lenient." He narrowed his eyes. "My brother is the constable, you see."

"Surely grateful I am," Eamon said. "You can trust me."

"And I too," Michael added. He turned to see the wagon on its way toward them, rumbling over the cobblestones.

"Ah, here's William now," Mr. Cousins said. "Well then, I'll stop by later to ensure all is well." He turned to leave.

Michael shook hands with Eamon and exchanged glances, feeling pleased with his good fortune. "I just arrived in town. To be sure, I'm going to America first chance I get."

"I've been here for a week with no work and no place to stay, so this is great luck."

"How've you managed? What've you eaten?"

"Och! You use your wits, and move fast," Eamon said evasively. "My ma and pa died, so I'm on my own for the past year. Needin' a job, to be certain, d'na want to land in the workhouse. Terrible place, that. You'll never pay your way out of it once you're in, to be sure, and the poor girls throw in with a bad lot just to get free of it."

They turned to inspect the pile of crates, sacks, and kegs they had found themselves charged with protecting and moving. The huge cargo wagon pulled up, drawn by two large draft horses. In the back were a wheelbarrow and a pile of ropes and poles.

"So you're the new men, are ye?" the driver said skeptically. "Barely men, I'd say."

"I'm nearly twenty, and I'm not afraid of hard work," Michael said and introduced himself. He reached up, took the reins from the driver, and secured the horses to a post.

"I'm William Cousins," the brawny, middle-aged man said as he set the brake and stepped down from the wagon. "My da' said to have a look and see if you'll do."

Eamon introduced himself and offered his hand, and William sized him up as they shook.

"Well, Eamon, bring down that wheelbarrow and load the sacks in it. We'll see if you're stronger than you look. The crates go in along the sides back here." William turned to Michael. "The kegs in between."

They brought down the wheelbarrow, and Eamon struggled to load the heavy sacks of grain. Michael helped William stack the crates in the wagon. Then they arranged the kegs on their sides in the middle, securing the load with ropes crisscrossed over the top and through iron rings on the sides of the wagon.

"The warehouse is up the hill, just six blocks away," William said, climbing back into the driver's seat. "It's up on Barracks Lane."

Michael had no idea where that was and hoped that he and Eamon could last that long pushing the overloaded wheelbarrow behind the wagon.

It took them several hours to unload the cargo and reload the wagon with smaller boxes, crates, and kegs as William read from the list of the next day's deliveries. Out of the wind for the first time in three days, Michael worked up a sweat and took off a layer of his clothing. He couldn't read the markings on the sides of the crates, but as William pointed them out, he started to recognize similarities. If he wasn't sure, he called back while pointing at the crate, "This one?"

"Well, I think you'll do," William said, handing them each a sixpence as they finally finished up the work for the day. "Here's some money to get you started. You'll get paid in full at the end of each week. My room is in the front with the office. At night and on Sunday, one of you has to stay in the warehouse to keep an eye out for crooks. I stay here at night most of the time, but I go home to eat. You can sleep here." He showed them a tiny room in the back of the warehouse, near the door to the alley, that was just big enough for two bunks. "We had a whole family staying in here last year. Five of 'em. Took a long time to work up all the money they needed for their passage to America." He opened the back door and led them out into the alley. "There's a firepot out here to cook if you need. Make sure it's well out when you're done. Privy at the end of the row. Just remember: no drink. And if anything goes missing, it'll be between you and the police. Ye understand?"

"I do, sir," Michael said.

"You can trust us," Eamon added.

They worked six days a week, moving goods from the docks and unloading and reloading for deliveries. Michael and Eamon got by on just enough food as they could manage from the market. They usually only had bread for breakfast but sometimes got meat and potatoes for supper, often buying what was half-bad or left over from the day's sales. Mr. Cousins paid them on Monday morning for the prior week's work. He said it was to help them avoid drinking it on Saturday night, but Michael found himself so exhausted by the end of the week that his boss needn't have worried. Besides, one of them always had to be in the warehouse, so that kept them out of trouble, too.

Weeks turned into months, and Michael and Eamon became friends, working hard and saving just shillings and pence each week.

Tuesday, June 21, 1842

The Quay, New Ross, Ireland

Michael waited for Mr. Cousins' goods to be unloaded from a newly arrived ship. He tied the horses to a post and reclined in the back of the wagon, enjoying the sunshine and the warmth while he kept watch for his employer to come take the delivery.

Nearby, a barque prepared to sail for America with a hundred and thirty passengers and six crew. Loaded with all its provisions for the journey, with all the passengers' luggage and goods and nearly overflowing with people, the ship sat low in the water. The excitement and emotion both on the ship and among the crowd at the dock grew as the time for departure neared. On board, families lined the rail at the top deck. Excited children ran about on the deck, while most of their parents looked apprehensive, waving to those gathered at the dock, many of them crying. Well-wishers called out encouragement.

Someone yelled a reminder. "Write us a letter!"

"We'll send for you!" a young man called to a relative in the crowd.

Passengers who had overpacked found that they had to leave some of their belongings on the dock, and scavengers rummaged through them while the crew pulled the gangplank back from the upper deck. They cast off the last ropes and pushed against the pier posts with long poles as the ship *Hannah* inched away from the dock to start the journey down the canal toward the River Barrow and then to the sea. Michael walked alongside as she slipped away.

Suddenly, a bundle about the size of a hogshead keg flew over the rail from the port side, landing with a thud on the wharf. Michael heard the protests of an unseen woman on board.

"Only get ten cubic feet of stowage," a crewman said gruffly. "You took nearly twice that. Whatever that was, you won't need it on board, and you can replace it when you get to America."

Michael quickly hoisted the bundle onto his shoulder and turned away from the crowd, moving alongside the ship as it crept downstream. He broke into a jog, heading back to town, leaving the others to follow the boat. After ducking down an alley, he doubled back to the horse and wagon, where he pushed the canvas-wrapped bundle under the seat.

After Mr. Cousins arrived to inspect his cargo, Michael wrestled the crates and kegs from the delivery onto the wagon and returned to the warehouse, where William and Eamon helped him unload and sort. When the wagon was almost empty, Michael stashed the bundle in their room and pushed it far back under his bunk.

They finished work at sundown, and Michael and Eamon sat out in the back alley, cooking potatoes and a bit of ham in an iron pot over the fire.

"At the dock today," Michael said, "the ship *Hannah* was departing, and a crewman threw some poor woman's luggage back on the dock. Heard her squawk for a mile, to be sure. Got the bag hid under the bed now. We'll have some new things, I hope. Be needin' some newer shoes soon."

"Maybe I'll get a new frock," Eamon said with a grin.

Michael retrieved the bundle from their room, untied the corners, and unrolled it in the alley. They found a few plain dresses, two books, a Bible, and several pants, shirts, and undergarments meant for much smaller boys. They couldn't wear any of the clothes themselves. However, the items weren't worthless. They'd trade them in the market for meat and potatoes and would be able to eat for at least two weeks on the earnings.

Michael tossed the dresses together onto the cobblestones. When he picked up the third one, its weight surprised him, and when it hit the ground, it gave a decided thud and a clink. "Hey, what's this now?" he asked, retrieving the plain blue dress.

The garment was unexpectedly heavy. He turned it inside out, revealing buttoned pockets sewn into the shirtwaist of the skirt. Inside them, he found six handkerchiefs, each tightly tied around folded bills and stacks of coins! The men grabbed up their belongings, hurried back inside the warehouse, and secured the door before counting out the money on Michael's bunk.

"Nearly seventeen pounds!" Eamon said in amazement. "Surely enough for passage to America!"

"Aye," Michael said. "The best of luck for us." He smiled briefly, but then recalled the scene at the wharf. "But that woman. They'll have troubles now wi' their money lost."

"Nothin' to be done about that now. 'Tis surely a gift from heaven for us."

As he looked at the largest pile of money he'd ever seen in his whole life, Michael thought about his mother. She'd wash and mend all year and still never accumulate a full eight pounds in cash. "Maybe you could go on this summer and I'll wait. This bit here'll keep my whole family set for the winter with some to spare, surely. I'll stay wi' Mr. Cousins and make the passage in the spring."

"Och! We've worked hard—this is what we've been waiting for! Me and you, we're a pair now, said Eamon. "'Twill be easier with one lookin' out for the other."

After a moment Michael nodded in agreement, and they tied the funds back into one of the handkerchiefs.

WILLIAM GRAVES & SON

The Quay, New Ross

PASSENGERS' CONTRACT TICKET

*Ship Dunbrody of 458 tons register
burthen, to sail from New Ross*

For Savannah on the 22d day of September1843

I engage that the Parties herein named shall be provided with a Steerage Passage to Savannah in the Ship Dunbrody with not less than 10 cubic feet for Luggage for each Statute adult, for the sum of £ 8.50 including Head Money, if any; at the place of landing, and every other charge; and I hereby acknowledge to have received the sum of £ 17.00 in full payment.

Water and Provisions, according to the annexed scale, will be supplied by the Ship as required by law, and also fires, and suitable hearths for cooking. Bedding and utensils for eating and drinking must be provided by the Passengers.

Signature, William Graves   Date, August 19, 1843

SCALE OF PROVISIONS AND WATER THAT WILL BE SUPPLIED TO EACH ADULT BY THE SHIP.

(Per Week, Issued not less often than twice a week)

3½ lb. of Biscuit; 3½ lb. in all of Flour, Oatmeal, or Rice, or a proportionate quantity of Potatos, (5lb. of Potatos being computed as equal to 1lb. of other articles above enumerated)

3 quarts of Water per day

NAMES	Ages
Michael Haley	20
Eamon McGinn	21

Friday, September 22, 1843

The Dunbrody, The Quay, New Ross, Ireland

Since they didn't have as much luggage as the other passengers—and had no children to mind—Michael and Eamon scrambled into the midship deck to claim their space first. The unfriendly crew pointed them down the steep ladder into the steerage compartment. The loading of freight and boxed cargo had been completed yesterday, leaving the lower section of the ship full. Deep in the hold, crates, large luggage, kegs, and boxes formed walls—so tightly packed that nothing was accessible. Stores of water and food were filled in afterward and kept closer to the entrances.

Michael pointed to a bunk near the hatch. "Let's take this top bunk here. Better air, to be sure." He set his wooden bucket on the floor and tossed his bag onto the bunk. Then, stepping on the bench fastened to the floor by the narrow table in the middle of the room, he climbed up after it.

"Aye," Eamon said, "and close to the middle. The hands said midship is better. Less of the motion as the ship rocks." He passed Michael's bucket up to him, then his own. One was half-filled with salted fish wrapped in layers of paper and covered with small potatoes. The other had salted pork arranged similarly. He threw his bundle up onto the shelf and climbed in.

They turned around with their feet to the wall and lay on their stomachs on the thin, straw-stuffed mats. It had evidently been a long time since they'd been changed or washed, Michael thought. They smelled sour.

Over the course of the morning, the rest of the passengers crowded the between deck. Amid a maze of luggage and bundles, scores of passengers arranged belongings into tiny living spaces. Stacks of deep shelves along the hull were sectioned off for families. Mothers draped skirts and blankets over ropes tied between the beams to create a bit of privacy. It was already uncomfortably warm, and the stale air smelled like a barn. Aside from the main hatch, four portholes in the ceiling served as the only source of light for the entire midship deck.

One of the crewmen came through barking orders, knocking on the uprights with a belaying pin to punctuate his directions. "Four to a berth. Fill in. There's no extra space." Behind him, a middle-aged man made his way down the narrow, unlit passageway. "You there. If you can climb up to this berth, that makes three here." The crewman pointed to the space where Michael and Eamon sat watching their fellow passengers work their way into the compartment. He leaned over and peered in on the family of six overflowing the berth below. They were piled on top of one another with all their belongings. "Put the biggest boy up here," he said to the father, tapping the pin on the beam above them.

A boy of about ten, as agile as a monkey climbing a tree, eagerly scrambled in with them from below.

The middle-aged man, meanwhile, reached the bunk and looked up at Eamon. "You mind?" He hoisted his belongings up to the rail.

"Not at all." Eamon grabbed the bundle and pushed it back to the wall.

The man stepped on the bench and pulled himself up into the berth, though not nearly as easily as the others had done. He worked his way up to sitting. The underside of the flooring of the main deck was just above them, and the space was enough for Michael to sit upright. Eamon had to hunker over.

Michael shook hands with the new man, who looked old enough to be his father. He didn't appear to be well-off—if he had been, he wouldn't have been in steerage—but he didn't look like a laborer, either.

"I'm Michael Haley."

Eamon did the same. "Eamon McGinn."

"I'm James Kines."

"Saw you in town last week," Michael said, "at the ticket office."

"Aye. What are you going to do in America then?"

Michael shrugged. "Don't know. Grew up farming, I did. I'll find some work, to be sure. Need to save and send for me ma and brothers and sisters. And you? What will you do?"

"Don't know, either, but I can't stay here anymore. Sometimes it gets to be too much, and you've just got to go."

The man's answer left Michael with more questions.

"Awright, awright!" The crewman beat the club on the table for quiet. The chatter stopped, and the occupants of the berths peered out at him. Even the babies stopped crying.

"We'll sail in two hours." The bearded seaman was enormous. His head nearly touched the ceiling, and his broad shoulders filled the entire space as he paced the aisle. "Listen up! Here's the rules. First and foremost, all passengers will obey the orders of Captain James Smith and the crew. On the top deck, you will not speak to the man at the helm. No passengers in the crew's cabins, and crew members will not come on the passenger deck except for work. All your gear should be secured to the walls. If you don't know why, you'll figure it out soon enough." He paced as he continued bellowing. "Fire on the top deck stove lit at six in the morning in fair weather. Rations for water and dry goods handed out Tuesdays and Saturdays at seven. Be up by then if you want your food. Ladies will organize themselves to cook for their families and must keep clean. No cooking or smoking below decks." He knocked his club on one of the vertical beams toward the middle of the room, indicating where the lantern hung over the table. "The lantern is only lit at dusk, weather permitting, and is put out at ten o'clock. Air out the bedding each week on the main deck when the weather is good. Keep the midship clean. There's a mop under the ladder. If you don't know why, you'll figure it out soon enough.

He pointed at a collection of buckets in the corner. "Down below, use those for *leithris,* up top, the head for steerage passengers is on the main deck, forward—one on the port side, and one on the starboard. Mind the little ones, as it drops straight down to the water, and only use the one that is leeward. If you don't know why—"

"You'll figure it out soon enough," Eamon said.

The seaman wheeled around. He took a step over to the bunk and poked the end of the club at Eamon's chest. "I think I just heard you volunteer to scrub out the buckets."

Even in the dim light, Michael could see Eamon's face turn red.

Saturday, October 21, 1843

The Atlantic Ocean

It was completely black in the compartment, the hatch and the portholes having been sealed for the storm. Light had been replaced by the sounds of retching and the stench of vomit. The ship pitched back and forth—not rolling in a rhythm but jerking suddenly, violently, in random directions. Babies and children cried. Grown men called out to God and called for their mothers. Women screamed at random intervals, their cries louder than even the howling of the wind.

He'd lost track of the time, but Michael figured this was at least the second day of the storm. They hadn't had rations, but one of the crew had come down to extract single ladles full of water from a keg in the hold and pour them into whatever bucket was offered to him. Moisture dripped intermittently from the timber over Michael's head. Initially, this had been an annoyance, but now he realized it was a blessing. He pressed his face up against the ceiling in just the right spot to collect the drops in his mouth. The mixture of seawater and rainwater took the edge off the bile in his throat.

Michael lay on his side next to Eamon and braced one hand against the floorboards above him, hugging the upright that supported their shelf with his other arm while pressing his feet against the wall of the hull. Under his fingers, he could feel letters that had been scratched into the wood by someone before him. Mr. Kines had told him it was an *R* and a *D*. He had been looking at those letters every day for the past month. *Maybe I'll take lessons and learn my letters.* He passed the time by imagining who had carved them. *What happened to him? Where did he come from? Where did he go? Did he have to endure this too?*

Saturday, November 4, 1843

Savannah, Georgia

The *Dunbrody* sailed slowly into the harbor at first morning light after sitting offshore overnight. The passengers—two hundred strong crammed below deck—had been at sea for six weeks. Six hot weeks of crowded conditions and foul odors. Six weeks of seasickness and no privacy. Six weeks of boredom and worry. Six weeks of cold meat and boiled potatoes.

Weary from the journey and ready to begin his new life, Michael stood with Eamon and gazed out over the rail as they approached the harbor. Other passengers crowded the top deck, each wrangling for a view of the shore. He couldn't believe all the changes he'd made in his life during the past year.

Tuesday, April 18, 1848
The Southern Recorder (Milledgeville, Georgia)

*Signature of the Cross—The mark which persons who
are unable to write are required to make instead of their
signature is in the form of a cross and this practice having
formerly been followed by Kings and nobles, is constantly
referred to as an instance of the deplorable ignorance of
ancient times. This signature is not however, invariably a
proof of such ignorance. Anciently, the use of this mark was
not confined to illiterate persons, for among the Saxons
the mark of the cross, as an attestation of the good faith
of the person signing, was required to be attached to the
signature of those who could write, as well as to stand in
the place of the signature of those who could not write . . .*

Saturday, August 19, 1848

Bibb County, Georgia

Michael spotted thunderclouds in the distance darkening the horizon. They rolled in as the afternoon wore on, and when the heat and humidity made the air so heavy it couldn't hold water any longer, raindrops began to splatter the ground. The whistle from down the tracks signaled a halt to work for the day, prompting the men to put away tools and supplies and head back toward camp.

Michael didn't mind getting wet, for it meant a respite from swinging a hammer, dragging ties, or pulling rails. Eamon worked on the logging-and-clearing crew nearly a mile forward of where the track was being laid, and between them, a third team prepared and leveled the bed for the track. The steam engine followed on the new rails, bringing forward the long steel beams and crossties for the construction as well as the food and water and supplies for the crew. The big black machine with a funnel-shaped smokestack always had a fire going and was the center of camp every night. This new leg of the Southwestern Railroad, which crept forward up to a quarter mile per day and would soon connect Macon to the city of Oglethorpe, was destined to reach Mobile eventually.

Michael and Eamon queued for a dinner plate, each receiving a single ladleful of hominy and venison from a huge pot manned by an enormous black man who'd been cooking all afternoon. They sat under the shelter of their tent to eat.

"Five years now thi' summer." Michael wiped the edge of his tin plate with his finger and stuck it in his mouth to get the last bit of gravy. "Did ye ask th' foreman about going to th' courthouse?"

"Aye," Eamon said. "Said I could have a day. Need to go on Sunday, do business on Monday. Back that night. Heard any more about what will happen? What will we have to pay?"

"No, no costs. You have to tell about yourself and have a witness so they know you're being truthful."

They started out the next morning with bedrolls and two days' worth of food, walking along the tracks they themselves had built toward Macon. They made camp in a field outside of town under a lean-to.

Bugs, heat, and excitement kept Michael awake despite his fatigue.

"Will they let us in?" he asked when he realized Eamon, too, was still awake. "Some folks don' like Irish."

"We aren't the first, and we won't be the last Irishmen, to be sure. Five years' hard work and no wrongdoings. We'll be fine. Go to sleep."

"'Tis been a long time, but worth it, I'd say. When I'm a citizen and have some money, I'll go back and get Ma and my brothers if they want to come."

Eamon snored softly.

~

After rising with the sun, the men walked to the square and climbed the steps of the large brick courthouse building. They inquired at the first office they found near the lobby.

"G'day," Michael removed his hat. "Here for the court to declare for citizenship, we are," he said proudly.

The clerk behind the desk looked askance at their workers' clothes, unkempt hair, and obviously humble station. The sour look on his face suggested he had noticed Michael's Irish accent.

"Follow me." He led them out another door, down a corridor, and into a courtroom already half-full of all sorts of people. "Talk to him." He pointed at one of the scribes seated at the tables along the wall and departed abruptly.

"Next." A bespectacled man turned to a fresh page in a large leather-bound book.

Less confident than before, Michael approached with subdued eagerness. "Good morning. We're here to declare for citizenship?"

The man didn't look up. "Have you lived in America for at least five years?"

"Aye, I have, sir."

"Print your name, where you're from, and when and how you arrived in America." He pushed a square of paper and a stub of a pencil across the table.

"Well, you see 'tis a bit of a problem," Michael said sheepishly.

The scribe retrieved the paper. "Tell me," he said, now irritated, "and I'll write it."

"I'm Michael Haley. Born in Ireland in 1823, and I'm twenty-five years old. We came to Savannah in 1843 on the *Dunbrody*."

"How do you spell your last name?"

"The regular way, to be certain," Michael said.

The clerk made an exasperated face. "H-E-A-L-E-Y?"

"Aye, if that's the regular way."

"And the names of your two witnesses?" he asked, writing intently and not looking up.

"Eamon McGinn and . . . um . . ." Michael turned to Eamon, surprised. He hadn't known they would have to have two witnesses. He had thought they could vouch for each other. He looked past Eamon's shoulder, and his eyes met those of another man who was standing by himself and had clearly overheard the conversation.

"And Andrew Wilson," the man said with a British accent.

Eamon turned around, and the three men exchanged glances.

The clerk eyed the group with mild suspicion and then took the same information from Eamon and from Andrew, with each of them serving as a witness for the other two. The clerk pulled out his pocket watch. "Judge will be here in one hour. Court will begin then. Don't be late." He looked past them and called forward the next man in line.

They returned in plenty of time and took seats in the back of the courthouse on long, dark benches, worn shiny and smooth from years of use. As the seats filled up, they found themselves closer together and eventually sat shoulder to shoulder when the courtroom reached its capacity. The still air intensified the heat.

"All rise," called out a voice. "Court is in session with Honorable Judge John Henry Akins presiding."

Chairs scraped the floor as the men seated at the tables near the front of the room stood, and the crowd in the pews behind them noisily worked their way to their feet.

A short man in a black robe entered the courtroom. He wore a thick beard and had dark curly hair, combed straight back. Squinting slightly, he studied the audience before climbing the steps to the elevated desk at the front of the room, where he took his seat facing the crowd. "Be seated," he said, to no one in particular.

The people settled back into their seats.

Judge Akins shuffled papers and gestured to a clerk, who brought one of the large ledgers, opened it, and pointed out the first issue of the day. The court session proceeded through a variety of cases, each called out by the clerk, prompting one or two people to rise and come forward to stand in front of the judge. Most concerns seemed to be quickly resolved with minimal chatter. The clerk documented the decisions in the big book, which he then passed to the judge, who finalized the matter with his signature and blotted the page before turning to the next case.

As the hours passed, the room gradually started to empty, allowing those remaining to spread out a bit more. Michael's stomach growled, and he nibbled on a heel of bread—the last of the food that he'd had tucked inside his knapsack. His eyelids drooped. Eventually, he heard the clerk call his name.

"Michael Haley, an Irishman, here to declare for citizenship." The clerk looked back at the group of men and waved them forward.

Michael and the other immigrants rose and approached the judge, who reviewed the entry in the court record, with the details now documented in a compact cursive handwriting.

The judge looked up to inspect the men. "Which one of you is Michael Haley?"

"I am, indeed, sir," Michael said, stepping forward.

"And you're from Ireland?"

"I am, sir."

"So you are a subject of Queen Victoria?"

"I am, sir."

"Do you have a title of nobility?" the judge asked with a hint of a good-natured smile. "Because if you do, you'll have to renounce it to become a citizen of the United States."

"Oh, wouldn't that be something now." Michael chuckled. "I don't, sir."

"And you've been in America for five years now?"

"I have, sir."

"And how do you make your living?" Judge Akins asked.

"I work on the railroad," Michael said. "Building the line to Oglethorpe."

The judge looked at Eamon and Andrew and then asked them about Michael's good character. "Does he have a family here? Does he indeed have a job? Does he drink too much?" Turning back to Michael, the judge finally said, "Michael Haley, do you intend to be an honorable citizen of the United States, and will you renounce your allegiance to Ireland and England and to Queen Victoria?"

"I will, sir."

"Then your request is approved. It'll be documented here at the courthouse. Come back to the court in three years to be examined again and swear an oath for citizenship." The judge passed the ledger to the clerk, who laid it out on a table.

Michael took the pen and made an X where the clerk pointed.

The clerk signed his name and passed the book back to the judge, who made his final signature of approval for the court's action. They repeated the sequence for Eamon and then Andrew, each of them vouching for someone he'd never met before—in Andrew's case, *two* people.

"Thank you, sir," Michael said when they finished.

"Gentlemen, do what's right in the eyes of the Lord. Do good and you'll do well," Judge Akins said. We'll see you here again at court in three years' time. Good luck."

"To be sure, sir," Michael said. "Thank you, sir, but I'm less countin' on luck and more countin' on hard work."

"True enough,' the judge agreed. "True enough."

They left through the swinging banister gate separating the gallery from the front of the court, and as they exited through the main door, Michael heard the clerk call the names for the next case.

Once outside on the lawn, Michael exchanged grins with the other two men. He turned to Andrew and offered his hand. "Well, thank you very much."

"And thanks to you both." Andrew accepted Michael's handshake. "Farewell, then."

"Aye, and to you as well," Eamon said.

Michael and Eamon turned and started south toward the railroad for their afternoon trek back to the steam engine.

Chapter 3

Georgia, DeKalb County:

To any minister of the Gospel, Judge, Justice of the Inferior Court or Justice of the peace, you are hereby authorized to join Michael Haley + Sophronia White in the holy State of Matrimony according to the Constitution and the laws of the State and for so doing this shall be your sufficient license, given under my hand and seal this 21st day of Feb'y 1852 (sic)

Allen Johnson, C. Co

Georgia, DeKalb County:

I do certify that Michael Haley and Miss Sophrona (sic) White were duly joined in matrimony by me this 29th (sic) day of February 1853

John J. Fain. J.P.

Tuesday, February 29, 1853

Atlanta, Georgia

The doorman of the Trout House Hotel welcomed Sophronia and Michael into the lobby, smiling warmly.

A smartly dressed gentleman in a dark jacket with an ascot at his neck greeted them at the reception desk. "Good evening. Welcome to the Trout House."

Sophronia, confident and excited, marched to the desk. "We'd like a room for the night. We're taking the train out tomorrow morning for Chattanooga."

Michael glanced at their surroundings as they approached the desk. He seemed a bit uncertain about staying in such a fancy place.

"Wonderful. One room and two for dinner?" The receptionist smiled at the baby in Sophronia's arms as he slid a card across the desk to Michael. "Please provide this information for our register and then sign here in our guestbook." He gestured to the leather-bound ledger open on the desk and then turned to a large pigeon-hole cabinet against the back wall, where keys hung on hooks over each vacant room.

Michael didn't move.

Without hesitating, Sophronia handed him the baby and stepped forward to pick up the quill from the writing set and dip the nib into the inkwell. On their registration card, she wrote *Mr. and Mrs. Michael Haley, infant Katherine Haley.* For their place of residence: *Whitehall, Atlanta, Georgia.* In the guest book, she wrote simply, *Mr. Haley.*

She replaced the quill and glanced over at Michael, who still looked uncomfortable. "Don't worry," she whispered. "I can teach you."

The desk clerk returned and smiled at them. "We have a lovely corner room at the top of the stairs on the left for you."

He gave the key to the young man in a red waistcoat who had appeared behind them.

The bellboy took the large bag and asked them to follow him up the stairs to the second floor, where he opened the door to their room. He put the bag at the foot of the bed and then pulled back the floor-to-ceiling curtains, letting in the light from the setting sun. "Dinner is at half past six," he said, handing Michael the key.

The pleasantly appointed room had printed wall coverings, wide, darkly stained baseboards and window casings, a wrought-iron double bed, an armoire, and a bedside table with a lamp. In the corner, Michael inspected a porcelain basin with a tap handle, seemingly impressed by the flow of water that appeared when he turned the knob.

Sophronia opened the door to a small room containing a toilet. "Look at this." She shifted the baby to the other hip and, with her free hand, pulled the chain on the lever connected to the white porcelain box that hung high on the wall. Water poured down through a pipe into the basin below and then disappeared with a gurgle.

"What's this now?"

"It's an indoor privy," she said. "The water washes everything down."

"Well, I'll be."

"It's quite modern. The newspaper advertises that many new hotels have them."

The baby started crying.

Sophronia pulled a rag doll from the carpet bag and waved it at her, but Katherine wasn't comforted or distracted by the toy. "She's hungry. Let's go to the kitchen to see if they have anything to feed her."

Downstairs, Michael asked the bellman to direct them to the kitchen. The cooks hurried about, busily preparing dinner, but one of the women happily mashed a spoonful of peas and some milk in a dish and cut a corner of the freshly baked cornbread for the baby. Katherine ate hungrily.

"Sho a swee' baby." The smiling cook clearly enjoyed watching Sophronia feed her. "How ol' she be?"

"She was one year in January," Michael said.

"Sho is swee'," the woman said, returning to attend to the stove.

When they came back to the room, Sophronia changed into fresh clothes. For their honeymoon dinner, she chose a dress that she was certain Michael had never seen before. He did seem pleased and impressed when she stepped out from behind the changing screen. The green patterned silk, the bustle, and the fitted waist made the most of her subtle curves. The gold cameo brooch at her neck gave her an air of maturity and sophistication. Next, she fixed her hair differently by pinning it with decorated combs. The effect, she decided after studying herself in the mirror, was quite lovely.

When Sophronia entered the dining room, she felt the eyes of the waiters and other patrons as they took notice. Michael, carrying the baby, followed her to a private area between a window and the fireplace, where they had their dinner presented on beautiful white china plates with delicate flowers on the rims. Katherine sat on Michael's lap as Sophronia cut tiny bits of roast beef and potatoes for her. They marveled at the delicious almond cake served for dessert.

"Our first dinner together as a family," Sophronia said.

"Aye, my heart is so full of joy."

She reached across the table and held his hand. "I'm so happy too. I know we'll have a good life together."

"I promise I'll be a good father and a good husband, to be sure."

"Oh, I have no doubt about that."

"A man needs a family. *Déanann an teaghlach tú láidir*—family gives you strength."

She smiled. "We'll be strong together."

When they rose to depart, Sophronia noticed Miss Weathersby, the old lady from church, seated at a nearby table. She sat up high in her chair and waved at Sophronia, who pretended not to see and quickened her pace to make straight for the lobby.

"Miss White!" the older woman called after her. "Sophronia, dear!"

Sophronia was startled when she glanced back to see Miss Weathersby rising from her chair to follow them. Michael carried the baby and followed Sophronia as she briskly headed for the door. The trio made it out of the dining room, through the grand hallway, up the stairs, and out of sight, avoiding an awkward greeting. The elderly neighbor had no doubt been slowed by the crowd and the waiters in the busy dining room.

Sophronia ducked behind a column at the top of the stairs and leaned against it to catch her breath. Michael stopped and turned, but she motioned for him to go back to their room. "Hurry. Go on."

She peeked around the column and down into the lobby and saw Miss Weathersby looking around for her among the guests near the reception desk.

Miss Weathersby approached the desk clerk. "I'm quite certain that I just saw Mr. James White's daughter, Sophronia, a moment ago. Is she a guest in the hotel?"

The clerk turned to the ledger, put on his reading glasses, and drew his finger down the column of names. "No, madam, we don't have a Miss White staying with us this evening."

Sophronia returned to the room. Inside, she leaned against the closed door, hand on her heart. "Oh, my. Everyone will know now. She's such a gossip."

"Aye, but everyone will know—eventually." Michael gently took her hands in his. "Having second thoughts, are you?"

"No, I'm not really. It's just that Father will be so mad." Unable to keep a look of concern from appearing on her face, she took a deep breath. "But I'm not a girl anymore. I'm a grown woman, and I can make my own decisions."

With the extra blankets from the armoire, she made a bed on the floor for Katherine, changed her diaper, then rubbed the baby's back until she fell asleep.

Michael sat, seemingly mesmerized by watching the bedtime routine. He smiled. Sophronia could sense his contentment and joy. She wondered if now, perhaps, he might be able to put the sad memories of Katherine's mother away.

"Michael, I'm truly happy," she said as she tucked the blanket around the baby. "I promise." She stood, smoothed her dress, and removed the combs from her hair, letting it fall long on her shoulders. "Would you unbutton the back of my dress?"

Michael obliged. The new bride pulled aside her hair for him, revealing the long line of her neck and her beautiful skin. He kissed her gently behind the ear.

Saturday, May 12, 1855
City Coroner Records (Memphis, Tennessee)

List of Deaths in the City of Memphis

#2830

Date	Name	Age	Disease
May 12, 1855	*Child of Mr. Haley*	*1*	*Not known*

Saturday, May 12, 1855

The Pinch, Memphis, Tennessee

Everyone in the tiny clapboard dwelling and several of the neighbors startled awake when Sophronia screamed.

Michael leapt out of bed and bolted through the door into the main room to find his wife shaking with sobs, holding the baby close to her chest. He reached toward her, but she jerked away. Then, turning back to him, she revealed the lifeless gray-blue body of their baby, Sidney. Her first child—not yet a year old—was wrapped in the patchwork quilt she'd sewn while awaiting the arrival.

Michael took his wife by the shoulders and softly guided her to sit down, just as Mrs. Delaney, their neighbor, knocked. When he opened the door for her, he could tell that she knew immediately what had happened.

"Oh, dear Sophronia, oh dear, oh dear," she said, pulling up the only other chair and wrapping an arm around her. "So many babies in heaven. So hard for us here, to be sure." They rocked back and forth.

Little Katherine cautiously peered into the room, frightened by the disturbance. Michael picked up the toddler and took her outside into the alley.

"Is Sidney all right?" she asked.

Michael cried.

The morning wore into the afternoon, and word of the tragedy spread throughout the poor Irish community known as the Pinch, on the northern outskirts of Memphis. Other friends came to the little house to offer hugs, to cry with Sophronia and Michael, and to perhaps provide some comfort. Mrs. Delaney cooked what she could find in the Haley house on the small potbelly stove in the corner of the sad two-room shack and then sent her oldest boy to their own house to bring some of their meager resources before she had to return home. That evening, Katherine lay in bed with her father, dozing restlessly and waking often.

Sophronia sat up and held the cold baby in silence all night.

The next day, Michael returned with the undertaker. A somber man in dark clothes, he arrived in a black wagon pulled by a black horse. Sophronia wrapped the quilt tightly around Sidney's now-stiffening body and gave over the precious bundle to seal into the tiny coffin. As the sharp sound of the hammer rang out, Sophronia suddenly fainted. Michael caught her before she hit the floor and laid her on the daybed in the tiny front room.

"Put her feet up," Mrs. Delaney said, taking charge of the situation. "Michael, get me a wet cloth."

Michael watched helplessly as their neighbor fanned his wife and rubbed her face with the cool rag. Eventually, Sophronia's eyes fluttered open, and over the next few minutes, she improved enough to sit up.

"When is the last time you ate?" Mrs. Delaney asked.

"I don't know."

Michael brought a glass of water and a cold biscuit. "Take a bite of this if you can."

An hour later, the family followed the undertaker outside, where he put the box into the back of the wagon.

The somber man leaned in as if to console Michael and put a gloved hand on his shoulder. "I'll be needing seven dollars."

Michael motioned for the man to step away with him, just beyond the small crowd that had gathered. "I already paid the sexton at the cemetery."

"Aye, that's for the grave and the digging. A coffin this small is just five, but there's an extra charge for coming out on Sunday. Seven altogether."

"Can I pay you next week?"

"I can't very well retrieve my goods if you don't come up with the money later now, can I? Services and coffins have to be paid up front."

Michael glanced over at his grieving wife and his little daughter sitting on a bench outside the door to their house. None of his friends met his eye. Michael looked at the undertaker uncomfortably, then moved to where Sophronia sat with Katherine in her lap and took a seat on the bench. He wrapped his arms around them and whispered into his wife's ear. In a moment, without looking up, she nodded slowly. Michael returned to the somber man keeping his back to the small crowd. "We've got a small gold pin. Would that do?"

"Not usually in the habit of trade. Let's have a look."

Michael went back into the house and dug around in the drawer with his wife's things, looking for her brooch. He brought the gold-framed cameo out to the undertaker and passed it to him in a handshake.

The black-clad man looked discreetly into his palm at the offering. "We can make an exception for today, I suppose," he said as he pocketed the pin and turned to climb up into the driver's seat.

After the chime at the Catholic church struck noon, the priest finally arrived to lead the procession. The family, now just three again, and a few mourners followed the black wagon to the cemetery six blocks away. There the clergyman led the solemn group through the rituals this community knew too well, repeating the words that were meant to comfort. Everyone gathered there had lost a little one before—a baby, a young sibling—so the scene was familiar, but for the novice, it was exceptionally painful.

Michael wrapped his arm around his wife, who leaned forward to put her head on his shoulder as she wiped her eyes. She held little Katherine's hand through the brief service.

"May this dear little soul and the souls of all the faithful departed, through the mercy of God, rest in peace," the priest said.

"Amen," the group murmured in unison.

The priest nodded to the two men attending the coffin on either side of the grave. They lowered the little box on two ropes down into the hole. One of the men pulled the shovel from the pile of dirt nearby and handed it to Michael, who tossed in the first scoop of earth. It landed on the coffin with a hollow thud.

Saturday, June 12, 1858

The Pinch, Memphis, Tennessee

Michael, who only worked a half day each Saturday, came home at noon for lunch.

Sophronia handed him a piece of yellow paper as he entered. "I saw this posted on a notice board today. It says they are looking for crew to hire on a new railroad line they are building—the Mississippi and Tennessee."

He took the notice and studied it. Sophronia had worked with him some on reading, but he was always too busy or too tired to stick with it. The letters looked jumbled and never really made much sense to him. On printed things like this, he could sometimes make out some words. It was easy enough getting along without writing, but not being able to read frustrated him.

"Says here that the pay is a little more than what you get now," she said, "but there might be days away from home. Crews will live in Hernando. That's a nice town. Clean and new—a good place to have the baby." She put a hand on her belly, which was growing bigger every week.

Michael knew that she had always blamed the dirtiness of their neighborhood and the city for Sidney's death. The loss of that child had nearly destroyed her. After the funeral, she had stayed in bed all the time and had gone days without getting up except to go to the privy. In those first six months, Michael had done the cooking in the morning and at night—and occasionally the cleaning too. He'd sent Katherine to the Delaneys every morning and asked her to make sure that both Sophie and little Kate had some lunch—even giving her money for groceries and laundry every week. Over the next year, very gradually, his wife had come back to life. Each week she became more and more like the girl he had married. She smiled more and occasionally laughed. Only in the past few months had their marriage returned to normal.

"Perhaps we could get a piece of land, keep some animals," she said. "I always loved having chickens."

"Sophie, dear, if that will make you happy, then that is what we shall do. I'll go hire on tomorrow. Where is the office?" He gave the paper back to her.

"It says to apply in person at their office on Union Avenue, near Court Square. You know where that is. Tomorrow is Sunday, though. I thought maybe we'd go to church and then to the park."

"Aye, I'll go on Monday then." He put his hand over hers as it rested on their new baby.

Tuesday, August 7, 1860

The Semi-Weekly Mississippian (Jackson, Mississippi)

MISSISSIPPI & TENNESSEE RAILROAD

FALL ARRANGEMENT

On and after Wednesday, April 30*th* 1860,

trains will run daily (Sundays excepted) as follows:

MAIL TRAIN

Leaves	*Leaves*
Oakland at 6:15 AM	Memphis at 2:30 PM
Pope's at 7:00 AM	Horn Lake at 3:10 PM
Panola at 7:27AM	Hernando at 3:43 PM
Sardis at 7:57 AM	Coldwater at 4:15 PM
Como at 8:15 AM	Senatobia at 4:37 PM
Senatobia at 8:38 AM	Como at 5:00 PM
Coldwater at 9:00 AM	Sardis at 5:18 PM
Hernando at 9:32 AM	Panola at 5:48 PM
Horn Lake at 10:05 AM	Pope's at 6:15 PM
Arrives at	*Arrives at*
Memphis at 10:45 AM	Oakland at 7:00 PM

FREIGHT AND ACCOMMODATION TRAINS
Will leave and arrive as follows:
On Mondays, Wednesdays, and Fridays

Leave	*Arrive at*
Memphis at 5:35 AM	*Oakland at 2:10 PM*

On Tuesdays, Thursdays, and Saturdays

Leave	*Arrive at*
Oakland at 8:00 AM	*Memphis at 4:32 PM*

Trains arriving at Memphis connect with the
Memphis and Charleston
and the
Memphis and Ohio Railroads.

Trains arriving at Oakland connect with a daily line of stages for
Grenada and the Mississippi Central Railroad.

R. HOUGH
General Superintendent

Saturday, October 13, 1860

Hernando, Mississippi

The little town was laid out in a grid at right angles around the DeSoto County Courthouse, located on a pleasant square in the middle, where the leaves on the hardwood trees shading its lawn were just starting to turn. The area buzzed with activity as shoppers and Saturday visitors to town milled about on the raised boardwalk that ran the length of all four sides of the square.

Michael had bought a piece of land south of Hernando, where the family lived in a cabin that they'd built near the Hickahala Creek. It was closer to Senatobia, but the family came north to shop and do business in Hernando at least once each month.

"Mr. Fort, sir." Michael waved to the older man as they passed each other on the boardwalk. "Can I speak to you for a moment?"

"Hello! Michael, how are you? Please, do call me David." David Fort was a prominent local farmer who had a daughter about the same age as Sophronia. The ladies were friendly, and their children sometimes played together. He was very nice, but his manner and appearance reminded Michael of Sophronia's father and made him a little nervous.

"Yes, sir—I mean, David, sir. Well, indeed, thank you, sir. I was wondering if I could ask you a favor."

"I suppose that depends on what it is," David said with a laugh.

"Well, sir," Michael said, smiling with what he hoped was a confident look, "I have been in America now for seventeen years, and back in Georgia, I declared for citizenship. That was over twelve years ago. I can be sworn a citizen here at our courthouse, but I'll be needin' two witnesses who are Americans and who can stand for my character."

"I'm honored that you'd ask, Michael. Judge Campbell is a friend, and I'd be glad to go with you to see him."

"Can you come to the courthouse wi' me on Monday? John Vanhorn, my mate from the telegraph company, will be there, too, and he's also agreed to stand for me."

"Oh, interesting! A telegraph man, you say?"

"Aye, we knew them in Memphis when we first came from Georgia. His wife is Sophie's friend."

The couples had met at church when they'd first arrived in Memphis. Every week the ladies sat next to each other to visit and chat, while the men sat on the outside and didn't say much. Michael had felt awkward around John. He'd attended school somewhere up north and worked in the railroad office. If John could tell that Michael couldn't read, he never let on, and perhaps he purposely avoided situations where it would become obvious and embarrassing to Michael.

"I'd be glad to do it," David said. "I'll meet you there at the courthouse in the morning."

"Aye, thank you so much, Mr. Fort. I'm truly grateful, to be sure."

~

On Monday morning, Michael donned his best shirt and pants and cleaned his shoes with some wax polish.

"Come sit here and let me trim your hair." Sophronia brought a pair of scissors and a comb and draped a towel over his shoulders as he sat on the front porch. She smoothed out his wavy curls with some hair tonic and trimmed the ends, cutting his hair a little shorter over the ears.

"Look here at me." She held his chin and turned his head side to side to make sure that the cuts looked even.

Two-year-old W. D. watched curiously from the doorway, sucking his thumb.

"You look nice, Daddy," said Katherine, who came out onto the porch with baby Mickey. She was eight now and growing like a weed.

"Thank you, dearest," he replied. "Not too fancy, am I?"

"You'll be the most handsome new American in the country today," Sophronia said and planted a kiss on his cheek.

"Let's go on then. I surely don't want John and Mr. Fort to have to wait on us."

Probate Court October Term

The State of Mississippi, DeSoto County

    This day appeared in open court David W. Fort and J. W. Vanhorn, citizens of the United States after being duly sworn say that they have known Michael Hailey for and during the space of six or seven years in the States of Tennessee and Mississippi and that during that time he has behaved as a man of good character attached to the Principles of the Constitution of the United States.

    Sworn and subscribed before me this 15th October 1860

G. D. Campbell

Probate Judge

The State of Mississippi

Desoto County

    This day personally appeared in open court Michael Hailey an Irishman by birth and after being duly sworn sayeth that sometime in the year 1848 he made application before the Judge of the District court in the county of Belltown of Macon Georgia that it was his bona fide intention to become a citizen of the United States and to renounce forever all allegiance and fidelity to any foreign prince, potentate, state or sovereignty and particularly to Queen Victoria of England of whom he is a subject.

    Sworn to and subscribed before me the 15ᵗʰ Oct 1860

G. D. Campbell

Probate Judge

The State of Mississippi

Probate Court

DeSoto County   *October Term 1860*

 I Michael Healey do solemnly swear that I will support the constitution of the United States of America

 Michael Healey {seal}

 This day Michael Healey appeared in open court + took + subscribed the above oath.

     < signed> G. D. Campbell {seal}

       Probate Judge

Probate Court October Term 1860

The State of Mississippi, DeSoto County

Michael Healey, a subject of her majesty the Queen of England and Ireland appears in court having made his declaration in oath before said court of his nativity emigration and intention to become a citizen of the United States and now here proof being made to the satisfaction of the court as required by Law, that the said Michael Haeley is of good moral character attached to the principles of the Constitution of the United States and desiring to preserve the peace and harmony + promote the prosperity of the same and proof having been made to the satisfaction of the Court that he has been a resident of the United States now more than eight years and was here the court permitting. He on his solemn oath renounces and abjures all allegiance to her Majesty Victoria Queen of England and Ireland and to all foreign princes, potentates, sovereignties or states whatever, and that he will support the Constitution of the United States. And now he is by the court admitted a citizen and invested with all the rights privileges and honors which to him under the Constitution may appertain. Ordered adjudged and decreed in open court this 15ᵗʰ day of October AD 1860.

G. D. Campbell

Probate Judge

Chapter 4

Saturday, April 13, 1861

The Memphis Appeal (Memphis, Tennessee)

THE CIVIL WAR BEGUN!
The Conflict Inaugurated at Charleston!

FORT SUMTER ATTACKED!
The Fire Returned by Anderson!
A Breach Effected by the Charleston Batteries!

TWO OF THE SUMTER GUNS SILENCED!
Base Treachery of the Administration Disclosed!

TRIUMPH OF THE SOUTHERN FORCES PROBABLE!

. . . *CHARLESTON, April 12.—The batteries of Sullivan's Island, Morris Island and other points opened on Sumter at 4 o'clock this morning. Sumter returned the fire, with brisk cannonading kept up. No information from the seaboard. Military under arms. The whole population on the streets. The harbor is filled with anxious spectators . . . Firing continued all day. Two of the Sumter guns have been silenced, and it is reported that a breach has been made through the south-east wall. No casualty has yet happened to any of our forces. Only seven of the nineteen batteries have opened fire on Sumter. The remainder are held ready for the expected fleet. 2000 men reached the city this morning and embarked for Morris Island.*

Monday, April 15, 1861

DeSoto County, Mississippi

Sophronia looked up from her needlework when Michael stepped through the door. She couldn't tell whether he was excited or afraid.

"Sophie, dear, I have news." He paced the floor, rubbing his hands through his hair.

"What, dear? What is it?" His agitation was alarming. She'd never seen him like this.

He stopped and looked at her, then took a deep breath. "I joined up with the army to fight the Yankees. Some of us on the crew signed up for a year."

She stared at him, trying to comprehend what he'd just said. "Why? You've got a family here."

Michael stopped and thought for a moment but didn't come up with an answer.

Sophronia pressed him. "All that business in South Carolina is so far away—is it really any of our concern?"

"Others been sayin' that the government can't tell the state what to do. Everyone was so excited an' all of 'em volunteered right there. I sorta had to. My responsibility, they say." He didn't seem convinced.

Sophronia shook her head. *Just nonsense.* "When will you leave?"

"We'll go to Nashville for training in three days. Won't even last a full year, to be sure—done by Christmas, they say."

Sophronia didn't relax. Her head was spinning, and she couldn't think of any reply. She couldn't help but imagine the worst. *What are we going to do without you here? Who is going to take care of us?*

"I won't need money," Michael said, perhaps sensing her discomfort. "The army gives us rations and such. You'll collect my pay here. And we got money saved."

She snapped back into the moment. "We'll be fine here." The words, she thought, sounded unconvincing in her ears even as she tried to reassure herself. She put down her work, forced a smile, and took his arm before he could pace. "I'm sure we'll be fine. It's you I'll be worried about." She stepped back to meet his gaze. "The newspaper said the South will surely win. We'll be here when you return home."

She put her head on his shoulder, not the least bit comforted by what she'd just said. *What if he gets hurt? Or killed?* She had a sinking feeling in her stomach. *A year! What will we do?* Sophronia's only concept of war came from romanticized stories and thirdhand tales, but she remembered the man back in Georgia who had lost an arm during the Indian War.

The next two days were full of activity and unspoken anxiety. He prepared for his long journey—packing a few things, making repairs on the house and barn that he'd put off, teaching and showing her things she'd need to know. She made mental preparations for a long and worry-filled wait, but one morning, while collecting the eggs from the chicken coop, she became so overwhelmed that she cried. They spent the next two nights together with few words between them. Sophronia wondered if they might be their last—but didn't tell Michael of her concern.

Friday, February 17, 1862

DeSoto County, Mississippi

Sophronia passed the time over the long winter by keeping busy with work around the house and tending their chickens, a few goats, and the mule. *Will Michael be home in time to plow?* She'd watched him do that and thought she probably could—but wasn't certain. She'd have to start soon, doing that and more if they were going to have any crops this year. Whenever she had a quiet moment, her mind instantly spiraled into worry about Michael, and that was enough to distract her from her sewing work. *Where are they? I hope he has enough to eat.*

She had received one short letter, written to her by one of Michael's campmates. She'd read it a hundred times before, but she pulled it out of her Bible and unfolded the sheet of paper, reading it once more to draw the encouragement she needed to face yet another rainy day with the children.

Dearest Sophronia,   *January 25, 1862*

We are doing fine and have been up in Kentucky for a while and didn't fare too well there. We are now back in Nashville. I've heard word that we'll be moving south soon. Plenty of training and drilling, and the sergeants sure are a bossy lot, but all in all I am fine. The food is sometimes enough but never very good.

I want so to be home with you soon. I miss you and the children terribly and will be happy to be there so I can get hugs and kisses from Katherine and W. D. and Mickey. Tell them that I would like to take them fishing. Remind them all that they are to be strong while I am away. I truly miss you and our times together.

Private Levy is writing this letter for me and will read for me any reply that you send.

Lovingly,

Michael Haley

The flour was gone. The bag with the cornmeal sat in the cabinet by the stove, drooping more sadly each week. There was one more small bag of meal stored away, but after that, there would be no more. She shook the sack vigorously, working every tiny piece to the bottom, then picked out the remaining fragments of corn from the cloth, collecting them in the pot as though they were gold.

She made sure the children always got the most of what she'd prepared to eat, but by making do with less herself, she could tell she had lost some weight and she felt tired all the time. The collards they'd planted, as well as the dandelion and alfalfa she'd found in the area, had been picked over as soon as they had leafed, but the children weren't fond of the stewed greens, especially with no salt or fatback for seasoning.

She had been frugal during Michael's absence, but the money had run out sooner than she'd expected. She'd only bought food staples and other necessities—though she had indulged the children with a few pieces of candy and some toys at Christmas. Katherine had gotten a new doll. The soft body had little boots, hands, and a head made of porcelain sewn onto it. Sophronia had intended to teach her to sew, starting with a new dress for the doll, but her daughter had lost interest when one of the boys broke the doll's head in two. W. D. had not confessed to the destructive act and had blamed it on two-year-old Mickey. Sophronia had bought W. D. a top, spun with a cord, which he played with on the wood floor of their small cabin when the weather wouldn't let them play outside. The loud buzzing of the spinning top was enough to drive her crazy sometimes. Mickey was disagreeable and cried incessantly. He refused to use the chamber pot or the privy, and Sophronia felt like she was constantly cleaning up after him.

"Katherine, will you please read to the boys? I have to go out and get the chickens in for the night. Then I can fix something for us to eat."

"I don't want grits again. Can we have an egg for supper?"

"If we eat the eggs tonight, then we won't have them tomorrow, and we'll get grits for breakfast."

"Do we have any meat?" W. D. asked. "We could have chicken."

"Think about that, dummy," Katherine said. "If we eat them chickens, then we don't get no eggs."

Sophronia took a deep breath, put her elbow on the table, and leaned her hand against her forehead. She'd been having headaches more often now, and she could feel one starting. "Katherine, be kind to your brother, please. You're right, though. If we eat *those* chickens, we don't get *any* eggs. Those chickens are about the only thing we've got going for ourselves here, so yes, we have to take care of them."

"When will Daddy be home?" W. D. asked.

"Sometime this summer is all I can tell you." Sophronia looked down at Mickey. "Did you pray for your father today?"

The little namesake nodded at his mother with a somber face.

*HEADQUARTERS ARMY OF THE MISSISSIPPI,
CORINTH, Miss, April 3, 1862*

Soldiers of the army of the Mississippi! I have put you in motion to offer battle to the invaders of your country. With resolution and disciplined valor becoming men fighting as you are for all that is worth living for, you can but march to decisive victory over the agrarian mercenaries who have been sent to despoil you of your liberties, your property and your honor. Remember the precious stake that is involved in this contest, remember the dependence of your mothers, your wives, your sisters and your children is upon the result. Remember the fair, broad, abounding land, the happy homes and the ties that would be dissolved and desolated by your defeat. The eyes and hopes of eight millions of people rest upon you. You are expected to show yourselves worthy of the women of the South, whose noble devotion in this war has never been exceeded at any time. With such incentives to brave deeds and in the trust that God is with us, your generals will lead you confidently to the combat, fully assured of ultimate and glorious success.

A. S. JOHNSTON, Gen. Com.

Saturday, April 5, 1862

North of Corinth, Mississippi

The rain wasn't constant, but with no long days of sunshine to dry the landscape, they'd been mostly wet for the past two weeks. That, combined with the persistent cold since the retreat from Nashville over a month ago, made everyone miserable.

Michael was thankful his enlistment was almost over. He'd had to sign up for only one year because of his age. At forty, he was the oldest man in his unit. When he and his railroad gang had traveled together to Nashville to enlist, they'd been assigned to an artillery unit because they had some experience with machinery. The Confederacy's unsuccessful push north into Kentucky in the winter had been a demoralizing failure. They'd even been forced to leave their cannons during a retreat across a river. Back in Nashville, the officers reorganized and retrained the troops, and their reconstituted crew was cobbled together from the leftovers of several units. Now called Company No. 16, they were attached to Captain McClung's Light Artillery and had a new twelve-pounder.

It had been three days now since they'd started back into Tennessee from the railroad junction at Corinth, and the going had been painfully slow. The road was a muddy mess, so narrow in places that men could only march two abreast, and the horse-drawn artillery traveled single file. Their movements started and stopped in fits as the mass of men and machines and animals crept forward with the undulating motion of an enormous earthworm. They finally made camp in a field just off the road by propping up poles and slinging wide tent flies over ropes tied between them. They laid damp blankets out beneath the open shelter. A small fire nearby warmed only their outstretched hands, but when it started raining again, they abandoned it to huddle under the canvas. The bacon from the day before was a distant memory, and they had only hardtack—cracker-like biscuits of flour and salt—to eat from their knapsacks that night. Michael couldn't remember when he'd last eaten a proper meal.

Private Applewhite rummaged through his sack to pull out another piece of hardtack. The boy, a new addition to their crew who worked supplies and horses for their unit, had become a bit of a pest since they'd left Nashville. Between voicing his frustration about not working the sequence on the gun and his eagerness to engage the Yankees, it seemed that he never stopped talking.

"Yankees 'round here for sure," he said. "See it soon. Gonna see that elephant tomorrow."

Reclining on the opposite side of their shelter, Michael didn't bother to turn around. The youngster's enthusiasm was maddening.

"Shut up already," Corporal Bowen said. "You'll see it soon enough, and then you'll wish you hadn't."

Don' know no better yet, Michael thought. He'd seen the elephant, the actual engagement with the enemy, plenty enough. He'd seen the fury and fear in the eyes of his comrades and in the eyes of the enemy. He'd seen the blood and the vomit and the tears and the destruction. He'd smelled the powder of the gun and the stench of the dead. He'd seen enough of the elephant in the past ten months to know he was ready for this year to be over and to go home to his family.

The proximity to the Yankee army brought them under orders for silence, so despite the noise that seven thousand men and hundreds of horses made, there was no revelry, even from the new recruits that evening. As he shivered in his tent under a damp blanket, Michael swore he could hear a band playing somewhere off in the distance.

Sunday, April 6, 1862

South of Pittsburg Landing, Tennessee

While it was still dark, Michael awoke to the sound of distant gunfire. Before he could get his boots on, he heard Captain McClung hollering.

"Come on, boys. It's started!"

They left most of their belongings in the tent, grabbing only guns, canteens, and knapsacks. Applewhite harnessed the horses to the limber as the crew found each other in the darkness. They rolled the four wheels forward, and the horses labored toward the sound of gunfire. After a half mile, they pulled aside with other artillery units to make a firing line in a field and then swung around and unhitched the gun from the limber to face the battle.

Seven of the men worked in sequence, just as they'd been trained—position the gun, clean the bore, pass the round, load the muzzle, ram it down, set the fuse, sight, and aim. They stepped back in unison and turned away, putting their fingers in their ears before the command to fire. A corporal pulled the lanyard to ignite the powder, blasting the shell from the muzzle. Just a second later in its trajectory, it exploded to launch twenty-seven iron balls toward the enemy. The crew did this with the calls of the sergeant directing each step, over and over, while others in the unit kept the supplies coming. After a few rounds, they fell into a rhythm, firing one or even two times in a minute.

Michael saw the forward line of infantry as the morning light grew brighter and the mist over the fields cleared. Captain McClung relayed orders down the line from Captain Hodgson and watched with a field glass to direct their targeting. They received no return artillery fire, so after an hour they were given a cease-fire order.

Throughout the morning, they limbered the gun three times more to reposition. While moving north, they encountered more and more wounded. First a few Confederates, then more, then a mixture of blue and gray uniforms. Eventually, bodies littered the field. The smell of blood reminded Michael of hog slaughtering in December. Then he thought of the other dead and wounded he'd seen in the past year. Fallen soldiers struggled to crawl to the shelter of a tree. One of the Confederates called out for water, and a member of their crew grabbed a canteen from the ground and brought it to him.

As they reached the edge of a swampy area, they hauled the gun down through a shallow creek and back up the bank to cross the road, moving toward the east, where they entered a Union camp, one of their targets from earlier in the day. The white circular tents hung shredded with bullet holes on broken poles, and the Yankees' abandoned equipment and belongings lay scattered. The devastation and death were gruesome. They navigated the horses through the destruction, pulling their cannon around and over wreckage of the camp. Personal belongings and supplies were strewn everywhere. Kettles and pots still sat over dwindling embers, as though the cook had just stepped away for more firewood. The hungry Confederates grabbed what they could of the food as they passed through, stuffing mouths, pockets, and knapsacks.

Michael averted his eyes when he nearly stepped on the mangled torso of a Union officer. The remaining hand still clutched an unfinished letter to his chest.

"We've got them on the run, boys!" Captain Hodgson called as he rode forward to the unit.

On the northeast side of the camp, the artillery units formed again, creating a firing line that stretched west toward a little log cabin church. They fired north at the Union lines for two more hours, keeping the rhythm and working in rotation, changing aim periodically as Captain McClung ordered.

A wounded Confederate soldier wandered past to the rear of the cannons. He was a boy, really, barely old enough to shave. He seemed unfazed by what was going on around him, stepping around and over the dead, staring blankly out into the distance. The shirt that his mother had made him from homespun cloth had a big gash in the left sleeve. It was bloodied all the way to his wrist, and he cradled his left arm with his right.

"Where's a doctor?" he asked Private Applewhite, who was working the supply line for the cannons.

The boys looked like they should have been carrying schoolbooks instead of rifles and cannonballs.

"Pro'ly some down that away, nearer the front line. What happened to you?" Applewhite eyed the boy's limp arm.

The boy stared into the distance, toward the sound of the gunfire in the east, and ignored his injury. "Bayonet. Don't hurt much. Just can't lift it." He turned toward the direction Applewhite had pointed and wandered off.

The captain directed them to move once more, through the trees and across another field. After pushing out onto a road running east toward the river, they met up with several other artillery units moving in the same direction and eventually stopped along the upper edge of a sloping meadow. Thousands of Confederate troops amassed to create a sea of gray uniforms. Beyond and below, at the other side of the field, the Yankees fired at them from inside a densely wooded area where the brush and undergrowth were so thick the only indication they were there was the flash and smoke from the rifle fire. The line of Confederate cannons extended to the left and the right as far as Michael could see in either direction, as their unit prepared for the next assault.

"Fire! Fire!" McClung called as the orders came down the line from the left.

The deafening cannonade lasted a full half-hour, punctuated with the sound of small arms fire, the shouts of charging troops, and the cries of the wounded. In the left side of the distant thicket, a fire started as the shells tore down limbs and shattered trees. Waves of men in gray uniforms worked their way forward, finally reaching the thick forest barrier at the opposite side of the field, and the return fire thinned as the Union troops were forced to retreat. The counterattack from the Yankee artillery farther beyond slowed to a stop.

That night, word quickly spread through the Rebel camps that they'd captured thousands of Yankees, and a hint of celebration floated in the air, despite the horror of the day's battle. Exhausted and numb, ears ringing, the unit bedded down in a field on the south side of the road and took turns keeping watch, eating whatever they had in silence. Groans and cries from the still-living came from all directions as men collected their comrades from among the dead to bring to the surgeons. When Michael was finally able to sleep, he heard them in his dreams, too.

Near midnight, he went to the edge of camp looking for a place for relief. A young lieutenant and two other men grabbed him.

"You there, Private, come with me," the lieutenant said. "The colonel has a mission for you. Take this." He thrust a long, dark-blue coat into Michael's hands.

Michael and the others followed the young officer at a brisk pace and arrived at the next encampment, where the lieutenant spoke to the guards as they passed. He ducked into one of the tents and, after a moment, emerged with a colonel who had chiseled features, fierce eyes, and a black goatee.

"I found a spot on the edge of the river where you can see the landing," the lieutenant said. "We can get an idea of the strength of their reinforcements."

The senior officer said nothing but jerked his head to get them moving. Suddenly he turned and squinted at Michael in the dim light of the nearby campfire. "Do I know you?"

"Private Michael Haley, sir," Michael said, straightening to attention and raising his hand in salute.

"Yes, you're from Hernando. I'm Nate Forrest." He returned the salute.

"Yessir. Well, below Coldwater, Sir." Michael dropped his hand to his side but remained at attention. "McClung's Light Artillery, working a cannon here."

"Good. Seems you're well then. Glad to see you."

"Yessir." Michael smiled slightly and nodded, pleased to have been recognized by the officer.

Colonel Forrest turned back to the lieutenant. "Let's get on then."

They set out to the northeast, through a cotton field, past the remnants of a peach orchard, and around a pond, now crimson with the blood of dozens of men, stepping over and around the dead. At the edge of the forest, they put on the dark-blue coats before continuing into the woods.

The thick mist became a drizzle and then a downpour. As they descended into a gully to follow a creek flowing toward the river, sporadic artillery fire sounded from the north.

"The gunboats," the lieutenant whispered. "You can see them from the top."

Near the mouth of the creek, they climbed the steep bank and came into an open area, thinly wooded, scattered with flat-topped Indian mounds—earthen structures, each taller than two men. As they sneaked around and between the man-made hills, they came to the largest at the edge of the steep embankment bordering the river.

"Keep watch here," the lieutenant said.

Lightning flashes and the burning fuses of artillery soaring overhead illuminated the officers as they scrambled up the mound and knelt atop it to stare down at the river landing.

"Union troops," the lieutenant whispered from his perch, "fresh and itching for a fight."

They've never seen the elephant before, Michael thought.

Minutes passed before the officers came down and the reconnaissance party backtracked to camp.

Tuesday, April 8, 1862

The Memphis Daily Appeal (Memphis, Tennessee)

THE SECOND DAY'S CONTEST!

Battlefield, April 7, 2 p.m. –We slept last night in the enemy's camp. Immense spoils and two thousand prisoners in our hands. The enemy, reinforced by a division seven thousand strong from below, engaged us again this morning at sunrise. The battle was desperate all the morning, our center and left being engaged. The enemy was driven back at ten o'clock, but renewed the attack with great vigor, and fresh troops probably from Buell's column. The battle is raging now and the fire terrible. Loss in number very heavy. Gens. Bowen and Clark are wounded, and Gen Cheatham has been injured in the shoulder. Col Blythe of Miss., is killed. Sanford's Mississippi battery was captured by the enemy, except one gun. Our troops are behaving nobly.

Monday, April 7, 1862

South of Pittsburg Landing, Tennessee

Gunfire from the direction of Michael's midnight excursion woke the artillerymen before dawn the next morning. Captain McClung moved them out of camp and across the road, positioning their guns in the woods between two fields not yet fully prepared for spring planting. On his order, they commenced firing toward the peach orchard and the pond where the blue uniforms had gathered in the distance. Throughout the morning, the intensity of the battle increased.

Small arms fire drew closer, whizzing past them like giant insects before smacking trees or taking down targets. On Michael's right, Corporal Bowen crumpled as a ball took off his left arm at the shoulder. Applewhite now had his chance on the firing team, and he stepped forward to take Bowen's place, but the private's head disappeared in a cloud of blood as he turned to insert the ram into the bore of the cannon.

On horseback behind the line, Captain McClung traded his field glasses for his pistol, and the others in the unit took up guns and knives to face the mass of blue uniforms now only a hundred feet away.

"Retreat! Retreat!" McClung screamed when a great wall of men in blue rose up from the field and raced toward them.

The Rebels abandoned the fight and sprinted back across the road and down into the woods, leaving the artillery where it stood.

Thursday, April 10, 1862

Hernando, Mississippi

Trying not to look so much like the beggar she felt she was, Sophronia wore her nice dress—the one with the fine print of tiny yellow flowers. It fit more loosely on her now, but she couldn't remember when last she wore it. As she tucked her hair up and pinned her hat to her head, the image in the mirror dismayed her—weatherworn and aged. She noticed her fingernails. *Oh, mother would just be so furious.* Working at the dirt under a thumbnail with a hat pin, she examined her calloused and leathered hands, then sighed and turned to retrieve a pair of gloves from the bottom of a nearby drawer. They didn't really match her outfit—something that would have bothered her before—but now she just resigned herself to it. Most of the women she knew here didn't even have gloves to begin with.

Butterflies and hunger pangs fought in her stomach as the family arrived in town and within sight of the store. They paused just down the covered plank walk from Watkins' so she could see through the window to time her entry.

When there were no customers inside, she turned to Katherine. "Keep an eye on your brothers and keep them out of the street. Remember to act like a lady and be polite. People are watching you, even though you might not know it."

"Can I come in the store, too?" W. D. asked. "I want a piece of candy."

"No, honey, no extras or treats, I'm afraid. Y'all wait here and behave nicely."

W. D. scowled and crossed his arms over his chest in frustration.

Sophronia opened the door and approached the counter, where Mr. Allen Watkins was reading a newspaper spread out before him.

He looked up when he heard the bell over the door announce her arrival. "Good morning, Mrs. Haley. How are you and the children?"

"We are all fine. Thank you. And how is Mrs. Watkins?"

"She's very well, thank you. Have you had any news of Mr. Haley?"

"No, just that letter from Nashville in February. He seemed to be well and said that they might be going south, but that was so long ago. I really have no idea."

"Well, look here in the Memphis paper. Says there was a battle over at Shiloh. A little place in Tennessee just north of Corinth. It seems things went pretty well for us. Here, read this." He folded the paper and put it on the counter, pointing to the article.

Sophronia removed her gloves and picked up the paper to read the second column on the first page.

Wednesday, April 9, 1862

The Memphis Daily Appeal (Memphis, Tennessee)

THE VICTORIES ON THE FIELD OF SHILOAH!

April 7, 1862

It is our proud privilege this morning to congratulate our fellow citizens throughout the Confederacy on the success that has crowned our arms on the corse-heaped plain of Shiloah. For two days have the brave soldiers of the South stood the utmost efforts the finest troops the North could make against them. Men well drilled, armed with the most perfect weapons modern skill can produce, and in possession of those numerous advantages which the expenditure of unstinted millions and free access to the workshops of Europe impart, were driven before them in ignominious flight. Breast to breast our gallant boys stood before the confident foe; but unawed by their proud array, their pompous panoply, they charged them with a weapon no art can produce, no money can buy— the chivalrous attribute of Southern COURAGE. With sparkling eye, cheek unblenched, eager step and unfailing soul they marched upon the opposing ranks—they baffled their mightiest efforts they subdued their loftiest rage they drove back their seried files and taught the vaunting legions that brave hearts and iron will stung by a sense of wrong and fired with the ardor of patriotism cannot be conquered. In the pages of history the hard-won field of Shiloah will have a name among the great battle-grounds of the world.

"That sounds pretty encouraging, I'd say," Watkins said.

"I suppose so, but I won't be able to stop this worry until I see him home safe again. Sometime this summer, I hope."

"What can I help you with today?"

"We're out of flour and meal and lard." Suddenly nervous and embarrassed, she felt her mouth go dry. "But we're also out of funds, so I was hopeful that perhaps you could extend a line of credit for us—just until Michael comes home." She wanted to look away, to run from the store, but she kept her head up and tried to maintain a pleasant expression while bracing herself for disappointment.

"Well, ma'am—times are certainly tough, even here in town. I can't offer credit anymore, because we have to keep funds on hand to bring in goods from Memphis. Supplies there are down, and prices are way up. We're running on a thin margin. I'm sorry."

Sophronia smiled pleasantly, despite the sinking feeling in her stomach and the humiliation that she felt. "I certainly understand. Thank you so much." She swallowed the lump in her throat and turned quickly to go, afraid that she might cry.

As she approached the door, she saw W. D.'s face pressed against the front window of the store, his hands cupped around his eyes. Katherine, who was holding Mickey, tried to pull him away.

Sophronia opened the door, ringing the little bell again, and turned to gather the children. They had traveled a dozen steps down the plank sidewalk when she heard the bell ring once more.

"Mrs. Haley," Mr. Watkins called, "one moment, please!"

She turned to see him standing on the walk.

He held the door open and waved her back toward him. "Please. Come back."

Sophronia motioned for Katherine and the children to remain where they were and then, holding her breath, went back inside.

Already back behind the counter, Mr. Watkins picked up his spectacles and turned to the bins and shelves behind him. Sophronia breathed a sigh of relief as the storekeeper scooped some flour from one of the barrels. He poured it into a bag, filled another bag with cornmeal, and then weighed each. After unwrapping a brick of soft lard, he cut off a generous piece, wrapped it in waxed paper, and put the bags and the package on the counter. He retrieved an accounts book and made some notes.

"Two dollars fifty for meal, four dollars for flour, and a dollar for lard. Seven-fifty altogether. Is that all right? You can pay when Michael gets home."

"Oh, Mr. Watkins. I'm so thankful. You just can't imagine what a relief this is. God bless you, sir."

"Well, we've got to take care of each other while our boys are away fighting for us. One minute." Mr. Watkins turned to a jar on the shelf and pulled out three pieces of taffy, each wrapped in a small piece of paper. "For the children later."

A lump welled up in Sophronia's throat. "Thank you. Thank you so very much."

Mr. Watkins smiled warmly, put the candies in her palm, and closed her fingers around them. "You come back if you need more."

Thursday, April 10, 1862

North of Corinth, Mississippi

Michael and his unit trudged up and down the hills on the road they'd marched five days before. The long walk back was nearly over. Their unit—minus two men, two cannons, and four horses—walked together on either side of the muddy ruts dug deeply into the wet earth by wheels and hooves. Wounded men in wagons passed them, groaning and crying as their injuries and broken bones were jostled. At dusk, they rested on the side of the road in the rain, still far out of sight of Corinth.

In one of the passing wagons, a soldier—a boy, really—nursed the stub of a freshly amputated arm. He looked over at the officer walking beside them. "Lieutenant, did we get whipped?"

They trudged quietly in retreat, having seen the elephant at last, the men much fewer in number. Downcast faces provided an answer.

"I guess that's one way to put it."

Wednesday, July 16, 1862

Vicksburg, Mississippi

"Haley," Sergeant Jackson called as he lifted the tent flap. "Private Haley."

"Aye," Michael said, rolling over in his bunk. "Tryin' to sleep here. Can't stay up all night watchin' if'n I got no sleep. What?"

"Captain McClung wants to see you. Said come right away if you want the train out of here this afternoon."

Michael scrambled to his feet and grabbed his hat. He pulled on his boots, hopping in place. "Discharge papers?"

"Sounds like it."

Michael grabbed his rucksack and gun and ran toward the commander's tent. When he arrived, he could see the captain seated at his field desk inside, working on a sheaf of papers.

The sentry nodded for him to enter.

"Captain McClung, sir? Private Haley. You sent for me, sir?"

"Yes, Haley. Here you go," he said, riffling through the stack of completed work at his side. "Discharge order. You're due to travel to Nashville, where you enlisted. Train'll get you to Chattanooga. Then you go overland with funds. But you don't have to go that way. You're from Mississippi, right?" He handed Michael the paper.

"Aye, sir, near Memphis."

"Well, you can go north from Jackson, instead. Train leaves in two hours."

Michael took the paper, then stood at attention, right hand at his brow.

"Go by the paymaster to collect the funds. Be careful going north. The Yankees took Memphis last month." He returned Michael's salute.

"Thank you, sir."

"Thank you, Private Haley. Good luck." He shook Michael's hand.

Outside, Michael walked between the rows of tents, head down, staring at the form. He recognized his name near the top and breathed a sigh of relief. A broad smile spread across his face.

He approached the paymaster's tent, where a short line of men waited. He showed the paper to the scowling guard charged with protecting all the money in the camp.

The guard took it from him and studied it. "Haley?"

"Aye. It's a discharge order, is it not?"

"Yeah." He thrust the paper back at Michael and nodded for him to pass.

After the others were attended to, Michael approached the desk where an officer was flanked by two more guards. The officer took Michael's form, read it, and made notes in a book. He turned to lift the lid on a small lockbox, counted out a few bills, and turned back to Michael. "Two and a half months' pay is twenty-seven-fifty, plus fifteen dollars travel. Forty-two-fifty all together. Sign here."

Michael picked up the pen and made his mark.

I CERTIFY, That the within named Michael Haley, a private of Captain H.L.W. McClung's Company of Artillery, born in Ireland, aged forty years, five feet six inches high, dark complexion, grey eyes, dark hair and by occupation a laborer, was enlisted by Lieut. Halecourt at Nashville on the 14th day of May 1861, to serve one year and is now entitled to discharge by reason of an act called the "Conscript act" approved April 16th 1862.

The said Michael Haley was last paid by paymaster Sullivan to include the 30th day of April, 1862 and has pay due from that date to the present date. There is due him fifteen Dollars traveling allowance from Chattanooga, (the place to which transportation is furnished) to Nashville, the place of enrollment, transportation not being furnished in kind.

Given in duplicate at Vicksburg, this 16th day of July 1862.

H. L. W. McClung, Capt

Commanding Company

Sunday, July 20, 1862

DeSoto County, Mississippi

As she went down to the creek with the buckets, Sophronia heard something unusual: the train whistle echoing through the woods behind her. The train stopped south of them in the town of Senatobia—and north of them at Coldwater—but rarely in between. When it was quiet, and if the wind was right, they might hear the train as it passed about a mile from their house, but it wouldn't whistle unless it stopped.

Sophronia carried two buckets of water up from the creek to the barn, poured them into the trough for the mule, and then went to the barn to check on the last two laying hens. There had been more. She didn't know exactly how old these two were. Among the first group they'd bought after moving from Memphis, they were at least five years old, but now they were wiry and lean and there were days when they didn't lay. She'd been diligent about keeping an eye on them, but their resources in the house had dwindled and the birds had been forced to forage farther in the fields and the woods. Over the months, fewer and fewer made it back to the coop in the evening. After a fox got the only rooster, there were no more chicks.

Sophronia unlatched the pen and shooed the birds away from where they sat. They squawked and ducked out the door into the yard, leaving in the corner just two eggs. Even *they* seemed puny and smaller than usual.

With an egg in each hand, Sophronia turned toward the door, but she caught her skirt on a nail that reached out from the side of a stall. Though the fabric ripped some, the nail hung on. As she turned and stooped to release it, she tripped on the bucket and fell forward against the chicken coop. Sophronia threw her arms forward to break her fall, and the eggs broke in her hands. Wet and sticky, the contents streamed through her fingers and formed a shiny puddle of yellow that slowly oozed away between the floorboards, dragging dirt and bits of hay with it.

"No!" she cried. "*Oh no!*"

That was it for the day. There was nothing left to eat.

Sophronia rolled over and looked at her hands. Dirty bits of eggshell stuck to her palms. She wiped them on her skirt and gave it an angry yank to release its hem from the nail. Once seated on the bench outside the door to the barn, she began to cry. *I don't know how much more of this I can take.*

It was then that she saw a man coming up the road. She blinked the tears from her eyes and recognized his stride. The man waved to her with both arms.

Michael!

Overwhelmed with surprise and relief, she ran to him.

As he saw her running, he began to run, too.

She wrapped her arms around his neck. "Oh, Michael, you're home! Thank God you're home!" She held him by the shoulders, stepping back to look him in the face, and then hugged him again.

"I've missed you so!" he said. "I'm so glad to be home!"

"Oh, I just can't believe it! I just can't believe it! Are you all right?" She stepped back again and looked him over once more, convincing herself it was really him, reassuring herself that he was whole. She felt his arms and his hands. He'd changed. Thinner. Aged more than one rightfully should in just a year. But he was here, in one piece—her husband. He was home.

Joy and relief washed away the anxiety she'd held on to for the past year, and tears filled her eyes and spilled down her cheeks. She sobbed, shaking uncontrollably.

"I'm here now." Michael wrapped his arms around her. "We can be a family again."

Thursday, September 11, 1862

DeSoto County, Mississippi

"Kate, run for the barn and find your father! Take the boys! Hurry! Tell him the Yankees are comin' to the house." Sophronia hoisted the three-year-old Mickey up onto Katherine's hip and pushed them out the back door. "Hurry and be quiet!"

She watched as her daughter, carrying the toddler and practically dragging W. D., ran to the barn. Thankfully, the ten-year-old had just obeyed this time, instead of asking dozens of questions as she usually did.

Sophronia quietly closed the back door, hurried across the room, and stepped out onto the front porch. She stood at the rail and raised her hand to shade her eyes from the hot afternoon sun.

A dozen men led by an officer on horseback came up the dusty road toward the house at a trot. The rider pulled back on the reins, stopping outside the gate twenty yards from the little unpainted wood house.

"Good afternoon, ma'am!" the officer called. "We're here on orders of General Smith! Lookin' for anybody who was in on killing our lieutenant last week!"

A nervous wave rolled through her stomach. She remembered how the Yankees had killed one of the local citizens who'd had no part in the skirmish that occurred when the Confederate picket tried to rescue the prisoners being taken from Hernando to Memphis.

"Just me and the children here now." She folded her arms across her chest.

"So you're Rebels then, I take it," the officer said. "Husband off to fight?"

"My husband is not in the army. He works for the railroad, repairing all the damage you've done." She glanced in the direction of the barn. "He should be home anytime now."

"And where was he last week?"

As Sophronia opened her mouth to reply to what sounded like an accusation, Michael rounded the corner of the house.

"I'm here now, and I was here then," he said. "What is it that you want?"

"What do you know about the gang that ambushed our soldiers last week and killed an officer?"

"Nothin', but I hear your men killed Mr. William White, even though he didn't have nothin' to do with it, neither." Michael stepped up on to the porch and put his arm around Sophronia's shoulder.

They hadn't known William White, but the skirmish had occurred near the man's plantation in the north part of the county. White had helped collect the dead Yankee officer and had sent his body back to Memphis with some other Union troops, but later, a large contingent of cavalry came back to exact revenge for White's supposed involvement. They beat him and killed him in his front yard while his wife and mother and sister watched.

"He was hiding supplies for the Rebels. Are you?"

Before Michael could reply, the officer nodded to two of his men, who kicked in the gate and entered the yard. The other men in blue uniforms followed.

The officer on the horse trotted up to the house and looked down at the couple from his mount. "We'll just check to make sure," he said with a sneer.

Three men climbed the porch and pushed their way into the house while two others grabbed Michael and Sophronia by the arms, pulling them from the porch into the yard. They drew pistols and cocked them. Furniture and dishes crashed inside as the Yankee soldiers wrecked Sophronia and Michael's home. The other men spread out across the property.

Sophronia screamed when she heard four gunshots in succession.

The officer pulled his horse around and kicked forward to investigate.

"You're a pretty one," hissed the Yankee who was holding her by the arm.

Michael clenched his fist and pulled away from his captor, trying to step forward and intervene, but he was felled by a swift kick from behind that buckled his knee and sent him face first into the dirt.

"Michael!" Sophronia screamed in fear for his life. "No, don't!"

The Yankee knelt on Michael's back and pulled his arm behind him, pointing the pistol at his head.

Sophronia tried to jerk away, but she, too, had her arm pinned behind her. "Animals!" she said through gritted teeth.

The Yankee chuckled. He holstered his pistol, reached around her with his free arm, and squeezed her breast through her shirt. "You know what all animals do, don't ya?" He thrust his hips back and forth against her from behind, and the other men laughed.

Michael struggled, but his captor kept him pinned down in the dirt.

The officer returned from behind the house, followed by the troops. The young cow that Michael had just purchased followed them obediently on her rope. They carried sacks of flour and corn over their shoulders. One had a bucket carrying all the eggs. The chickens they'd shot dripped a trail of blood behind them. They brought W. D. and Katherine, still carrying little Michael, and pushed the children over to the porch.

"Daddy!" Katherine said, clearly alarmed at the scene. The little boys began to cry.

"No guns," the officer said, "but General Smith certainly thanks you for the food and provisions. Your support is appreciated. Let 'em go."

As Michael got up, Sophronia ran over to comfort the children. The family watched as the raiders left the yard and headed south on the road with their stolen provisions.

Monday, September 15, 1862

The Memphis Daily Appeal (Memphis, Tennessee)

THE FEDERALS IN NORTH MISSISSIPPI

We have received some particulars of the late raid of the Federal troops into De Soto county, and they are outrageous, as might have been expected. The cavalry entered Hernando on Wednesday, the 10th inst., about three o'clock' P.M., and took position in the public square where they kept all the citizens and others whom they found about the streets under guard until after dark. The infantry arrived about five o'clock, P.M., and marched through the town, flaunting their flags and singing snatches of ribald songs to the fairgrounds south of the village.

On Thursday morning very early they proceeded to the Cold Water, where they destroyed all the trestle work and the railroad bridge, and also committed other outrages upon private property . . . Several families were totally stripped of every servant. Nearly all the valuable horses and mules that fell in their way were unceremoniously appropriated. They cleaned out all the poultry they could find—took corn and fodder without offering to pay, and many of them went into private houses and imperiously demanded victuals to be prepared for them. They entered many houses between midnight and day, and searched rooms and closets, and even turned over the beds, under pretense of looking for arms . . . They gutted every store, shop and office on the square that contained anything they could appropriate, scattering and smashing whatever they did not want. Two personal outrages were committed by the fiends—the sickening details of which are too revolting to be thought of, much less printed.

Saturday, August 20, 1864

DeSoto County, Mississippi

Michael startled awake when Sophronia bolted upright in bed and grabbed his arm. He'd been sleeping soundly, thanks to the constant hum of the showers on the roof. The heavy rain had displaced the intense heat from the prior weeks.

"Someone is at the door!" She grabbed his shoulder and shook him vigorously. "Go check."

He heard the pounding and wondered how long someone had been outside. "Go check on the children. Close the door." He put on his trousers and retrieved his pistol from the bureau.

The visitors pounded again, more urgently.

Michael loaded and cocked the weapon. "Coming!" he hollered.

In the front room, he peeked out from behind the curtain onto the porch. Four men stood in the dim light, bedraggled and muddy. The saturated brims of their hats sagged over their faces.

Michael was reassured to not see blue caps but was still alarmed to have visitors well before dawn. "Whaddaya want?" he hollered.

"Sorry to wake y'all up. Need help crossin' the river. That your ferry down there at the landing?"

"I only run it during daylight. Too dangerous otherwise. Who's askin'?"

"General Forrest sent us up from Senatobia to scout the crossing."

More certain then that it wasn't Yankees, Michael opened the door a crack—but kept his weight against it and his foot firmly planted on the floor. "General Forrest? From Hernando?"

"Yeah. Headed north. Restin' the horses in Senatobia now. Got a bunch a troops but the bridge is out."

"Yankees wrecked 'em months ago. I been ferryin' folks here, but you still gotta cross the Coldwater. Five mile north. No bridge there, neither."

Through the crack in the door, he made eye contact with one of the privates, then a corporal. Their Southern accents were further reassurance.

He opened the door wider. "General Forrest? I was with him at Shiloh. Colonel then."

"We heard he's from 'round here."

Michael uncocked his pistol and picked up his boots from inside the door.

The strangers stepped back from the front door and removed their hats.

Michael stepped outside and closed the door behind him. The rain drummed on the porch roof and poured off its shingles into the mud in front of the house. Michael sat down on the bench, to put on his boots, then pulled a jacket from the peg where it hung.

"Come on. I got an idea."

The group tromped across the yard and through the nearest field. The downpours of the previous week had swollen the creek so that it had jumped its banks and was now at least twenty yards closer to the house than usual, swallowing half of the garden. They continued along the edge of the water on the south side of the creek, moving upstream. After sloshing across the cleared land through ankle-deep water, they entered the woods and continued on toward the destroyed train trestle.

"Dry spot up here. Stays pretty clear down to the break in the road below my barn." Michael pointed toward two tall pines, straight and nearly limbless, that stood like sentinels on higher ground. Just three feet from the water in a slight curve of the creek, with roots already exposed on the edge of the bank—they'd fall in a few years, after the creek tore away the soil beneath them. "Look here. Two here. Long. And two more there." He pointed the men to the sentinels' twins on the opposite bank.

"They won't reach across," the private said.

"Fell these two in on this side," Michael said, "and those in on tha' side. Like rails for a train, they are. Pull the ferry up on top of 'em in the middle."

"We'll need mor'n that," the corporal said. "How will we secure 'em?"

"Find some lumber. Telegraph poles even. Bind 'em wi' those muscadine vines." Michael pointed to the gnarled, twisted vines, thick as a man's arm, climbing in the nearby trees. "Woods are full of 'em."

The soldiers looked at each other and shrugged.

"Worth a try, I s'pose," the corporal said. "Let's go back and tell the officers."

In the late morning, as the last of the lashings were placed on the boards and the first horses and wagons were hesitantly led across the new bridge, one of the privates found Michael among the crowd of men and the piles of leftover lumber and supplies. "You there, sir. The general wants to see you."

Michael followed him through the crowd toward a cluster of officers standing with their horses.

The private approached the general and saluted. "General Forrest, sir. Here's the man you wanted to see. It's his land and his ferry raft in the middle there. He showed us the spot and the trees."

Forrest turned and appeared to recognize Michael immediately. "Haley! Well, I'll be damned."

Michael saluted. "Aye, sir. Welcome home, I suppose."

"Glad to be back here. This is your place, is it?" The general returned the salute.

"Aye. I knew this high spot would be a good place for a crossing. There, down below's my house." He motioned over his shoulder toward his house and barn across the flooded field.

"Well, thanks to you for the good idea and the loan of the lumber."

"All the sides off our barn and every other'n in the county, to be sure." Michael grinned.

"When we're off, will you help to make sure that folks get their lumber back?"

"I will, sir. Been making some money on the ferry operation since the bridge was down last year. Guess I'll be back at it soon enough."

"Ha, I suppose so." The general mounted up, and the other officers followed suit. "I hear we'll need to be crossing the Coldwater in a bit. Now I'll know how we'll do it. Good luck to you."

"To be sure, sir," Michael said. "Good luck to you too."

Tennessee and Mississippi (detail), Map of the United States, Calvin Smith, 1852. Courtesy of David Rumsey Map Collection, www.davidrumsey.com.

Chapter 5

Thursday, September 5, 1867
Hernando Press (Hernando, Mississippi)

DRS. HALL & SAUNDERS
Office over
Smith and Monroe's Drug Store.

We respectfully solicit the patronage of the public in the various branches of our profession, and in hope to merit it by fidelity to the trust imposed in us. Twenty percent will be deducted from medical bills if they are paid when cases are dismissed.

L. H. Hall, M.D., *Residence at the house formerly occupied as an office by Drs. Hall & Mobley and A.W. Stokes, Attorney.*

L. L. Saunders, M.D., *Residence on Holly Springs street, (former residence of Mrs. Connelly).*

RATES OF MEDICAL CHARGES

*WE PHYSICIANS. . . MUTUALLY AGREE TO CHARGE
AND REQUIRE FEES NOT LESS THAN THE FOLLOWING
IN THE CASES HEREAFTER SPECIFIED*

VISITS

(Including one prescription)

For a visit within the city	*$1.00*
A visit beyond the limits of the city and not exceeding two miles	*$1.50*
For each additional mile beyond two	*.33*
Visits unavoidably made in failing weather	*33% extra*

*Night visits shall in every instance be double the price
of day*

PRESCRIPTIONS

Office:

Acute case	*$1.00*
Chronic case	*$2.00 to $5.00*

*Where there are several patients in a family,
provided there are no chronic cases.*

For the second and third case, each	*$1.00*
Each subsequent case	*.50*
Letter of advice, patient not under the writer's care	*$5.00*

OBSTETRICS

Delivering a White woman of a single child	$20.00
Delivering a Black woman of a single child	$10.00
Delivering a White woman of Twins	$30.00
Delivering a Black woman of Twins	$20.00
Difficult or Instrumental Delivery	$20.00 to $100.00
Delivery of Placenta, Fœtus not delivered by the Physician	$10.00 to $20.00
Miscarriage to be charged as Labors	

If a Physician is summoned to attend a woman in Labor and is in the house but does not officiate, he shall receive the same fee as if he did.

ATTENDANCE

Necessary attendance on a patient for a period longer than two hours to be charged:

For every additional daytime hour	.50
For every additional nighttime hour	$1.00
A day's attendance	$5.00
A night's attendance and sitting up	$10.00

FRACTURES

Setting Fractured Clavicle, Humerus, Forearm, Patella or Inferior Maxillary	$10.00
Setting fractured Thigh	$20.00
Setting fractured Leg	$15.00
Setting fractured Fingers or Toes each	$5.00
Compound fractures double the above rates	

Thursday, October 15, 1867

DeSoto County, Mississippi

W. D. saw his mother wince. Katherine put down the dish and pulled out a chair for her. The labor pains had come on abruptly after breakfast. Sophronia suddenly cried out, and he saw the puddle of greenish water pool on the floor.

Sophronia bit her lip and began to cry. "Something's not right. It's too early."

"How much too early, Mama?" Katherine asked.

"I think a month at least, and I never had green water before. W. D., go to town to see if one of the doctors can come. If they can't come, go by Alford Beall's house on the way back. See if his mama can come over."

W. D. set out running, but he tired out after the first mile and walked the rest of the way to town. Just ten years old, he knew what was happening. He remembered when his little brother Robert had been born nearly two years before. The crying and moaning and the blood and the mess were upsetting, but within a day, everything got back to normal, and he was intrigued with his newest little brother. He didn't remember anything about when Mickey was born. It seemed he'd just always been there. When Thomas came, he and Katherine and Mickey had all gone for a couple of days to stay with a friend of their mother's in town.

W. D. reached the physician's office on the upper floor in the same building as the druggist and climbed the stairs to the entrance. A bell over the door announced arrivals, but no one was sitting on the benches in the front room today.

"Good morning," the tall doctor said, drying his hands as he came in from the back room.

"Good morning, sir. My mama's gonna birth a baby today. Sister said to ask you to come help if you can."

"Does everything seem okay at your house just now? What's your name?" The doctor adjusted the spectacles on his nose.

"I s'pose. I'm W. D. Haley. My daddy's at work on the railroad, and my sister's home with Mama."

"Oh, you're Michael's boy. Well, let me get some things. How far is it to your house? If it's more than ten minutes' walk, we can go in my buggy." The doctor pulled out two different bags and tucked a box under his arm. He put a sign on the door saying he'd be out for the day as they departed.

"You turn at the road past the station and go out across Hickahala Creek," W. D. said.

In the stable at the back of the store, the doctor untied the horse and hitched the animal to a two-seat carriage. W. D. climbed in beside him.

~

When they arrived at the Haley home, Dr. Hall heard the end of an agonizing groan coming from inside. A thin curtain hung in the doorway. The door had been propped open so that air could circulate, but the curtain hung limply in the heat.

Dr. Hall pushed it back. "Hello! Dr. Hall here! May I come in?"

"We're back here!" Katherine called.

He found Sophronia lying on the bed in the back room with Katherine beside her, mopping her brow. Robert Lee, nearly two years old, stood by the bed with a worried look and held his mother's hand. It was unseasonably warm, and the hottest part of the day was yet to come. With no breeze, the still, damp air hung over them like a blanket.

"Good morning, ladies."

Katherine and Sophronia appeared visibly relieved by his arrival.

"Well, I think today is the day," Sophronia said, smiling weakly.

"When did your water break? Was there blood?"

"Maybe three hours ago. No blood, but it was green. What does that mean?"

"Not to worry about that right now," he said. "We've got to get this baby delivered first." Though he tried not to show alarm, he could feel his brow wrinkle with anxiety. "About how long do the labor pains last?"

His question was interrupted by Sophronia's grimace as another contraction came on. He pulled out his pocket watch, noted the time, and measured its duration. "How long have you been pregnant?"

"I figured it out in March."

"And how many prior pregnancies and deliveries? Any problems with them."

"This is six. No problems before."

"May I examine you?"

Sophronia nodded.

Watching and touching told him a great deal. Her pulse was strong at the wrist—not too fast, not too slow. No fever. The uterus was softer now that the contraction had passed. No tenderness in the belly, and no swelling of the feet or legs.

Dr. Hall pulled a wooden horn from his bag. It had a flat plate on the small end. He placed the bell of the horn on Sophronia's side and then pressed his ear against the small plate to listen. He repeated this several times in different places on her belly. He assessed the situation confidently and was generally reassured. "Sounds good," he said, smiling.

Katherine shooed W. D. away. "Go find your brothers and go wait on Daddy at the Senatobia depot."

W. D. put the toddler on his back and set out to find Mickey and Thomas. "Bye, Mama. I love you."

"Bye-bye, sweetie. Your father will come back this evening with the last train. Kate, give the boys some money to get something at the store."

Katherine fished a few coins out of the jar on the top shelf of the kitchen cupboard and gave them to W. D. "Stay out of trouble and mind the little ones."

Dr. Hall addressed her as soon as she was finished instructing her younger siblings. "Young lady, will you gather me some sheets and towels and a large basin of water?"

When she brought them, he took a bar of soap from his kit, rolled up his sleeves, and scrubbed his hands and arms in the basin.

"Bend your knees and pull your feet back for me." He maneuvered Sophronia's legs wide and then lifted the bottom of the sheet and draped it over her knees to examine her. He felt around inside with two fingers. "The baby's down low now. Won't be too long before he arrives." He turned to Katherine. "You'll have a new little brother later today, I'd expect."

Katherine wiped her mother's brow again. "Or maybe a sister," she said hopefully.

"Indeed, maybe a sister."

Before dark, he told Sophronia to start pushing with each contraction. Katherine sat behind her mother, supporting her and mopping her brow. Sophronia had drenched the sheets with sweat, and her saturated hair stuck to her face.

An hour later, Michael arrived home, surprised to find the baby nearly delivered. He knelt beside his wife and held her hand.

Dr. Hall pulled a large metal syringe from his bag. It had a T-shaped handle and a carved wooden nozzle on the end.

"What's that for?" Katherine asked with a tone of worry as she inspected the frightening-looking tool.

"I'm going to have to suction out the baby's nose and mouth before it starts to breathe. I have to get that meconium out so it doesn't get into the lungs."

"The what?"

"The green stuff."

The next push delivered the baby's head.

"Okay, stop. Stop pushing, and just breathe."

Sophronia panted.

Dr. Hall put the nozzle into the baby's nostril, holding the syringe and the baby's head awkwardly with one hand and pulling up on the plunger with the other. He did this again and then suctioned out the baby's mouth several times in the same fashion. "Okay. Now one more big push and that should be it."

With a final, agonizing groan, she delivered the baby.

"It's a girl," Dr. Hall said.

The baby was limp, slippery and purple, covered with a greenish slime. He held her with her head downward and rubbed her back.

Nothing.

"Is she all right?" Sophronia asked, sitting up to see. "Is she going to be all right?"

After patting her on the back several more times, Dr. Hall laid the baby on the bed. He felt her arm. "Heartbeat is slow—but there. Now breathe."

Sophronia sat up, eyes wide in alarm. Michael and Katherine peered over the sheet draping Sophronia's knees and watched for any sign of life from the newborn. They all held their breath.

Dr. Hall picked up the big syringe and used it to suction her mouth and nose again.

The infant coughed and took a little breath.

"There you go. Come on, come on." He turned her upside down again and rubbed her back some more.

Two more shaky breaths, then a cough. Then she started to cry.

Sophronia exhaled with a sigh of relief and collapsed back onto the bed.

Thursday, January 2, 1868

The Hernando Press (Hernando, Mississippi)

GREAT COMBINATION

of the

BARNUM & VAN AMBURGH

MUSEUM & MENAGERIE Co. &

DAN CASTELLO'S GREAT SHOW

Hernando, Monday, January 6ᵗʰ, 1868,

Afternoon and Night

A BRILLIANT STREET PAGEANT, in this Grand Cavalcade and moving Picture will appear a series of the most elaborately finished Chariots, gorgeously decorated Platform Cars, artistically finished Cages and dens, containing the whole of the Zoological Collection, the Band Chariot of original design and resplendent decoration, called the Throne of Appollo, and a cavalcade entitled the Crusader's Triumph, consisting of over one hundred and fifty Mounted Knights, clad in Burnished Steel Armor, with their Banners, Pennons and Insignia, and accompanied by their Ladies in Costumes of Medieval ages, all preceding the Crowning Feature of the procession, a large living Lion borne on the elevated platform of the Splendid Tableau. Carriage loose, unchained, untrammeled and free in the public streets. This sight forms the Great Sensation of the times.

Doors open at 2 and 7 o'clock. Admission One Dollar. Children under Ten years old 50 cents.

Saturday, January 4, 1868

DeSoto County, Mississippi

"No, Robert, don't!" little Mickey hollered as Robert Lee pulled at the newspaper laid out on the kitchen table. "You're gonna tear it! Daddy, make him stop!"

The boys gawked at the drawing, fascinated by a large advertisement printed in a wide column on the inside of the second page. The older boy pushed Robert away a little too firmly, and the two-year-old cried.

"Och, don't hurt him now," Michael admonished. "Oughtn't be so rough. He's just as interested as you are." He sat down and put the little one in his lap, wrapping his arm gently around him to contain his reach, and then pulled the paper closer for all three of them to see.

"What's that, Daddy?" Mickey pointed at the sketch of a spotted animal with a long neck.

In the top corner of the advertisement, an elephant stood with a tiger, an ostrich, a zebra, and a lion in a jungle scene. Down the other side of the column, ladies in fancy dresses stood on the backs of running horses, acrobats held twisting bodies aloft, and a donkey bucked a clown from its back.

"To be sure, that's a giraffe," he said. "Never seen one. Supposed to be very tall. They eat the leaves from the tops of the trees, they do."

Katherine entered the room and peered over the group clustered at the table. "Oh, a circus! What fun! Daddy, can we go?"

"I think that might be all right. W. D., figure out here what it'll cost."

The oldest boy stepped closer to study the paper. "Says here it costs a dollar, and children under ten are just fifty cents, so that makes a dollar for you, a dollar for Mama, a dollar for Kate, and a dollar for me, but just half a dollar for Mickey and Thomas and Robert and Fannie, so that will be"—he paused to work out the math on his fingers—"six dollars for all of us."

"Well, how about we all go for free?" Michael said. "I've work with the crew on the railcars on Sunday and when they leave on Tuesday. This'll get us all tickets for the first day!"

"Oh, that's great!" W. D. said, beaming.

Sophronia came in carrying baby Fannie, and Thomas followed. "What's so great?"

"We're going to the circus!" Little Mickey jumped up and down. "On Monday night!"

Five-year-old Thomas looked up at his mother. "What's a circus?"

"Ah sure, 'twill be grand," Michael said as he pulled the boy onto his other knee to see the advertisement. "The likes of which we've never seen before."

~

Michael was amazed himself when he saw the menagerie on the train on Sunday afternoon. A small crowd, bundled up in overcoats, braved the rain to watch the arrival. The steam engine pulled brightly colored cars with circus scenes painted on the sides. The first train brought lots of people, a few horses, some stock, and supplies. After the circus boss and some of the men walked around in the nearby field to survey the site, they directed the others to unload the gear and haul it to the field in some wagons. The grass was trampled in a few hours, and there stood two large red-and-white-striped tents, with several smaller tents nearby. A second train arrived that night with two dozen more men and several women, as well as the rolling wagon cages holding the animals. They had a different smell than the horses and cows and goats to which the small town was accustomed.

The giraffe's cage had an opening at the top from which the tall animal's head protruded. The cages with the lion and the tiger and the elephant boasted decorated covers like barn doors that swung open to display the animal behind the bars. The crew uncoupled the railcars, lowered the rear gates, and attached ramps for the rolling cages. They harnessed the horses—and even the zebra—to pull the wagons to the campsite. Some of the cages were so heavy that the crew laid down planks for them to roll across, keeping them from bogging down in the soft earth. The big elephant lumbered behind his trainer. They pulled the caravan to the field, keeping the excited children at a distance, and stowed away all the animals inside the tents for the evening.

Monday was cold and drizzly again as the Haley family waited with the rest of a gathering crowd to enter the circus tent. The tent flaps were lifted outward at intervals and suspended on poles, letting in the afternoon light and creating more space for the crowd. Long benches arranged in a circle around the ring began to fill up with people.

"One of the hands told me to come to this side here," Michael said, "so we can see the animals up close."

They made their way behind the benches and picked seats on the front row, near the back entrance. A man with a painted face was dressed in brightly colored clothes and sold large paper cones filled with popcorn. W. D., Mickey, and Thomas each got a cone for a penny. Sophronia and Michael held the littlest ones in their laps and sat with Katherine behind the boys, who wiggled with excitement on the front row, eating their popcorn.

At exactly three o'clock, a man in a suit and top hat ran to the middle of the ring and called out through a megaphone. "Ladies and gentlemen, *mesdames et messieurs*! Please take your seats. The most incredible show that has ever been imagined is about to begin! The parade you will see before you includes the most exotic animals from across the globe, brought together here for your amazement!"

He delighted the crowd with a description of the parade and the acts they were about to see and of the *"Artiste Equestrienne,"* here on her first tour in America. At the other side of the ring, a band started up with trumpets and drums and cymbals. The spectacular parade entered the tent near where the family sat, beginning with knights on horseback, clowns, and jugglers. The animals followed, led by the ostrich and then a small monkey riding on the zebra.

When the ten-feet-tall pachyderm lumbered in, draped with a huge tapestry, the crowd gasped. The dark-colored man riding on its back didn't look like any of the black people they'd ever seen before. As it passed in front of them, close enough for the children to touch, W. D. stood up and reached out with a handful of popcorn. The thick gray trunk swung sidewise to take the offering with its fleshy finger.

"Careful, son. Don't let him carry you off!" Michael grabbed the straps of the boy's overalls and pulled him back.

Thomas and Mickey recoiled as the elephant extended its trunk toward them, searching for more. From the safety of his daddy's lap—and while his parents chuckled—little Robert gaped at the sight.

Suddenly, the animal left a large deposit, dropped with a splat from a height of six feet.

"Phew!" The three older boys held their noses and laughed, pointing at the mess.

After the giraffe and more acrobats, the parade culminated with the lion, which roared in its cage atop the wagon. They made two rounds inside the tent and then exited the way they had come. Circus hands with big shovels followed to clean up after the animals.

The next two hours amazed them all. They wondered at feats by the acrobats, who tumbled and swung from the trapeze; laughed at clowns doing funny tricks with little dogs; and clapped for Mademoiselle Pauline in a sparkling dress as she danced on the backs of her horses trotting around the ring.

～

On the way home, Sophronia listened, amused, as the boys recounted the spectacular things they'd seen. She smiled at little Robert Lee, riding on his daddy's shoulders. "Robert, what did you think of the circus?"

"Effant poop!" he said, wide-eyed.

Michael chuckled and put his arm around her.

She squeezed baby Fannie and kissed her and then kissed Michael's cheek. She was so happy! She loved her family so much. They made any hardship worth it. All they'd been through together these past fifteen years came flooding back to her— the joy of getting to keep baby Katherine, the thrill of a secret courtship with Michael, the excitement of their elopement, the joys of the births, the fears and anxiety of the war.

There had been sadness during the tough times. The loss of their baby Sidney was heartbreaking still, and the periods with little money seemed overwhelming. Her mind drifted to how things might have been had she chosen differently. If they'd stayed in Memphis, she might have been a teacher or maybe even a nurse. She knew she'd missed out on some things by leaving Georgia. She didn't get a coming-out party or a big wedding. She didn't have house help. Without a doubt, though, the joy of her life was Michael, and the love in their home made up for whatever she might have forfeited.

Sophronia thought about her family in Georgia and wondered how they'd managed through the war. She'd received one letter from her mother, but her father had never written. She knew she'd been his favorite, the apple of his eye. No doubt he had been crushed by her elopement. The sadness and pain from the loss of her father's love was a quiet burden she'd borne—and something she had never shared with Michael, lest he feel guilty somehow.

That feeling had faded over the years, but it came back pointedly now, like the cold wind blowing in her face. She resolved to ask her father for his forgiveness, but she was also determined to let him know that things had turned out well for her and Michael and that she was happy. Her sense of contentment returned.

They returned home after a long wagon ride and settled the exhausted children into bed, Sophronia lit an oil lamp and sat at the kitchen table with a pen and some stationery.

"Comin' to bed?" Michael asked.

"I'll be there in a few minutes. I need to write a letter."

Senatobia, Miss.

January 6, 1868

Dearest Father,

I know how much you love all your children, and I am sure that any grandchildren you may now have are equally cherished. So it is with that same great love that I write to you and to Mother to tell you about your grandchildren and the family we have here.

After the loss of our firstborn in 1855, we now have had five more children. There are four boys and a baby girl in the house now. Whitten David is ten, Michael Junior is nine, Thomas Jefferson is five, and Robert Lee will be three this year. The baby is a little girl, Fannie, whom I know you would love dearly. She will be a year old in October and looks so much like little baby Camilla as I remember her.

Katherine is sixteen and has grown to be a lovely young woman. Father, I don't know if Ruth ever told you this, but when she found her in the barn, it was Michael who had left her there. His first wife had died just after her birth, and he was bereft and without any means whatsoever. Perhaps you may have suspected it then, but you certainly would know it now. She resembles her father greatly in many respects.

Michael has been so good to me over these years, and I want you to know that we are happy. We moved from Memphis and now live in DeSoto County, Mississippi, where Michael works for the railroad.

There have been difficult times, certainly made more so by not having family nearby to be of help, but you raised me to be strong, and we have done well. I know that while our children did not have some of the material blessings that being your daughter afforded me, they are equally loved and cared for.

As the years have passed, I hope you've found that you can forgive me for leaving. Now, since I, too, have lost a child, I understand more fully the pain my elopement must have brought you. I deeply regret causing you that pain, but still, I know the decision I made to marry Michael was the right one.

Father, please do write and tell me how you and Mother and the family are. Share my love with them and with Ruth and all the others there.

With tremendous love,

Sophronia

Thursday, September 16 (sic), 1868

The Hernando Press (Hernando, Mississippi)

LOCAL NEWS

Our patrons, we hope will excuse us this week for giving them a half sheet. We have labored under many disadvantages during the past four weeks, caused by sickness in our family and the loss by death, of our infant boy. Being absent from the office several days the compositor's work has fallen in the rear. If no unforeseen calamity occurs to draw us off again, we can safely promise our readers a full sheet hereafter.

During the past month, and up to this day, we have heard enquiries hourly regarding the health of this or that individual and reports of deaths unprecedented in Desoto county have greeted our ears with the sad tidings. There have been in this short space of time forty-eight deaths of infants caused by diarrhea and pneumonia. Out of fifty cases but two remain with but slight hopes of their recovery. With adults chills and fevers predominate, but as yet we have heard of but a few fatal cases.

We cannot say we are well, but we manage to keep up and hope for better times in the future.

J.P.M. Pullin

Contractor, Builder

and

Undertaker

Hernando, Miss

*Is prepared at all times to contract for building
houses, etc., at the lowest figure*

Keeps constantly on hand

Wooden Coffins of all kinds

Orders promptly attended

to all the cemeteries

Thursday, September 17, 1868

DeSoto County, Mississippi

"Are you all right, Sophie, dear?" Michael came in from work to see his wife in the rocking chair with her feet up on the sofa and a damp cloth over her eyes.

Katherine worked in the kitchen, simultaneously preparing for supper and keeping an eye on baby Fannie, while W. D. organized his little brothers for a game of blind man's bluff in the yard as the sun set.

Sophronia awoke at the sound of Michael's voice. "Hello, dear. I lost track of the time. I guess I was sleeping. I haven't even started cooking."

"Don't worry, Mama," Katherine said. "I've been keepin' up with it. You were finally sleepin'. Figured I'd get it goin'."

"Today I started with an upset stomach and that fever again. It's just been so hot. I haven't had any energy at all. Feeling so weak."

"To be sure," Michael said, "you've been low sick for several days now. I'm goin' to send for the doc to see on you."

"No, don't," she said. "I don't want to bother him. Katherine has been such a big help, and I'll be fine tomorrow. Think of the expense."

"Well, then, if you're not much better in the morning, I'll stop in town to ask him to come by, for sure." Michael poured hot water from the kettle and made tea for his wife.

Katherine brought her the toast she'd asked for.

While the rest of the family ate their supper, Michael watched Sophronia as she lay on the sofa sipping the tea. She couldn't eat a bite of the toast. He couldn't help worrying. He had heard that many others in the area were down with illness and that a number of children had died.

"Mama sick?" almost three-year-old Robert asked, using one of the dozens of words he now knew. He had a worried look on his face.

Sophronia pushed back the damp cloth and opened her eyes, smiling at the toddler. "Hey, sweetie." She caressed his face. "I'll be all right."

~

Near dawn, a crash outside woke Katherine. She rushed from the children's bedroom and found the back door wide open. Alarmed, she hurried outside and down the steps, only to find her mother lying facedown on the ground. It appeared that she had tumbled on her way to the outhouse.

"Daddy!" Katherine shouted. "Help!"

Her father dashed outside, and as they reached Sophronia in the yard, she cried out and her bowels let loose, fouling her sleeping gown with a horrible green liquid.

"Oh, Mama! It's going to be all right." Katherine tried to help her mother into a sitting position. "Daddy, go put on a kettle, and I'll fill the washtub from the pump." She untied her mother's nightdress, peeled it off, and used it to wipe away the foul liquid. She then led her, naked, to the water pump, where she rinsed off her legs with a bucket of water.

Despite the warm summer air, the chilly water and fever set her mother's teeth chattering.

Michael brought a lamp when he returned with a quilt that he wrapped around Sophronia. They led her back to the porch to sit. When the kettle was ready, Katherine filled the washtub with several buckets of water from the pump and warmed it with the hot water. Her father helped her mother to stand while Katherine bathed her.

"Daddy, look." Katherine pointed to several large pink spots on her mother's chest and belly. "Mother, what are these spots on you?"

Sophronia tried to look but couldn't answer. Her head was wobbly, and she swayed back and forth, clutching the porch rail.

Michael brought a towel and some fresh clothes so they could dress her and help her back inside. Then he dressed himself and set out toward town to find Dr. Hall just as the sun peeked through the trees.

~

Over the next two days, Sophronia had some lucid intervals but was mostly delirious with fever. Michael and Katherine took turns sitting beside her for hours, mopping her brow, trying to get her to take sips of water. She didn't have any more diarrhea, and she didn't eat anything, but her stomach grew more and more distended, which made her miserable.

Dr. Hall came by twice each day to examine her and give some advice, but he didn't smile much. He used the horn to listen to her belly for a long time and then shook his head slightly as he put the instrument back into his bag.

"Those spots are one of the signs we've seen in the more severe cases. She's not out of the woods yet." His serious tone revealed his worry.

"Isn't there anything else we can do?" Katherine asked.

"Use some willow bark tea to try to break the fever—if you can get her to take some."

Katherine and Michael took turns tending to her. She couldn't eat or drink anything—not even the thin broth or tea they'd made. She barely spoke. Her breathing became fast and shallow.

Late in the afternoon of the third day, Michael sat holding his wife's hand and resting his head on the end of the sofa while Katherine tried to stay busy keeping the other children occupied and fed.

"Mama, can you take some broth?" Katherine sat down in the chair next to her again with the bowl.

Sophronia couldn't even open her eyes.

All evening, Michael sat beside her as Katherine put the little ones to bed. He felt so helpless, and he tried to push the worst thoughts out of his mind. He couldn't remember the last time he'd prayed, but as his wife became sicker, he pleaded with God. *Please, please. Let her get better. I don't know if we can make it without her.*

"Ruth?" Sophronia cracked open her eyes, and she turned her head to the side to look at her husband. She smiled weakly. "Ruth." Her voice was raspy, her lips cracked and bleeding. "Would you make me a sweet potato pie? You make the best sweet potato pies."

"It's me, Sophie. Michael. You want Kate to make you a pie? She can do that."

She didn't answer.

Michael let go of her hand and went into the other room. "Katherine, can you make Mama a pie?"

"Yes, Daddy. Did she say that's what she wanted? Is she getting better? Getting an appetite back is good." Katherine got up from the bed and followed Michael back into the front room. "Mama," she said, approaching the sofa, "do you want me to make you a pie?"

Sophronia was dead.

Monday, September 21, 1868

DeSoto County, Mississippi

The rain had come down in heavy sheets, making a muddy mess of the yard. From his chair by the window, Michael watched as Katherine brought down the money jar from the kitchen shelf, where it stayed next to the china soup tureen they rarely used. It was the only piece of nice tableware they'd ever had. White with green handles on the sides, it was painted with delicate pink roses. The lid was missing—another victim of the Yankees' barbarism. He had brought it back from Memphis for Sophronia just after they'd moved to DeSoto County. Part of their new beginning, he'd thought.

"There just ain't enough for a marker, Daddy." Katherine pulled out the one-dollar bill and spread the coins on the kitchen table to count again. She looked at the handwritten bill from the undertaker, crumpled it up in her hand, and threw it on the floor.

After they'd had to pay twenty-five dollars for the simplest coffin at Pullins', there were only four dollars left. They still hadn't paid Dr. Hall.

"This ain't fair. No funeral cards. No notice in the paper. We shoulda least had a notice in the Memphis paper. Mama was a real lady, and people knew it. Her daddy *was* somebody!"

Michael knew she didn't mean that he wasn't somebody, but the words still stung. He looked out the window toward the creek in the distance. "We'll have to work out somethin' with Dr. Hall for getting him paid."

He got up and went out onto the back porch. The past week had been exhausting. He hadn't slept, and he'd wandered through the days like he was in a bad dream—one that he'd endured before. All those other cemetery stones he'd never bought haunted his dreams at night—his father's, and certainly by now his mother's too. Here in America, a baby and now two wives. He crossed the yard where the chickens gathered toward him hopefully, as if he might be bringing some feed to scatter. At the gate, he just kept walking.

"Daddy, where you goin'?"

He didn't turn around.

"I might want to go to town, too!" Katherine hollered after him in frustration.

A quarter mile up the road, he took the path through the woods that led to the clearing on the north side of their property. In the back corner, next to the pile of fresh dirt, Michael lay down next to his wife, put his arm over his face, and sobbed.

Monday, October 8, 1868
Senatobia, Mississippi

When Michael arrived in town Monday morning, he was surprised to see it. Workers from the other rail lines had been talking about just such a contraption for the past year. Passersby were curious, too, and a small group gathered around the new railroad handcar. It was bigger than he had imagined it would be—probably about ten feet long, a little wider than the rails, with wheels about as big as the forward wheels on the steam engine. The front end of the car had a hand crank on an offset handle that rotated a large wheel inside a casing, which turned a reduction gear on the axle underneath the car.

"Well, I'll be!" Henry Taylor said. "Never thought we'd get a handcar. Can't carry as much as the wagon, though. S'pose we'll have to leave stock out on the road?"

"Aye, but this'll get us out and back a sight quicker," Michael said.

"And we'll get a better gauge of the rails." Henry chuckled. "'Cause if they go wide, we'll be derailed ourselves."

"Right," Michael said. "But better this little car than the engine. Wonder how much it weighs. The crew's gonna have to lift this thing on and off the track."

"Let's see," Henry said.

They each took hold of one end of the car and tried to lift it but could barely get it off the tracks.

"Takes four men, for sure," Michael said.

For the next two weeks, the gang used the wagon and mules to position supplies alongside the tracks, stacking the ties and rails at intervals. When the tracks needed repair, they took crowbars, hammers, shovels, spikes, and buckets of pitch out on the handcar to do the work, making quick time out and back. Up to five miles an hour on the flats, slower on the upgrades, and faster on the downslopes. They took turns working the crank in pairs, keeping an eye on the pocket watch and an eye out in the distance so they could find a flat place to unload the car and lift it off the tracks if they saw a train approaching.

In town, Katherine passed the post office on the way to the general merchandise store. She ran into a friend she hadn't seen since before the funeral.

"Katherine, dear, I was so saddened to hear about your mother," Rebecca Dumas said, lowering her toddler to the floor so she could give Katherine a hug. "I'm so terribly sorry."

Katherine returned the embrace. "Thank you, Becky."

Ida, the three-year-old, looked at her mother and Katherine and then hugged Katherine's leg.

"How are y'all getting along?"

"Well, Daddy's gone back to work. Now I gotta be keeping the kids. There's so much to do now. It just seems like too much sometimes." Katherine followed Becky into the post office.

"I know your mother had been teaching the boys their reading and writing. Are they still doin' schoolwork? You think maybe your father could send the boys over to Thomas at the school?"

"They're all about as good at readin' and writin' as I am now, but I can't keep an eye on Fannie and Robert and teach the boys at the same time. I know Mr. Dumas can teach 'em more advanced books and things, plus math and history and such, but I don't know. Doctor bills and the funeral and all." Katherine didn't tell Becky that they'd had to open a line of credit at Lane's for necessities.

"I'll talk to Thomas and see if he can work something out on costs and payments," Becky said.

The Dumas family had a one-room school on their farm, near the Haley family's house, and Becky's brother-in-law did the teaching. Between their small farm and the income from the school, the Dumas family managed to keep food on the table for themselves—and for the two black boys who lived and worked on their land with them.

"Thanks, Becky. I'll ask Daddy and let you know."

The postmaster, Mr. Gillespie, handed Becky two letters and then turned to Katherine. "Miss Haley, there's a letter here for your house too. Came last week addressed to your mama. I'd just been waitin' to see one of y'all in town. Otherwise, I was gonna bring it out to your house. I sure am sorry about her dyin' an' all. She was a real nice lady."

"Thank you so much," Katherine said, taking the letter with a pained smile. She glanced at the small envelope but didn't recognize the neat cursive handwriting on the front. The letters *S* and *H* in her mother's name and in the name of the town had beautifully formed, tiny flourishes decorating the script. She put it in her pocket.

～

That evening after dinner, Katherine cleaned up while W. D. and Thomas gave Robert and Fannie a bath in the big tub out near the well pump. Michael sat on the back porch, smoking his pipe.

"Daddy," Katherine said, "I saw Becky Dumas in town today, and she asked if you'd send the boys to school on their place. I don't know how much it'll cost, but Becky said she'd ask Mr. Dumas to work somethin' out."

"To be sure, it won't be cheap," Michael said. "Three boys to school. Where are they in their learnin'? Can you keep on teachin' 'em?"

"Daddy, it just takes too much time. I can't keep the babies and teach three boys *and* do all the cookin' and cleanin'." Her grief fueled her frustration, which boiled over into tears as she sat next to her father on the porch. "I don't get to do nothin' anymore." She leaned forward and put her face in her hands. "All this is too much, and I'm just a girl."

Her father touched her shoulder. "You be strong now. The younguns need us to be strong. I'll talk to Tom on Sunday and see what we can do about school."

"I miss Mama."

Her father put his arm around her and wiped his eyes. "Me too."

As Katherine got dressed for bed, she remembered the letter and retrieved it from her coat pocket. She went back to the kitchen and sat down next to her father. "I forgot to tell you that a letter came today. It's for Mama."

"Who's it from?"

"I don't know." She opened the envelope, held it under the light, and glanced at the back of the page to see the signature. "It's from Grandmother White." She read it out loud:

September 30, 1868

My Dearest Sophronia,

We received your letter in February. I am finally writing back to you after so long a time because I could never get your father to write a letter. Many times I would plead with him to write to you, but he just delayed. Last month, I even got out his pens and paper for him, but he just sat and stared and then left them on the table. I decided then that I would write back for both of us.

We moved west and rebuilt in Haralson County after the Yankees burned Whitehall. The new house is smaller than the one you remember, but we are happy not to be living in a barn anymore. Jesse had buried much of the silver beforehand, so we had some resources to start over with.

"Damn that Sherman to hell," Michael said as he sat back in his chair and relit his pipe.

The crop this year is better than last year, since there was more rain. The business dealings are so complicated now that we have to pay the slaves who stayed on and came with us. Each family has a parcel of land to work. They get a portion of the proceeds from the harvest. I get confused by it all.

I was happy to hear about your family but sad about the loss of your first child. I have faith that the arms of Jesus cradle that baby. You must take joy in those other children and cherish them every day, because, as you know, we are not even promised a tomorrow. I wish I could be there, seeing you as a mother. I know that you must be doing well raising your family.

Katherine turned the page over and continued.

Ruth is still with us.

Katherine's eyes traveled to the next sentence, and she stopped.

"Go on," Michael said.

Katherine hesitated and skipped the rest of the next paragraph. She made up the next sentence. "Ruth is still with us, and she still makes those delicious sweet potato pies." Then she finished reading the rest of the letter aloud to her father.

Sophronia, your father will surely forgive you for running off, but I think his heart just aches. Can you come visit us? That might do him some good.

With love,

Mother

Tears ran down Michael's face, and he pulled out his handkerchief to wipe his eyes. "You'll have to write back to her and tell her that Sophie died. That will just break their hearts, I'm afraid."

"I need to go to bed," Katherine said abruptly, folding the letter and sliding it back into the envelope. "Good night."

"Good night, dear."

In the kids' room, Katherine lit the lamp, changed into her nightgown, and lay down. She looked at the letter again. The part she hadn't read to her father startled her. She didn't understand.

. . . Ruth is still with us. It was about two years ago that she finally told me it was Michael who left Katherine in the barn. Did you ever learn more about her mother? Watching you with baby Katherine when you lived here, still as a young girl in my mind, is a fond memory for me. Before I showed him your letter, I had to tell your father about Katherine too. I think that was another setback for him . . .

She had to read it again. *More about her mother?* As the meaning sank in, Katherine felt stunned. Her mind raced. *If Sophronia White Haley wasn't my mother, then who was? Where is she? Is she still alive? Why didn't anyone tell me? That's why nobody ever says I favored Mama like they tell Thomas and W. D.*

She didn't cry. She wasn't angry. She just felt numb. Katherine put the letter on the table and stared at the ceiling. Many minutes later, she rolled over and blew out the lamp.

Tuesday, October 16, 1868

Sardis, Mississippi

"Aye, there's a spot," Henry said. "We just crossed it back there. The tie's got a split an' the spike's let loose. The rail bounces."

Michael and Henry stopped cranking the handles and let the handcar roll to a stop. Michael jumped off and pushed it to start back in the opposite direction, while Henry started cranking the handle in reverse. They stopped the car again, just beside the tie with the missing spike.

Henry inspected the fault with George Gates and Joseph Crawford. He jumped on the split wood, and the crosstie, no longer fastened by the spike, bounced against the ground under the rail.

"Need to lay in a new tie under here," he said, grabbing a shovel and crowbar from the car. "Y'all go down to the next stack and bring a new one." He turned to Joe and George. "We'll dig this out."

Michael pushed the car to get it started in the right direction for Joe and George as they cranked the handle. Henry used a long crowbar to pry the remaining spikes from the opposite side of the heavy wooden beam, and they started digging out the dirt and gravel from beneath the wood. After positioning the jacks to brace the rails, they were nearly ready to pull out the old crosstie with a pair of giant pincer tongs when they heard George yelling.

"Hey, hey! Train! Train coming!"

Henry and Michael looked down the track and saw their partners turning the car handle furiously and gaining speed on the way back toward them. A northbound train came around the bend in the distance.

Michael instantly recognized the crisis. Joe and George couldn't leave the handcar on the track where it would damage and could possibly derail the train if it got hit, but with just two men there, nearly a half mile away, they couldn't lift the heavy car to get it off the tracks themselves.

Michael and Henry dropped their tools and sprinted toward the handcar. They intercepted it, and the men on board let go of the spinning handle as Michael and Henry pulled on the back of the car to bring it to a stop. The train engineer, meanwhile, indicated he had spotted them by giving the whistle a long blast and applying the brakes on the locomotive.

When the handcar finally slowed to a stop, they could move it out of the way, but the ground on either side of the tracks was uneven, requiring Michael and Joe to lift it even higher so the other two could keep moving across the tracks. Joe stumbled in the gravel and dropped his corner. A wheel caught in the dirt, and the car was left straddling a rail.

"Roll it over!" Henry yelled over the loud whistle screeching from the engine bearing down on them.

As Joe and Henry lifted their side of the car over the track, Michael and George pushed up on either end. When the heavy car reached the tipping point, they gave a final heave and scrambled to get out of the way. Michael fell down the bank, landing face first in the dirt. He tried to roll away from the tumbling car but wasn't fast enough to keep the gear handle from pinning his left arm to the ground. The bone in his arm snapped, but he couldn't hear his own scream over the train whistle as the engine rushed by.

Thursday, September 16, 1869

Hernando, Mississippi

Michael paced the lawn outside the ruins of the DeSoto County Courthouse. The one room that remained after the Yankees had burned the building still served as a hub for county business.

"If this don't work," he said, "I've truly no idea what we'll do." He rubbed his left hand, which he carried in his right to relieve the pressure on his elbow. Initially, he had done it to help ease the pain, but now it had just become a habit.

The break in his upper arm had healed pretty well. Dr. Hall had set the bone to get the ends of the break together and had bound it with wood slats and strips of cloth that he'd covered in plaster. "You're very lucky the skin stayed intact," he'd said. "If the bones stuck out, it would've required an amputation."

Weeks later, by the time the cast came off, the muscles had all shriveled. Michael could bend some at the elbow but couldn't move his hand, which dangled limply at the end of his arm. Dr. Hall wasn't hopeful that Michael would ever get that hand to work again.

Even though the accident had involved an unscheduled train, the investigation board had faulted the crew for not staying together with the handcar, so Michael had received some injury pay but no damages in the settlement. That money had lasted for a while, but eventually the railroad had let him go because he couldn't work.

He'd heard in town that the county would take bids on the poorhouse job, so he made some inquiries. He convinced the board of supervisors that he could still work to keep up the place despite his bad arm and pointed out that he had Katherine and several able-bodied boys to help. When he went with her to the courthouse to put in a sealed bid for the monthly wage, Katherine was upset.

"Daddy, it's terrible. Living at the poorhouse? It's just so embarrassing."

"I don't like it, neither," he told her, "but it pays, and it keeps a roof over our head, and it keeps our family together. We got no other choice right now. Just think of it as workin' for the county."

Mr. Fort opened the door and stepped out onto the lawn. He surveyed the small group gathered before him, made eye contact with Michael, and gave a tiny nod. "The bid for the board at the poorhouse for this year goes to Michael Haley." He turned to speak to Michael and Katherine. "You can move in on the first of October."

Chapter 6

Thursday, March 24, 1870

Public Ledger (Memphis, Tennessee)

Taking the Census.

We learn from Colonel Eaton, the United States Marshal, that applications for appointments as census takers are numerous. An exchange says: "As Congress has resisted all new plans, the census this year will be taken on the same basis as in 1850 and 1860. The law of 1850 provides that the census shall be taken by the United States' Marshals of the respective districts, with the aid of such assistance as shall be required. Each state is divided into census districts to be composed of not less than twenty thousand persons. The assistants for taking the census are appointed and commissioned by the Marshall, and are paid for their compensation as follows: Two cents for every name taken, ten cents for every farm, fifteen cents for every productive establishment of industry, two cents for every deceased person and two percent of the gross amount for names enumerated for social statistics, and ten cents per mile for travel. The enumeration must begin the first day of June, and the census must be completed and the returns all sent to Secretary of the Interior by the first of November following."

Thursday, June 9, 1870

Hernando Press (Hernando, Mississippi)

Taking the Census

    An exchange makes the following suggestions in regard to the census: Next month the work of taking the census of the United States will begin in all parts of the county, and it is very important that the statistics should be accurate. The other questions relating to persons, ages, births, deaths, marriages, professions, occupations and trades can readily be answered by any intelligent member of the family—only requiring care that the dates are correct.

Thursday, August 18, 1870

Hernando Press (Hernando, Mississippi)

BOARD OF SUPERVISORS

August Term 1870

The Report of R. D. Fort, County Treasurer of Desoto county Miss., on account of the several funds in his hands showing a balance as follows to wit:

On account of County Fund Cash on hand   *$2,320.99*

   Pauper Fund,   *$1,649.97*

Appropriations out of the Pauper Fund.
Dr. Tom Jones, for medical attention
to Pauper at Poor House,   *$53.50*

E. H. Flynn, for goods furnished Poor House,   *$9.20*

M. Haley, for board of Paupers at Poor House $67.00

E. J. Lipsey for services as Commissioner of
the Poor for the 5th District 12 months
and conveying Paupers to the Poor House   *$52.00*

Wednesday, September 14, 1870

Township 3, Range 8, Hernando, Mississippi

Sitting far off the plank road, ugly and unpainted, the main house was low and flat with a sagging porch. Its tin roof was rusted through in so many places that it was patched more than not. Behind it, a collection of smaller shacks huddled together on the piece of land between the Memphis plank road and the railroad tracks. A few sorry rows of corn sagged under the heat in a dusty patch of garden. This was the poorhouse, home to those with no family to care for them—the crippled, the very old, the sick, the crazy. Katherine hated it.

She'd just hung the last of the laundry on the line when she turned to see a man with a blue jacket down on the plank road. He removed his matching hat, mopped his brow with a handkerchief, and then stuffed it back into his pocket, surveying the house before crossing the logs bridging the ditch to approach.

A Yankee soldier! Katherine picked up the clothespins and the basket and ducked through the back door. "Thomas, Mickey! Come here, quick!"

She looked around the corner into a bedroom and found Mrs. Duglis holding little Fannie in her lap, but there was no one else with them.

"Where are the boys?" Katherine whispered loudly.

The frail old woman responded only with a blank look.

Katherine could hear the man at the front of the house now. She peeked out from behind the coarse fabric of the limp and yellowed curtain tacked up at the window.

"Well, hello there, little man." The short, middle-aged man stooped forward as he spoke to her wide-eyed little brother. "Is your mother home?"

Robert stared, turned, and ran back behind the house.

The man waited for a moment and looked around. When no one came back, he stepped onto the porch and knocked on the door.

Fannie ran in, clomping on the wooden floor. Katherine put her fingers to her lips to quiet her little sister and then picked her up and put her on her hip.

He knocked again, more loudly. "Hello. Is anyone home?"

"What do you want?" Katherine called from behind the door.

"I'm here to see the man or the woman of the house, to take the census."

"My daddy's not home. Come back later."

"Oh, to be sure. May I talk to you for a few minutes then? My name is Patrick McLernon." He opened a little folder to show a card with his name on it and stamped by Marshal Daley in Oxford. He held it out in front of him, leaning to the side toward the window.

For months people had been hearing that the census taker was coming. Some seemed eager to help, but others were suspicious. A census taker in Winston County had been shot at and had narrowly escaped. It hadn't helped that his blue uniform coat really had made him look like a Yankee soldier. For her part, Katherine didn't know what to make of it.

"I'm taking the census to make a list of all the people in the county. Just a few questions. I'll sit outside here, if that's all right."

Katherine peeked out the door, slightly reassured by an Irish accent much like her father's. "What do you want?"

"Just a few questions for the census." He turned his back to the door, stepped down, and sat on the porch, opening his bag between his feet. He carried blank report pages in a thick leather folio, rolled lengthwise, and he had a kit with several pens, nibs, and inkwells. He took out a pen and an inkwell, uncorked the little bottle, and set it on the porch beside him. Then he pulled out a board with what appeared to be a form clipped to it.

"What's a census?" Katherine opened the door a bit wider but still kept her foot firmly planted against it on the inside.

"Oh, an account of all the people, to be sure. The state and the whole country. Collect this information every ten years." Mr. McLernon turned a bit and leaned against the post on the porch to look over his shoulder at Katherine. "You didn't hear about this in school? The whole country knows about it, to be sure."

"You're travelin' over the whole country?"

"Oh no," Mr. McLernon said. "Me and some other fellas are doin' this part of Mississippi between Memphis and Clarksdale. Good weather so far this summer, but lots of walkin' and ridin'. Had to get new shoes twice since June."

Katherine let her guard down a bit. Mr. McLernon was congenial and seemed eager to talk but wasn't overly formal or pushy. It was clear he'd learned how to approach people in a friendly way. And he was Irish.

"What is the surname here?" he asked.

"What?"

"Your family name, lass? Your last name?"

"Haley," Katherine said, opening the door a bit wider. "But this is the poorhouse. There's others here, too."

Mr. McLernon wrote down her answer without looking back over his shoulder. "Aye, let's talk about your family first. Are you the head of the household?"

"No, my daddy—Michael Haley—is, but he's not here now."

The man kept writing. "How old is Michael?"

"He's forty-six." She thought she remembered him saying that. She stepped outside onto the porch to see what Mr. McLernon was doing, but stayed far enough away to be out of his reach.

The man nodded. "Where was he born? Where were his parents born?"

"He came from Ireland. His parents, too, but I don't know their names."

"Oh, not to worry then." He made notes and tick marks on the big sheet of paper. "And what is his occupation?"

"He's the keeper here." Katherine took a step closer. "We don't really have to live here, though. This is just my father's job. He could get another job in Memphis or somewhere, and we could live there, ya know."

Mr. McLernon wrote *Keeper of Poorhouse* in the box for occupation as Katherine looked over his shoulder.

"He gets paid by the county, so put in there this is the *county* poorhouse. He works for the county."

Mr. McLernon squeezed the word *county* over the writing in the block he'd already filled.

Katherine stepped down from the porch and out into the sunshine. Robert emerged from his hiding place at the corner of the house and ran to hide behind her. He peered at the man from behind her skirt.

"Did your father go to school? Can he read and write?"

"No, no school. Can't read really. But he's good at lots of other things."

Mr. McLernon made more little marks on the paper. "What about your mother?"

"She died."

"'Tis a shame for sure. I'm sorry for your troubles. And so you are a Haley too?"

"Aye." She stood in the yard, and Mr. McLernon collected the same information about her and recorded it in quick scribbles and ticks mostly without looking up. Then they went through the rest of the family—W. D., Michael Junior, Thomas, Robert, and Fannie.

He took down their names and ages. "And is anyone afflicted in any way? Blind, deaf, dumb, or slow?"

"No," Katherine said indignantly. "We're not here because of any of that. Mr. Brown is afflicted, as you say, but we just live here because Mother died and my father broke his arm and lost his job at the railroad. He had to keep all of us together, and this worked out best for us."

"Well then, that's fine. Now who else lives here? Can I talk to them?"

"Mr. and Mrs. Duglis stay with us in the house. The others stay in the cabins."

Katherine took him to see each of them so they could answer his questions. First the ancient and frail white couple with them in the main house, then the black folks in the little shacks by the railroad tracks. Phyllis Goodman stayed in a one-room shack with Susan Bell, the cook; old Mr. Stevenson, a blind widower with no family, lived in another; finally, there was the mulatto, Mr. Brown, who usually just wandered around the place talking to himself. He was short and fat, with an odd, flat face and a protruding tongue. Katherine had initially been afraid of him, but as the months wore on, she figured that he probably wasn't dangerous. Still, she kept Fannie and Robert Lee away from him.

Oh, how I hate this place, she thought. *I can't wait to get out of here.*

October 8, 1870

Weekly Panola Star (Sardis, Mississippi)

The Board of Supervisors of DeSoto County let out the contractt (sic) for building the courthouse at Hernando. It is to be a $40,000 building This settles the Senatobia division about moving the county seat from Hernando.

Tuesday, March 15, 1871

Hernando, Mississippi

The townspeople, buzzing with excitement about the new building project, stopped every day on their errands to see the progress of the demolition and construction.

Katherine spent a few minutes watching the activity before heading back up the plank road toward home. She hated the walk. None of her friends lived out this way—not that too many were still friendly anymore. People were still polite, but something had definitely changed after her father had taken the job.

Someday, I'll live somewhere nice, she thought, admiring the last of the big houses she passed as she left downtown.

A mile farther up the plank road, Katherine reached the turnoff to the poor farm as a large wagon, filled with debris from the demolition, rumbled past. She stepped aside and turned to watch. She was wearing her favorite blue dress, which made her feel tall and slender.

Two men on the front seat removed their hats, smiled, and nodded to acknowledge her. One of them spoke to the other in Gaelic and wagged his eyebrows.

Her ears perked up when she heard the familiar sounds. She waved.

"Good day, m'lady," the driver said.

"*Dia duit*," Katherine said, using one of the few Gaelic phrases her father had taught her—Hello. She giggled and gave an exaggerated curtsey in return.

The young men hooted with delight.

The driver's companion returned the greeting. "*Agus dia duit!*"

On the end of the wagon, another young man sat, legs dangling, as the load bumped along over the plank road. "*Cad is ainm duit?*" he yelled as they pulled away.

"*Katherine is anim dom!*" she called back. "Katherine Haley!" She wondered if he could hear her over the noise of the iron-clad wagon wheels on the planks.

He smiled and waved.

Katherine waved back and watched the tall, dark-haired boy on the back of the wagon until they passed over the next hill. Then she turned back up the dirt path toward the sad house that she hated so much.

Wednesday, March 23, 1871

Hernando, Mississippi

When Peter McHugh saw the young woman across the street with her little brothers, he dropped the bricks and dusted off his hands on his trousers. He and his friends, Thomas Kearns and Thomas Flynn, were working on the courthouse construction project. Their job consisted mostly of cleaning up and hauling off debris, but Peter had apprenticed as a blacksmith before being hired for the job. They had all moved to Hernando from Memphis last year.

"Lookee there," Peter said to Kearns. "That girl we seen on the road. She's a pretty one." Peter had been riding on the back of the wagon when he first spotted her.

"Aye. And she don't look like such a fancy type, so ya might have a chance wi' 'er. Go on then. Go talk to 'er."

Peter took his bandana from his back pocket, dunked it into the water trough, and wrung it out. He wiped his face and hands. "How do I look?" he asked Kearns.

"Still just as ugly as ever ya were, but you'd better go talk to 'er, nonetheless."

Peter punched his pal on the shoulder with a grin and then walked across the street to catch up with the girl and her brothers.

~

Katherine stopped outside of Smith and Monroe's clothing store to look at the beautiful green dress in the window. It boasted a tight waist, a fitted bodice, a slightly lowered neckline, and puffy shoulders—the new style now. The skirt hung straight down the front, and a big bow sat above a small bustle in the back. The mannequin in the window stood by a small table displaying the matching hat and gloves. It reminded her of the pleasant dream she often had—and never wanted to end.

In the dream, she was at a party at a big hotel in Memphis with nice people in a pretty room that had beautiful furniture and carpeting. She had her hair pinned up and wore some jewelry. She and her friends sat by the fountain in the lobby and listened

Chapter 6

to the music playing in the ballroom. A waiter brought them little sandwiches on pretty plates, and a nice young man brought her a lemonade and asked her to dance.

"Good morning," someone said. "Lovely day for bein' out, to be sure. Nice spring weather."

Katherine, startled from her daydream, whirled around. "Oh, good morning. Yes, out for a few things from town today."

"I saw you last week—we were riding out on the wagon. I asked you your name, but I couldn't hear you answer."

"I'm Katherine. Katherine Haley."

"Well, nice to meet you then, Miss Katherine. I'm Pete McHugh. What has your mother sent you for today? Are you out for one of these new dresses then?" He turned toward the window. "That green dress there would look lovely on any Irish girl."

Katherine felt her ears burn with embarrassment. "Our mother died more than a year ago now, and no, there'll be no store-bought clothing in our house, to be certain." Feeling flustered, she turned to continue down the walk.

Peter took off his hat and walked backward in front of her. "Oh, sorry then to hear about your ma."

W. D. and Thomas returned to Katherine's side, no doubt feeling protective.

"These are two of my brothers, W. D. and Thomas," Katherine said. "I have two other little brothers and a little sister at home."

"Aye, a house full of young men and lovely girls," Peter replied, smiling at her brothers and then at her.

She blushed. "You're Irish. From where?"

"County Leitrim. Came here in sixty-six and apprenticed to a blacksmith in Memphis. Working on the new courthouse here."

"My father is from Ireland, too, but I don't know where."

"Well, it's always good to meet a fellow Irishman. I should come along with you so I can talk to him. We might know some of the same people, mightn't we? Where do you live?"

Katherine looked away. "I need to get on back home."

169

"Well then, I should come out with you to meet your pa. Perhaps we're from the same county, to be sure."

"Oh, it's a long walk. You need to get back to work, and we've got to go now." She ducked past him on the walkway. "It was nice to meet you."

"Aye. 'Twas certainly lovely to meet you, as well."

She hurried the boys off toward home, glancing over her shoulder once.

He waved.

~

As Peter crossed the street to the worksite, his buddies hooted at him.

"Well, is it a match then?" Flynn asked. "Shall we send word up to Memphis for a priest?"

"Och, no. Her name is Katherine, and her pa's from Ireland, but she didn't say where. A bit secretive, she was."

"Ha, I'll bet you scared her," Flynn said.

"She's just got to warm up to the idea of having a man fancy her," Peter said.

"What man would that be?" Kearns asked.

Peter scoffed at his friend. "She might just warm up to me yet."

Monday, March 28, 1871

Hernando, Mississippi

Michael exited the hardware store with W. D. As he donned his hat and looked across the street to survey the construction, he saw a young blacksmith suddenly drop what he was doing and run toward them.

The young man removed his hat. "Mr. Haley, sir?"

"Aye," Michael said, taken aback and wary of the too-friendly stranger.

"I'm Peter McHugh. Came down from Memphis, I did, to work on the courthouse last year. I'm from Ireland too." He offered his hand.

"Aye, lots of Irish in Memphis," Michael said. They shook his hand. "What do you need then?" He half expected a request for a favor or a loan.

"Well, sir," Peter said, hesitating, "I met your family last week when they were out here on the square shopping." He nodded to W. D. "I recognized your son here. That's how I knew it must be you."

"Aye, 'tis then." Michael turned to go.

"Sir?"

Michael stopped and turned back to the earnest young man.

"I've completed an apprenticeship—in Memphis—with a blacksmith." Peter spoke rapidly. "Of course, I'm just starting out. I'm just doing wagon fittings and wheels here with this part of the construction project, but I've done hinges and tools and repaired broken hardware. I'm quite good at it—er—not to boast sir, but Mr. Robinson is a master blacksmith, and he taught me in Memphis, and it's him that said I'm quite good. What I mean to say is that I'm not a slouch like many. I'm a hard worker, and I have a good trade, and I know that, um . . ."

"Go on," Michael said.

"Sir, I was wondering." The young lad paused. "I mean, I'd like to ask if I can call on your daughter Katherine. That is, if you approve, sir."

Michael studied the tall, skinny boy for a moment. Had he had the chance, he wondered, would he have been brave enough to approach James White in the same way?

"All right then," he said and turned to go.

Thursday, May 16, 1872

The Hernando Press (Hernando, Mississippi)

THE BALL—*The members of the Memorial Society will give a Ball, on to-morrow Friday night the 17ᵗʰ inst., at the Male Institute. The proceeds of which will be devoted to the erection of a Monument to the Confederate dead.*

Friday, May 17, 1872

The DeSoto County Poor Farm

Peter helped Katherine up into the wagon and then climbed in beside her. Mrs. Duglis watched the couple silently from the porch. The memorial ball at the boys' school had been the talk of the town for several weeks. Katherine had been evasive after Peter had invited her, but he had managed to deduce the reason and had bought her the green dress she had been eyeing in the storefront window the day they first met. He'd gotten a new jacket and pants for himself too and looked handsome. She was thrilled to be attending the event with him.

They smiled at each other as they set out from the house, but before they crossed the bridge over the ditch and turned onto the plank road, she spotted her father walking back from town.

He appeared confused, then irritated. "Why are you dressed so? Where do you two think you are going?"

"We're going to the ball at the boys' school. Peter got me a dress so he could take me."

"Sir, I—"

"Hold your tongue, young man. You should have asked me about all this first." Michael turned to Katherine. "You can't be out at night with a young man without a chaperone. People will talk. What would your mother say about all this?"

Katherine feared that she might not be allowed to go to the dance. Her frustration, her humiliation at living at the poorhouse, and the anger about the secret that her father had kept from her spilled out before she could stop herself. "I don't know who my mother is, so I wouldn't know what she'd say." She felt the blood rushing into her face.

"What are you—"

She cut him off. "Do you mean my *real* mother? The mother you never told me about?"

Her father's shocked expression softened.

Katherine saw the recognition in his face. "The letter was right then? It's true, isn't it?"

He looked away from them and furrowed his brow in thought, leaving an uncomfortable silence. "Your mother died when you were born. Sophie cared for you ever since you were just two weeks old. She was your ma—you've never known another. She loved you so much. We didn't think that really mattered. That's why we never told you."

"Still, you should have. If I'd known when I was younger, it probably wouldn't have mattered, and I'd have had time to talk to her about it. Now it seems like my whole life has been just a big secret up until now. A big lie."

Her father stared at her blankly. "I'm sorry."

"Peter, let's go on now."

"Mr. Haley, sir," Peter said as the wagon lurched forward, "we won't be late. I promise."

Saturday, November 23, 1872

The Weekly Panola Star (Sardis, Mississippi)

We glean the following items from Desoto county as furnished by the Hernando Press and Times for the last week, that will interest our readers:

The grand jury in their report to the court last week, state that the county has never been so free from crime, and that peace and good will prevails. They compliment Judge Fisher and District Attorney M. C. Brady.

The Board of Supervisors passed complimentary resolutions to the contractor of the new courthouse upon completion of his contract.

Friday, December 6, 1872

The DeSoto County Poor Farm

Katherine knelt down, kissed Robert and Fannie on the cheek, and then hugged them both to her. When she broke their embrace, she held them at arm's length. "I'll be back in a while, and I'll come get you. I promise."

"Where ya goin'?" Robert asked.

"Me and Peter are going away, but we'll be back. When Daddy gets home, you can get one of the boys to read him this letter." She held up the folded piece of paper for the littlest ones to see and then placed it on the table.

"What does it say?" Fannie asked, seemingly unconcerned as she skipped across the room to pick up the cat. The calico sagged in her arms like a rag doll.

Katherine didn't answer.

"When will Daddy and Thomas and Mickey and W. D. be back?" Fannie asked.

"I don't know. They went to town early."

Katherine heard footsteps on the front porch. The door opened, exposing them to a blast of cold air and the morning sunlight. Peter came in, and Robert ran to see him.

"Hey, little man." Pete put a hand on the boy's shoulder and turned to Katherine. "You ready then?"

She hugged the children again. "You're family. Always take care of each other and stay together." She wiped away a tear that rolled down her cheek.

After fetching her things from the bedroom, all wrapped in an old skirt, Katherine hurried back through the front room, where she tried not to look at the little ones again. Peter took the bundle from her and followed her out onto the porch.

Mrs. Duglis sat in the corner near the stove with a quilt on her lap, observing silently.

"When ya comin' back?" Fannie called just as Peter closed the door.

~

When Michael and the boys returned after lunch, he found the letter lying on the table. He picked it up and asked the old woman, "What's this for?"

Mrs. Duglis watched Fannie as she teased the cat with a feather on a string but remained mute.

"Katherine left it," Robert said. "She said for W. D. or Mickey to read it for you."

"Where is she?"

"She went with Mr. Pete."

Michael stepped out onto the front porch. The boys weren't in the yard, but he could see them down at the pond. "Thomas!" he yelled for the nine-year-old. "Come up here for a minute."

When Thomas returned, they went inside, and Michael gave him the letter.

"What's this?" Thomas asked.

"From Katherine. Read it out."

Daddy,

Me and Peter are in love, and we're going to marry. He is a good man and got a good trade and works hard, and I know that he can work wherever we live. Don't be angry. I am twenty now. I'm big enough to make my own decisions. I know he'll be a good husband. When we get settled, I will write you a letter again.

Katherine

"What does it mean?" Fannie asked.

"It means she's not comin' back," Michael said.

"Uh-uh," Fannie protested. "That's not true. She said she was." Fannie waved the string in front of the cat again.

Michael stared out the window at the row of forlorn shacks that housed the most pitiful people in the county. He knew that he was now truly one of them. Katherine must have thought so too. Otherwise, why would she have fled? He turned to survey the room and saw that it was the same as what he'd run away from in Ireland—disability, squalor, despondence. Too many children, too many wants, not enough hope. *I can't much blame her.*

"People can't always do what they say they want," he said to Fannie. "Sometimes it's just too much, and they have to go."

"What's too much?"

"Life."

Fannie stopped and looked up at her father with genuine concern. "Well, we're family. We have to stay together. That's what Katherine said."

Sunday, August 10, 1873

"Happy Hollow" District, Memphis, Tennessee

William Davis staggered down the gangplank from the barge tug *Bee*. For the past two days, he'd had a fever with unbearable headaches in the front and back of his head, like someone stabbing him with a knife from both directions. He was delirious. His mouth was parched, his tongue a thick white slab. His eyes watered and burned.

Slowly and unsteadily, he made his way up the alley from the waterfront toward the house of Fergus Riley in the poor Irish district squeezed between the Chickasaw Bluff and the river. Ankle-deep in muddy filth with the runoff from the city above, the whole neighborhood smelled putrid. He had stayed with Fergus and his family on prior trips through Memphis while working steamboats up the river and back to New Orleans, where they'd been last week. He hoped he could make it to their place. *If I could just lay down to rest.*

When he reached the tiny shack, he eased himself onto the front stoop and leaned against the wall. Nausea overtook him, and he felt the contents of his stomach rise into his throat, then black vomit spewed from his mouth and nose.

The mosquitoes from the rain barrel swarmed around him.

William fell forward into the stinky muck. His heart raced, and his breathing grew shallow.

A winged vector from the rain barrel alighted on his neck, searching for her next blood meal. Others gathered too. They drank deeply, uninterrupted by the now-unconscious man. She left him in search of a mate, and the next day, she laid her eggs in the rainwater standing in an unused pot under the edge of a house down the street.

Sunday, September 14, 1873

The Memphis Daily Appeal (Memphis, Tennessee)

THE YELLOW FEVER

NOT EPIDEMIC IN MEMPHIS

We publish this morning the resolution of the board of health declaring the presence of the yellow-fever in the city. Why the declaration should be made will not be clear to many of our citizens. According to the resolution itself the disease is not epidemic, being confined to one locality; therefore we think it would have been more prudent for the board to have published the specific causes of death in the regular weekly mortuary report and let the facts speak for themselves . . . We regret the resolution, but trust the facts will be taken as full interpretation of it. Yellow-fever is not epidemic here. When it is, the APPEAL will say so.

Saturday, September 27, 1873

The DeSoto County Poor Farm

Thomas looked up as his father entered the house and sat at the small table. Michael Haley didn't look well. He was flushed and sweating profusely. His whole body shook.

"What's wrong, Papa?"

"Headed to courthouse to collect, but Jæsus, my head hurts so. Didna think I'd get home. Where are the others?"

"W. D. and Mickey are in the garden. R. L. and baby Fannie are out back with Mrs. Duglis."

Thomas heard the footsteps of his siblings as they bounded up the porch and through the open front door.

"I'm not a baby!" Fannie said indignantly.

Robert Lee closed the door behind them.

"Papa," Fannie said as she stepped closer, "are you okay?"

"Och, I just need to lie down." His knees buckled as he tried to stand, and he collapsed beside the table.

Thomas leapt up to help and scrambled around the others to where his father lay. He grabbed him by the arm and shoulder, trying to pull him back into a seated position, but his dead weight was too much. Fannie and R. L. stood a few feet away, dumbstruck.

"Stay here," Thomas said as he bolted out the door. "I'll get Mickey and W. D." When he spotted his brothers working in the garden, he called out to them. "Daddy fell, an' he looks sick! Come quick!"

W. D. leaned his hoe against the fence and ran toward Thomas. Farther off, Mickey grabbed the basket with the beans he'd been picking and headed for the house.

Their father had a hand over his face and didn't look up when the three boys clambered up the steps and into the room. He was breathing heavily, and his mouth hung open.

Mr. Duglis, older and even more feeble than his wife, crept over to assess the situation as he peered in from the doorway.

"Better go fetch the doc. He got the fever. Fannie, get some water and a rag an' we cool him off some."

After the three older boys helped Michael to the bed, Thomas took off toward town to find Dr. Hall. At the train station, he noticed a crowd that had either just gotten off the train that was now preparing to depart or couldn't get a ticket for the trip out. A good number of folks he recognized, but many more he didn't. At the big house where Mr. Banks lived, the black help were dragging a mattress out to a burn pile, already alight with bedding. On Commerce Street, Mrs. Elizabeth Merriweather stood outside of Dr. Hall's closed office. Her wide hat shielded her from the afternoon sun, and she had a fist-sized bag hanging by a cord around her neck.

"Mrs. Merriweather, ma'am," Thomas said between breaths, "we need Dr. Hall at our house. You seen him? Papa took sick."

"No, child. He's out on a call now to Mary Nelson's. She's sick too. What's wrong with your daddy?"

"Don't know, ma'am. Took a fever today when he come back from town. Mr. Duglis told me to get the doctor."

"Oh my. Does he have the Bronze John?" She lifted the bag to her face and wrinkled her nose as she took a step back.

"What's a Bronze John?"

"You hadn't heard? It's the yellow fever, child. People who get it turn orange as a pumpkin if they real sick. Some folks'll get better, but lots of 'em die. All these ones comin' from Memphis are gettin' out of town 'cause they's lots of it there." She waved in the direction of the train station. "Been goin' on for weeks now."

"Oh, thank you," Thomas said, now apprehensive. "Do you know where Mrs. Nelson's house is?"

"Down the Belmont Road, on the right. Before you get to Mussacuna Creek."

"Thank you," he said and hurried off in that direction.

After another half mile of walking, Thomas found Dr. Hall's buggy outside the Nelsons' house. He heard people crying inside, so he waited in the nearby shade. Soon, the door opened, and the doctor came out with Mr. Nelson. They both looked somber. Dr.

Hall put his hand on Mr. Nelson's shoulder as he stared at the ground, and they talked together for a moment.

"We know you don't catch it from another person," the doctor said. "You won't get it from having nursed her, and those who recover from a mild case won't ever get it again. I'm terribly sorry for your loss." He finally turned to depart.

As the doctor loaded his bag into the large basket fastened across the back of the buggy, Thomas approached sheepishly, hat in hand. "Dr. Hall," he said in the most grown-up way he could muster, "I'm Thomas Haley, sir, and I got sent to ask if you could please come see our daddy. He got sick with a fever today."

"Haley?"

"Yes, sir." Thomas stared at the doctor's boots. "We keep the poor farm."

"Yes, I've known your father for several years now. Well, hop up here beside me, and let's get on out there. Is anyone else in the family sick?"

"No, sir."

"Are any of the house residents sick?"

"Not so's I can tell."

They covered the mile back to town in just a few minutes and again passed the station, where the people Thomas had seen earlier were still milling about. The poor farm was a mile farther north.

"These folks are evacuating from Memphis," Dr. Hall said. "There's lots of fever up there. Some of them are probably sick with it right now."

Thomas looked at the crowd with a new sense of unease as they passed. "The Bronze John?"

"Why, yes, that's what some call it," the doctor said, glancing down at Thomas. "It gives you bad liver trouble."

"What was that thing that Mrs. Merriweather had on a string?"

"What do you mean?"

"She had this thing around her neck, and she stuck it up to her nose when I told her that Papa had a fever."

"Oh, that's an asphidity bag. Some people think that it will keep the yellow fever away, but I don't think it works. Not sure about putting powder lime on the streets either, like they're doing in Memphis."

"What causes it—the yellow fever?"

"I don't know. Dr. Saunders thinks we ought to burn the bedding of people who died, but from what I can tell, you can't catch it from someone else, even if you sleep in the same bed with the sick person. Somehow it spreads, though."

They rode the rest of the way in silence. Thomas worried about what would happen if he got yellow fever. Who would take care of his bean plants?

When they got back to the poorhouse, Thomas led Dr. Hall in through the front door. In the back room, Thomas found his father, barely conscious.

Dr. Hall took Michael's wrist to feel his pulse and put his other hand on his forehead. He lifted one of Michael's eyelids. There was a yellowish tinge where white should have been.

"He has the yellow fever," the doctor announced to the room.

No one said a word.

Dr. Hall gave some instructions to Mr. and Mrs. Duglis on how to nurse him. "Rest is most important. Be sure he stays in bed. He may get delirious and try to get up and walk around, but keep him bundled up to burn off the fever." He took a cup from the table. "Get him to drink half a cup of cool water every hour, and try to keep track of how often he passes water. Ma'am," he said to the old woman, "make some thin, salty soup and give it to him when it cools off."

He turned to Thomas's older brothers. "You boys go and collect up some dogwood bark and willow bark for Mrs. Duglis to brew some tea for him." As if noticing the little ones for the first time, the doctor knelt beside Fannie and R. L. "Look at how big you are now."

"I'm gonna be six," Fannie said.

"I remember bringing you into this world just like it was yesterday. Would you two come stay at our house for a few days 'til your daddy gets better?"

R. L. glanced over at Thomas and W. D. for approval.

"I think that'll be okay," W. D. said. "We'll be busy here till Papa gets better. Then you can come back home."

R. L. seemed reassured by his brother's confidence and nodded silently to the doctor.

"Our daughter, Loulie, will be happy to have someone to play with, and we have new puppies at our house that are really fun." Dr. Hall smiled at Fannie. "I'm sure you'd like that."

The doctor gave some more instruction to the boys and then to Mr. and Mrs. Duglis. "Send word to let me know if he has black vomit or if he stops making water."

Thomas helped R. L. and Fannie into the buggy and then tucked a rolled-up collection of extra clothes into the basket on the back. "We'll come fetch you in a couple of days when Papa's better. Be good. Mind the doc, and watch out for each other." He kissed Fannie on the forehead and squeezed Robert's hand.

Dr. Hall prompted the horse, and it lumbered forward, jolting the buggy to a roll. The children waved at their brothers, and Thomas watched as they grew smaller and smaller in the distance.

Friday, October 3, 1873

Public Ledger (Memphis, Tennessee)

SCENES OF DISTRESS

The unutterable woe and distress depicted upon every face that peers out of the lonely houses in Happy Hollow and Pinch and appeals for sympathy and help will never be known to the outside world or even to our refugees, scattered over West Tennessee and half a dozen states waiting for two or three white frosts . . .

Case number one, last night a sister of charity found a woman very low with the yellow fever. Her feeble moan was the only response that answered the voice of mercy. By her side, on the same hard, narrow bed, lay the contracted form of her dead husband, who died not long before of yellow fever. This in the only bedroom and the only bed in the humble little shanty they had known as home. A sickly light from a feeble lamp, placed there perhaps by some tenant neighbor struggled to throw its pale sallow rays over the ill-furnished apartment and in the faces of the dead and dying. No nurse or doctor or kind, courageous neighbor was found there by the gentle Sister. She procured a mattress somewhere for the sick woman and caused other comforts to be provided.

Case number two was in a dingy, dilapidated old rookery with a sickening odor as if from the depths of a charnel house. No one had sought them out for days. Their neighbors had their own funerals and sick ones to attend, and when they found by an angel of mercy, the husband, all pinched and shriveled, with his last mortal agony, lay dead, and by his side was a wan and hollow-eyed wife, not able to rise, but holding to her parched-up bosom a wailing skeleton of an infant not yet two hours old. These two cases properly authenticated are enough for one day. Many others might be described. The heart sickens at the thought and we turn to the public to ask relief.

Monday, October 6, 1873

The DeSoto County Poor Farm

In the haze of the fever, Michael saw Dr. Hall leaning over him as he lifted an eyelid.

"Michael. Michael?"

He couldn't respond. The light went out, and the voices faded to garbled noise. He was suddenly so cold.

Oh, there—Sophronia.

Wasn't she so pretty and so much fun to be with? She was holding baby Sidney.

I miss you so, dear. The children are so big now. Fine, they are—all of 'em. 'Tis been so hard since you left. Oh, I love you so.

Then the sadness and embarrassment burned. He had to tell her.

But Katherine's gone an' left—I don't know where she is. Ran off with Peter. Same age you were when we left Georgia. Och! Sophronia, I'm sorry. 'Twas so hard for her after you died.

Sophronia smiled and caressed his face. She was so pretty. Suddenly another lovely young woman appeared as Sophronia faded away.

Oh, there you are, Katherine. Where did you go? We all miss you. Is Peter good to you?

She waved at him and smiled. And then there was her mother, too, standing with her arms around their daughter before they faded away.

No! Don't go! Stay. Oh, please stay. I was so sad when you died. I was so lost. Didn't know what to do. But I found her a mother, and I did my best for her—I promise. I did my best.

He turned down the lane and strolled between the stone walls toward their tiny plot of emerald-green land.

Mother. Mother? Oh, Mother, I'm here now. I couldna come before, but I'm back. I came back for you. Can you come to America wi' me now?

The woman took a step from the corner of the house and looked up the lane when she heard him call, but she wasn't old. She wasn't stooped over and crippled anymore. She waved and smiled when she saw him.

Where are my brothers? Did they grow up fine? And my sisters—did they marry?

Suddenly W. D. ran from behind the little cottage out into the tiny narrow lane. An elephant lumbered behind him, reaching out toward the boy with his long trunk. Michael tried to take chase, to help his son, to distract the elephant.

"Here! Hey, hey! Over here! Run, W. D.!"

Suddenly Michael's feet were freezing cold. He couldn't move. He tried to lift his legs, but they were stuck. He looked down at his uniform boots and pants, stuck in the muddy road to Corinth. He couldn't pull his feet from the deep mud. When he looked up, he saw Private Applewhite and Corporal Bowen riding away on the elephant's back, chasing W. D.

Run! Run!

Wake up, W. D.! Wake up!

~

Wake up, W. D.! Wake up!

The yelling and commotion from the other side of the house pulled Michael back from his hallucination. His head swam, and his nausea was overwhelming. He tried to swallow but couldn't. Through bleary eyes, he saw the boys' empty beds.

Where are they?

Sunlight poured through the window, and he could just make out Thomas, who was standing in the big room and shaking W. D., who lay on the sofa.

"Wake up!" Thomas yelled. He turned to speak to someone. "I think W. D. is sick."

Dr. Hall came into view. He examined W. D. and then put his hand on Thomas's shoulder, but the boy flung his arm away.

"What's wrong? Wake up! Wake up!"

Michael made an effort to rise but couldn't even lift his head from the pillow. *Got to get to the boys.* He gave up, exhausted, and his vision faded again.

Then, suddenly, everything was light.

~

Mickey and Thomas had already started digging the second grave in the late afternoon, well before Dr. Hall returned that evening.

Thomas had been trying to keep his brother cool with a wet cloth, but when he returned from the well, W. D.'s breathing had stopped. Thomas sat for several minutes on the edge of the bed in the big room with his brother, silently thinking. W. D. had taught him to fish and how to skin a rabbit. One time, W. D. had taken the blame when Thomas had broken a window in the house.

Thomas reached over and ran a hand down his brother's face, closing his eyelids. *I don't know why he did that. Katherine was madder at him than she would have been at me.* It wasn't until he thought about Katherine—then Daddy, then Mama—that the tears started. They welled up in his eyes and then came in a torrent.

When Dr. Hall returned to the poorhouse before dusk, Thomas met him on the plank road. "W. D. is dead."

The doctor's mouth wrinkled into a frown. He stepped down from the buggy, put his hand on Thomas's shoulder, and wrapped his arms around him. Thomas felt the tears rushing down his cheeks.

Dr. Hall helped Thomas and Mickey wrap W. D. in a sheet, and they took him on the back of the buggy to the pauper's cemetery, beyond the garden, and over the hill behind the poorhouse. They lowered his body into a grave next to their father, whom they'd buried that morning. They fashioned two crosses out of wood, and Mickey used his pocketknife to scratch a name into each one.

~

Dr. Hall mounted the steps at the back door with a lantern, where he saw the children sleeping on the floor in the pantry.

He'd been out on other calls all day, after which he'd had to give the report at the relief committee meeting, so when he finally came home, it was very late.

He knelt on the floor beside Fannie and Robert and woke them gently.

The children sat up on their makeshift mattresses.

"Miss Fannie, Robert, I have to tell you some bad news. You know he had the yellow fever, like so many other people now, and this morning he . . . well, your daddy was . . . he was so sick. He died today. When I went by to check in on him and your brothers this morning, he was so sick. Now it seems that W. D. had the yellow fever, and he died, too."

They both looked blankly at him in the lamplight. Then Fannie's face contorted in sadness, and she cried.

"When can we go back home?" R. L. asked.

"Well, let's give it a few more days."

"I want to go home now." Tears poured down Fannie's face, and snot ran from her nose. "I want to see Thomas and Mickey."

"We can't," R. L. said. "It's the middle of the night." He reached over, took her hand in his, and put his arm awkwardly around his little sister in a manner much older and more mature than a seven-year-old.

Dr. Hall pulled together the two pallets and helped them lie back down together, tucking the sheet around them both. "Tomorrow, I'll go over to check on them," he said as he smoothed Fannie's hair away from her face, "and we'll decide what to do."

Fannie sobbed inconsolably. Robert stared at the wall in silence.

Monday, October 13, 1873

Hernando, Mississippi

Dr. Hall opened the door and was immediately set upon with a barrage from his wife.

"Lawrence, you've got to do something," Helen said. "Initially, I didn't mind keeping these two since you said they'd just play with Loulie all day. But I thought they'd be back home in a week. But now they're so loud. It's always something with one of them."

"You just go on about your business," he said, trying to calm her. "Parthena can look after them." He sat down next to her at the kitchen table.

"Lawrence, I have, but two extra children to watch keeps her from all her other work. Honestly, dear, we just can't keep them any longer. You're gone all the time now, and I know this fever can't go on forever, but, Lawrence, really, think. What if *you* get sick? Think of your children and me. What will we do? We can't take on every orphan in the county."

He took his wife's hand. He'd been so busy these past six weeks that he'd hardly been home, often leaving the house before his wife and children woke up and returning home after they'd gone to bed. He sighed and looked out the window, exhausted. As soon as the hard frosts came, they would bring an end to the spread of the fever. But there was no telling when the chillier weather would arrive.

"The Haley boys can barely care for themselves, Helen," he finally said. "There's no one else at church who can take them, and every day we risk having more orphans in town. The county will find someone else to run the poorhouse, and the older boys can stay there, but these two—I don't know. They're so young."

"Lawrence, please. I just can't take it anymore. And I worry so about you."

"At the relief committee meeting, they said that the Catholic orphan home in Memphis is still taking children. I can tell Moses to carry them up there tomorrow."

"Oh, thank goodness. That'll be better for them, and we can try to get back to normal here."

Part II
Robert and Fannie

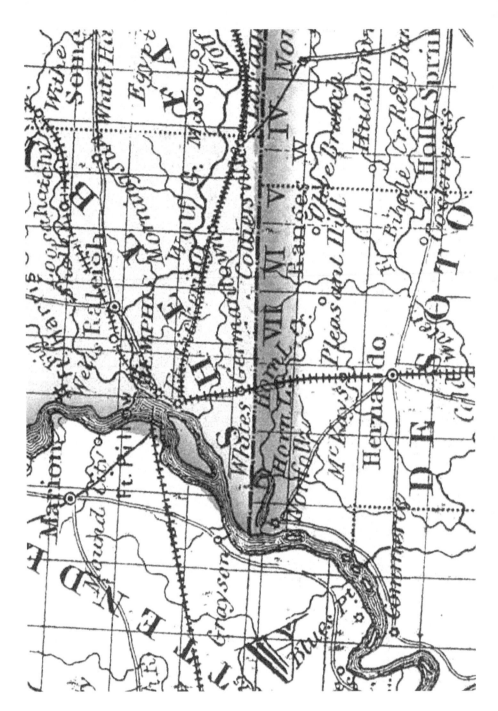

Tennessee and Mississippi (detail), New Illustrated Family Atlas, Johnson and Ward, New York, 1864. Courtesy of David Rumsey Map Collection, www.davidrumsey.com.

Chapter 7

Tuesday, October 14, 1873

Public Ledger (Memphis, Tennessee)

Sister Laurenta, of St. Peter's orphan asylum, informs Major Busby that they can accommodate 100 or even 200 orphans if the committee will supply clothing, bedding, and provisions.

Tuesday, October 14, 1873

The Memphis Daily Appeal (Memphis, Tennessee)

Intelligent yellow fever doctors and nurses are much encouraged by the frost of last night and the night before to believe that "yellow jack" has had his back broken. We hope so sincerely.

The Board of Health are working well. The principal streets were yesterday cleaned and sprinkled with lime. Carbolic acid will follow today. The people have only to be prudent and obey the health laws and all will soon be well.

We cannot too strongly impress our citizens with the importance of continuing the beneficial work of disinfecting. Although the cool nights may do much to dissipate the scourge, still disinfectants should be continued. Anyone knowing a dereliction of sanitary duties or a violation of sanitary laws is requested to report the same under real signature to The APPEAL.

Leith orphan asylum has not been filled simply because there were not means to support more children. If the Citizens Relief Committee or others, will furnish necessary subsistence, the managers will gladly fill the building with orphans, even to its utmost capacity.

One of our compositors informs us (and we can direct the attention of inspector O'Bannon to it), that the body of Mrs. Wilkinson, who died on Sunday evening last, on Clay Street, between LaRose and De Soto St., is still unburied, and the neighbors say they cannot stand the odor. Her son is also in an adjoining room suffering from yellow fever and without a nurse.

Editor's appeal – please call the attention of the board of health to the yellow fever bedclothing on the rear roof of 101 Jefferson St. Also, a dead animal in the rear of the same. The secretary of the board of health and sanitary sergeant have been notified twice.

Wednesday, October 15, 1873

The Memphis Daily Appeal (Memphis, Tennessee)

According to your suggestion that every man should report any infringement of the rules of the Board of Health, and which I think, is proper: there is a Negro lying dead since Saturday on Pontotoc Street near Hernando, and not buried yet, the bedding and clothes in which he died being exposed to the open air, breeding contagion and disease to the neighboring.

Friday, October 17, 1873

Hernando, Mississippi

Before the sun rose over the trees, Mrs. Hall wrapped some bacon and biscuits in a piece of paper and gave them to old Moses, who had pulled the wooden wagon to the back door. Without questioning, the two little Haleys climbed into the back with their meager belongings. Loulie stood on the porch clutching one of the puppies and waved. Fannie hesitated before waving back to her.

After they'd been riding for half an hour, Robert realized that they'd left Hernando, but he had no idea where they were. "Mr. Moses, where we goin'?"

"Goin' to Meh'fis. They's some church ladies there take care of li'l chirrens who parents gone."

"Will Mickey and Thomas be there?"

"Ah s'pec' so," Moses said.

"Oh," Robert said.

They rode in silence the rest of the way, crossing the Nonconnah Creek near noon. As they came into town, the sour-sweet smell of sickness and decay grew thicker. The streets were empty, save for wagons stacked three and four high with coffins, and on every block, piles of bedding burned in smoky fires in open spaces. White lime powder covered the main thoroughfares.

Moses stopped to ask for directions. After a few more turns and another half-hour of riding over the bumpy plank and cobbled streets, he stopped the wagon in front of a large brick building with a tall steeple on the roof over the front entrance. Robert had never seen such an enormous structure. It was three stories high and surrounded by a tall iron fence that extended in both directions as far as the eye could see. A few other smaller buildings were visible on the grounds.

At the front gate, a yard man stood holding a rake. He peered out at them and hollered to Moses. "What you want?"

"Dis Saint Petah Orphan home?" Moses called back. "Got two chirren heah from H'nando. They daddy died of the fever an' they mama dead for a long time. Dr. Hall wife say fo' me to take 'em up here for the orphan home."

"Yeah, dis da orphan home. You wait. I'll get Sister."

Robert held Fannie's hand and peered over the side of the wagon.

The man returned with a tall woman wearing a long black dress and a strange white hat. She seemed to be just a face on top of a dress.

Where are her arms? Robert wondered. *Why does she have her hair covered up like that?*

The man unlocked the gate and opened it, stepping aside for her as she floated down the steps to the street.

"Children, welcome," she said sweetly. "Let me help you down. Are you hungry? Do you need something to eat?" She uncrossed her arms, pushed her hands out of her sleeves, and reached into the back of the wagon for them.

Robert was relieved to see that she had hands.

She smiled as she helped them down. "What are your names?"

"Where's Thomas and Mickey?" Robert asked.

"What, dear?"

"Are my brothers here?"

"Why, there are lots of brothers and sisters here for you."

"Is Katherine here too?" Fannie asked brightly.

"You poor dear. Such an angel." The sister smiled and brushed Fannie's hair from her face. "I'm Sister Laurenta. Please come this way. Let's get you something for lunch." She turned to the groundskeeper. "Thaddeus, bring this man in so we can get the details from him." She shepherded the children up the stairs and into the building.

Thaddeus brought Moses and closed the gate behind them.

In a room off the kitchen, one of the servants brought Robert and Fannie some cheese sandwiches. While they were eating,

Robert heard a bell and then the sound of children scrambling out onto the playground. He stood up on the chair to look out the window.

A different black-dress woman entered from the kitchen. "Sit down!" she snapped. "We do not stand on chairs. Chairs are for sitting."

Fannie looked up from her plate. "Well, how's he gonna see out then?" she said, innocently.

The woman shook her head at Fannie and then took Robert by the arm and helped him down. "Hurry up and finish eating. You need to take a bath before the doctor sees you."

"I'm not sick, am I?" Robert said, concerned. "I don't need to see the doctor."

"We don't know that. Before we can put you in with the other children, you have to be clean, and we have to examine you."

After they finished lunch, she ushered them down a long hallway that smelled of lye soap and into a tiled room with several tubs and many buckets. There was a pump in one corner with a floor drain and a stove in the other corner where kettles steamed. Two more black-dress women entered and poured two buckets of water and a kettle of hot water into two different tubs.

"Let me have your clothes. We'll wash these, and you can have them back if they're all right, or we'll get you some different ones."

Robert and Fannie undressed, and the women put them each into one of the tubs. Robert closed his eyes tightly as one of the women knelt beside him and scrubbed him with a scratchy cloth. She poked her soapy fingers into his ears and nose and scrubbed every inch of his body. She raked her fingernails across his scalp and inspected his hair, then rubbed the bar of soap on his head and washed it thoroughly. Before the suds could settle, she rinsed him and dried him and then led him and his sister, each of them towel-wrapped, through the side door and into the doctor's suite.

"They don't have lice," the black-dress woman announced to the doctor who was waiting there.

The doctor sat on a stool and examined Fannie first. When it was Robert's turn, he stood still as the doctor peered into his mouth, pulled down his eyelids, and probed his neck and under his arms. The doctor inspected Robert's skin, listened to his chest, and felt his belly. "They're both fit," he pronounced when he was finished.

The black-dress women brought them back into the tub room, and Robert and Fannie put on a different set of clean clothes before being led out onto the playground. It was a big yard, with hard-packed dirt and big trees, and was surrounded by a brick wall that seemed to go on forever.

Bewildered, Robert stood with his sister until a girl older than Fannie and about the same size as Robert noticed them.

She came bounding up, excited. "Are you new? I'll be your friend. My name is Eleanor. What's yours?"

"Fannie."

"Let's go skip rope," Eleanor said, taking Fannie's hand and leading her away to meet the other little girls.

Robert stayed put and searched the yard for Thomas and Mickey.

∼

After playtime, they went into a big room where everyone had to sit and then kneel. A statue of a woman with her arms stretched outward stood in the corner, and on the wall in front was a carving of a sad man hanging by his hands. Several of the black-dress women—in unison with many of the children—murmured things that Robert couldn't understand. This went on for a while as they said the same things over and over.

"*Ave Maria, gratia plena . . .*"

Later that evening, a black-dress woman let Robert and Fannie sit together for dinner. It wasn't the norm, apparently—usually the boys and girls all sat separately—but it was their first day. Robert ate hungrily. This was more food than he could ever remember eating in one sitting.

"What is this?" Fannie asked, also enjoying the meal.

"Some kinda soup with some kinda meat," Robert answered.

They also had stewed greens and cornbread. He liked the saltiness of the stew, and it was hot.

Robert was nervous. No one had talked to him at the playground, and now dozens of eyes peered at them from both the girls' and boys' sides of the room.

Fannie had to line up with the girls when one of the women finally took them to bed.

"Say good night to your sister," the woman said. "You'll see her again in the morning."

Robert waved at Fannie as he was led up one more flight of stairs.

"Good night, Robert," Fannie said over her shoulder, apparently more confident than he was about the situation.

In the boys' hall, Robert was given the empty bed at the end of the room. A set of sleeping clothes was waiting there for him. He'd never had a pair of pajamas before. He watched the other boys fold their clothes and lay them at the foot of their beds, and he did the same before crawling under the covers.

The black-dress woman walked up and down the row of beds with her carry lantern, checking on each boy. "Let's say our bedtime prayer, please." She led them in some more words that everyone but Robert seemed to know.

"Father, unto thee I pray. Thou hast guarded me all day. Safe I am while in thy sight. Safely let me sleep tonight."

After making her final inspections, she turned to the boys. "No misbehavior," she announced to the room. "I am listening outside, and Jesus is watching you."

The dancing light faded as she walked toward the door.

Robert rolled over to face the wall. *I have to find Thomas and Mickey.*

Saturday, January 17, 1874

Memphis Daily Appeal (Memphis, Tennessee)

WANTS

ROOM—Furnished for two gentlemen near Court Square. Address this day. C.L.M., Appeal office.

NURSE—For a baby eleven months old; white preferred. Apply to PEOPLES' INS. Co., 16 Madison, St.

BOY—Immediately, a respectable lad, aged thirteen years, with good references. Apply at 291 Main Street.

HOME—Any Catholic, in comfortable circumstances wishing to adopt an orphan girl three or six years old, will please call at this office.

SITUATION—A young German of business qualifications wishes a situation; will work for small wages. Address H. O. B. Appeal Office.

BOY—A sprightly cotton office boy, from twelve to fourteen years old. Apply at 222 FRONT ST., Upstairs.

Monday, May 17, 1875

St. Peter's Catholic Orphanage, Memphis, Tennessee

The nun in a long black habit watched the children from the porch of the school building, surveying the playground through narrowed eyes. Clusters of little girls skipped and played. One scratched lines into the dirt, and the others took turns tossing a white pebble out onto the grid, indicating which of the squares they had to avoid as they hopped. Nearby, a girl skipped rope, her long braids flopping up and down with each jump as her playmates turned either end of the rope for her.

"Fannie, your turn," the girl with the braids called when the rope got caught around her ankles.

Seven-year-old Fannie handed over her end of the rope and swapped positions to take her turn in the middle.

Farther out in the yard, nine-year-old Robert and the bigger boys chased each other in a game of roundball. Robert sprawled face first into the dirt while trying to escape being tagged by the boy chasing him with the ball.

The nun pushed her hand from the long sleeve and rang the bell for the children to come to dinner. She frowned at Robert as he trotted up the stairs. "Robert Haley! Completely filthy you are, really. You can't come in for dinner like that. Go up to the dormitory to change your shirt."

Robert stared down at his dirty shirt. He brushed at the dust but managed only to spread it around. "Yes, Sister."

"And wash your hands and face!" the nun added as he turned to go.

At the washbasin in the boys' room on the third floor, he gazed out the window, past the hedge and the fence guarding the orphanage. A boy on the sidewalk on the far side of the street peered up at the building.

Startled, Robert looked again—it was his brother Thomas!

It can't be!

The boy on the street turned around again, surveying the imposing brick building, home to nearly two hundred parentless children.

It is him!

Robert pounded on the window. He screamed and waved, but Thomas didn't look up. In a flash, he'd turned the corner and was gone, headed in the direction of downtown.

Robert threw on his clean shirt and sprinted to tell the sisters. The crowd of children was just as noisy as always, and the frustrated sisters flapped around, trying in vain to quiet and organize.

"Sister, I saw my brother outside! I have to go get him!"

"Robert, in line for supper, please," the novice said. "Are your hands clean?" She pulled up an arm to inspect. "All right," she said, satisfied, and turned to go.

Robert grabbed her sleeve. "Daddy said we always have to stay together! Please! We got to go out and get Thomas! He's out there! I seen him!"

"Robert, lower your voice. We don't yell inside. Stand in line here, and we'll file in and say grace before dinner."

Thomas is out there!

Determined to tell Fannie that he had seen their brother, Robert searched the faces on the other side of the room where the girls were forming a line, but he didn't spot his sister in the small swarm waiting to be seated for the evening meal.

From the hall, Robert had a view of the corridor leading to the classrooms, and he noticed sunlight streaming across the floor. A door to the outside had been left ajar. Without another thought, he ducked out of line and ran down the hall and out the door, with no plan but to find Thomas.

After peeking around two corners before continuing, he made straight for the groundskeeper's shed, behind which he knew there was a pile of wood and broken furniture. He climbed the stack of junk, mounted the brick wall on the backside of the property, scrambled up and over in a flash, and landed outside the orphanage grounds. With no way to get back over the wall, he was committed to pursuing his brother now. He'd be in big trouble if he rang the bell at the front gate.

"Thomas!" he screamed, racing to the end of the alley and out onto the street. Downtown loomed ahead of him.

Friday, June 11, 1875

Memphis, Tennessee

"Paper, sir? Do you need a copy of today's paper?" Robert stepped in front of a fat businessman who puffed and grunted as he worked his way down from the trolley, book and cane in hand.

The well-dressed man didn't look very old, but he had a stiff-legged limp that made him teeter with every step. Robert recalled that he'd seen this man three days in a row now at the trolley stop near the Cotton Exchange.

The man peered down at him over pince-nez. "Those papers are wrinkled. You're reselling papers you've picked up from the train station," he said, with an accusatory tone.

"It's today's paper," Robert said defensively, not admitting to his scheme. "You need a paper to read or not? Just three cents."

"Well, I won't pay full price for a used paper. Just one penny, that's all."

"Three cents." Robert thought for a second. "Okay, how 'bout two cents then? You need a paper, and I'm gonna need some money to get lunch today."

"Ha, ha!" the man roared. "You are a cheeky little one. You'll be a businessman yet." He dug two pennies out of his pocket and traded Robert for one of the papers. Upon pocketing his glasses, he turned Robert around by the shoulder to walk with him. "How old are you?"

"Ten," Robert guessed. He thought that he was about as big as the boys at the orphanage who *did* know their birthdays, and some of them were ten.

"Not in school today? Where are your parents?"

He hesitated, but the man seemed nice enough. "I got no parents, sir. They died. I was in the St. Peter's home, but I ran off. Been lookin' for my brother, but I ain't found him yet." He held his hand to shield his eyes from the sun and squinted, giving the man what he hoped was an endearing look. "I been out here for three weeks now but ain't seen him. Gotta make some kinda work to get something to eat." *I just might get that extra penny yet.*

"Well, that's certainly most unfortunate." The man stopped to put his hand on his hip and then arched his back with a grimace. He fished a small brown bottle from his vest, uncorked it, and took a sip. He surveyed Robert again. "I'll tell you what. I've got a business south of here. If you can do some chores at the house and work in my store, you can stay with us. There's a school in our town you can go to."

"Nah. I gotta find my brother and get me an' our family back together."

"What have you been doing to try to find him for the past three weeks? He could be anywhere."

Robert had no answer.

"Do you even know if he's still in Memphis?"

"I don't, I guess."

"Precisely," said the fat man with an air of triumph, as though he'd won a debate contest.

Robert thought for a minute. *Maybe he's not here anymore. What if he went south back to Hernando? I could look for him there, maybe.* He looked up at the man again then glanced at his surroundings. The deal seemed better than the switches he knew he'd get from the sisters for running off. The prospect of eating regularly was appealing and he was tired of hiding in cow sheds to sleep. *Fannie will be ok there with the Sisters till I find Thomas,* he told himself.

"Well, son, what's it going to be?"

"All right then."

"I'm A. J. Black." The man extended his hand.

"Robert Lee Haley."

They shook.

"Oh, our beloved general's namesake, are you? Come with me. Let's get a sandwich, and then I have two more stops to make before we head home."

A few hours later, the fat man took him to Union Station, where he bought two tickets on the afternoon southbound run of the T & M Line. Hoisting himself onto the train was difficult for Mr. Black. He pushed his briefcase out for Robert to hold as he grabbed the rail and heaved himself up the steps, breathing heavily. When they finally took their seats on the hard folding benches, he had to leave his stiff leg stuck out in the aisle. He took a swig from the little brown bottle again.

"What's that?" Robert asked.

"Medicine. I took a minié ball to the leg in Atlanta. Pains me all the time, but at least I still got two legs. Doc Maury wanted to amputate, but I wouldn't let him."

Robert didn't respond. He recalled that Dr. Hall had talked about the possibility of amputating his father's arm after the accident. As the train started rolling south out of the station, he stared out the window and wondered what happened to a leg or an arm after it was amputated. *Where do you keep it? Will you get it back when you get to heaven?*

Mr. Black fell asleep before they'd even reached the Horn Lake stop. His head fell forward on his thick neck, and he snored most of the trip. When he was awake, he didn't say much but took sips from the little bottle every few minutes.

Wednesday, November 17, 1875

St. Peter's Catholic Orphanage, Memphis, Tennessee

The room was still, and the bright light from a full moon streamed through the window. While the other girls slept, Fannie sat up in her bed, uncertain what had woken her. She walked barefooted to the honey bucket, which sat behind a curtain in the distant corner of the room. The sisters had issued stern instructions: a child was only to make water at night; other business was for the outdoor privy.

Fannie trod softly back to bed but stopped when she heard someone crying. It was the newest addition, who had arrived the day before. She was curled up under the thin blanket with her back to the room.

"Hey, it's all right," Fannie whispered, patting the little girl on the shoulder. She sat on the edge of the bed. "Don't cry. It's all right. Did you have a bad dream?"

The tiny girl rolled over and, sniffing, wiped the hair from her face and the tears from her eyes. Her right thumb never left her mouth.

"I used to have bad dreams when I got here," Fannie said. "It's scary at first. I know. I came here when I was six. I'm eight now. How old are you?"

The little girl used her free hand to hold up four fingers.

"What's yer name?"

"Margaret," she said, removing her thumb from her mouth just long enough to answer.

"Where you from?"

The wide-eyed little girl didn't respond.

"I'm Fannie. You come here by yourself?"

Margaret nodded and then rolled back over to face the wall. She started to cry again.

Fannie lifted the edge of the blanket and lay down, wrapping her arm around the newcomer. She covered them both with the blanket. "I'm by myself now too," she whispered. "I came from M'sippi. Don't remember my mama, but my daddy died, and my brother died, and now my other brother who was here is gone."

Minutes passed, and Margaret's crying gradually gave way to shaky breaths and sniffling.

"Let's be friends. We can take care of each other. Sorta like family. Will that be all right?"

Margaret nodded almost imperceptibly.

In the morning, Fannie was awakened by a poke in the shoulder from a single bony finger. She heard the purposeful sound of the sisters' shoes on the floor and the swish of their long skirts as they pulled back the window curtains to greet the new day.

"Fannie, wake up," Sister Francis said sternly. "Each child must sleep in her own bed. You know the rules. Get up now and get dressed. It's almost time for morning prayers."

Not fully awake, Fannie sat up and looked around. It took her a moment to remember how she had ended up in the wrong bed.

"Did you hear me? You must stay in your own bed at night."

"She was sad," Fannie explained, earnestly, "and she misses her mama. She needs someone to be nice to her right now."

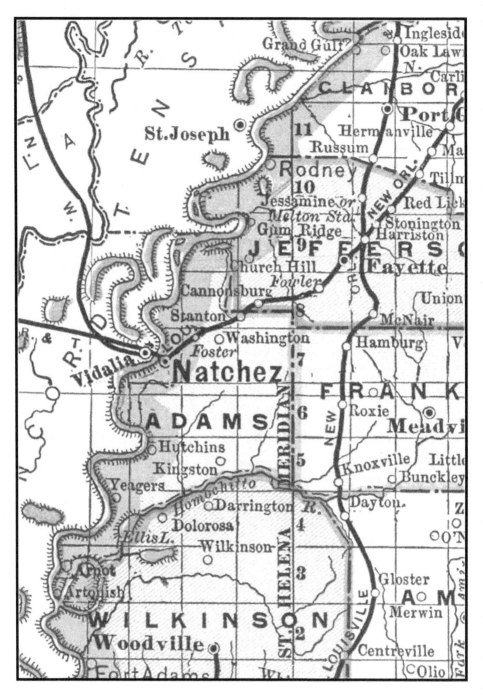

Mississippi (detail), The Library Atlas of Modern Geography, Appleton & Co., Buffalo, New York, 1892. Courtesy of David Rumsey Map Collection, www.davidrumsey.com.

Chapter 8

Sunday, April 2, 1876

Memphis Daily Appeal (Memphis, Tennessee)

THE ORPHAN'S PRAYER

Orphaned and lonely I wander about

Homeless and friendless, beginning to doubt

Even the Savior, whose promise I've read.

All seems so dire and sad since thou art dead.

Mother, I think that if I could just once more

Feel your dear arms around me as in days of yore

I would battle to gain the crown for the just

And humble my proud, haughty soul in the dust

Before the infinite father above,

And pray for His pardon and bountiful love,

A home where for ever and ever with thee

And my dearest brother together we'd be.

Sansouci

Saturday, July 20, 1876

St. Peter's Catholic Orphanage, Memphis, Tennessee

After recess, the children came in to wash before dinner. In the girls' wing, Fannie got in line with the others, the smallest girls in the front and the older ones behind. They filed down the main corridor, past the hallway to the boys' wing, where they, too, were waiting to go to prayers. The sisters shushed them, poking and prodding their charges to keep order and move things along, but the group was still fidgety and unsettled, not nearly as reverent and pious as the nuns would have liked.

Most days, Fannie was hungry by this time, and taking forever to say a whole rosary before they could go eat was maddening, but the novices irritated her even more today.

The orphans entered through a back door, moving single file along the wall to fill the long pews stretching from one side of the small chapel to the other. After the first four pews filled, Fannie started down the fifth row. She could see Sister Theresa standing in the doorway across the room. A well-dressed couple peered in at them over the nun's shoulder. *More of them fancy church ladies bringin' us old clothes.*

With their charges in place, two new sisters took their positions on kneelers at the front of the room before a large crucifix mounted on the wall. One of them rang a small bell to indicate that the children should kneel, too. The novices pulled rosaries from the pockets of their black robes, made the sign of the cross, and started the prayers.

"In nomine Patris, et Filii, et Spiritus Sancti. Amen."

The children had been taught how to make the sign of the cross, but most of them looked like they were swatting at flies.

The sisters continued. *"Gloria Patri, et Filii, et Spiritus Sancti. Sicut erat in principio, et nunc, et semper—"*

A much bigger boy seated on the aisle behind Fannie reached forward and pulled Margaret's hair.

"Ouch!" She began to cry.

Fannie got up from the kneeler, went back one pew, and punched the boy square in the face. Blood gushed from his nose, and he clamped his hands over his face as he howled.

"I been tellin' you all day to leave her alone." Fannie leaned over the crying boy. "I told ya you'd get it, and now you did!"

The students stopped mid-*Gloria* and turned, craning to see the commotion. One of the sisters up front looked over her shoulder and then stood to investigate.

From her concealment, Sister Theresa stepped into the chapel to intervene. "Sister Mary Joseph, I have this under control. Please continue." She grabbed Fannie and the boy and pulled them out the side door by their arms. After standing them against the wall, she closed the door to the chapel.

Fannie crossed her arms defiantly while the bigger boy cried, blood running from his nose and down his chin.

The nun addressed the visiting couple first. "Mr. and Mrs. Sims, I must apologize. We do our best, but sometimes children do misbehave." She turned to the children. "Fannie Haley, what have you to say for yourself? We're supposed to turn the other cheek. Jesus would not approve of your behavior!"

"Well, I wouldna had to do it if Jesus woulda told him to stop pulling our pigtails," Fannie said, glaring at the boy.

Mr. Sims chuckled. "A little David and Goliath," he said to the nun.

Mrs. Sims, however, appeared horrified. The rail-thin woman wore a tailored jacket over a matching dress. She had beautiful shoes and was dotted with gold jewelry. The look on her face, though, suggested that she'd smelled something bad.

"Gillie, dear, I think we need to go. The trip up was so tiring, and now I need to go rest." She leaned toward her husband and spoke out of the side of her mouth. "Perhaps this wasn't such a good idea."

The short, stout man muttered under his breath to his wife, "Irene, dear, we've talked about this. I thought we'd decided."

The woman cut her eyes at Sister Theresa, indicating that she wanted some privacy.

Sister Theresa pursed her lips in almost a half-smile, nodded slightly, and pushed Fannie and the boy down the hall a few steps to wait.

The woman turned her back to them and, after bringing her dainty lace handkerchief to her face, spoke into her husband's shoulder. "I know, but still. Now that we're here, it just seems so, so . . ." She struggled for the right word. "So institutional. The ladies at church are all for it, too, but now I don't know. I feel like we're just giving in to never having our own children. Gillie, what if these children didn't come from nice families? What if— "

"We can't know if they *came* from nice families, but we know that the child we bring home will be *going* to a nice family. Think of it that way." Mr. Sims turned his wife around, guiding her by the elbow. "Sister Theresa, I do apologize. Shall we go back to the office to discuss this further?"

"Yes, certainly." Sister Theresa turned to Fannie and the boy. "Fannie, go back in for prayers—*quietly*. I can assure you that this conversation is not over. Oliver, come with us. I'll take you to the nurse."

Saturday, April 20, 1877

Deer Creek Plantation, Washington County, Mississippi

"Gillie, honestly. We shouldn't even bring that girl with us. She won't sit still. She doesn't mind what I say. I don't think I could bear the long trip with her. Just leave her here with the slaves." Irene made no pretense of liking the little girl that they had adopted.

From what Sims could see, that feeling was mutual. "Not 'slaves,' dear. 'Servants.'" He took a deep breath and responded with patience that was wearing thin after eleven years with this woman. "We have to take her. I told Eleanor and William about her, and they're expecting to meet her. Besides, it would be unseemly for us to leave our child here."

"I don't see why. No one would know."

"Word would get to town, certainly."

Irene shook her head in frustration and gave a little sigh. "I don't care if your brother and sister meet her or not. I don't want to have to fret with her." She turned her attention away from her jewelry box, which she'd been sorting through to pick out pieces for the trip. "And I've changed my mind. I don't want to ride on a train. It's so tedious and exhausting. I want to take the riverboat instead, so there won't be a bed for her in our stateroom."

"What if we brought Luvalia with us as well? I'm sure she could keep Fannie on the deck quarters."

She paused, contemplating this. "Let's do that. It would be good to have Luvalia, anyway, and I don't know if your brother's slaves will manage things the way I prefer. Oh, and I want to stay Saturday night in Natchez. We could go to church there and meet some people before we go down to Woodville. When we get to your brother's, there won't be anyone interesting to talk to."

Sims sighed. When he'd met Irene in Georgia after his release from the Yankee prison camp, he'd thought that marrying her would provide a good familial and political benefit, but instead, she'd become a liability. After they'd come home to Mississippi, he had struggled financially for the first few years, and she had complained bitterly. Since then, she'd strained their relationships with many of his friends and acquaintances. He was certain that the only reason they ever received invitations anymore was that he'd been elected from his area to serve on the county's board of supervisors. When they had failed to produce children, she'd become temperamental and moody, and now she gave him no attention at all.

"Not slaves, dear. You have to call them servants now."

Sunday, April 28, 1877

Natchez, Mississippi

Confined in a brand-new dress that she already hated, Fannie squirmed and scratched. The tight dress wasn't the most uncomfortable thing that Ma'am was making her wear, and neither were the tight bloomers and petticoats. It was the new shoes. They pinched her feet terribly.

Luvalia worked at the buttons on the side of the shoes with her short, fat fingers while Fannie squirmed. "Chil', sit still a minute."

"Luvalia, they too tight. I don't like 'em," Fannie complained.

"Ma'am say you gon' wear 'em, so you gon' wear 'em. If you'd wear 'em more, they'd fit better from stretchin'. Now then, stan' on up."

The shoes were nearly unbearable: pointed toes, tight all around, and thick, scratchy seams on the inside.

"Mr. Sims, she ready now."

"Thank you, Luvalia." Mr. Sims came in from the adjoining room. "My, don't you look pretty? I know that Mother would love for you to dress up so nicely more often. Don't you like your new dress? Let's go meet her in the lobby and walk over to the church."

"She ain't my mother."

"Yes, but remember we said we were going to try." Sims knelt beside Fannie, and his expression softened. "We can be a nice family if we all try a little more."

Fannie scowled and looked to Luvalia for some support.

"You be good now," the black woman said.

Fannie followed Mr. Sims down the hall, all the while fidgeting with the bound-up waistband that held the binding layer of undergarments against her skin. She reached beneath her dress, pulled down the tormenting underwear and stepped out of them, one foot at a time. She ran them back to Luvalia. "I ain't wearin' this."

The black woman took the drawers, shook her head and smiled. "Be good, you hear?"

"Come on, dear," Mr. Sims called from the top of the stairs. "We don't want to keep her waiting."

They found Mrs. Sims pacing impatiently in the hotel lobby.

"Good, the new dress fits," she said. "Let's go. I want to be sure to get there early so we can meet some people." She turned to Fannie. "Remember: you don't speak unless spoken to, sit still in church, and for heaven's sake, don't tell anyone that you're an orphan."

Mr. Sims gave Fannie a conciliatory look and put a hand on her shoulder, guiding her in front of him as they followed his wife. The four blocks to the church were agony for Fannie. The cruel shoes pinched with every step and squeaked as she walked. She stopped and rubbed her foot against the ground, trying to work out a vexing wrinkle in her long sock.

"Stop that!" Mrs. Sims said, turning to look. "You're scuffing your new shoes and getting them dirty. Let's go!"

At the enormous white church, well-dressed congregants greeted each other politely as they entered. Mr. Sims and Fannie followed Mrs. Sims up the steep steps and through the big doorway, where she stopped—right in the middle of the entryway. She pulled her husband beside her to face the other worshippers arriving through the main door, awkwardly positioning herself as though everyone was coming specifically to meet them.

Mrs. Sims forced introductions from the others entering, shaking their hands and smiling. *"Yes, originally from Georgia. And what is it that you do?"*

Since she wasn't introduced to anyone, Fannie said nothing. Invisible and tortured by her footwear, she stood behind the pretentious woman and pulled on Mrs. Sims' sleeve. Perhaps she could take off the shoes now that they were inside.

Mrs. Sims reached behind her back to wave Fannie away. *"We met after the war. He's in cotton now."*

"Ma'am," Fannie said, pulling at her sleeve again.

Mrs. Sims stepped sideways so that her bustle and big dress obscured Fannie. *"No, no children yet."*

Fannie couldn't take standing in the painful shoes anymore. She moved to the corner and sat down on the floor with her back against the wall, where she unbuttoned the side of her shoe and labored to remove it. When she was finally relieved of it, she pulled her aching foot up onto her leg and rubbed at the raw spots on her heel and toe.

"Oh, yes. He won't say so, since he's so modest, but he's on the board of supervisors. People have asked him to run for sheriff, and I do think he will." Mrs. Sims smiled at her husband approvingly and put her hand on his arm. Then her eyes widened as she spotted Fannie sitting on the floor in the corner, legs akimbo, on display. She grabbed her husband's arm, a horrified grimace on her face. "Gillie!"

Before Mr. Sims could rescue Fannie, his wife flew across the room and grabbed her by the arm with a vicious pinch, pulling her to her feet. "Oh, how could you? You horrible little urchin! We should have never brought you into our home! So embarrassing. For heaven's sake, stand up right this minute and put your shoe on!" Her fingers burned Fannie's arm like a hot poker.

Fannie screamed and tried to shake loose from her grasp. "Ouch!" She wrenched her arm away from the snarling woman. "I hate you! I wish I didn't never come to your house, neither!"

"Stop it!" she hissed back. "You are making a scene!"

Everyone standing in the vestibule of the church turned to look. With the shoe in hand, Fannie swung out at the woman, still bent over her with curled lips and flying spittle. The heel caught her over the eye, opening a cut that promptly gushed red.

Mrs. Sims straightened and staggered back, shocked. She wheeled around toward her husband and released the full force of her rage and humiliation. "This is all your fault!" she screamed. "I never wanted to bring that wretched little girl into our home to begin with!"

While everyone else watched the shocking tirade, Fannie ducked under the arm of a man holding the door for his wife and ran.

Thursday, June 10, 1880

Census Report, Franklin County, Mississippi

Page No. 11

Supervisor's Dist. No. 3

Enumeration Dist. No 144

SCHEDULE 1.—Inhabitants in Supervisors District Beat No 2, in the County of Franklin, State of Mississippi, enumerated by me on the 10th day of June, 1880.

Dwelling	Family	Name	Color	Sex	Age	Relationship	Profession
		D'Arnon, L. H.	W	M	27		Farmer
		--- M. E.	W	F	27	Wife	Keeping House
105	106	--- Chas. H.	W	M	6	Son	
		--- Frederick H.	W	M	2	Son	
		Simms, Fannie	W	F	11	Orphan	

Chapter 9

Sunday, March 26, 1882

The Natchez Democrat (Natchez, Mississippi)

May God hear the prayer of His orphans and grant an abundance of spiritual and temporal blessings upon their benefactors.

Friday, July 21, 1882

Rural Southwest Mississippi

Without any real understanding of where she was headed, Fannie worked her way east. She followed roads generally, but only walked on the roadway itself when there was no one visible. Whenever she saw or heard anyone approaching, she ducked into the woods and hid. Nobody had been good to her—none of the folks who had taken her in had been kind. She'd had to work hard, she'd been poorly fed, and she'd even been beaten. Leaving these people had gotten easier each time she'd had to do it; she'd been optimistic that someone else would help her. These last folks though; that was the last straw.

When the midnight visits had started, she hadn't understood what was happening—she just knew it was awful. As the months had worn on, she realized it was the same sort of thing that the bigger boys laughed about whenever they'd seen animals behaving oddly. This, though, Fannie thought, wasn't funny at all.

She was determined to strike out on her own. *Ain't nobody gonna touch me again. Not one more time.* She was ill prepared for a long journey. No food, no coat. She just ran. The only thing she carried were the clothes on her back and a steely determination. She got better at scavenging. She ate the ripening blackberries until her stomach ached, but picking through them for weeks left her cut by thorns, bitten by bugs, and tormented by chiggers. It was hot, and the sun beat down on her and left her blistered and red.

~

Fannie inched forward on all fours in the tall grass, watching for anyone to exit the back door as she crept toward the garden. The grasshoppers sprang this way and that before settling back down behind her as she moved forward—an easy tell for any savvy observer. Fifty yards of open space, in full view of the house, lay between her concealment and the first row of tomato plants.

A tall girl came out the back door carrying a white enamel pot by its side handles. She walked toward the garden and then turned and proceeded down the backside of the barn. At the pigpen, she poured the contents of the pot into a trough and then retraced her steps, stopping beside the outhouse. After setting the pot on top of the woodpile and stepping into the privy, she turned around to face the garden, pulled up her dress in back, and gathered it around her waist to sit. She pulled the door shut.

In a flash, Fannie leapt up and silently made the distance to the garden in just a few steps. She kept running, turning toward the woodpile at the end of the row of tomatoes. The logs there had already been split—raw splintered faces on two sides with dark stripes of bark down the back. She took a short piece with a split on the end and approached the outhouse, jammed the notched end under the edge of the door, pushed it into the ground, and wedged the door firmly shut by stamping it down into the dirt.

"Hey! Who—?" the girl inside said. "Jimmy? This ain't funny! Jimmy!"

While the girl struggled inside the outhouse, Fannie ran back to the garden and pulled three of the ripest tomatoes she could see from the nearest plants.

"Boy, when I get you! Ooh, you are such a brat! I'm gonna tell Papa, and you're gonna get it for sure!" The girl pushed on the door from the inside. It rattled some, but the stick held. "Jimmy! Jimmy! I mean it! Lemme outta here right this minute!"

As she made her escape behind the barn, Fannie spotted the kitchen scraps in the hog trough. An apple—mushy on one side—a dried end of a loaf of bread, two cobs of corn that somebody hadn't finished, and a ham hock.

She ran back to the woodpile and grabbed the pot, returned to the trough, and picked the best pieces out of the pile. After dropping the food scraps in the pot, she made a beeline for the woods.

Thursday, October 12, 1882

Oakland, Mississippi

"Come on, y'all. Let's get on with it," Robert Lee said. "Your mama don't like us taking so long to get home."

Only halfway home from school, the three children had another mile to go.

"Don't matter," said Julia, who was in first grade. "There's nothing to do when we get there nohow."

"Nothing for *you* to do, but I got chores 'fore supper, so let's go."

"Can we go down to the creek?" asked Willie, Julia's older brother.

"We'll get home first, and you can go if your mama says you can." Robert knew Mrs. Black wouldn't let the children go to the creek, and so did they.

Willie scowled and kicked at a rock.

"I don't like school," Julia said. This was her first year to go with the boys to the one-room schoolhouse in Oakland. Willie was in third grade, and Robert was in sixth.

Robert didn't like school, either. He would rather have been out on his own, exploring in the woods or fishing. Living with the Black family was better than being in the orphanage, but he wasn't happy about it. Robert had been thinking more about his brothers and sister over the past few months too. He realized that his memories of them grew fuzzier every year, and he felt bad about that. Somedays he daydreamed about what would have happened if he'd found Thomas, or if he'd stayed at St. Peter's with Fannie. He wanted to find them and Mickey, too, but he was stuck here without any money. Today at school, though, he got an idea and wrote a letter.

They finally reached the house, and the dog came out to meet them, wagging the entire back half of his body. Willie and Julia stopped to scratch him behind his ears.

Robert opened the door on the back porch to enter the kitchen.

Sina was there. The black woman's back was to him. With her sleeves rolled up, she mixed dry ingredients in a bowl on the table in the middle of the room. She looked over her shoulder at him when he entered. "You hungry? I'm makin' yo' favorite. Fried chicken tonight."

"Thanks," he replied without enthusiasm.

"Whas de matter?"

"Nothin'." He leaned against the table, frowning. "Sina, it ain't fair that I got to do all the morning and afternoon chores, and Willie ain't got to do none. And workin' on the weekend for nothin' when them other folks get paid."

On Saturdays, Willie and Julia got to play and do what they wanted, while Robert had to clean floors and move boxes and do whatever other dirty work Mr. Black could think of at his store in town. The first time Robert had mentioned not getting paid like the other staff did, he got the old man's cane across his back.

Sina put a hand on her hip as she turned to Robert. "Not much in this ol' world fair. You better just put that notion right out of yo' head. What you gotta do is think on the good things that you do got and be thankful for 'em." She wiped her flour-dusty hands on her apron and then spread blackberry jam across a cold biscuit. "This ought to sweeten you up some. Get on and get them chores done while I cook this supper, or Missus Black gon' be mad at us both."

Robert went back outside and walked to the small cottage a hundred yards behind the house. He pulled open the screen door to find his roommate sitting at a table by the window in the larger room.

"Mr. Ladd, when you go to the post office tomorrow, can you mail my letter? I got a penny for the stamp." Robert pulled out a folded piece of paper and put the coin on the table, where the young man sat reviewing a column of numbers in a big book.

"I won't be going into town until late," Mr. Ladd said, not looking up from his work, "and the mail train from Grenada runs in the morning, so if you want your letter to go out tomorrow, you'd better take it on your way to school."

Mr. Henry Ladd was the bookkeeper for Mr. Black's businesses. He and Robert shared the small two-room cottage behind the house. Mr. Ladd had a bedroom to himself, while Robert slept on a smaller bed in the main room. They lived there rent-free and ate their meals with the Black family, but Mr. Ladd also got paid each week after he reviewed all the ledgers with Mr. Black on Saturday afternoon. Robert only got room and board. In the evenings, after dinner in the house, he and Mr. Ladd sat at the table in their little cottage and worked by lamplight. Robert did his homework lessons, and Mr. Ladd worked on the ledgers or read the newspaper.

"To whom are you sending a letter?" Mr. Ladd inquired with a faint accent, a remnant of his English parents. The sound was different from the brogue Robert remembered from his own father.

"Well, I been thinkin' about the orphanage, an' I wanted to see if my sister Fannie's still there. I'm gonna ask the sisters where she's at now, and maybe I'll go live by her."

"You mean 'where she is,' " Mr. Ladd said, putting down his pencil and looking up. "What does your letter say, if I might ask?"

Robert handed him the paper, which he unfolded and held in the afternoon sunlight to reveal penciled words printed in neat rows.

Mother Superior

This is Robert Lee Haley I ran away from the orfan home a few years ago and now that I am older I want to know if my sister Fannie is still there or if she got adopted and can you write to me and tell me where shes at? I live in Oakland Miss now with Mr. Black and you can write back here and tell me where she is because I am going to go live near her.

Please write back

Robert Lee Haley

p.s. I am sorry for running away but I am doing fine now thank you

"Well, I think that will get the point across," Mr. Ladd said. "Orphan is spelled with a *ph* and not an *f*, and I'll encourage you to work with your teacher at school on some punctuation rules, but the letter is otherwise quite adequate." He got up to look through a drawer in the bureau against the wall and returned with an envelope, a tiny bottle of glue, his pen, a bottle of ink, and a blue one-cent stamp bearing the profile of Benjamin Franklin. "Here's a stamp," he said, pocketing the penny from the table. "Let me write the address in ink on the envelope so that it doesn't get rubbed off."

Robert put the letter in the envelope, sealed it, and affixed the stamp with the glue. Mr. Ladd addressed the envelope to *St. Peter's Orphanage, Memphis, Tennessee*, with his pen.

The next morning, Robert got Willie and Julia to the schoolhouse on time and made sure that the teacher, Miss Lilly Barnes, had seen the three of them present for the day. When she turned her attention elsewhere, he ducked back out the door and ran three more blocks over to the train depot office that housed the postal clerk's desk. He pushed on the door to enter, but it was locked. He couldn't wait around for someone to open it—and he couldn't leave school again once he'd gone back—so he wedged the envelope into the jamb just above the doorknob so that when Mr. Crenshaw arrived to open, he'd put the letter on the clerk's desk.

Robert made it back to school just a little bit tardy and averted his eyes to avoid the stern look from Miss Barnes as he sneaked in the door.

Days went by, and Robert wondered what had become of his letter. *What if someone didn't get my letter to the clerk? Would they know who to give the letter to if it made it to the orphanage? Will they send someone to come get me and bring me back to Memphis, now that I've told them where I am?*

He didn't share his worries with Mr. Ladd, but twice Robert asked for him to check with the clerk to see if a reply had come.

Monday, November 13, 1882

Rural Southwest Mississippi

During the summer, Fannie had only moved early in the morning and had spent the hot afternoons resting in a shady spot or down at the cool edge of a creek. She had been relieved when the weather had grown cooler, but now the pleasant days were turning into uncomfortably cold nights. They'd had a frost last week.

In the purple dusk, with a cool breeze at her back, Fannie sat silently and watched from the far side of a cornfield that had been picked over. The farmer watered the horses and then put them in for the night. When he stepped out of the barn, he put the bar across the door. He washed his face and hands in the trough and then, shaking his hands free of the water, wiped them on the bib of his overalls. He headed up toward the house, where lamplights were being lit inside and a wisp of smoke rose from the chimney in twisting curls before disappearing in the wind.

The bird dog started to follow him but stopped suddenly to stare at Fannie's hiding spot. The man stopped a moment later and turned to the dog. "Scout, come on. Let's go."

After looking over his shoulder at the man, the dog barked once, paused to look again in Fannie's direction, and then ran up the hill after his master.

Fannie stayed in her hiding place and dozed. The cold woke her. She could see her breath in the moonlight. Her teeth chattered, and she rubbed her arms and legs. The lights were out in the house, so she figured she could warm up in the barn for a minute or two.

She got up and crossed the field swiftly, putting the barn between her and the house before slowing down. When she reached the barn, she lifted the bar on the door, pulled it open a crack, and then ducked inside. It was warmer there.

She pulled the door closed, but it swung open with an alarming squeak when she let it go. It wouldn't stay closed unless the bar on the outside was in place. After a couple of attempts with the door, she studied her surroundings and noticed a lamp hanging from a nail on the doorpost. By running her hand along the brace on the inside wall, she managed to find the small tube of matches that she hoped would be there. She lit the lamp and was able to see the saddles on the stall rail with the harnesses and bridles hanging nearby. She needed only one harness, which she used to pull the door shut by looping it around one nail in the door and one nail on the opposite doorpost.

She raised the lantern again, and the horse nearest her turned her head and gazed at Fannie. The mare's breath was visible in the chilly air, too. She and her teammate had blankets over their backs. More horse blankets, folded and stacked, lay on the bench near the door. Fannie took one and wrapped it around herself. It was blue and had apparently been someone's quilt long ago. The pattern was small, light-blue squares surrounded by darker blue borders. It must have been pretty once, but now its holes and tears were roughly patched with burlap and odds and ends of other cloths and shirts.

Fannie put the other two blankets on the floor and sat down on them. Under the bench she found two pairs of work boots and a pair of smaller boys' shoes. She pulled off the shoes she'd been wearing for the past six weeks and rubbed her sore feet, then slipped on the new shoes and stood up to take a couple of tentative steps. They flopped on her feet, but they were better. With two handfuls of straw folded neatly and stuffed into the toes, they worked just fine.

Fannie wrapped the blue quilt around her and lay down on the blankets on the floor. In her dream, she was at home with Thomas and Mickey. They all played outside with Robert and W. D. while Katherine cooked them a delicious supper. They all sat down to eat together after Daddy returned home in the evening.

～

The dog whined and scratched at the door, waking her. As soon as Fannie sat up, he bayed.

"Whatcha got, Scout?" The man sounded like he was far up on the hill.

She leapt up from the floor. The lantern had gone out, and in the predawn darkness, she didn't remember where she was or how she'd gotten there.

The dog continued pawing at the door and bayed again. The horses nickered and whinnied.

The man's voice grew nearer. "Attaboy! Got a possum in there?"

She couldn't see another way out. She'd have to escape through the door and get past the dog somehow.

She grabbed a broken hoe handle in one hand and balled up the blanket under her other arm. She peeked out the crack in the door at the baying dog. In one swift motion, she pulled the harness off the nail and kicked open the door, pitching the dog back onto his back legs. She sprinted outside and down the side of the barn, hopefully unseen by the man who was now just around the corner.

The dog was right on her heels.

As he barked, Fannie swung the hoe handle and caught the dog on the jaw. He yelped and retreated one step, giving her just enough time to turn the corner. She sprinted as fast as she could down the backside of the barn and into the woods. She was near certain the farmer had stopped to attend to his injured animal.

Tuesday, November 14, 1882

Oakland, Mississippi

As they sat down to eat supper in the big house, Robert stood behind his chair at the farthest end of the table beyond Mr. Ladd, waiting for Mrs. Black to come down for dinner. Sina brought in a large tureen of stewed meat and vegetables, which she placed on the table next to a big plate of cornbread. Mr. Black came downstairs with his wife and seated her on his left side. He then pulled out the head chair and winced as he dropped his weight onto the seat.

After what seemed like the longest prayer yet from Mr. Black, they started in with the food. Sina ladled the stew into bowls for the family and then for Mr. Ladd. At the end of the table, Robert was always the last to be served. The conversation was always the same, always boring, and never included Robert, but today he was startled to hear Mr. Black mention his name.

"Robert," Mr. Black said, pausing to look up from his meal; "Mr. Crenshaw came to the store today. Brought me a letter addressed to you."

Mrs. Black turned to gaze down the length of the table at Robert. "Whoever in the world is writing to you?"

Mr. Black took a letter from the inside breast pocket of his jacket, broke his stare at Robert, and handed it to Willie on his right. "Pass this to Robert."

Willie didn't wipe his hands, so when he held the letter closely to inspect it rather than passing it on, he got a greasy thumbprint on the pale-blue envelope. "I can't read cursive handwriting yet. Who's it from?" He turned to look down the table at Robert without passing the letter to Mr. Ladd.

"We won't know until he opens it, now will we?" Mr. Ladd said, holding out his hand for the envelope.

Willie jeered at Robert. "Is it from a girl?"

"That's none of our concern," Mrs. Black said. "William, pass him the letter."

Mr. Ladd took the letter from Willie and handed it to Robert, who put down the spoon he'd been holding suspended above the bowl since Mr. Black had first pulled out the letter. He wiped his mouth with his sleeve and gawked at the envelope.

"Use your napkin, Robert," Mrs. Black said.

"Yes, ma'am," he said, staring at the letter in disbelief. It was addressed to *Mr. Robert Haley, Oakland, Mississippi*, in flowing cursive and boasted a blue stamp in the corner, just like the one he had put on the letter he'd sent. On the back, he saw the words embossed in script, *St. Peter's Orphanage, Poplar Street, Memphis, Tennessee.*

Robert addressed the head of the table. "May I please be excused?"

Mr. Black stared at him for a moment and then looked at his wife and shrugged. He tucked back in for another bite of his dinner. "I suppose so," he said to Robert. "You're past fourteen now. They can't make you go back."

"Yessir." Robert pushed in the chair and went through the kitchen, where he passed Sina on his way out.

She smiled at him and handed him another piece of cornbread.

In the cottage, he lit the oil lamp on the table and moved it to the bureau, where the light shone on his small bed. He peered at the letter with fresh waves of anxiety. After tearing open the envelope unevenly with his finger, he withdrew a single sheet of matching light-blue paper.

St. Peter's Orphanage   *October 28, 1882*

Poplar Street

Memphis, Tennessee

Dear Robert,

Your sister, Fannie, was adopted by the Sims family from Carrollton, Mississippi, in 1876, shortly after you left us. We have not heard from them since, so we have no further information to provide.

We are pleased to hear that you are well, and we wish you the very best.

With the blessings of our Lord Jesus Christ,

Sister Mary Joseph

Lying in bed that night, Robert listened to the owls' rhythmic hoots in the darkness. Somewhere in the distance, an animal shrieked. He made up his mind to go find Fannie and decided he'd better start out pretty soon before it got any colder. They'd already had one frost in the past week. He had put a second quilt on his bed and kept his socks on at night.

He lay awake, wondering about his sister. The questions running through his mind tied his stomach in knots. *Is she still in Carrollton? If I find her, will she remember me? Did she get adopted by a rich family? If they are, could I stay with 'em? If I don't find her, should I come back to Oakland and live here again?*

Carrollton was forty miles away, south of Grenada, and he figured it would take him maybe two days to get there walking. Many minutes later, he rolled over and blew out the lamp.

In the morning, Robert went to school with Willie and Julia as usual, but he didn't bring home his schoolbooks, despite having homework assigned for the evening.

As he did his afternoon chores, he retrieved from the barn an old saddlebag that hadn't been used in years and gathered some things he thought he might need: a knife, a flint, a candle, some extra clothes, and a corked bottle to fill with water. He wrapped them in an old blanket that no one would miss. At dusk, he tucked everything behind a bush. Then he came around to the back of the house and started toward the cottage to get ready for dinner.

"You should appreciate what we've done for you."

Robert started when he heard Mr. Black's voice. He turned to see him sitting in a dark corner of the back porch. His pipe emitted a soft glow, partly obscured by the haze from its smoke. His tone made Robert wary.

"Yessir. I do."

The fat man hoisted himself up from the chair with a grunt and came down the steps with his cane, holding the porch rail to keep the weight off his painful leg. "Seven years of room and board. Do you know how much that would cost?" He used the cane to hobble over to where the boy stood.

Robert knew what was coming, but he dared not move away. That strategy hadn't served him well in the past. "No, sir."

"A damn lot!" Mr. Black swung the cane and struck Robert on the back of the thigh.

Robert winced. "I know, sir."

"And supplies for school. And clothes." He struck him a second time.

"I 'preciate all them things, I do, sir."

"What was that letter from the orphanage about?"

"I had wrote a letter to my sister Fannie, but they said she wasn't there no more. Said she got adopted. That's all."

Mr. Black glared. "You should appreciate what we've given you. Maybe someday I'll give you a job in the store if you work hard." He turned to make his way back inside.

Not a chance, Robert thought.

~

After dinner that evening, Robert followed Sina when she went out to the well, and he told her about his plan. "I'm goin' away, and I wanted t' let you know I pro'ly won't be back. I'm gonna find my sister."

"That's what the letta' was?" she asked, putting down the bucket and turning to look at him.

"Yeah. Said she got adopted by a family in Carrollton. That's not too far away. I just gotta go find her." *Pro'ly shouda never left the orphanage*, he thought. *We coulda got adopted together.*

"When you leavin'?"

"Tonight, when Mr. Ladd goes to bed. I ain't gonna tell nobody, neither, but I don't want you to worry 'bout me."

Sina looked at Robert and smiled. She pulled him close and wrapped her arms around him. "You a swee' boy." She held him by the shoulders at arm's length and added, "I'm gonna put you some food on top of th' wood box on the porch, so you get it when you leavin'."

"Thank you, Sina. I'm gonna miss you."

"I know Jesus gonna look after you, an' I know you gonna fin' your sister," she said. "You be good." She picked up the bucket and turned away—but not before Robert saw the tears gathering in her eyes.

After Mr. Ladd went to bed, Robert slipped out the door, retrieved his stash from behind the house, and grabbed the food Sina had set aside for him. With the moon mostly obscured by clouds and a chilly breeze blowing, he set out, avoiding the main street in Oakland just in case someone else happened to be out at that hour.

He cut back to the railroad tracks about a quarter mile below town and followed them south, walking most of the night. With his head on the saddlebag and wrapped in his blanket, he tried to rest for a couple of hours in the dark and then started out again just as the sun rose. Later that day, outside Grenada, he slept some behind a barn, warmed by the sun.

When he arrived in Carrollton that night, it was well after the residents of the town had gone to bed. Robert wrapped up in the blanket and spent the rest of the night tucked out of the breeze on the porch of a law office across from the courthouse. Excitement and hunger kept him from sleep. Despite his rationing, the food that Sina had given him was nearly gone. All that remained was a chicken wing, which he ate down to the bones. This left nothing for the rest of the day, but tomorrow he figured he would have supper with his sister and her adopted family.

Friday, November 17, 1882

Carrollton, Mississippi

Morning rose on the square, and sunlight crept down the side of the courthouse, gradually warming the small town. Robert opened the gate of the courthouse lawn and approached the gray brick building. He was surprised at the enormity of the front doors. The first floor boasted two open breezeways running perpendicular to each other, with offices in each quadrant and a stairway to the courtroom upstairs.

A clerk arrived to open one of the first-floor offices. He looked at Robert as he pulled out his keys. "Good morning."

Robert nodded, followed the man inside, and waited for him to get situated at the desk before he approached.

"What can I do for you?"

"G' mornin'. I'm lookin' for my sister, Fannie." For the next ten minutes, Robert told the man the story of Hernando, Memphis, and the orphanage. Then he showed him the letter. He didn't share the envelope, since it identified that he was from Oakland, and he left out any mention of the Black family, in case word got back to them and somehow he might get in trouble for running off.

"Well," the clerk said, "that's some adventure. I can tell you, though, that I've worked here for ten years. I know everyone in the county, and I've never heard of a family named Sims, nor of a girl named Fannie."

Robert felt the air rush out of him. His heart sank. *This can't be. The letter said she got adopted and came to Carrollton.* "Are you sure?" he asked, his voice rising in panic.

"Oh, yes, I keep the voter rolls and the tax digest, so I'd know if there was a Sims family."

"Maybe they were here before and moved away. Could you find out that?"

"Well, from what you told me, ten years ago you lived in Hernando with your sister and your family, so I'm sure there's been a mistake. We don't have any white people named Sims in

Carroll County, and if there had been, it would have been before you were even alive."

Robert's shoulders sagged as he turned to go. Outside, he crossed the street and sat on the steps of the law office again, watching as the businesses opened and the town came to life. He hung his head. When he had run away from the orphanage seven years ago, he hadn't known enough to be scared, but now he knew his tenuous situation was of his own making. With his hopes dashed, sadness, anger, and anxiety enveloped him in a confusing cloud. The teenager wanted to be brave now, but despite his efforts, his emotions didn't cooperate, and he began to cry.

"Hey, now, young sir," someone said in a grown-up voice as a pair of dark-brown boots stopped in front of him. "Whas de mattah heah?"

Robert looked up into the face of a tall, elderly black man in worn overalls and a workman's jacket.

"This th' day de Lawd is made!" the man said. "S'posed t' be rejoicin'."

Robert wiped his eyes with the sleeve of his shirt, sniffed, and did his best to stir up some courage. "I'm fine," he said, turning his head away.

"Don' look like everythin' fine to me."

"Well, it is," Robert said defensively. "I just got to figure out how to get me a job and a place to stay."

"Young man like yo-sef ain't got no place to stay?"

Robert stood and looked around. "I got somewhere. I just don't know where it is yet."

"Well, how you come to be not knowin'?" the man asked.

Robert's emotions came to the surface again, and his voice broke as he blurted out the story. "I wrote to the orphanage sister, and she said my sister was here, and I walked for two days, and now I'm here, but the man inside says she don't live here, and I know Mr. Black'll be real mad, and I don't want to go back there nohow, and I already ate everything that Sina gave me and don't got no money, so now . . ." His voice trailed off, and he took a deep, shaky breath.

The old man surely couldn't understand all the pieces of what he'd just heard, but he could clearly see Robert's desperation. "So you don' got no place to stay an' nothin' to eat, an' you need you a job?"

"Yes," Robert said, wiping his eyes again on his sleeve.

"Well, let me get these here things, an' we'll see what we can do. I know summody who might can help." The old man pulled out a key to the law office, unlocked the door, and went inside. After he came back out with a coat and some books, he locked the door and tucked the key back into his pocket. "Up here to fetch this jacket and these here books for Senator George. Come on wid' me, young sir. We'll ride on up to the house and see 'bout getting you a job."

Robert followed the old man to the corner and watched as he climbed up into a short wagon hitched to a blue-gray mule. A man came up the hill on the boardwalk porch and unlocked the door to the store facing the main street. Through the big plate glass windows and the glass door, Robert could see shelves nearly all the way to the ceiling crammed with merchandise and boxes.

"Mornin', Mr. Gee," the black man said.

"Good morning, Jake. Is the senator in the office today?"

"Nah, sir. I'm goin' up to G'nada today to get him from the train. Been out makin' speeches for more 'n two weeks now."

"Well, do give him my best regards."

"I surely do that, Mr. Gee. I surely will."

"Who's your young charge there?"

"Dis young man new in town. We gonna fin' him a job."

The merchant offered his hand to Robert. "J. J. Gee."

"I'm Robert Haley."

They shook.

"New in town, you say?"

"Yessir."

"Well, I'm sure that Jake and Senator George will take fine care of you."

Robert looked up at the old black man, who nodded.

"Yassuh, we'll need to go on directly so I can make it to G'nada in time for the train. Don' want to keep the senator waitin'." He reached down from the seat and gave Robert a hand, pulling him up onto the bench beside him.

"Well, better get on then," Mr. Gee said. "Take care, Jake."

"Yassuh, Mr. Gee. You have a good day now."

The mule-drawn cart jostled them from side to side as they rode down the hill, across the low wooden bridge at the edge of town, and back up the road north. Less than a half hour later, they started up the drive to the most enormous house Robert had ever seen. The six tall columns supported a high roof that sheltered a large porch running the whole way across the front of the two-story wooden house.

Jake drove the wagon around to the back. After stepping down and walking toward the log-cabin kitchen, he motioned for Robert to follow. They went inside.

"DeDe, got some more breakfast for this young man here?" Jake asked as he sat down at the table.

The brick-floored kitchen was comfortably warm and filled with the aroma of bacon and coffee.

The short black woman covered the pot she'd been stirring and put the spoon down on the hearth before she turned to face them. "Who you got here?"

"My name is Robert."

"I'm DeDe," the cook said. "Let me get you somethin' to eat. Sit right on down here."

"He need a job and don' got nowhere to stay," Jake said, "so I figured I'd ask the senator if he could work in the barns."

The cook pulled back the cloth covering the skillet that sat on the table and used a fork to cut off a piece of cornbread, which she put on a plate for Robert. "I know if you the one doin' the askin', he sure to say yes," she said to Jake. She smiled and turned to Robert. "You want some bacon too?"

Tuesday, November 28, 1882

Rural South Mississippi

The old turkey hunter looked twice but still couldn't tell what the blue thing was in the distance. He got off his horse, tied him to a sapling on the side of the road, and then stepped through the undergrowth and into the woods. The forest floor, which was clear of any understory, lay beneath the canopies of giant pines. He could see his breath in the chilly morning air.

He drew closer, stepping silently and carefully through the woods until he could make out a piece of cloth hanging over a fallen log. Closer. A person in there—a girl. Alive. Asleep.

"Hey." He stepped closer still. "Hey."

The girl lay wrapped in a ragged, dirty quilt, cradled in a cleft between the trunk of the tree and large branch that had broken off when the massive oak fell. She didn't stir.

He put a hand on the girl's shoulder and shook her gently. She startled awake and reflexively swung at him.

He caught her by the forearm. "What in th' blazin' hell is a little girl like you doin' all the way out here by yerself?"

"You let me go!" she said, swinging a leg at him. "I'll kick you hard!"

He maintained his grip and held her at arm's length. "Hold on now, girl. I ain't gonna hurt you."

Her scrawny frame, dirty face, and tangled hair made her look like a wild animal. When she calmed down and quit squirming, he let go, backing up a good bit to put some distance between them.

"You got any food?" she asked.

"Yeah." He rummaged through his sack and held out a biscuit.

She snatched it and jumped back several steps before gobbling it down.

"You lost?"

"No," she said with a sneer.

"Well, what the hell are you doin' out here?"

"Got any more?"

"Here." He tossed her his knapsack. "There's more in there. Deer meat too." He leaned his gun against the tree behind him and sat down. "Long way to town. Your folks know where you are?"

"None of yer business."

"Ha! Sassy little one, ain't ya?"

Her ragged dress was pitifully thin and too small, revealing her knobby knees and skinny legs, which were covered with cuts, bruises, and insect bites. She stepped forward to grab her quilt and then retreated again to wrap it around her shoulders. She crouched next to the big log.

"Gonna make us a fire." He cleared out a spot on the ground and arranged some pine straw, pinecones, and small sticks into a little lean-to. "There's matches down in that bag. Toss 'em here."

She kept one eye on him while she fished through the sack. Then she threw the little cardboard tube to him.

He lit the kindling and gradually added bigger sticks to fuel the flames. When she moved a little closer to the warmth, he scooted back to give her some more room. "Lemme have some of that meat. I'm hungry, too."

She took another piece for herself and threw the bag back to him.

That afternoon, she told him a story of hard work, of mistreatment at the hands of mean people, both rich and poor. She told him how she had been forced to strike out on her own at a too-young age. She concluded with a defiant ultimatum.

"I ain't stayin' with them no more. I'll run off again and again. They can keep on beatin' me till they beat me to death, but I ain't gonna stay. I'd rather die than stay with them."

"I ain't never heard of such complete horseshit!" he said. "No wonder ya had to run off. If I ever run into any of them bastards, I'll kick their asses all the way to Luzianna."

"I aim to find my brother and go live with him," she said. "We gonna be a family again."

"Well, that sounds like a good idea. But you can stay with me and Elisa until you get some sort of a damn plan."

Six hours later, in the early evening, they finally made it back to the barn at the Smiths' farm. While the man fed and watered the horse before putting him in for the night, Fannie stood just inside the door, and even with the ragged blanket around her, began to shiver as the temperature fell. A woman came across the field with a lantern and called out to the barn.

"Bill Smith, where have you been?" She had a slightly irritated tone. "I was 'bout ready to send the boys out lookin' for you! It's late and I was worryin'."

"Took a helluva lot longer to get home, since she wouldn't ride on the horse with me. Walked the whole damn way," the man replied as the woman came in.

"What? Who?"

"Her." Bill pointed to Fannie in the corner behind her.

The woman turned and lifted the lantern, letting the light fall on the bedraggled girl. "Mercy, child! Just look at you. Where'd you come from?"

Fannie said nothing.

"I found her in the woods. Says she run off from some pretty bad folks. I mean—I'd like to string them bastards up."

"Papa, watch your language in front of the girl. She don't know you like the rest of county does." The woman chuckled and smiled warmly at Fannie. She was petite and thin and had a kindly face. She nodded her head toward Bill. "If you don't count all the cussin', he's a real good sort. No bad folks here honey, so don't you worry none. You look a sight! You hungry?"

"Yessum," said Fannie reservedly.

"Oh honey, you can call me Elisa. Come on inside, and we'll get you some supper and put you to bed."

"I cain't stay here," said Fannie. "Gotta go find my brother."

"Told her she could stay with us till she got some sort of a damn plan."

"Well you can stay the night here where its warm, and we'll figure all that out in the morning," Elisa said, as she put her arm around Fannie and led her toward the house.

Saturday, April 5, 1883

Harrison County, Mississippi

Fannie sat in the big round washtub after dinner on Saturday night, enjoying being warm after a good dinner, and looking forward to a soft bed. When she first came to stay with the Smiths, she couldn't sleep—remaining vigilant in the house nearly all night and ducking away to sleep, hidden in the barn during the day. As the weeks wore on though, she'd grown more comfortable with the family, especially Elisa. In addition to the three boys still in the house with them, all of whom were older than Fannie, the couple had three older boys and two older daughters. Those grown ones were married and lived on their own places but were all within walking distance of the cabin. Five months of regular eating made her feel stronger, and now that it was spring, Fannie thought about heading back out to look for Robert but realized that she'd really miss the folks here.

Despite her persistent nervousness around a crowd, Fannie was beginning to enjoy their community church at Red Creek. She had roused Bill's ire with her initial refusal to attend, but Elisa had shushed him and told him that she didn't have to go if she didn't want to—adding that if he was so worried about holiness he ought to start with his own tongue. The first time Fannie had reluctantly agreed to go, Elisa had gotten a nice dress, Sunday shoes, and a coat from the extended family for her to wear. Those shoes didn't really fit her either, but when she kicked them off under the pew at the service, Elisa just smiled and put her arm around her, telling her that they'd find her a different pair that would work.

Getting baths for everyone in the house on the night before the Sunday service was a production. Bill had fixed a drain in the wash tub so that the water ran out through the floor and away from the house in a pipe, but they still had to carry buckets in from the pump and add hot water from kettles on the stove. Elisa insisted that Fannie get the first bath, telling the others that, in addition to being polite to have ladies and guests go first, the men were always dirtier, and it saved at least one change of the water.

"Is it warm enough?" asked Elisa as she peeked in on her. Stepping between the two quilts strung up on a line across the back corner of the cabin, she brought in another warm kettle and a towel.

"Yessum."

"Here's you a towel."

Fannie stood, taking the towel to dry her arms and legs as Elisa stepped back outside the curtain. She saw it on the towel first and then looked at her arms and hands to find the source. It was the pink tinge in the water and a trickle running down the inside of her leg that alarmed her. "Oh!" she exclaimed, startled by the blood.

Elisa stuck her head back in. "What is it, honey?' she said with concern.

"I'm bleeding." Tears welled up in Fannie's eyes as anxiety gripped her.

Elisa quickly assessed the situation. "It's OK, honey. Don't you worry none," she said. "Everything's fine. Wash off and step out. I'll be right back." She returned momentarily with some strips of dark cloth and some safety pins. "You ain't had this before?"

Fannie shook her head.

"Here's what you do." Elisa folded the cloth over and over, pinned it to the inside of the pants, then helped Fannie step into them. While Fannie put on her night dress, Elisa drained the tub and washed it out, then called to the boys to come in and get washed as she pushed back the quilt.

"Where's the water?" asked Donan when he came into the room.

"Gonna have to go get your own this time," said Elisa. She took Fannie by the hand and led her into the bedroom, where Bill sat dozing and waiting for his turn in the tub.

"Get on outta here," she told him. "Girls gotta talk."

"What the hell?" He worked himself up from the chair and went out toward the kitchen.

"An' close the door," she called after him.

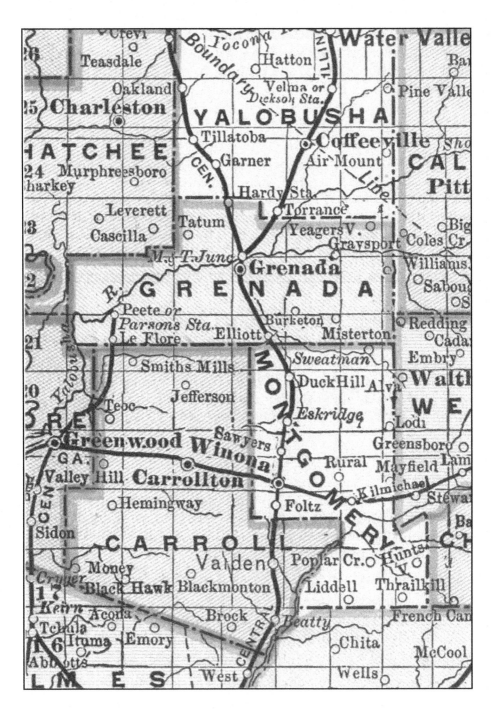

Mississippi (detail), The Library Atlas of Modern Geography,
Appleton & Co., Buffalo, New York, 1892. Courtesy of David
Rumsey Map Collection, www.davidrumsey.com.

Chapter 10

Saturday, February 20, 1886

The Conservative (Carrollton, Mississippi)

A shooting affray occurred on our streets about 7 o'clock last Saturday evening, in which some twenty or more shots were fired. It seems that Mr. James Liddell, a gallant young lawyer and editor of the Valley Flag, had had some hot words in the evening with Ed Brown (c). Ed and his brother and one John Johnson (c), it seems, went off and armed themselves in anticipation of what followed.

Directly after eating his supper, Mr. Liddell started down the streets when he saw the Brown brothers with a host of their colored friends around them and, it is said, he asked Ed what they were doing there and received a very insulting reply, whereupon Liddell slapped him, when Ed and Charlie Brown and John Johnson opened fire upon Liddell. Mr. Liddell returned the fire with a double action Colt's revolver, and for a few seconds the noise resembled a regular picket charge. Mr. Liddell received two wounds, one in the right elbow and one in the thigh. Ed Brown received a slight wound in the stomach while Charlie

Brown got a painful shot in the shoulder. It is a miracle how the parties escaped death, as they were only a few feet apart, and the weapons used were all of large caliber and of the best make.

Mr. Liddell is getting along finely, and with proper care and attention will soon be out again. The parties to the affray, with the exception of John Johnson, who is still at large, have all given bond for their appearance at circuit court, and until after that time we forbear further comment.

Wednesday, March 17, 1886

Cotesworth Plantation, Carroll County, Mississippi

When the heifer didn't come back to the barn with the others, Robert went out to look for her, since he knew she was due to calve soon. He found her in a secluded area of the pasture down by the lake. Panting and drenched with sweat, she had finally lain down. She looked up when he approached but didn't seem to feel threatened in the least bit.

He knelt and patted her on the side. "Hey, Matilda." He noticed the calf was presenting a hind leg and a tail. "Uh-oh. That's not good. Come on, girl. Gotta get up." He looped a lead rope around her neck and pulled her to rise.

She struggled but finally got up, back feet first.

Robert looked around for something to secure her to and spotted a tree with two large limbs growing from a single trunk about three feet off the ground. "Come on over here," he said, leading her to it.

She followed, and he passed the lead through the V in the tree, pulling her forward until her head was between the trunks like an upside-down yoke. He secured the rope around the tree and back to her neck, pinning her head there. "Now let's see what we can do here," he said as he removed his shirt.

He stood with his chest beside the cow's hind quarter and pushed his right arm inside her along the calf's protruding leg. He found the other rear leg, which was folded up beneath the calf and blocking its descent. After pushing the calf's body up and forward inside the heifer as she bawled, he grabbed the inside leg and straightened it. He then paired the two legs together and worked them out. He delivered the calf in breech position by pulling down on both legs, one in each hand.

The wet calf was heavy and fell to the ground with a thud.

Robert rolled it over and watched, but it didn't breathe. "Come on, buddy," he said and rubbed the calf's chest.

When it still didn't move, he stood and pulled a thin, flexible shoot from a branch of the tree and stripped its leaves. He pushed it deep into the calf's nose and twirled it around.

The calf coughed.

"There you go." He stuck the branch deep into the other nostril.

It coughed twice more and then took a deep, wheezing breath and coughed some more. After a few spastic gasps and coughs, the breathing became regular.

Robert dragged the calf from behind its mother and then untied the heifer and turned her around to see her new baby. She leaned down and licked the newborn's head and ears. A half hour later, the calf stood on wobbly legs and nursed for the first time.

When it was done, Robert hoisted it onto his shoulders and carried it up to the barn, leading the heifer on the rope.

On his way back from the barn, Robert heard people arguing as he approached the kitchen. He stopped at the pump, cranked the handle several times, and then picked up the wash bucket to catch the gush of cold water that followed. The back and forth of the argument grew more intense. He hung the bucket on the post, and grabbed the wad of soap to wash off the dirt and grime. He could tell it was Jake, and he heard DeDe crying.

The argument reached a peak. Then the door flew open and DeDe ran out, tears streaming down her face. She slammed the door behind her. When she saw Robert, she turned away and hurried off in the direction of the servants' quarters, picking up the front of her skirt and quickening her pace.

Robert pulled open the kitchen door, and a wave of warm air and the aroma of dinner poured over him as he stepped inside. Jake was sitting at the small table.

"What's the matter?"

"She upset."

"Well, I can see that," Robert said. "What about?"

"Her sister's boys. They them ones got mixed up with that Liddell in town." Jake got up from the table and crossed the room to fetch two bowls from the cupboard. After handing the bowls to Robert, he used the iron poker to pull forward the swing-arm hanging inside the long fireplace. He ladled some stew into a bowl and handed it to him before filling his own bowl and turning toward the table.

"Well," Robert said, "I thought I'd go down there tomorrow afternoon and see about the trial. Even if I can't get into the courthouse, there'll be a big crowd and lots of excitement."

Jake wheeled around to face Robert with a look on his face that fell somewhere between anger and panic. His eyes widened, and he grabbed Robert's arm with his free hand, staring him in the face. "Mr. Robert, you gotta promise me you won't go down there, no way." He set his bowl on the table.

"But I could bring back the news on what happens."

"The only news we gon' hear tomorrow is bad news."

"Jake, why? What's the problem?"

"Talk among black folks on what they hearin' at different places. It won't be no good. Some folks' white people know already an' they tellin' 'em not to leave the house even."

"What do you mean? Word is that them boys spillin' the molasses was all just an accident, and Liddell hit them first and started all the fightin'."

"That's all true, but them boys takin' it to the judge gon' cause trouble."

"That's how the law works, though, Jake. The brothers have a right to take it to the court."

"Court only for white folks. Ain't gon' be allowed for them boys to stand up to a white man like they be doin'. Black people free now after the war, but it ain't real. We still gotta do like summody else say. Can't make no way for ourselves."

"Well, let's go on down there to let 'em know we think they're right. When we all speak up, then things can change."

"Whas gon' happen is trouble. I know. We been hearin' at different places, an' it won't be no good." The old man braced himself against the back of the chair, his grip tightening. He shook Robert's arm. "We friends, Mista Robert?"

"Jake?" Robert gave him a quizzical look. "Of course we are. You practically saved me when I got here. You the best person I know."

"Then you promise me you'll stay here tomorrow." Jake had tears in his eyes.

"I will." Robert put his own hand on top of his old friend's. "I promise."

Thursday, March 18, 1886

The Clarion-Ledger (Jackson, Mississippi)

RIOT AND KILLING AT CARROLLTON

A telegram was received in this city at a late hour last night, stating that a riot occurred in Carrollton yesterday, and that ten men were killed, and three wounded, in the court-house. No particulars as to the origin of the trouble.

Friday, March 19, 1886

The Vicksburg Herald (Vicksburg, Mississippi)

CARROLLTON'S TRAGEDY

THE CAUSES WHICH LED TO THE SHOOTING.

A Detailed Statement of the Manner in Which
the Fight Started and the Names of the Killed.

*New Orleans, March 18. – The Times-Democrat Winona
special says:*

*Since my last special I visited the Carrollton to get
particulars, and gleaned the following: Some months
ago, Robert Moore, a young man from a Leflore County
came to Carrollton and met there Ed. Brown, colored.
They had some words and the negro smeared and poured
on him molasses, which he carried in a jug. Sometime
afterwards J. M. Liddell, Jr., of Greenwood, a friend of
Moore, happened to meet with Ed. Brown and made
some allusion to his treatment of Moore. Brown gave him
impudence and Liddell started at him, but was prevented
by bystanders from attacking him. The negro then went
and armed himself and induced others to do likewise.
They stationed themselves on the streets, some behind
trees, and when Liddell came after supper from the hotel
he saw them, and asked what they meant, whereupon Ed.
Brown responded: "It was none of his damn business." At
that Liddell struck at Brown with his fist, and Ed and
Charles Brown, his brother, both simultaneously fired
upon Liddell, one ball striking the elbow of his right arm.
About this time some fifteen to twenty shots were fired
from different quarters. Liddell pulled his pistol and hit Ed
Brown in the abdomen, and received one shot in the fleshy
part of his leg. Chas. Brown was shot in the shoulder. All
remained quiet and the parties who had taken part in the
affray were brought before the mayor forthwith, waived
an examination and were bailed to appear before the next
circuit court . . .*

Upon calling the case the courthouse was filled with negroes, who stationed themselves around and about the Brown brothers. The attorneys, while proceeding, were suddenly surprised by the appearance of about one hundred white men well armed. Perceiving the noise of the entrance, Ed. Brown at once drew his pistol and fired in the direction of Liddell, who was between his attorneys. Thereupon the firing began in general. The result was that ten were instantly killed and two have died since Some escaping by jumping through the window, a distance of at least twenty feet. On most of the dead bodies arms was found. The room was completely filled with smoke. The judge's bench is on the north side of the room and the benches facing it were towards the south. It is a very large courtroom, with windows all around. I counted on the wall one hundred thirty five shots, in the wall and on the benches thirty shot holes. One shot struck the northeast window sash and glanced into the wall. Five other shots show on the north wall from the direction of the benches. The blood was in streams on the floor in the court room. The mob left as quietly and quickly as they came in.

The general impression is that this will end in further trouble . . .

The following is the list of the killed, Andrew Robertson, Charles Brown, Ed. Brown, Joe Long, John Money, Simon Kane, Jim Harris, Amos Matthews, Scott Moore, French Hughes, Coley Little and Jim Johnson. The following were wounded Will Donald, Jim Keys, Christian Preacher, Jim Hows, and Jake Kane. Very seriously; Bill Ewing, Chas. Price, Henry Cole, and Coley Thompson badly shot and reported dead.

Peyton Hemingway and Walter McHand jumped through the window carrying the sash along. The former was shot slightly in the hand but is otherwise unhurt. Amos Matthews, was shot dead while trying the same mode of escape. One colored man rolled himself out of one of the west windows, fell out on the brick pavement, got up and made his escape unhurt. As he was going out three shots were fired at him and struck the windowsill, *and one shot went through the glass. Now all is quiet. The main leaders of gang were Charles and Ed. Brown who were amongst the killed.*

It was impossible to get anyone to state any names of the mob, and it will be very difficult to ascertain such, for nobody in the excitement took any notice of any of the parties who entered the courthouse and no arrests have been made yet.

Wednesday, 24 March 1886

The Clarion, (Jackson, Mississippi)

The Carrollton Massacre

In another place in this paper we print the Picayune's account of the horrible massacre at Carrollton, which tells how eleven citizens of Mississippi were shot to death, and nine others mortally wounded. We are far from believing that this account contains "the whole truth," but its sickening details, with what measure of truth it does contain, present a spectacle of butchery hideous enough to curdle the blood of the most phlegmatic. The story, though terrible and ghastly, is simple . . .

But why consume time in discussing disputed matters? Enough is admitted to damn that hideous affair. It is admitted that the Browns had given bond to answer at the circuit court for any offense the laws of the state of which they had been guilty. It is admitted that they had caused the arrest of Jas. Liddell and others on an affidavit charging them with a felony.

It is admitted that these defendants had been arrested and were being tried by a lawful officer of the State, holding a lawful court in the very sanctuary of the law, when one hundred armed men then appeared upon the scene, surrounded to the temple of justice and shot to death under the eye of the court, eleven citizens of Mississippi and mortally wounded nine others. It is admitted that not one white man was hurt . . .

Do the people of Mississippi realize that at the door of the court room in Carrollton in Carroll County, the bloody bodies of its slain citizens lie heaped one upon the other? They have not been removed. They cannot be removed. There they will stay as a monument to the folly and wickedness of their ruthless slayers. There can be no adequate punishment for the injury which has been *inflicted upon the good people of Mississippi, by the murderous mob at Carrollton . . .*

Saturday, July 16, 1887

Northwest Harrison County, Mississippi

From the front porch, two hundred yards away, Fannie looked out across the road into the field where sixty-eight-year-old Bill Smith stood near his wife's grave. His eleven-year-old grandson, Monroe, stood by and held his grandpa's hand while the boy's father and uncles unloaded the marker from the wagon. The simple white stone was set into a cement block. They lifted it with the ropes and sidestepped to the hole in the ground at the head of the grave, now two months old. The rain streamed down the pile of dirt like tears.

Elisa Smith, wife of Bill Smith

An hour later, the boys had all gone back to their barns. The work didn't stop, even for grief, and if there was to be a day of rest tomorrow, then there was still much to be done today. On Sunday, they'd be up before dawn to feed animals, milk cows, and gather eggs before going to Red Creek Church for services.

After standing alone in the cemetery for a while, Bill walked back through the field toward the house. From the kitchen, Fannie heard his footsteps on the porch. He took off his coat and shook it before hanging it on a peg near the door.

"Mr. Smith, I was wonderin' . . ." She hesitated, unsure how to word it. "Please don't ask me to leave here. Would it be all right if I stay on with you?" She couldn't look him in the face to ask such a thing but called to him from the kitchen.

Bill came inside and gave her a stern look. "What the hell are you talkin' 'bout, girl?"

"Well, the boys are all grown up now. Married and gone. And now Elisa. It might be that I ought to move on, too."

"Ho-lee crap! You're stayin' here. This is your home. I ain't never thought of any other way. You're one of us."

Tears came to her eyes. Overcome with relief, she gave the old man a big hug. Since she'd been taken in by the Smith clan nearly five years earlier, she'd never let anyone see her emotions, but this unexpected reassurance overwhelmed her. She was older now but still felt like a child in his presence. "You been the best daddy I ever had, an' I don't want to leave you. Y'all are my people. I love livin' here and goin' to church an' all." She cried in earnest. "And when I die, you can bury me out there in that field too."

"Well, we're in this together. You're family, and we all gon' take care of each other. That's what we do." He put one arm awkwardly around her and wiped his eyes with his other sleeve.

Sunday, July 17, 1887

Red Creek Church, Harrison County, Mississippi

The little wooden church was filled to capacity—as it was every Sunday—with families named Smith, Ladner, and Dale, all loosely connected by marriage.

As they milled about and visited after the service, Sarah Ladner approached Fannie, who stood apart from the clusters of men and women still talking. "Good morning, Fannie. So nice to see you."

"Good morning, Sarah. How are you?"

"Things are fine with us. This next baby should be here in another month or so." Sarah patted her belly. "Are you and Mr. Smith getting along all right without Elisa?"

"Yes, he seems to be doin' good as can be expected. Havin' all the boys so close by makes things easier. Always got children in the house to mind—and family right beside. Elisa taught me all her best recipes, so we're eatin' fine."

"Well, I'm sure that Mr. Smith is thankful for you bein' there, too. Will you be goin' to live with one of the brothers and his family?"

"No, we talked yesterday. I'm gonna stay with him."

Sarah raised an eyebrow. "Oh. Well, are y'all gonna marry?"

Fanny chuckled. "No, that's silly. He's like a father to me."

"But y'all aren't really kin."

"Well, no," she said, suddenly feeling wary.

~

Fannie was doing laundry on the front porch two days later when she saw a wagon making its way down the road toward their house in the early evening, She felt a wave of nervousness wash over her. The preacher and his wife, the highly esteemed spiritual leaders in the community, were always serious and somber. He looked even older than his seventy years—always dressed in black, small and thin, with wild gray hair and a long, wiry beard.

His wife helped him down from the wagon and silently followed him as he grabbed the post to step up onto the front porch. His wife didn't smile.

Fannie hung the last pair of pants on the porch rail and dried her hands on her apron. "Good evening, Reverend." She stepped forward to offer him a hand and help him up the steps, but he waved her away.

He straightened himself to his full standing height and looked at Bill, who appeared in the doorway.

"Reverend, to what do we owe this honor?"

"William Smith, I'm here to tell you that if you're gonna stay in the house with this girl—or if she's gonna stay in the house with you—then y'all need to be rightly married in the sight of God."

Despite the warning from Sarah on Sunday, the consternation and finality of this pronouncement surprised Fannie.

Bill's eyes flashed anger. "Fannie here's been livin' with us since she was just a girl. Near to five years now. You know that."

"You and Elisa done right by her when you took her in—that's so—but she's not your daughter, and she's not your granddaughter. She's not kin to you at all. Neither of you is married, and there's no chaperone in this house, so you can't live with her unless you are man and wife." The ancient minister opened his worn black Bible and pointed to a passage, which he quoted without looking. "Second Corinthians, chapter eight, verse twenty-one. *'Providing for honest things, not only in the sight of God but in the sight of men.'* It ain't right—you two livin' together. If y'all don't marry, all the wagging tongues won't be good for neither of you!"

Fannie could see Bill clench his jaw. She knew he tried extra hard to hold his tongue around the preacher and his wife, but she suspected this might be one of the days that he couldn't.

"Dammit, Preacher, she's young enough to be my granddaughter! This is just them old biddies at church stirrin' things up."

"William Smith! Don't you use your unclean lips to justify more sin!" The minister's wife raised a scolding finger at him. "Your children think it's right, as do I. And so you must."

Fannie protested. "But I'm just a girl!"

"That's precisely the point," she said, turning on Fannie. "You're too young to be caught up in a life that has the appearance of sin and wickedness. Surely, you don't want that, do you?"

"Well . . . no . . ."

"Then you must do what is right," she said. "You need to get this matter resolved or go find somewhere else to live that won't be a discredit to us all."

They stood in awkward silence for a moment.

"Deacon Elijah Ladner will go to the courthouse with you on Thursday to make the marriage bond." The preacher tottered down the steps, holding on to the rail and his wife's shoulder.

After she helped him up into the wagon and climbed into the driver's seat, they drove off without another word.

Thursday, July 21, 1887

Mississippi City, Mississippi.

Mr. F. S. Hewes, the clerk of the court, pulled out the bond book after Elijah Ladner explained to him why they had made the long trip from the north part of the county to the courthouse near the beach.

Cussin' Bill Smith, indignant about the ultimatum from the preacher, was still struggling to remove the scowl from his face.

"So, William Smith and Elijah Ladner." Mr. Hewes checked the date on the paper wall calendar, which advertised a smiling man with long white hair and a top hat promoting the quality of Quaker Oats. "Today is the twenty-first." He filled in more blanks on the page. "Who are the bride and groom?"

"William Smith and Fannie Haley," Deacon Ladner said.

"And how do you spell Miss Haley's name?"

The deacon turned to Cussin' Bill.

"Regular way, I suppose," Bill said with a shrug.

Fanny Healy, Hewes wrote. "And what are the ages of the couple?"

"I'm sixty-eight. She's nineteen."

Mr. Hewes looked at Bill in surprise, then at the deacon. "Your daughter?"

"No, she's a foundling," the deacon explained. "Orphaned. Bill here took her in years ago when his whole family was in the house, but now the boys are all married out and Mrs. Smith has passed. This is what we need to do. It's a custodial marriage. All perfectly righteous and moral. Keepin' the standards for our community."

Mr. Hewes shook his head. He completed another form for Deacon Ladner to attest to Fannie's age and then turned the book around on the counter and indicated where the two men should sign.

The deacon signed his name, Bill made his mark, and Mr. Hewes finalized it.

"The bond is for a hundred dollars," Hewes said.

"A hundred *what*?" Bill felt his face burn red as he struggled to speak. "What the hell for? You didn't hardly do nothin'!"

"You don't pay the bond now, Mr. Smith," Deacon Ladner said in a placating voice. "That's what you're committin' to pay if for some reason the marriage can't go through. You normally make the bond with the father of the bride—like a penalty if you don't get married and leave somebody jilted." Elijah turned Bill around by the shoulders and pushed him toward the door. "Thank you," he said over his shoulder as they left. "The couple will come down on Tuesday for the proceedings with the justice of the peace."

Tuesday, July 26, 1887

Northwest Harrison County, Mississippi.

"Well, let's get on then if we're goin'!" Fannie heard Bill call from the porch as a hint of light peeked over the trees.

"I'm comin'." Fannie grabbed her hat and blew out the lanterns in her bedroom.

Samuel met them outside with two horses hitched to the fastest and most comfortable buggy the extended family owned.

"It's more'n thirty mile to get there from Perkinston," Bill said to Samuel. "If'n we don't show, I'll have to pay Elijah Ladner a hunnerd damn dollars. I mean, ain't this some kinda crap!"

"Just a formality, Pa. Don't change nothin'," Fannie said as she climbed into the back seat. "But if it keeps the preacher happy and keeps his wife outta our business, then the whole trip is worth it."

She noticed that Samuel had put on Sunday clothes and that Bill had combed his hair flat with tonic and was wearing his nice jacket. It made her feel better about fixing up her hair this morning and borrowing a hat from Mary.

They arrived late morning at the courthouse in Mississippi City and walked to the clerk's office.

"We're for a weddin'," Bill said to the clerk at the counter. "Made the bond last week."

"Well, that's lovely." The girl at the counter didn't appear much older than Fannie. "You've come to the right place. Councilman Bond is here this morning and can get this all settled before lunch. Bride's name?" She turned several pages in the bond book, searching for the entry.

"Fannie Haley," Samuel said.

She found the right page. "And you are Mr. Smith?" The girl looked to Samuel for a reply.

"Yeah, but I'm not the groom." Samuel shook his head and pointed at his father. "He is."

"Sir?" She looked at Bill.

"William Smith. How long is this gonna take? We got farmin' to attend to. Cows ain't gonna milk themselves."

The clerk looked confused for a moment. Then a hint of a smirk crept across her face.

Fannie scowled at the girl and leaned across the counter. "This ain't no shotgun wedding, if that's what you're thinkin'."

"Oh, of course not." The girl turned pink. "I'll go get the councilman right away." She hurried off with the ledger.

A few minutes later, a door opened and a balding man stuck his head through the doorway. "William Smith and Fannie Haley."

William, Fannie, and Samuel followed the man into his office, where they stood in front of his desk. An open window let in the fresh saltwater breeze from the beachfront, just a block away.

"Who is the groom?"

"I am." Bill raised his hand as Samuel pointed at him.

"Miss Haley?" The councilman looked at her.

She nodded.

"Please stand together and hold hands."

Samuel moved to Fannie's right side so that she was between him and Bill.

"Do you, William Smith, take Fannie Haley to be your lawful wedded wife, to have and to hold from this day forward until death you do part?"

"I do," Bill said flatly.

"Do you, Fannie Haley, take William Smith to be your lawful wedded husband, to have and to hold from this day forward until death you do part?"

"I do."

"By the power vested in me by the State of Mississippi, I pronounce you man and wife. You may kiss the bride."

Fannie and Bill exchanged glances, and Bill shook his head slightly. She hugged him and kissed him on the cheek.

"Aw, hell," said Bill. "I'm gonna need a copy of that certificate for when we get home, 'cause I sure as hell ain't gonna pay Elijah Ladner no hunnerd dollars."

MARRIAGE BOND

The State of Mississippi, Harrison County

KNOW ALL MEN BY THESE PRESENTS:

That we, *William Smith and Elijah Ladner,* of the County of Harrison, and the State of Mississippi, are held and firmly bound unto the State of Mississippi aforesaid, in the sum of ONE HUNDRED DOLLARS, for the payment of which, well and truly to be made we and each of us do bind ourselves, our heirs, executors, administrators and assigns, jointly severally and firmly by these presents.

Sealed with our seals and dated this 21st day

of July, A.D., 1887

The condition of this obligation is such, that whereas a MARRIAGE is shortly intended to be celebrated between the above bound *William Smith and Fanny Healy.*

Now, if there be no lawful cause to obstruct the said Marriage, then this obligation to be void, otherwise to remain in full force and virtue.

Signed, Sealed and delivered in presence of

William (his mark X) Smith {Seal}

Elijah Ladner {Seal}

F. S. Hewes affdt of age of parties made & filed

THE STATE OF MISSISSIPPI, HARRISON COUNTY,

To Any Judge, Minister, Justice or other Person lawfully authorized to celebrate the Rites of Matrimony:

You are hereby licensed to celebrate the Rites of Matrimony between Mr. *William Smith and Miss Fanny Healy,* and for doing so, this shall be your warrant.

Given under my hand and official seal, this 21st day of July in the year of our Lord one thousand eight-hundred and *eighty-seven.*

{Seal}   *F. S. Hewes*

The State of Mississippi, Harrison County,

In virtue of a License from the Clerk of Court of said County of Harrison, I have this day celebrated the Rites of Matrimony between Mr. *William Smith, and Miss Fanny Healy.*

Given under my hand and seal this 26th day of July A.D. 1887

A. J. Bond, M. B. Supervisor {Seal}

Sunday, October 16, 1888

Carrollton, Mississippi

The annual picnic in Carrollton was a well-attended event, scheduled for the fall, when it was cooler, and for a weekend when all the churches had their circuit-riding preachers in town simultaneously. The whole county looked forward to the event for months, and politicians from all over the state kept the date for speechmaking. The level ground along the south bank of the Big Sandy Creek, shaded by trees that hadn't yet dropped their leaves, provided a perfect spot for the townsfolk to set doors on sawhorses and stack them with food. After lunch, there were games and contests. Awards were given for the best pies and cakes. It was standing room only as the crowd gathered to watch the younger boys in the three-legged race along the length of the field.

Twenty-two-year-old Robert crowded in with the others to watch but was bumped from behind and lost his balance. He waved his arms wildly to keep his footing at the edge of the slope, but the earth gave way under the heel of his boot, and he tumbled down the bank toward the creek, taking down someone with him.

"Hey!" the young lady said indignantly as she rolled over and scrambled to her feet.

Robert looked up to see who he'd just knocked over. "I'm so sorry. I fell. Are you okay?"

"I'm fine," she said as she brushed herself off. "Good thing we didn't go down in the water."

Robert got to his feet. "I'm awful sorry. I don't know what happened."

"It's okay. No harm done. No injuries except to my pride." The woman looked at Robert and laughed. She was petite and wore a pretty autumn-patterned dress for the occasion.

Robert was taken immediately by her smile.

She tucked a stray curl of dark, wavy hair beneath the hat pinned to her head. "You have dirt on your face. Here. Use this." She offered her handkerchief—a dainty white thing embroidered with flowers.

"Uh, I've got this instead, but thanks." He pulled out his own, a scrap of an old calico dress that DeDe had hemmed for him. "Something more appropriate for a farmhand." He suddenly became aware of his appearance and wished that he'd worn a nicer shirt and a better pair of pants.

"Well, since we've bumped into each other, we should trade formal introductions. I'm Annie Corley."

"I'm Robert Haley." He offered his hand, but it was dirty, too. He glanced at his palms and waved a hand instead.

She laughed again.

He thought she was beautiful. "Would you like some lemonade?"

"That would be lovely. Thank you."

An hour later, an older gentleman approached Robert and Annie. Robert had noticed the man keeping a close eye on them as they talked. He was clearly Annie's father.

"Annie, dear, it's time for us to go home. Will you please go collect your mother and sisters?"

Robert stood and extended his hand. "Sir, I'm Robert Haley."

"Silas Corley. Good to meet you. I've seen you on occasion in town." The man was taller than Robert, with deeply set eyes and chiseled lines framing his mustache.

"Yes sir, I work the cattle at Cotesworth. Stay in one of the old cabins there."

"I farm too. East of town. McCarley area. Hard work."

"Hard work's good for you," said Robert. "Builds character."

"So they say."

The men stood, not really looking at each other, until the silence became uncomfortable.

"So, you know the senator, then?" asked Annie.

"He's so busy all the time. I see him sometimes when he's home. He's really nice, but mostly I know Jake."

"Yes, a fine man."

MARRIAGE BOND

The State of Mississippi, Carroll County

Know all Men by these Presents

That we *R.L. Haley and A. R. Corley* of the County of Carroll, and the State of Mississippi are held and firmly bound unto the State of Mississippi, in the penal sum of ONE HUNDRED DOLLARS current money of the United States of America, which payment, well and truly to be made and performed, we, and each of us, do hereby bind ourselves, our heirs, executors, administrators and assigns, jointly and severally, firmly by these presents.

Witness our hands and seals, this *26* day of *Dec* A. D. 1889

The Conditions of this Obligation is such, that whereas application has this day been made to the Clerk of the Circuit Court of the County of Carroll and State aforesaid, for the granting and issuing of License for the Marriage of *R.L. Haley* and *Wife Annie I. Corley.*

Now, therefore, if there shall be no lawful cause to obstruct the Marriage for which this License is granted, then this obligation to be void, otherwise to remain in full force and effect.

Signed, sealed and delivered in the presence of *R.L. Haley* {seal} *A.R. Corley* {seal}

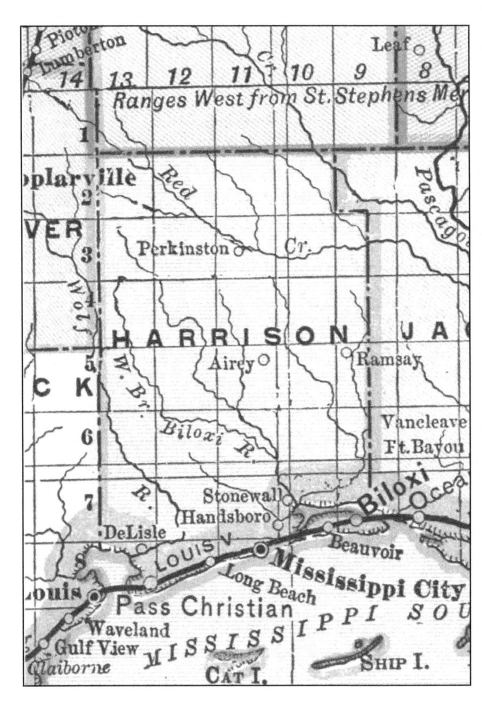

Mississippi (detail), The Library Atlas of Modern Geography,
Appleton & Co., Buffalo, New York, 1892. Courtesy of David
Rumsey Map Collection, www.davidrumsey.com.

Chapter 11

Friday, November 1, 1895

The Vicksburg Evening Post (Vicksburg, Mississippi)

The wise way, the proper way, the Christian way, to care for the orphans is (to) let kind-hearted people, who are childless adopt the little ones, and they will be repaid a thousand fold in the love and affection that will be bestowed upon them in their old age.

Tuesday, December 17, 1895

Northwest Harrison County, Mississippi.

Most of the time, worry and anger kept her awake, but they'd worked her so hard the past two days she'd slept deeply this night. Still, she heard the creak when the door to the shed opened, and the fear struck immediately. Hands touching her. Pressure, suffocating, pain. Hot breath smelling of liquor. She tried to keep her head turned away, tried to be somewhere else.

Fannie cried out and opened her eyes. Outside, the moonless night provided just a trace of light, so only the dim outline of the window was visible. *Just that dream.*

She heard Bill struggling down the hall with the lantern, and a second later he opened the door to her room. "You all right?" He leaned against the door, gasping after the short walk.

Fannie jumped up from the bed and took the lantern from him. "What are you doing up?"

He took her arm for support and leaned on her as she guided him into the kitchen, where he collapsed into the big chair.

"I'll make us some coffee." Fannie turned to set the lamp on the wood box. "But first let's get your feet up." She balanced blankets on a stool, lifted his swollen legs, and wrapped his feet inside.

"Bad dream again?" he asked, breathlessly.

"Yeah, same ol' bad dream. Been a while. Last time I had 'em was after Elisa died." Now that Bill had chest pains nearly all day and shortness of breath, the nightmares were back. She knew it was a leftover from previous tough times that always seemed to show up in new tough times—the one thing that didn't get left behind when she ran away.

Back then, she'd been too ashamed to tell anyone—and wouldn't have, even if the man hadn't threatened her. Other than Elisa, she'd never told anyone about all of the terrible things that had happened to her before she had come to live with the Smiths. When she was younger and had cried in the night, Elisa would lie down with her and rub her back till she fell asleep. Now, whenever the nightmare woke her, she just sat up and waited for morning. It made for tiring days.

"What happens in the dream?"

"I don't know," she lied. "Just makes you real 'fraid."

Bill couldn't work anymore, but Fannie did her best to keep up with the chores in the barn while continuing with the cooking and managing the house. It was good to have all the family so close. They helped out and took turns sitting with Bill, but even after these long days, she had difficulty falling asleep. She dreaded the dream.

"I'll be fine. You rest while I make us some breakfast." Fannie tapped the handle of the firebox on the stove to test its temperature, then turned the latch and let down the door. She put some small kindling on the nearly dead embers and blew gently, coaxing them to flame.

"I seen this before. I know what's coming."

Fannie took the kettle, ladled water from the bucket, and set it on the stove. "What are you talking about?" She turned back to him.

"I'll be seventy-seven in January if I make it to my birthday."

"Papa, don't talk like that—"

"Listen, I seen this. Hell, nobody lives forever." He paused to take a few breaths, exhaling slowly through pursed lips. "And I don't want to. I'm ready to go be with Elisa." He stopped to catch his breath again. "I told Samuel. I want you an' Monroe to have this house."

"What?"

"I know. Y'all two have a spark. I seen it." He winced and took another slow, deep breath. "Y'all should marry when I'm gone. Have a family. That'd be good."

She sat down beside him, putting her hand on his arm. "*You're* my family."

"You're a Smith. Been one for fourteen years. You belong here."

Saturday, January 18, 1896

Northwest Harrison County, Mississippi

Word of Bill's death spread quickly. His sons and the men from the church spent the night making a coffin in the Ladners' barn, while Fannie and Mary sat up with him. They stopped the clock and covered the mirrors. After washing his body, they put him in his best suit of clothes and set his arms and hands in a reverent position on his chest. Fannie trimmed and combed his hair, setting aside a long piece to form into a flower with glue and string to keep under glass with those of the other family members they'd collected over the years. Finally, they cleaned the whole house and changed out all the laundry, putting the dirty linens out in the barn to wash in the coming days. They were already exhausted from nursing him night and day for the prior week. Nevertheless, they felt relieved to get breakfast going for the men when they returned. It gave them something different to do to take their mind away from the sadness.

George and Calvin lifted the casket from the back of the wagon and brought it inside. It was hexagonal, wider at the shoulders than the foot. They put the box on the floor next to the bed and leaned the lid against the wall. The funeral service would be at noon. The brothers gathered around the bed and looked at their pa once more.

Monroe went back out on the front porch and sat by Fannie. "You okay?"

"I'm glad he's not sufferin' no more, but it's real sad anyhow. That man was so good to me. After all the bad times I been through, he was the first good man I ever knew since my real daddy died." She started to cry and put her face in her hands.

"I do know. He was a good man."

Samuel came to the door. "Monroe, we need another set of strong arms in here."

Monroe joined his father and his uncles and helped lift the old man by the sheet on the bed and lay him inside the coffin. They put the box in the front room on four chairs facing each other.

Three other uncles came in from the cemetery, where they'd been digging the grave next to their mother's. They stood for a minute to stare at their father's body.

"Looks just like he's sleepin'," Monroe said.

"He's resting now, but he's not here," Samuel said. "He's with Jesus and Mama."

At noon, the community came to support the Smith clan as they gathered to bury their patriarch. The family filled the house and spilled out onto the front porch and into the yard. Neighbors and friends came, surrounding the little cabin with wagons and horses, greeting each other with somber faces, bearing food and love and condolences. They filed through the house to see their friend one last time.

The ancient and frail preacher spoke at length from the front porch. He finally concluded as the crowd started to fidget. "'God is my refuge and strength, an ever-present help in time of trouble.' The words of the psalmist are a comfort to us all. In these days as we gain strength from our family, strength from our neighbors, strength from our friends, remember that for all of us, God is the source of that strength." He closed his Bible and turned to step down from the porch, indicating that it was time to move on to the cemetery across the road.

Inside, Calvin and George covered the coffin and began to nail the lid shut. This prompted more crying from family members. One of the women started to sing, and the tune caught with the crowd.

"Shall we gather at the river, the beautiful, the beautiful river . . ."

Two men helped the preacher down the steps from the front porch. When he reached the road, he turned to face the cabin, where the women filed out behind him. They lined an open path and waited for the men to bring their father to the cemetery. The singing continued. Samuel, Hezekiah, George, Calvin, Bruno, and Donan struggled to lift the casket and arranged themselves with it on their shoulders. As they approached the door, it became apparent that not only could they not bring it out with the pallbearers two abreast, but the shoulders of the casket wouldn't even fit through the narrow cabin door.

"Can we pass him out the window?" Calvin asked.

George held his hands out as wide as the casket and then moved to the window to estimate the width. "No."

"Well, we can't open it back up," Donan said.

"Turn him sideways," Samuel said.

The men stepped back into the room. Calvin and Hezekiah went out the front door, while their four brothers turned the box onto its side and passed it to them through the door, feet first. George and Donan ducked under the coffin to get out to the porch, while Samuel and Bruno held the shoulders of the box.

The singing faded as the surprised crowd stopped to watch the unusual procession.

The brothers passed the coffin outside. Then the six men reorganized themselves on the porch, returned the casket to its back, and made their way down the front steps.

A hint of a smile crept across the preacher's face. "Well, I'm sure that ol' Cussin' Bill would have something to say about that."

A wave of chuckles passed through the crowd.

Saturday, February 15, 1896

Perkinston, Mississippi

Fannie perused the new dresses for sale at the Perkins and Lott Mercantile, imagining what she might look like in something that was store-bought. She really liked the ones with lace edging on the neckline and the sleeves. Her future mother-in-law, Mary, was handy with sewing, and there was no doubt this dress would come out beautifully for her wedding. Fannie would describe some of the details, and Mary would have no trouble making something just as pretty.

Fannie had known Monroe for nearly fifteen years. Growing up in the extended family had allowed their relationship to deepen. Their attraction had grown gradually and solidly. She knew his heart—that he was a good man. He made her happy, and she wanted to be around him. *That must be it*, she thought. *That's what love is.* During the year that Cussin' Bill had been sick, he'd told each of them—and Monroe's parents—that they should marry, so the announcement of this match didn't cause much of a stir among the family. The couple did set out a timeline for a long engagement, however. Fannie figured they'd better wait at least a year to keep things proper for the folks in town.

Outside, a tin peddler stopped in the dusty street. Fannie watched through the window as he climbed down from his wagon, strategically placed to attract the Saturday shoppers who had already begun to gather in the tiny town center.

She stepped across the street as he started to set up his display.

"Well, good morning!" He smiled and removed his hat. "What are you shopping for today, ma'am? Can I interest you in something from our wares? Frank Watson's my name. I got lots of things you need—and lots you don't even know you need yet!"

The hand-painted sign on the side of the wagon read *Watson's Goods* in not-too-even lettering. He lowered a side door, revealing shelves crammed full of all sorts of kitchen tools, housewares, children's toys, sewing notions, and baskets.

Fannie took a step closer to inspect several cards wound with lace trimming that she'd noticed tucked in the back of a shelf.

"Yes, I can see you'd like to look at some of our sewing things. You clearly have a fine eye for the quality of the merchandise. What exactly are you looking for, may I ask?"

"Well, I might like to look at some lace," she said, a little cautious of this man she'd never seen before.

"Perfect! We've got several kinds—all fashionable additions to a new dress. What will you be making?"

"Mary and I gonna eventually be makin' my weddin' dress. I was in the store just now lookin' at the new styles."

"That prospective groom is a fortunate man, indeed." He grabbed one of the cards. "I'm sure you and your sister will love this beautiful pattern here."

Taken by the salesman's flattery, she lowered her guard and became a little more talkative. "Actually, Mary will be my mother-in-law. I'm an orphan. I grew up here after I came down from Memphis."

"Oh, I see. I'm sorry to hear that. But everything does work out then, doesn't it? Now you'll have a whole family."

Fannie rubbed the lace between her thumb and forefinger, inspecting the tightness of the knots and the details of the work. "Had some brothers who were older, but just my one brother and me ended up in the orphan home after Daddy died in the yellow fever. I was six."

The man dug around in a bin for some other samples of lace. "Will your brother be coming for the wedding?"

"Well, no, he ran off from there, but I don't know where he went to. I got adopted and brought down here, but I eventually ran away too. Been with the Smiths for a long time now."

"Well, maybe your brother still lives in Memphis. It's a mighty big city." The salesman held out two other colors of similar lace for her to inspect. "You maybe could write a letter up there to the po-lice in Memphis. See if anybody's heard of him. Wouldn't it be something if he could come down here to see his sister's wedding?"

"How much for six feet of this here?" Fannie asked, handing back the card.

"Oh, a great choice! I think I could go for maybe seventy-five cents. You know it's from up in New York. Handmade, of course."

Fannie eyed the lace again and did some calculations in her head. "That'll be fine," she finally said and took out some coins from her purse.

~

While they sat after dinner doing needlework that evening, Fannie told Mary about the conversation with the tin peddler.

"Robert was just there one day and gone the next." She shook her head. "Never heard from him. Nobody knew." Fannie put her stitching in her lap and thought for a minute. "No reason not to write a letter up to Memphis and ask. Might hear nothin', but at least I'd've tried."

"Could get bad news too," Mary said in a cautious tone. "Might find out he got killed or somethin'." She stopped rocking in her chair.

Fannie had come to live with Bill and Elisa after Mary was already wed to their son, Samuel, and was already a mother to several children, including Fannie's fiancé, Monroe. The two young ladies had spent many years together as additions to the large Smith clan and had developed a comfortable, sisterly friendship.

"Maybe, but I ain't seen him in more'n twenty years. I guess I'd be sad about somethin' like that, but still, then at least I'd know somethin'." Fannie put her work down in the sewing basket and retrieved paper and pen from a cabinet drawer. She sat closer to the lamplight and penned a letter.

Thursday, February 20, 1896

Memphis, Tennessee

The letter from Perkinston arrived at its destination in Memphis and made it to the "In" box at the Memphis police station. After reviewing the records from the night before and speaking to the officers coming on duty for the morning, Officer E. B. Moseley stepped inside his office and turned his attention to the stack of correspondence. He dictated several letters to the secretary for typing, personally handled two issues with handwritten notes, and responded to several invitations over the next hour. Then he opened the letter from Perkinston.

> *Sir:*
>
> *My name is Fannie Haley, and I live in Perkinston, Mississippi. I am writing to know if you have heard of my brother Robert Lee Haley. When we were real little, we were sent to St. Peter's Orphanage home from Hernando after my father died in the yellow fever in 1873. Our daddy was Michael Haley. My brother ran off from the orphanage after a year, and I have not seen him since. Do you know about anyone named Robert Lee Haley in Memphis? If you do, could you ask him if he came from the orphanage and if he had a sister named Fannie? Ask him to write me if it is him. I live in Perkinston, Miss. I am getting married, and it would be good if he could come to the wedding.*
>
> *Thank you,*
>
> *Fannie Haley*

Moseley hadn't heard of a Robert Lee Haley, neither among the folks who frequented the jail and the courthouse nor among anyone he was acquainted with socially. He scribbled a note on the back of the envelope, gave the letter to the desk officer, and told him to pass it to the policeman who would be walking the beat near Auburndale and Poplar to drop off at St. Peter's that day.

When Patrolman John Griffin got to the orphanage, he left the letter in the main office.

~

Sister Mary Callahan, the corresponding secretary at St. Peter's, read the letter from Fannie on Saturday. She vaguely recalled that she'd filed a letter from someone named Haley a number of years ago when she had only been the assistant to Sister Mary Joseph. Every piece of correspondence was meticulously logged in and out of the office and then kept on file. She made an entry in the current book for the new letter and then took out two sheets of light-blue stationery.

St. Peter's Orphanage   *Feb 22, 1896*
Poplar Street
Memphis, Tennessee

Dear Fannie,

Your letter to the police department inquiring about your brother was forwarded to us here at the orphanage. We don't have any information about Robert, but we do recall that a number of years ago we received a letter from him requesting information about you.

I hope this information is somehow comforting to you, knowing that he, too, was thinking of you and wanted to see you again.

We hope that you are well, and we wish you the very best.

With all the blessings of our Lord Jesus Christ,

Sister Mary Callahan

Suddenly she remembered something else. She got up from her chair and riffled through another stack of correspondence on a bureau across the room. The envelope she was looking for had come from Georgia somewhere, from an attorney. When she had received it last month, she'd had no information to offer, so she had set it aside.

She finally found the piece she was looking for and opened the letter again.

R. G. Bentley, Attorney   *January 17, 1896*
Monroe Street, Tallapoosa, Georgia

To the St. Peter's Orphanage

Memphis, Tennessee

To Whom It May Concern:

I am the attorney settling the estate of a Mr. James V. White, formerly of Atlanta, Georgia, most recently of Haralson County, Georgia, who is now deceased. I am charged with disposition of his assets and distribution of funds to all of his living heirs and legatees.

Since I am advised that his daughter Sophronia has also died, I am obligated to divide her portion of the estate among her children. The DeSoto County Courthouse reports that two of those children were sent to your institution in 1873, a Miss Fannie Haley and a Mr. Robert Lee Haley.

It would be greatly appreciated if you would provide any information that you have on these two individuals so that we may send correspondence to them on this matter.

Sincerely,

R. G. Bentley, Esq.

The nun pulled out another sheet of paper and quickly wrote a reply.

St. Peter's Orphanage   *Feb 22, 1896*

Poplar Street

Memphis, Tennessee

Dear. Mr. Bentley,

    I write in response to your inquiry about Miss Fannie Haley and her brother Robert L. Haley. Though we have no information on the whereabouts of Mr. Haley, I can tell you that Miss Fannie Haley now lives in Perkinston, Mississippi.

With all the blessings of our Lord Jesus Christ,

      Sister Mary Callahan

Thursday, April 9, 1896
The Free Press (Picayune, Mississippi)

Pearls of Thought

Remembrance is very bitter, and useless as well; to play one's part out bravely in the world, it is necessary to have no memory.

Thursday, April 9, 1896

Memphis, Tennessee

After she received the letter from the orphanage, Fannie suffered through weeks of irritation, sadness, and outright anger. "I know very well them sisters kept record of every letter that came into that office," Fannie said. "They wrote everything down in them record books. They know, all right—they just won't take the time to look. They don't care!"

Finally, Mary gave her the money for a trip to Memphis. "You gonna have to go up there an' see them to get this all worked out," she conceded. "It's just eatin' you up an' you gotta get this worked out."

It took three full days to get to Memphis by train. But the alternative—riding all the way in a stagecoach—had been unthinkable. After riding the narrow-gauge train to the coast, Fannie went from Mississippi City to New Orleans and stayed overnight before changing to the Illinois Central line. She took another overnight in Jackson before catching the train that would finally take her to Memphis.

It stopped briefly in Hernando, and Fannie recalled that they'd lived there once. As she stared out from the car, she noticed the scenery created a vaguely pleasant sense of familiarity, but she didn't recognize anything.

They rolled north out of town and passed a cluster of shacks where tired-looking people sat listlessly. A little girl, barefoot in a dress that she'd long outgrown, waved excitedly at the train.

At Union Station in Memphis, Fannie took a streetcar to the Clarendon Hotel on Madison Street. The clerk gave her a key to a fourth-floor room and pointed her to the elevator.

She stood outside the little box for a moment, confused.

The bellboy hurried over and stepped inside first. "Right this way, ma'am," he said with a welcoming sweep of his arm.

"Where?" she said, unsure what to do. "What?"

"I'll take you up to the fourth floor."

She stepped inside hesitantly, having never ridden in an elevator before, and he shut the gate and lifted the lever to command the car upward.

The hot bath with running water in the room was a welcome change from heating kettles on the stove for the washtub at home. After washing away the grime from traveling, she went down to dinner and stared at the evening paper while waiting for her food. An article about an orphanage outing to the park, scheduled for the next day, caught her attention.

Never heard of such. Didn't have no fun days at the park when I was here.

After dinner, she strolled down Madison Street for a couple of blocks. The store windows and shops housed more clothing and commercial goods in one place than she'd ever imagined. She watched the busy city, marveling at the streetcars and the traffic and the crowds before heading back to the hotel as it grew dark.

That night, she lay in bed and stared at the ceiling. Mixed emotions kept her awake. Many minutes later, she rolled over to fall asleep. She slept fitfully and dreamt of her brother.

~

Outside the orphanage the next day, Fannie stood on the sidewalk and gazed up at the red brick belfry. The long black iron fence was still there, but the building wasn't nearly as big or imposing as she remembered it from all those years ago. Her heart raced, and her mouth felt dry. She wrung her gloves in her hands, twisting them tightly. When she'd calmed herself with a few deep, fortifying breaths, she rang the bell.

A young nun stepped out the front door to speak to her through the gate. "Good morning."

"Good morning." Fannie reached into her handbag to retrieve the letter. She glanced at the signature to remind herself of the name she needed. "I'm here to see Sister Mary Callahan."

The nun appeared to recognize the stationery. "Of course. Welcome." She opened the gate. "Most of the children and staff have gone to the park, but Sister Callahan is here today. Please follow me." She closed the gate behind them and led Fannie up the walk and through the front door.

The smells brought all the memories flooding back. Unbidden images and feelings crowded her mind: the fears of the first year as she struggled to grow accustomed to living with the others in the girls' hall, the aromas from the kitchen and the food that she had appreciated at first—it was hot and plentiful—before coming to intensely dislike eating the same things week after week, the lonely nights when she had cried herself to sleep after Robert left her without a word. She remembered with anger the day Mr. Sims smiled at her and took her away to live with them. Then she smirked to herself as she recalled the scene she'd caused at church before running away.

She followed the sister through the front hall and down a corridor to the administrative offices, where, after opening a door labeled *Correspondence,* they found an older nun sitting at a large desk and writing on blue stationery.

She looked up as they entered. "Yes, may I help you?"

"Good morning. I'm Fannie Haley. I was an orphan in here after my daddy died, and I got adopted out to the Sims family in seventy-six." She offered the blue sheet of paper to the stern-looking woman behind the desk. "I got this letter from you after I wrote up here a few months back."

The old nun read the letter. "Oh, I do remember writing this." She stood to retrieve a book from the shelf on the side of the room. "We register all the correspondence in and out as it relates to the children. We just filled the last book and started a new one." She put the leather-bound volume on the desk and opened it from the back. After turning through a few pages, she came to the line indicating Fannie's letter. "I received your letter on a Thursday when the policeman brought it, and I wrote back to you on Saturday. See there: *'No more information.'* I wrote it right here." She smiled unconvincingly. "Now is there anything else I can help you with?"

Fannie, determined to remain pleasant, replied in a measured tone. "Well, if you have this written down, then I'm sure you got somethin' in them books about when my brother wrote to you looking for me. I want to find in that book where he was when he wrote it."

"Oh, I'm afraid that's not possible," she said. "All our files are closed. We must protect the privacy of the children and everyone else concerned. I'm sure you can understand."

"But this is about me and about my brother!" Fannie struggled to contain her frustration. "Is it my privacy you think you're keepin'?" Her eyes flashed, and anger crept into her tone. "You remembered enough to tell me in the letter he was lookin' for me, but then you just quit? Why write anything down? Why keep any records in them books at all if you just put 'em away and don't let nobody look at 'em?"

"But—"

"I ain't goin' nowhere 'till I look through them books." She pulled out a chair, sat at the table, and set her purse in her lap with determination.

The sister, perhaps unaccustomed to being confronted, folded quickly. "Well, I suppose." She turned back to the shelves. "I have no idea when the letter came or when we might have replied. I suppose you can look through the records, but you certainly can't take any of them outside this room." She pulled five books from the shelf and put them on the table. "The records work in backwards order from here. Put them all back on the shelf when you're done, and don't get them out of order." She left in a huff.

Fannie spent the entire morning and afternoon sitting at the table, poring over the reports page by page. Her stomach growled when she detected the familiar smell of lunch, and she heard a few children, rambunctious, somewhere down the halls. Still, she searched. She didn't dare leave for fear of being kept from reentering.

As dinnertime neared, she turned a page in a book from 1882. Her heart leapt when she saw her brother's name.

Received:	From:	Reply:
Oct 22, 1882	R. L. Haley	Oct 28, 1882

Note: Fannie adopted to R. Sims, Carrollton, Miss.

Fannie ran her fingers over the handwriting on the page, committed the words to memory, and then replaced the volumes on the shelf. Her hopes dashed, she fished for a handkerchief in her bag to wipe away her tears and then turned to leave.

Sister Mary Callahan appeared at the end of the corridor in the main lobby. "Did you find an entry about his letter?"

"His letter was in 1882, but all the book said was you told him I got adopted by Mr. Sims and went to Carrollton." Fannie stuffed her handkerchief into her purse, straightened herself, and smoothed her jacket. "Thank you for letting me look through the books." She exited through the front door and didn't look back.

~

Sister Mary Callahan found herself unable to concentrate during Mass that evening. She couldn't focus on her prayers before bed. For days, she ruminated on her interaction with Fannie.

A week later, she dispatched her assistant to the basement files one morning with an assignment and some notes. Just before lunch, the young novice brought the sister a yellowed envelope bearing a blue postage stamp and containing the letter from R. L. Haley. Sister Mary Callahan read it and smiled at the grammatical errors and the juvenile handwriting.

After pondering what to do next, she took out a sheet of pale-blue stationery and began composing a letter.

Saturday, April 18, 1896

Carrollton, Mississippi

Robert and Jake finished loading the wagon with supplies that they'd purchased for Cotesworth: two sacks of flour, salt, a keg of nails, a spool of wire, and a new pair of scissors.

"You shoulda heard Mr. Gee in there," Robert said. "They got a new magazine at the store this week from a company called Sears. They sell things in the magazine and send it to you in the mail. He said if you can get anything you want by mail, it'll be the death of all the stores in town!"

"What kinds of things?"

"Everything you could imagine. Shoes, clothes, tools, kitchen things, medicine pills. He's worried that he can't keep all the things in the store that somebody might want and that it'll put him out of business."

Jake scoffed. "I wouldn't worry 'bout that too much. Still gotta go to town to get the mail, and if'n you need nails today, can't wait two weeks for the mail train. How's Miss Annie doin'?"

"Havin' that baby in a couple of weeks, I'd think."

"Good," Jake said. "Real good. She better?"

"She has a few good days now. Sometimes it's almost like it never happened."

Robert frowned as the memory returned. In October, about the time Annie had figured out she was pregnant with their third child, the oldest baby, three-year-old Hattie, had fallen ill. It had started with a fever but had worsened quickly, with red spots all over her body and sores in her mouth that kept her from being able to drink. The doctor had said it was measles. Within four days, she developed a cough and had trouble breathing. On the seventh day, she was unconscious. She had fits the next morning and shook uncontrollably on the way to a terrible, agonizing death. They'd buried her in the graveyard at the Hickory Grove Church. It had been the saddest day of his life.

"Can't just stop livin'," Robert said. "Gotta be strong to take care of my girls."

Jake put his hand on his friend's shoulder.

As they turned the corner off the square to start back north, Robert heard someone call out his name from just inside the newspaper office.

John Buckley, the postal clerk, hollered to him. "R. L., wait one minute. There's a letter in here for you. Came yesterday." He ducked back into the store and in a moment returned and handed the letter up to Jake, who passed it to Robert.

Robert was alarmed. "Who could that be from? I hadn't never got a letter here before." He inspected the envelope. It was blue, addressed to the Carrollton Postmaster, and on the bottom below the address, it read: *Give this letter to Robert Lee Haley*. The stamp had been canceled in Memphis.

He turned it over and saw the return address embossed on the back. "It's from the orphanage. What could that be all about?"

"Well, might better open it then." Jake pulled out his pocketknife and handed it to Robert.

Robert's hands trembled as he unfolded the knife and used it to slice open the envelope. He took out the single page and read it silently.

> *St. Peter's Orphanage*   *April 16, 1896*
>
> *Poplar Street*
>
> *Memphis, Tennessee*
>
> *Mr. Haley,*
>
> *If you are the Mr. Robert Lee Haley who was a resident of our home in 1873 and have a sister named Fannie, please know that she has recently been here to the orphanage and is looking for you.*
>
> *She now lives in Perkinston, Mississippi.*
>
> *We hope that you are well, and we wish you the very best.*
>
> *With all the blessings of our Lord Jesus Christ,*
>
>   *Sister Mary Callahan*

"It says here my sister went to Memphis looking for me!" Robert said, astonished. "She lives in Perkinston, Mississippi!" He put his hand on his head. He couldn't believe it. "I gotta go see her now! You take the supplies home. I gotta go!" He grabbed his hat and jumped down from the wagon.

"Hol' on now, Mr. Robert. Cain't just run off like that. Do you even know where Perkinston is? How you gon' get there? You gotta go tell your wife first, for sure."

Robert looked at his friend, then reread the letter. He laughed out loud. "Well, no. I ain't never even heard of it."

"Me neither, but I bet the senator knows. Let's get on home an' get some supper. We'll go talk to him tonight and figure it out."

~

At Cotesworth, Jake opened the back door to the big house and peered inside. DeDe was in the dining room, setting the table for dinner. He waved to her, but she didn't see him, so he scraped the bottoms of his boots on the brick step and stomped them several times before entering.

DeDe heard him and turned around.

"Where the senator?" Jake asked.

She glared at him and put her hand on her hip. "I want you to know I just cleaned that floor in there."

"My boots not dirty." Jake looked down at his feet to check. "We just been to town, and we got news. Where is the senator?"

"He was in the library workin' earlier. Supper in an hour or so. What's the news?"

"Mr. Robert's sister. He got a letter from Memphis. Say she lookin' for him."

"Oh, that's good." DeDe smiled and waved at Robert, who was still holding the door but hadn't entered. "See there, Jake? He a smart man, that Mr. Robert. He don' walk his dirty boots on my clean floor."

Jake gave her a playful scowl.

The men came around the back of the house and walked through the breezeway between the main house and the guest quarters, finally stepping out onto the front porch. Below them on the lawn was the senator's library. An unusual building, it had six sides, a pointed roof, and a cupola on top. It was painted white with green shutters to match the main house. They mounted its steps under a small porch.

Jake knocked at the screen door. "Senator?"

"Come in, Jake." The senator was seated at the desk in the middle of the room. Tall and portly, he had a shock of long gray whiskers around his mouth and chin, which was stained in places by tobacco spittle, as was his shirt. "How are things in town? Any news?"

Jake chuckled. "No, sir. Quiet today. I brought Mr. Robert." He gestured toward Robert, who stood just inside the door. "He got some questions."

"Yes, of course. Hello, Robert. Sit, sit." The senator returned to his seat and gestured to the other chairs in the room. "What can I do for you?"

Jake nodded to Robert.

"Senator George," Robert began, "I got a letter today. About my sister. We got separated in the orphanage in Memphis when I went out to look for my brother."

"Oh?"

"Well, the orphanage wrote and said she lives in Perkinston now." He proffered the light-blue envelope.

The senator inspected the return address embossed on the envelope and then looked back to Robert. "May I?"

"Oh, yes, sir."

He pulled out the sheet of paper and read the letter. "Well, this is good news, I suspect."

"Oh, yes, sir. I want to go see her, but I don't know where Perkinston is."

"Oh, I see. I've been through there. A small stop on the way to Biloxi. A lumber town." The senator stood again and pulled an atlas from one of the shelves. After moving over to a book stand, he placed the atlas atop the dictionary on display and leafed through the pages to find the map of the state. He pointed to a spot at the bottom of the page. "It's not labeled on this map, but it's about here—between Hattiesburg and Mississippi City."

Robert studied the map.

"Where are we?" asked Jake, who was staring over Robert's shoulder at the map.

"Up here." The senator pointed to Carrollton. "You'll definitely want to take the train. Winona to Jackson, then to Hattiesburg. Change to the Ship Island Railroad there for Mississippi City and get off at Perkinston." He drew the path with his thumbnail down the page. "When do you think you'll go?"

"Don't know, sir. Hadn't really thought about it yet."

Jake smiled. "Shoulda seen him in town. 'Bout run off right then when he got the letter."

"Write back to her first and arrange a time before you set off traveling," the senator said.

A bell rang from behind the house.

"That's supper." The senator retrieved a sheet of paper, an envelope, and a pen from the drawer and put them on the table as the dinner bell rang again. "Write to her, and make the arrangements. Leave it there on the desk, and I'll take it to town Monday when I go into the office." He turned to go.

"Thank you, Senator," Robert said as the screen door slammed and the big man descended the steps of the library.

"What you gon' tell her?" Jake asked.

Robert sat and stared at the paper. "I don't even know where to start."

Thursday, April 23, 1896

Harrison County, Mississippi

Fannie wiped her hands on the dish towel and used it to cover the two pans of bread she'd set next to the stove to rise. She heard the wagon roll to a stop outside.

Samuel called to her from the front door of the cabin. "Fannie? Fannie! Lookee here!" His voice was excited.

"What, Papa?" she said, alarmed as he came bounding up the steps to the cabin. "What's wrong?"

"You got a letter. *Two* letters, but this one here—look." He handed her the envelopes.

The first letter had a printed return address for *R. G. Bentley, Attorney, Tallapoosa Georgia.*

"What in the world? I got some lawyer-man writin' to me?"

"Don't worry about that. Look at the other one first." Samuel took back the attorney's letter. "There. Lookee there." He pointed.

She turned over the smaller envelope and suddenly recognized the name of the sender. Too stunned to speak, she stared wide-eyed and slack-jawed at her stepson and future father-in-law.

Samuel took her by the elbow and led her to a chair on the front porch.

Her hands shook so fiercely that she had no choice but to hand the letter back to Samuel, who opened it and read it aloud.

Dear Fannie: *April 18, 1896*

    I am writing to you after so many years because I got a letter today from the orphanage in Memphis that said you were up there to find me. It's a long story to tell, but I left the orphanage to look for Thomas and ended up living in Oakland, Miss. About twelve years ago I wrote to the orphanage looking for you, but they said you got adopted to people here in Carrollton, so I came to look for you here, but you were not here and I have lived here ever since.

I would like for us to visit. I live in Carrollton, Miss. I have a job and some money, and I could come down there to Perkinston on the train.

Please write back and tell me about yourself and when I could come visit.

Your brother, Robert Lee Haley

She grabbed up her apron, put her face in her hands, and burst into tears. "I just can't believe this. I just can't. Next month'll be twenty-one years since I seen him."

"We gotta go tell Mary and Monroe. Come on." Samuel helped her down from the porch and up into the wagon.

They made quick time down to his home, not more than half a mile away.

Fannie ran to where Mary was hanging laundry in the yard. "I found him! I found Robert!" she cried, waving the sheet of paper.

"What?"

Fannie bounced up and down as her future mother-in-law read the letter.

Mary hugged Fannie, who wiped the tears from her cheeks.

"He's gonna come visit!"

"Fannie, honey, this is so wonderful. I'm so happy for you."

Thirty minutes later, as they sat in the kitchen, Samuel gave Fannie the other letter. "I almost forgot."

She opened the envelope to find a typewritten letter and a check for $13.33, drawn on the Merchant's and Miner's Bank of Tallapoosa, Georgia. She passed the check to Mary as she read the letter.

R. G. Bentley, Attorney   April 15, 1896
Monroe Street, Tallapoosa, Georgia

Miss Fannie Haley,

I am the attorney settling the estate of your maternal grandfather, Mr. James V. White, formerly of Atlanta, Georgia, most recently of Haralson County, Georgia, who is now deceased. I am charged with the disposition of his assets to his heirs. Since your mother, Sophronia, has also died, a check for your portion of her inheritance is enclosed.

I followed the information recently provided to me by the DeSoto County Court to contact St. Peter's Orphanage in Memphis in order to locate you and your brother, Robert. They informed me of your whereabouts but did not have any information about him. If you know where he is, please have him contact this office, as he is similarly entitled to a portion of the inheritance.

Sincerely,

R. G. Bentley, Esq.

"Well, I can't believe all this," said Fannie. "We gotta get him to come visit." She looked up suddenly with realization. "I gotta tell Monroe. Where's he at now?"

"Down at the barn with Donan. I'll carry you down there and we'll go put up the wagon and the horse." He rose to go as Fannie stood up and hugged Mary.

"I'm just so happy for you, honey," said Mary. "When he comes to visit, we'll make everything real nice. You can get you a new hat with some of that money—maybe even a store-bought dress."

"I ain't wasting money on that sort of vanity. Every dress you ever made me has been just perfect. I could get something nice for Monroe for our wedding." She hugged Mary again and squeezed her tightly.

"This is an answered prayer," said Mary.

"I just can't believe it!"

Saturday, June 6, 1896

Carrollton, Mississippi

When Robert returned to the main house, he stopped to wash up at the pump.

DeDe appeared in the kitchen doorway. "Where you been? Senator's lookin' for you. He brung a letter for you from town."

"It's too soon for another letter from my sister. I just got one yesterday."

"He didn't say, but you better go see what it's all about."

Robert found the senator sitting in a rocking chair on the front porch. He was reading, as usual.

"Good evening, Senator."

"Oh, Robert, good. You got a letter here from a lawyer in Georgia." The senator removed an envelope from the book he was reading and handed it to Robert.

Robert looked at the senator, surprised and uncertain, and then tore open the envelope with his finger. He pulled out the letter and a check.

"Thirteen dollars. My portion from my grandfather's estate. Doesn't say when he died. I never met the man."

"Well, maybe Fannie knows. When are you going to visit?"

"We decided on Thanksgiving. She's gonna get married in the spring, so I'll go meet her new family."

Wednesday, November 25, 1896

Greenville Times (Greenville, Mississippi)

THANKSGIVING

"Chill November's surly blasts" reminded the poet
Burns that "man was made to mourn," but they remind us
rather that man was made to rejoice and give thanks. It
is a bitter lot that cannot find something in the experience
of twelve months for which to feel grateful, even though
the cares and disappointments may have outweighed
the joys and triumphs. It is the most appropriate and
beautiful of all our national holidays—a time not only for
thoughtless rejoicing and celebration of the safe garnering
of the harvest, but for the welding of broken ties of love
and friendship, the healing of the estrangements and the
meeting of those long parted . . .

Wednesday, November 25, 1896

Perkinston, Mississippi

The train labored up and down the wooded hills as it lumbered south out of Hattiesburg. The passenger car was more than half-full of travelers headed for the coast to visit family for Thanksgiving.

Robert had been studying the maps and knew it would be less than an hour until he was there, but it seemed that time was just creeping by. *Will she recognize me?* Out the window the scattered hardwood trees dotted the pine forest with yellow, brown, and red leaves, and Robert remembered those same colors on his trip to Carrollton to find his sister sixteen years earlier. So much had transpired since. Over the years, the nagging voices in his head had been quieted, especially since he'd found Annie and they'd had children, but as he stared past his reflection in the window, the past overcame the more recent memories of better times. "What if" and "why" and "why didn't you" all crowded in now. *What happened? Did I try hard enough? Would things have been better if . . .?* Never to be known.

～

Fannie's palms were sweaty despite the cool day. Seated in the wagon, she raised a hand to shield her eyes from the sun and peered up the tracks, straining to see the train she could just now hear.

A few minutes later, the whistle sounded as the steam engine hissed and slowed to a stop. The station at Perkinston was little more than a platform with stairs.

Fannie climbed down from the wagon and hurried over to the plank deck, her eyes searching the short row of cars for a familiar face among the windows. The porter jumped down from the last car and placed a step box in front of the door.

A short man with a bushy mustache was the first to exit. He passed his cardboard suitcase to the porter, who set it on the platform, and stepped down onto the box while holding the rail. He didn't look anything like she remembered—or like she'd imagined—but she knew instantly it was her brother.

"Robert?" She took a few eager steps, then hesitated. "Robert?"

He smiled. "Fannie?"

It was him!

She reached him in two more steps and wrapped her arms around his neck. "Robert Lee Haley! I can't believe it." She held him by the shoulders as she stepped back to look him in the face. Then she hugged him again.

"I'm so glad to be here."

"Oh, I just can't believe it! I just can't believe it!" She stepped back again and studied him once more. Her brother, changed by so much, missed for so many years. He was here—no longer a dream, a memory, or a ghost. A jumble of conflicting emotions came suddenly. The joy of this reunion, the grief of the loss of their family and the decades spent apart, the anger over his absence, the shame of what she'd endured. *Where have you been? Why did you leave me? We were supposed to take care of each other.* Tears came, and she sobbed, shaking uncontrollably.

"I'm here now." Robert wrapped his arms around her. "We can be a family again."

Monroe approached and picked up Robert's suitcase. When Fannie had calmed somewhat, he extended his hand. "I'm Monroe Smith."

"Robert Haley. Good to meet you." They shook hands as Robert kept his other arm around his sister.

They loaded up in the wagon and began the ten-mile journey back to the Smith farm.

Fannie sat next to her brother with her arm tightly wrapped around his. "How long can you stay?"

"I'll need to be back in a week. Annie's got the girls."

Fannie took his hand and searched his eyes. "I'm so sorry about your little girl. How old are the others now?"

"Helen is three, and Linnie was born in May, so six months now. Annie's sister is helping this week, so they'll be all right, but I'll need to get back to work eventually."

"A week will be great. We've got so much to catch up on."

"Big Thanksgiving dinner coming up," Monroe said. "The whole family—too many to sit down at one time, but plenty to eat. Papa got some turkeys this week."

"I made some sweet potato pies," Fannie said. "I just love a sweet potato pie!"

Saturday, August 19, 1911

Carrollton, Mississippi

Saturday afternoon was the usual time for a trip to town. Annie bought household goods and maybe a few items at the store. If there were extra vegetables at home, she'd bring them to trade with other ladies who did the same. Robert would buy the most recent copy of the newspaper, *The Carroll County Conservative*, and would visit with folks on the square. Coming to town was a treat, so the kids took turns going with their parents for the trip. Today the older girls, Helen and Linnie, stayed home with five other siblings.

After they'd finished for the day and were ready to head home, Robert hoisted ten-year-old Ruby into the back of the wagon, where she took her place beside her little sister Marie and little brother Sidney. They'd each gotten a candy stick today, and they stuck out their tongues at each other and laughed at the bright red color. Robert had a few more in his pocket for the kids at home.

Annie exited J. J. Gee's and crossed the street to the wagon, carrying her last purchases and their youngest baby, Ethel, on her hip.

"Got a letter from your sister," she said as Robert helped her up into the wagon. She slid over on the bench, and Robert climbed in beside her. Annie opened the envelope and began reading.

"What does she have to say?"

"Things are good. They want us to come down to visit."

Robert called to the horse, and they started the journey home.

Annie turned over the page. "She had the baby. Another boy."

"That's six now, right?"

Annie smiled and looked up. "And she named him after you!"

Epilogue

Perkinston, Miss. Route 10   *Jan 8, 1958*

Dear Ruby

I received your letter and was glad to hear from you. I will try to answer your request about your Dad + Fannie. I don't know to much I think they was borned in Memphis Tennessee. Theyr Dad & Momma died and they was put in a orphan Home. You dady ran away and a Man by the name of Black got him to go live with him and he lived somewhere in Miss. I don't know how long he stayed with him but anyway he was mean to him and he ran away one night and got to Caroltton at midnight and a Negro told him he could get a job with a man out where you all now live. The man's name I do not know.

As for Fannie a man by the name of R Syms got her out of the home and brought her to Caroltton. She was 6 years old then he moved to this community. When she was 12 years old she ran away & came to my Grandady and he gave her a home and she stayed there until me & her was married. We lived together 51 years and one month. We had 6 children, 4 boys and 2 girls, 4 of them is living Otho Luther Robert & Isabell and 2 dead Idabell and Marion.

Now I will try to tell you how they found each other. A foot peddler came along and told Fannie to wright to the chief of police of Memphis and give him her name and address so she did. Then he saw the man in the orphan home who wrote Fannie a letter and Fannie went to Memphis to see him. He told her where your dad was so in a few days she got a letter from your dad so they exchanged a few letters and finally your dad came to see her just before we were married.

Well Ruby this is about all I can say. I would like to see you all but I'm old now I am past 83. I give my love and best regards to you all.

Monroe Smith

PS I want some of you to come see me. Bye-bye

Afterword

Augusta, Georgia, 2020

Many of the details behind this story remain beyond my reach. I therefore invite descendants of the Haley, White, Smith, and McHugh families to share any other information, photographs, stories, or documents they may have by emailing me at *therunawayhaleystory@gmail.com.* I have compiled a family tree on Ancestry.com, which is open for review and contains many of the documents that I've collected.

As I alluded to in the *Author's Note,* the following details provided my rationale for creating this story.

Michael Haley was born in Ireland in about 1823. I don't know where his family lived in Ireland, nor his port of embarkation or arrival. I've chosen Savannah, Georgia, for his arrival in America in my story, since ships from Ireland did arrive there during this period, which was before the great Irish emigration caused by the potato famine. The Immigration Act of 1802 allowed newly arrived men of good character to declare their intent to become citizens by naturalization after just five years in the country, instead of fourteen, as had previously been required. After that, there was a three-year waiting period before citizenship could be conferred. The record of Michael's naturalization in 1860 states that he declared his intent to the court in 1848, so he may have sailed for America at about age twenty, putting him here in as late as 1843.

It seems that Michael lived in the Blackhall District of Atlanta (DeKalb County), Georgia, in 1850, when the railroad construction was booming and the Irish constituted a large part of the labor force. In the 1850 census of Atlanta, a twenty-five-year-old railroad worker named Michael Haley is listed in a family group with a fifty-year-old Irishman named James Kines. I haven't found out anything more about Kines.

Michael's marriage to Sophronia Adeline White is documented in the DeKalb County Courthouse and dated February 29, 1853, but there are several oddities in the marriage application and registration. The county keeps its registration and marriage documents in sequence among the other chronological entries from 1853. The application for marriage is clearly dated February 21, 1852, and the marriage is dated February 29, 1853. The year 1853, however, was not a leap year. It may be that the registrar miswrote the year as 1852 on the application (as one might erroneously do after the turn of the New Year), or it could be that the couple did, in fact, wait more than one year between the application and their marriage. Perhaps the marriage actually was on the twenty-seventh of February instead of the twenty-ninth, but that would have been a Sunday, when the courthouse was likely closed and a justice of the peace was probably unavailable. In either case, these date irregularities raise the possibility that Catherine was conceived or born before Michael and Sophronia were married—and perhaps before they even met—if, as I believe, she was born in 1852.

I don't know how or when Michael and Sophronia moved to the area around Memphis. We do know that our Michael Haley was naturalized in Hernando (DeSoto County), Mississippi, in 1860, as documented in the probate court records. There it states that Michael made his declaration of intent for naturalization in Bell Town near Macon, Georgia, in 1848. My searches in the Georgia state archives for this declaration were unsuccessful. Judge John Henry Akins, who presides at court in my story, was my own great-great-great-grandfather and was the judge in the Spalding County Superior Court in Georgia, just up the Macon and Western Railroad line from the city of Macon. Though he was on the bench in Spalding County when Michael Haley made his declaration in Macon, he obviously did not oversee the proceedings.

The DeSoto County naturalization record says that Mr. David Fort, who lived in Hernando, and Mr. John W. Vanhorn, a Memphian, "knew him in Tennessee and Mississippi for six or seven years." This statement places the couple in Memphis in about 1853. A one-year-old child of someone identified only as "Mr. Haley" is listed in the Memphis, Tennessee, death register in 1855, which could fit with the birth sequence of the other children and the timing of a move to the area. I have used this report in the story, although it could be a different Mr. Haley.

In Mississippi, Michael was probably a farmer rather than a railroad worker. The DeSoto County, Mississippi, land deed records show that he purchased acreage in the southern part of the county in April of 1859. This parcel of land is now in Tate County, where Mississippi Highway 51 crosses the Hickahala Creek. It's now owned by the Army Corps of Engineers as an easement for a flood control project associated with the downstream Arkabutla Lake, constructed in the 1940s. The area had previously been farmland but has never been developed otherwise, and today it is frequently used for hunting and recreational activities.

During my research, I was able to locate and contact Mrs. Marcia Kidder, who, with her husband, James, owns the property immediately southwest of this parcel. They report that they have not come across any evidence of an old homestead or cemetery in the area. During a 2019 visit to Tate County, I found that the land once owned by Michael Haley is now almost completely covered in swamp.

T. W. White, Trustee
to & Deed Michael Healey
NE ¼ S18 T5 R7 West

Know all men by the presents that I, T. W. White by virtue of a Deed of Trust to me made by Charles Whitehead for the benefit of C S Meriwether Recorded in the Book of Deed of Trust of the office of the Probate Clerk of DeSoto County for and in consideration of the sum of nine hundred Dollars to me in hand for and by Michael Healey, the receipt whereof is acknowledged have bargained + sold unto the said Michael Healey the North East quarter of Section (18) Eighteen Township (5) Five, Range (7) Seven West in said county. To have and to hold unto him the said Michael Haley and his heirs + assigns in fee simple except the 850 by 275 feet across from the water station and by virtue of the power vested in me by the Said Deed of Trust convey to the said Healey his heirs and assigns all the right + interest of the said Charles Whitehead in and to said land.

In testimony whereof I have hereunto set my hand this

9ᵗʰ day of April 1859

T. W. White Trustee {Seal}

Michael Haley almost certainly served in the military during the Civil War, although he was at least forty years old at the time. There are Confederate records of several soldiers named Michael Haley from Mississippi and Tennessee, so I can't be certain which unit he joined or where he served. I have saved documents from multiple Michael Haleys in my files on Ancestry.com. Documentation of a forty-year-old Private Michael Haley—noted to be a five-foot-six Irish immigrant with a dark complexion—from McClung's Battery of the Tennessee Light Artillery shows that this man was released from Confederate service in July of 1862 at Vicksburg after his one-year enlistment. That unit had seen action in Kentucky at the Battle of Mill Springs. Then, after reorganizing back in Nashville, it fought in the battle of Shiloh in April of 1862. There they were unattached to any brigade but supported the Louisiana Washington Artillery.

I walked through the Shiloh National Battlefield, following that unit's movements, and imagined our Michael's participation with them during the two-day battle. I have no idea whether or not Michael ever actually met Nathan Bedford Forrest, who was also from Hernando, but it is very likely that Forrest's 1864 crossing of the Hickahala Creek did occur on Michael's land. He almost certainly knew about it—and very well may have been a participant—but was not likely the architect of the bridge, as I have imagined in my story.

The Haley family's land was sold a decade after its purchase, in November 1869. The deed book shows that Michael apparently never learned to write, since he made his mark rather than provide a signature to complete the transaction. Sophronia's death, probably in 1868 or 1869, likely contributed to the family's dire circumstances, and sometime shortly after the sale of the land, the family moved to the poorhouse in Hernando.

Coincidentally, after I had completed work on this story, another element of the Haley family oral history surfaced—a report that Michael actually did lose an arm in an accident, which was a key factor in the family's relocation to the poorhouse. The report of this injury was apparently found in a newspaper by Leo Rasberry of Hernando (the husband of one of Robert's granddaughters), but no further details are available at this time. The fact that I had inadvertently foreshadowed this type of injury in the book, and then confabulated Michael's functional loss of an arm, gave me a strange sensation of harmony with him.

Michael Healey

to Deed J. B Wooten

NE ¼ S18 T5 R7 W

This Indenture made on the 28th day of November in 1869 between Michael Healey of the first part and John B. Wooten of the second part. (Illegible) for the sum of twenty-five hundred dollars to him in hand paid the receipt of which is acknowledged, has granted, assigned, sold and conveyed unto the said second party, the North East Quarter of Section (18) Eighteen, Township (5) five, Range (7) seven West in Desoto County Mississippi to have and to hold to him the said John B. Wooten his heirs and assigns in fee simple. And the said first party covenants with the said second party that he will forever regard and defend the title of the above granted premises to him the said second party, his heirs and assigns against the claim of all persons whatsoever. The testimony whereof the said first party has hereto set his hand and seal this Nov 25th 1869   Michael (his mark X) Healey {Seal}

The State of Mississippi, DeSoto County

Personally appeared before me J. C. Acree, Clerk of the Probate Court of said County, Michael Haley who acknowledged that he signed, sealed and delivered the written deed for the purpose herein contained, and on the day and year therefore mentioned as his own act and deed.

Given under my hand and the seal of said court at office the 25th Nov AD 1869.

J. C. Acree, Clerk by A. W. Smith DC

Our Michael Haley is last documented in the 1870 census in DeSoto County, Mississippi. The census taker, Mr. Patrick McLernon, documented him as the forty-six-year-old illiterate keeper of the county poorhouse, with his children Katherine (eighteen), W. D. (twelve), Michael (eleven), Thomas (seven), Robert Lee (four), and Fannie (two). The poorhouse in Hernando sat just north of the town, between the Tennessee and Mississippi Railroad and the plank road to Memphis (now Old Highway 51). Sources in Hernando report that the cemetery for the poorhouse was just to the north of this area, but its precise location has since been lost.

I was able to overlay a 1969 aerial photo of this area in DeSoto County with a current street map to estimate a location for the poorhouse. I shared this information with Mr. Arthur Broady of Memphis, whose family purchased the property and the house (not the original) and lived there in the early 1960s. He recalls a wooden main house with a tin roof, south of the pond, and a line of tenant shacks in a row that backed up to the train tracks nearby. During my research trip to Hernando in August of 2018, I walked the northern edge of the undeveloped property and watched as heavy machinery cleared that land for development and construction.

Given that Fannie and Robert were in an orphan home in Memphis when Fannie was six years old (according to the 1958 letter from Fannie's husband, Monroe Smith, to Robert's daughter, Ruby Haley Lott), the first of several deadly yellow fever epidemics in Memphis and the surrounding area in the late summer of 1873 could have taken Michael Haley's life at age forty-nine or fifty. The index case for the 1873 epidemic was an itinerant riverboat hand named William Davis, who brought the mosquito-borne virus from New Orleans to Memphis.

There is another Michael Haley, also an Irish immigrant and a widower, who died at his home on Vance Street in Memphis in June of 1902. In the 1900 census, though, that man's age is documented as seventy, which means he was born in about 1830. The census report also states that he had been living in the country for only forty years, had immigrated in 1860, and was not a naturalized citizen. The similarities here create some confusion, but since Monroe Smith told Ruby Haley that Fannie's parents had died, I do not believe that this man was our Michael Haley.

Sophronia Adeline White was born in 1833 to James V. White, a prominent planter of DeKalb County, Georgia. She married Michael Haley in February of 1853 and gave birth to her youngest child in Mississippi in 1867 or 1868. I haven't discovered much about her childhood or youth, nor have I learned how she came to marry an Irish immigrant and move to Memphis. However it came to be that Michael and Sophronia found each other, the socio-economic gap between them was surely wide, and it must have been a factor in their relationship—and possibly in their relocation to the Memphis area.

If she was nineteen or twenty when she married Michael, a man ten years older than she, and if she died perhaps at age thirty-six in 1869, then their marriage would have spanned sixteen or seventeen years. There are many unknowns.

It is certainly possible that Sophronia died as a complication from the birth of the last child, but in September of 1868, the *Hernando Press* reported on an outbreak of infectious diarrhea, which I have portrayed in the story as the cause of her death. The symptoms they reported and the high mortality rate in children could be consistent with typhoid fever due to Salmonella, which often causes the characteristic "pea soup" diarrhea and "rose spots" on the trunk of those afflicted. Sophronia is not found in the 1870 census, and I have found no death records, obituary, or grave site for her.

Margaret Catherine (Katherine) Haley's approximate year of birth varies in the available records, but it seems she was born in Georgia in 1852. I spelled her name with a *K* in the novel because her gravestone bears her first name as Kate.

The most reliable information about her actual birth year probably comes from the census data from 1870. In that year she was still living with her father in Hernando, Mississippi, in the county poorhouse, where she is listed as being eighteen years old. The census taker, Mr. McLernon, noted that she worked as the housekeeper there and that she was able to read and write.

Catherine married <u>Peter McHugh</u>, an Irish immigrant, in about 1872. I have no details about their marriage, but their first child was born in about 1873. Catherine and Peter moved from Hernando to Booneville, Mississippi, then to Dyer, Tennessee. She died in Tennessee in 1927.

Having tracked the locations and years of birth of the children listed in that census, I believe that the McHugh family moved from Mississippi to Tennessee sometime between 1880 and 1883. The 1880 census of Booneville, Mississippi, is also consistent with an 1852 birth. It reports Catherine as the twenty-eight-year-old mother of three and states that her mother was from Georgia. The 1900 census of Gibson County, Tennessee, differs significantly, and so it may have been information reported by someone else on Catherine's behalf. It states that she was forty-five years old (an estimated birth year would have been 1855), that she was born in Mississippi, that she could neither read nor write, and that her mother was from Georgia. The 1910 census of Gibson County, Tennessee, reports Catherine was sixty-three years old (an estimated birth year would have been 1847), was born in Georgia, and had eight living children from twelve births. It notes she was able to read but not write, and that her mother was from Georgia. Her death certificate, completed by her daughter in 1927, states she was seventy-four years old, perhaps born in 1853.

It seems possible that, as I've portrayed in this story, Catherine's mother was not Sophronia White. Two pieces of information caused me initially to consider this possibility. Catherine's siblings (or half-siblings), Thomas, Robert, and Fannie, inherited money from the estate of their maternal grandfather, James V. White, after his death in 1892, but Catherine did not. The portion of the estate allotted to each of J. V. White's children was forty dollars. The administrator of the estate was Mr. R. G. Bentley of Haralson County, Georgia, and was apparently the brother-in-law of Sophronia's baby sister, Camilla White Bentley (b. ~1852). He wrote in his 1894 report that Sophronia had died "having 3 children to share her inheritance," and he allotted each of them $13.33. Thomas received his share in 1894, and Robert and Fannie received theirs sometime before Bentley's July 1, 1896, annual report to the court (Georgia Wills and Probate Records 1742-1992, microfilm images 972, 981 and 1000).

It appears that either Bentley could not find Catherine, or that J. V. White's other legatees did not identify Catherine as an heir. This fact, combined with an 1852 birthdate (perhaps prior to an 1853 wedding of Michael and Sophronia), raises the possibility that Catherine had a different mother, as I've portrayed in this story. Alternatively, if the February 21, 1852 date of the application for her parents' marriage is indeed correct, then it follows that Catherine could have been conceived prior to the marriage and born out of wedlock. But again, there is no solid proof for either of these possibilities.

Some additional supporting evidence for my hypothesis comes from the genetic information in family DNA profiles that are now widely available. As of this writing, the only direct descendants of Catherine Haley with DNA available through the services of Ancestry.com are two great-great-great-granddaughters. It seems that they share genetic markers with Michael Haley and with all the descendants of Robert Lee Haley and Fannie Haley Smith, but do not appear to connect directly to Sophronia White or her parents, James and Martha.

W. D. Haley was twelve years old in the 1870 census and could have been born in either Memphis or in Mississippi, depending on where the family lived in 1858. I haven't found any other documentation of him after that, so I have imagined he, too, died in the yellow fever epidemic of 1873.

I don't know what his full name was, but there may be some clues in the family tree. Thomas Haley's oldest son was named Jacob Whitten Haley (1893–1958), and Sophronia had a brother named David W. White (b.~ 1840).

Michael Haley Jr., (in the story, I have called him Mickey) was eleven years old in the 1870 census and was therefore born in about 1859. If he was fourteen years old when his father died, he wouldn't necessarily have been sent to an orphanage.

He grew up to become a painter in Memphis. He married Annie McLean in 1884 but died just a few years later in 1887 of consumption (tuberculosis). It appears that Annie had at least one daughter, Etta, who was born around 1881, so her father was probably not Michael Haley Jr. Etta married Mike Fink, and in the 1910 census of Memphis, she had two children: James (eight) and Violet (four). Annie McLean Haley is found in the Memphis census of 1920 with her thirteen-year-old granddaughter, Violet Fink.

Thomas J. (Jefferson?) Haley was seven years old in the 1870 census, born sometime in 1863. The gap in the birth sequences of the children suggests that Michael may have been away at war before 1862. Thomas became the second husband of Mary Emmaline Moore (née Redus) from DeSoto County, Mississippi, in 1891. She had two children by her previous marriage (Elizabeth and Eugenia), and the couple had three children together: Jacob Whitten Haley (b. 1893), Charlie Acree Haley (b. 1897), and daughter Sidney Haley (b. 1900). He inherited a portion of his grandfather's estate in 1894, as documented in the Georgia court records.

Thomas and Emma are listed in the census of Tunica County, Mississippi, in 1930. Later, he lived with his daughter, Sidney Haley Rena, and her family in Arkansas, apparently after the death of his wife. Thomas died in 1943 in Memphis.

I don't know if Robert and Fannie ever found any of their other siblings after they left the orphanage. Robert Haley's 1934 obituary doesn't mention Thomas, and none of the Smith family members were aware of a connection.

I was able to contact Mr. Brian Rena, of Memphis, Tennessee, who is the great-grandson of Thomas and Mary Emma Haley. He had no details or family history to add to Michael's story, but it is interesting to note that his grandmother's name was Sidney Haley (1900–1974) and Robert's son, Sidney Thomas (Bud) Haley (1905–1951), was my wife's grandfather. It is because of this that I named the "child of Mr. Haley," who died in 1855, Sidney, but since that report did not specify a gender, neither did I. Though that is an actual death record, there is no definite connection to Michael or Sophronia.

Robert Lee Haley was born in DeSoto County, Mississippi, and I assume he was named after General Robert E. Lee. The headstone on his grave reports his birthday as May 16, 1868. If this was correct, he would have been only two years old in the 1870 census, which documented him as four years old as of the first of June 1870. Fannie was listed on that document as a two-year-old. The incorrect birthdates on their respective gravestones would make Fannie one year older than Robert; but if the census taker, Mr. Patrick McLernon, saw the children, he would have recognized the difference between a four-year-old and a two-year-old. Even if he didn't actually see them, whoever reported for the household would have known Fannie was the baby. I suspected that Robert was born in 1866—indeed, a later finding of a fragment from a family Bible confirmed that year.

After the death of their father, Robert and Fannie were taken in by one of the orphanages in Memphis, but after a period there, Robert ran away. *Carroll County, Mississippi: History and Families* (2001, Rose Publishing, Humboldt, Tennessee) contains an entry written by Mr. Yancey DeLapp Jr., that reports that the Haley children were sent to the "Catholic Orphanage" in Memphis.

During my research for this book, I contacted the archivist for the Archdiocese of Memphis, Father Richard Mickey, who had his staff review the intake records of St. Peter's Orphanage, but they did not find documentation of any of the Haley children there between 1870 and 1880. The staff at the Leath Orphanage in Memphis thoroughly combed through their records to determine that Robert, Fannie, Thomas, Michael Jr., and W. D. were not wards of their institution, either. There were other orphanages in Memphis during that decade, specifically "The Church Home," run by the Episcopal Church, where the sisters wore habits, but I was unable to find any organization that knew the whereabouts of any of the records from that institution. Robert and Fannie could have recalled and related to their families that there were sisters in religious garb, thereby making an assumed connection to the Catholic orphanage. Finally, the Tennessee Department of Children's Records (Post Adoption) had no information on Fannie Haley during this period. This element of the story remains a mystery.

Robert Lee Haley is next found in Oakland (Yalobusha County), Mississippi, on the 1878 Register of Educable Children. In the 1880 census, Robert is listed as the twelve-year-old ward of Mr. A. J. Black and lived there with the family, including eight-year-old Willie and several smaller children. The bookkeeper, Mr. Henry T. Ladd, the son of an Englishman, lived there also, as did multiple servants, including the cook, Sina Seviorener (thirty-five), and her two children. Mr. Ladd became the second husband of Mrs. Hattie Black after A. J. Black died in 1883. The Haley family oral history reports that Mr. Black had been a colonel in the army and was a "morphine addict" because of an injury he sustained in the war. Confederate soldier rosters document a Private A. J. Black from Oakland, Mississippi, who had been in the 28th Regiment of the Mississippi Cavalry and who was wounded in May of 1864. In the late 1800s, the newspapers of Memphis and Panola County, Mississippi, ran merchant advertisements that cited Mr. Black's association with the cavalry unit but gave his rank as captain.

It is not clear when he ran away from the Blacks' home, but Robert Haley was almost certainly living in Carroll County when the 1886 Courthouse Massacre occurred, and he would have been about twenty years old at the time. Aside from the letter to Ruby Haley, I haven't found any details about how Robert arrived in Carrollton, the identity of the black man who found him, or where he eventually lived and worked.

Senator James Zachariah George was frequently at his grand home, Cotesworth, between Carrollton town and the Jefferson community during this period. I looked through all the books and documents in Senator J. Z. George's library at Cotesworth but did not find any records of the plantation operations or staff during the 1880s. Senator George's lifelong friend was Jake, one of their former slaves. He and the senator were devoted to each other throughout their lives, and Jake was included with the family at J. Z. George's funeral in 1897, where he was overheard to have said that he'd lost his best friend. Katharine Saunders Williams, J. Z. George's great-granddaughter, reports that Jake was buried in the family plot at the Evergreen Cemetery in North Carrollton, but if he was, there is no headstone for him there now. I have imagined Jake and Senator George as part of this story.

Robert married <u>Annie Iona (or Idella?) Corley</u> in Carroll County, Mississippi, on December 26, 1889. The 1900 census reported that he was twenty-eight years old (the birth year would have been 1872). He purchased 120 acres of land across from the site of the old Friendship Baptist Church in northeast Carroll County for $800 in 1901. On that farm, Robert and Annie raised fifteen children. He died there on January 29, 1934, and is buried at the Hickory Grove Church Cemetery next to his wife and near a number of his children and grandchildren.

Friday, February 2, 1934

The Conservative (Carrollton, Mississippi)

Robert L. Haley Passes Suddenly

Robert L. Haley died suddenly at his home in the Hickory Grove community of this county on Monday, January 29th. He was 65 years old.

Mr. Haley was born in Georgia (sic) but came to Carroll county when a young man and soon afterwards married Miss Annie Corley, daughter of S. O. and Harriette Corley, pioneer settlers of Carroll County. After coming here Mr. Haley spent the remainder of his life as a true and faithful citizen of the county. He had, by dint of hard work and diligent effort made a success of farming in the northern section of the county. He was a member of the Hickory Grove Baptist church and his funeral was held there on Tuesday, January 30th, conducted by Rev. Joe Lott, longtime friend of the deceased, assisted by Rev. Henderson of the Grenada Baptist church and Rev. L. F. Fowler of Providence Baptist church. Interment was in Hickory Grove cemetery.

Mr. Haley is survived by the following: His wife, Mrs. Annie Corley Haley; five sons, Sidney, Earl, Kermit, Rogers and Rufus, all of McCarley; six daughters, Mrs. Ethel Lawrence, McCarley; Mrs. Helen Turner, Grenada; Mrs. Lennie Campbell, Carrollton; Mrs. Mattie Taylor, Grenada; Mrs. Rubie (sic) Lott, McCarley and Mrs. Tessie McDonald, Grenada. He is also survived by a sister, Mrs. Fannie Smith of Perkinston, Miss.

The Conservative extends sympathy to the bereaved family.

Fannie Haley was born in Hernando (DeSoto County), Mississippi, but her year of birth is not completely certain. Her gravestone reports her birthday was July 4, 1867, but the family history acknowledges that she didn't know when she was born and that she chose this date and year.

I don't know when or how the children ended up in an orphanage in Memphis, but the letter from Fannie's husband, Monroe Smith, to Robert's daughter Ruby says their parents had died. There's a report that the family had become so impoverished that Michael put the children there for their own benefit, but I don't think this is correct. The record of the Michael Haley who lived on Vance Street in Memphis and died in 1902 probably contributes to the confusion on this point. If our Michael had been alive and had left the children with the orphanage, Fannie would have been about six and Robert eight. If this were true, the children would have remembered this, and Fannie probably would have told her husband. This element would have figured more prominently in the Haley family oral history, and I think that the children would have tried to find their father when they were older.

Monroe Smith's letter says that Fannie was adopted by a man named R. Syms and moved to Carrollton. I didn't find any further clues on the Syms (Sims, Simms, Symes?) family in any of the census records for Carrollton for 1880. There is, however, a childless couple, forty-one-year-old Robert Gill Sims (b. 1839, m. 1865, d.~1896) and his wife Felixiana Sims (née Wingfield, d. after 1880), in the Washington County (Greenville), Mississippi, census in 1880. He had previously been documented in Wilkinson County, in southwest Mississippi, on the 1860 Slave Owner's Schedule. This may be a link because the 1880 census of nearby Franklin County, Mississippi, (east of Natchez) reports an eleven-year-old orphan named Fannie Simms living with the "L. H. D'Arnon" family in the Hamburg community. My research suggests that their name was probably D'Armond. I have not been able to work out any connection to Carrollton for Fannie, nor do I know how she came to live with the D'Armond family.

According to Smith family oral history, Fannie was mistreated and ran away more than once but was found and forced to return. It also recounts that Fannie hid in the woods and got her food from a pig trough. Somehow, Fannie came to live with Bill

Smith in northwest Harrison County, Mississippi. He found her sleeping on a log in the woods.

William (Cussin' Bill) Smith and his wife, Elisa Rouse Smith, are listed in the 1880 census as being aged sixty-one and fifty-one, respectively, with their five youngest children still living at home and ranging in age from twelve to twenty-two. After Elisa died in 1886 or 1887 (her headstone has no dates), Fannie and Cussin' Bill were married on July 26, 1887, when she was perhaps eighteen and he was sixty-seven. This was purportedly an act of propriety to allow her to remain in his home and meet the community's standards. Their relationship does seem to have been a strictly platonic one. Cussin' Bill died nine years later, in 1896.

Fannie Smith eventually married Monroe Smith (Cussin' Bill's grandson) on March 8, 1897, when she was twenty-nine and he was twenty-one. They lived in northwest Stone County (previously part of Harrison County), Mississippi, on the family land, where their descendants still live today. Throughout their marriage, they had six children. Monroe's 1958 letter to Ruby reports that they had lived together for fifty-one years and one month before she died.

Monroe reported in his letter that Robert came to visit them in southern Mississippi before he and Fannie were married. Since the siblings are reported together in the Georgia probate records of July 1896, when they inherited money from their grandfather, it seems that perhaps they had found each other before then. My research of newspapers from several archival sources found no report of this reunion.

Fannie's stepgranddaughter, Mrs. June Trehern of Pascagoula, Mississippi, remembers her grandmother as having been warm and kind, especially to the very young children. Fannie suffered from dementia in her later years and died on March 22, 1948. She is buried in the Smith family cemetery in Stone County.

MARRIAGE AFFIDAVIT

The State of Mississippi

County of Harrison

BEFORE ME, The undersigned authority, on this day personally appeared D. M. Smith, who being duly sworn according to law, deposes and says, that there is no legal cause to obstruct the marriage of said D. M. Smith to Fanny Smith, and that both _____ and the said _____ have arrived at the ages prescribed by law for marriage without consent of parent or guardian.

Sworn and subscribed before me, this 6ᵗʰ day of March, 1897.

Recorded the 8ᵗʰ day of March 1897

By F. S. Hewes, Circuit Clerk

Affidavit of age of parties filed

MARRIAGE LICENSE AND CERTIFICATE

The State of Mississippi

County of Harrison,

To any Person Lawfully Authorized to Celebrate the Rites of Matrimony:

You are hereby Licensed to Celebrate the RITES OF MATRIMONY Between Mr. D. M. Smith and Miss Fannie Smith, and for so doing, this shall be your Warrant. Given under my hand and official seal this 6 day of March, in the year of our Lord one thousand eight hundred and ninety seven.

F. S. Hewes, Clerk

The State of Mississippi

County of Harrison,

    BY VIRTUE OF A LICENSE from the Clerk of the Circuit Court of Said County of Harrison, I HAVE THIS DAY Celebrated the RITES OF MATRIMONY Between Mr. D. M. Smith and Miss Fannie Smith, GIVEN under my hand and seal this 8 day of March A.D. 1897.

F Damphdrill, M. G. {Seal}

    The foregoing Certificate of Marriage was filed for Record in my office on the 17 day of May A. D. 1897 at 8 o'clock and ___ minutes A. M.

F. S. Hewes, Circuit Clerk

Thursday, April 1, 1948

The Weekly Democrat (Poplarville, Mississippi)

Mrs. Smith Death Noted

Mrs. Fannie Smith, age 80, wife of Monroe Smith, died at her home in the Thomas Price community of Stone County Tuesday after a period of illness.

Funeral Services were conducted at the home Wednesday afternoon with Elders Lamar Dale and Tevis Ladner officiating. Pallbearers were Hinton Smith, L. L. Hickman, Jim Parker, Kentrel Jackson, Lloyd Davis, and Jim Dale. McDonald Funeral Home was in charge of arrangements.

Mrs. Smith was born on July 4, 1867. She has lived in the Thomas Price community for 70 years. She was a devoted member of the Red Creek Baptist church.

Survivors include her husband and four children: Otha Smith, Luther Smith and Mrs. Arledge, all of Perkinston, and Robert Smith of Lumberton.

<u>Monroe Smith</u> wrote to answer a letter from his niece, Ruby Haley Lott, in January of 1958. He related the story of the runaways, the families they stayed with, the siblings' sequential ties to Carrollton, Mississippi, and their eventual reunion through communication with the orphanage in Memphis. He died in August of that year in Stone County, Mississippi, and is buried next to his wife, Fannie.

The letter that Monroe sent to Ruby came into the possession of Cindy Rasberry Childs, one of Ruby's great-nieces, who, it seems, contributed it to a compiled family history document somewhere. The image of the photocopy that she sent to the author includes a label at the bottom of the first page that says "Contributed by Cindy Childs." Any family member with knowledge of the whereabouts of the original letter, or the compilation to which it was contributed, is asked to share this information with the author at *therunawayhaleystory@gmail.com*.

Thursday, October 22, 1992
The Conservative (Carrollton, Mississippi)

Haley-Corley reunion a success

On Sunday, October 11, 1992, 140 members of the
family of Robert Lee and Annie Corley Haley gathered at the
Carrollton Community House to renew old acquaintances,
meet new family members, share happy memories and
enjoy a bountiful meal prepared by the best cooks in the
world.

The weather was perfect, the Community House
was very comfortable and was decorated with large fall
arrangements of magnolia, cotton, pampas grass and
brown cattails. Three long tables covered with antique
quilts which were made by family members held photos
of early ancestors.

The only living children of Robert and Annie Haley are
Rogers Haley and Mrs. Ruby Lott, who were kept busy
identifying photos and answering questions about various
family connections. After registration was completed, and
church attenders arrived, dinner was served.

After lunch, Brenda Dunlap, daughter of Hermit (sic)
Haley led the group in sharing some of their favorite
memories, especially those fun times when everyone went
for a family gathering at the Grandma Haley's house, and
those times when "times were hard" economically but
because of hard working parents and good management,
no one went hungry or was not well-clothed.

Mr. Leo Rasberry of Hernando, whose wife (now
deceased) was Annie Frances Taylor, gave each one a

Descendancy Chart. From this chart, we find that Robert Lee Haley, son of Michael Haley of Ireland, married Annie Iona Corley, daughter of Harriette and Silas Corley, and from this union there were born into this family 15 children.

Their first child named Hattie was born in 1892. She died as an infant. During the next 24 years, they lost one son who was 11 years old, and a set of twins while infants. The remaining 11 children gave the Haleys' 46 grandchildren and a host of great-grandchildren who were in attendance. The oldest person present was John Taylor of Grenada, husband of the deceased Mattie Haley Taylor, and the youngest in attendance was his great-great-granddaughter Ashley, age three months, the daughter of Mr. and Mrs. Joe Evans. John will be 95 in December. Running a close second in age was Mrs. Ruby Lott whose birthday was celebrated on the day of the reunion, October 11. She became 91, had a cake and all the little ones present sang the traditional happy birthday song to her.

The grandsons of Robert Haley's sister, Fannie Smith, who live in south Mississippi were present. Several members of the Corley family were present. Everyone was thankful that Birteen H. DeLapp has recovered enough from her illness that she could be present. The Melvin Corley children were also present.

Future plans are to compile a book of Haley-Corley recipes and memoirs to share with each other at the next reunion. We cherish those good, wholesome times and look forward to the next one.

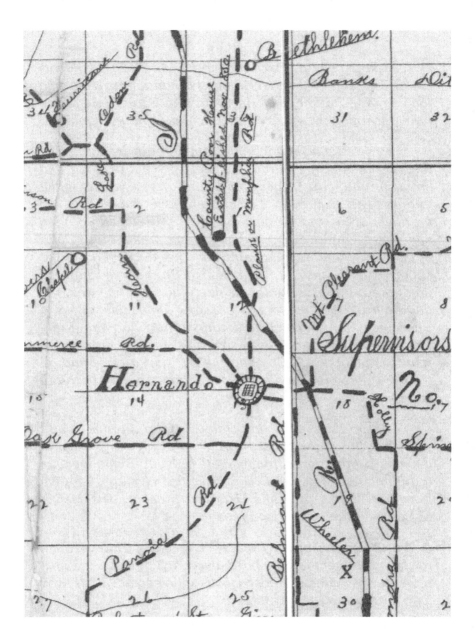

Detail: Logan's 1904 map of DeSoto County, Mississippi. Note the location of the poorhouse between the railroad tracks and the plank road to Memphis. (Courtesy of the Archives and Records Services Division, Mississippi Department of Archives and History.)

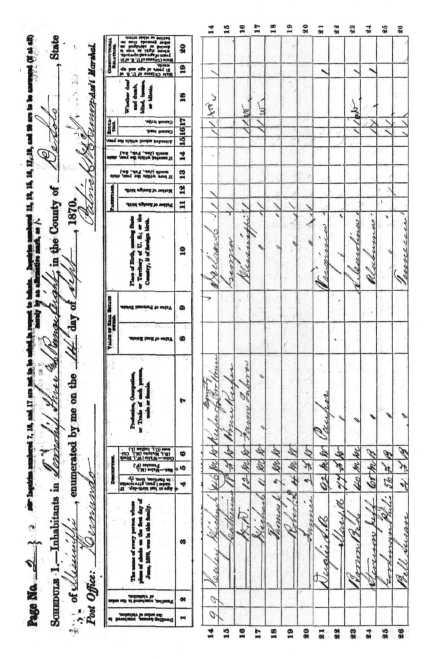

*Details from the 1870 Census Report, Hernando
(DeSotoCounty), Mississippi. (National Archives and Records
administration in association with Ancestry.Com Operations,
Inc, Provo UT, Year: 1870; Roll: M593_728; Page: 194B;
Image: 396; Family History Library Film: 552227.)*

*Robert Lee Haley family, (about 1910, Carroll County,
Mississippi). L-R: Sidney, Robert (with Earl), Mattie,
Silas, Annie (with Ethel), Helen, Linnie, Percy, Ruby, and
Marie. The original is a large colorized oval portrait owned
by Mrs. Terry R. Jones of Grenada, Mississippi*

Fannie Smith and Robert Lee Haley, (about 1927).
The location of this visit is unclear. Other photos in the series
show the siblings sitting on a front porch, and there is a
photo of Annie and Robert together, but none of Monroe.

Fannie and (L-R) Isabel, Otho, Luther, and Idabel,
about 1908, Harrison (now Stone) County, Mississippi.
Original photo unknown.

Monroe, Marion, Robert, and Fannie,
about 1914, Stone County, Mississippi.
Original photo unknown.

Three Generations of Descendants of
Michael Haley (1823-1873?)
and
Sophronia Adeline White (1833-1869?)

(Compiled from Various Sources)

1. Margaret Katherine Haley (1852-1927)

   m. Peter M. McHugh (1848-1920)

   1.1. William Thomas McHugh (1873-1904)

      m. Josie Lena Hearn (1874-1949)

      1.1.1. William Otto McHugh (1897-1981)

   1.2. Peter M. McHugh (1878-1951)

      m. Chloe Peeler (1885-1966)

      1.2.1. David Austin McHugh (1913-1917)

      1.2.2. Harriett Peeler McHugh (1917-1991)

      1.2.3. Robert Thomas Mc Hugh (1922-1946)

   1.3. Molly McHugh (1879-1879)

   1.4. Ella Mae McHugh (1880-1966)

      m. William Mace Hearn (1877-1932)

1.4.1. Della Mae Hearn (1899-1977)

1.4.2. Eva Lee Hearn (1901-1983)

1.4.3. William Gratis Hearn (1906-1960)

1.4.4. Margaret Lou Hearn (1911-2002)

1.5. John McHugh (1883-1883)

1.6. Katherine McHugh (1883-1932)

   m.   William G. Orr (1876-?)

   1.6.1. Naomi H. Orr (1904-1991)

1.7. Margaret Katherine McHugh (1885-1961)

1.8. Mary Alice McHugh (1888-1932)

   m.   Robert Thomas Wyatt (1890-1956)

   1.8.1. Infant Harold

   1.8.2. Alma Lurline Wyatt (1920-1986)

   1.8.3. Imogene Wyatt (1921- 2000)

   1.8.4. Mary Alice Wyatt (1926-2006)

   1.8.5. Mack Wilson Wyatt (1926-2011)

1.9. William Wallace McHugh (1890-1951)

   m.   Fredna Crockett (1901-1925)

   m.   Winnie Edwards (1906-1981) – had no children

   1.9.1. William Wallace McHugh. Jr. (1921-1996)

1.10. Edward Bruce McHugh (1893-1951)

    m. Hautie Mae Reed (1900-1981)

    1.10.1. Ruby Margarie McHugh (1921-2007)

    1.10.2. Helen Justine McHugh (1927-2001)

1.11. Charles Omega McHugh (1895-1938)

    m. Lois Gray Hale (1893-1968)

    1.11.13. Jules Rudolph McHugh (1925-1997)

2. W. D. Haley (1858- ?) Full name unknown.
No known marriage or descendants.

3. Michael Haley Jr. (1859-1887)

    m. Annie McLean, who had a daughter, Etta (Henrietta?)

No known children

4. Thomas J. (Jefferson?) Haley (1863-1943)

    m. Emma Redus Moore, a widow with two
children (Elizabeth and Eugenia).

    4.1. Jacob Whitten Haley (1893-1958)

        m. Mary Edith Wade (1896-1937)

        m. Katie Gertrude Franks (1894-1987)
        second wife–no known children

        4.1.1. Mary Lucille Haley (1918-1985)

        4.1.2. Annie Jean Haley (1919-1987)

        4.1.3. Dorothy Rose Haley (1927-2006)

    4.2. Charlie Acree Haley (1897-1963) — no known children

        m. Mattie Velma Holloway (1902-1984)

4.3. Sidney Haley (1900-1973)

    m.   Ila Hugh Rena (1895-1950)

    4.3.1. Ila Hugh Rena (1921-1992)

5. Robert Lee Haley (1866-1934)

    m. Annie Iona Corley (1874-1949)

    5.1. Hattie Iona Haley (1892-1894)

    5.2. Helen Iona Haley (1894-1978)

        m. Seabron Gray Turner (1885-1965)

        5.2.1. Robert Haley Turner (1914-1979)

        5.2.2. Dorothy Helen Turner (1916-1988)

        5.2.3. Annie Naomi Turner (1920-2002)

        5.2.4. Claudine Rebecca Turner (1921-1999)

        5.2.5. Hazel Emily Turner (1924-1981)

        5.2.6. Norma Gray Turner (1931-2014)

    5.3. Linnie Estelle Haley (1896-1988)

        m. Henry Grady Campbell (1895-1969)

        5.3.1. Eveline C. Campbell (1922-1953)

        5.3.2. Estelle Campbell (1920-)

        5.3.3. Lloyd Edwin Campbell (1923-1998)

        5.3.4. Sadie Lee Campbell (1927-)

        5.3.5. David Henderson Campbell (1929-2014)

        5.3.6. Mary Allen Campbell (1932-)

5.4. Robert Percy Haley (1898-1932)

   m. Florence Nail (1902-1991)

   5.4.1. Irene Haley (1919-2013)

   5.4.2. Birteen Haley (1922-2012)

   5.4.3. Louise Haley (1924-2015)

   5.4.4. Infant Haley (1926)

   5.4.5. Sarah Odella Haley (1929-1995)

5.5. Mattie Idella Haley (1899-1950)

   m. John William Taylor (1897-1996)

   5.5.1. Vera Iona Taylor (1917-2010)

   5.5.2. Noble Everett Taylor (1918-2012)

   5.5.3. Pauline Taylor (1920-2011)

   5.5.4. Hilda Taylor (1922-2008)

   5.5.5. Robert Earl Taylor (1925-1925)

   5.5.6. Annie Francis Taylor (1926-1983)

   5.5.7. Johnnie Dean Taylor (female) (1931-)

5.6. Ruby Lee Haley (1901-1996) – had no children

   m. Claude Roy Lott (1902-1990)

5.7. Tessie Marie Haley (1903-1974)

   m. William Robert McDaniel (1902-1975)

   5.7.1. Infant McDaniel (1933)

   5.7.2. William R. McDaniel (1936-1936)

   5.7.3. Edwin Lee McDaniel (1939-1960)

5.8. Sidney Thomas Haley (1905-1951)

    m.   Hilton Hull (1910-1935) – had no children

    m.   Sallie Rebecca Herbert (1915-2009)

    5.8.1. Christopher Lee Haley (1943-1990)

    5.8.2. Sidney Thomas Haley (1947-2000)

    5.8.3. Lanny Lynn Haley (1951-)

5.9. Silas Coleman Haley (1906-1918)

5.10. Earl Myrtis Haley (1908-1985)

    m.   Mayzelle Nail (1914-2006)

    5.10.1. Maxine Haley (1932-2018)

    5.10.2. James Robert Haley (1936-1995)

    5.10.3. Ocie Dale Haley (male) (1939-2008)

    5.10.4. Jerry Lee Haley (1944-)

    5.10.5. Sandra Faye Haley (1950-1966)

5.11. Ethel Cornelia Haley (1910-1938)

    m.   Sam T. Lawrence (1905-1966)

    5.11.1. James Coleman Lawrence (1929-1977)

    5.11.2. Ann Augusta Lawrence (1931-1997)

    5.11.3. Barbara Jean Lawrence (1935-2012)

5.12. Kermit Deward Haley (1912-1985)

    m.   Kate Brunson (1918-2010)

    5.12.1. Brenda Haley (1951-)

    5.12.2. Kermit David Haley (1957-2014)

5.13. Infant Twin A Haley (1914-1914)

5.14. Infant Twin B Haley (1914-1915)

5.15. Rogers Corley Haley (1916-2001)

    m. Nell Marie Miller (1922-2005)

    5.15.1. Robert Lynn Haley (1943-)

    5.15.2. Richard Wayne Haley (1947-)

    5.15.3. William Glenn Haley (1954 -)

    5.15.4. Martin Bruce Haley (1960-)

6. Fannie Haley (1867-1948)

    m. William Smith (1819-1896) – had no children

    m. Monroe Smith (1875-1958)

      (m. Nancy Ladner, second wife, m. after 1948)

6.1. Albert Otho Smith (1898-1975)

    m. Gussie Mettis Dale (1913-1936) – had six children

    m. Polly Yhetive Dale (1913-2001) – had five children

    6.1.1. James Harrison Smith (1921-1985)

    6.1.2. Cliff Thomas Smith (1923-1995)

    6.1.3. Howard Otho Smith (1925-1997)

    6.1.4. Juanice Melinee Smith (1927-2015)

    6.1.5. Gene Cody Smith (1931-2011)

    6.1.6. Jimmie Stewart Smith (1933-2009)

    6.1.7. Annie Mae Smith (1936-)

    6.1.8. Derril Monroe Smith (1942-2002)

6.1.9. Daisy Evelyn Smith (1943-)

6.1.10. Dennis Delno Smith 1946-2017)

6.1.11. John Haley Smith (1948-)

6.1.12. Fannie Greye Smith (1952-)

6.2. Luther Smith (1899-1982)

    m.   Grace I. Dale (1899-1971)

    6.2.1. Elvidge Monroe Smith (1924-2008)

    6.2.2. Doyle Preston Smith (male) (1926-2005)

    6.2.3. Mary Idona Smith (1932-2017)

6.3. Idabell Smith (1901-1918)

6.4. Isabell Smith (1904-1985)

    m.   Aldredge E. Smith (1905-1979)

    6.4.1. Allen Keaton Smith (1932-2003)

    6.4.2. Virginia Smith (1932-)

    6.4.3. Nobie Ruth Smith (1936-)

    6.4.4. Johnny Boy Smith (1937-2006)

    6.4.5. Harold Dean Smith (1945-)

6.5. Marion Monroe Smith (1909-1941)

6.6. Robert Edward Smith (1911-1971)

    m.   Flossie Olivia Davis (1915-1973)

    6.6.1. Gaynes Edward Smith (1937-2012)

    6.6.2. Marie Smith (1939-2011)

    6.6.3. Robbie Sandra Smith (1941-2018)

❖ References

Letter from Monroe Smith to Ruby Haley Lott, January 1958. Copy of original passed to the author by email from Cindy Childs.

The Federal Union, (Milledgeville, Georgia), 10 Feb 1852, retrieved from https://gahistoricnewspapers.galileo.usg.edu/lccn/sn86053071/1852-02-10/ed-1/.

The Weekly Chronicle and Sentinel, (Augusta, Georgia), 25 Aug 1852, retrieved from https://gahistoricnewspapers.galileo.usg.edu/lccn/sn82014777/1852-08-25/ed-1.

The Southern Recorder, (Milledgeville, Georgia), 19 Oct 1852, retrieved from https://gahistoricnewspapers.galileo.usg.edu/lccn/sn82016415/1852-10-19/ed-1/.

Bryan, Lettice, *The Kentucky Housewife, 1841,* Cincinnati, Shepard and Stearns, p. 268, retrieved from https://www.loc.gov/resource/rbc0001.2015ge n16076/?sp=276.

The Dunbrody Famine Ship Experience, New Ross, County Wexford, Ireland, reproduction of 1846 Passenger Contract Ticket from William Graves and Sons Shipping, Used with permission of the company.

The Southern Recorder, (Milledgeville, Georgia), 18 Apr 1848, retrieved from https://gahistoricnewspapers.galileo.usg.edu/lccn/sn82016415/1848-04-18/ed-1/.

Marriage Index DeKalb County, Georgia, 1840-1908, Ancestry.com. [database on-line]. Provo, UT, USA: Ancestry.com Operations, Inc., 2014.

Death Register, Shelby County, Tennessee, 12 May 1855, retrieved from http://register.shelby.tn.us/imgView. php?imgtype=pdf&id=28301855051 21%20YR.

The Semi-Weekly Mississippian, (Jackson, Mississippi), 7 August 1860, retrieved from https://www.newspapers.com/ image/223342164.

Probate Court Records, DeSoto County, Mississippi. Author's photograph of the original which is on file in archives of the Genealogical Society of DeSoto County, Hernando, Mississippi.

The Memphis Daily Appeal, (Memphis, Tennessee), 13 Apr 1861, retrieved from https://newspapers.com/image/39785706.

The Memphis Daily Appeal, (Memphis, Tennessee), 4 Apr 1862, retrieved from https://newspapers.com/image/39798245.

The Memphis Daily Appeal, (Memphis, Tennessee), 8 Apr 1862, retrieved from https://newspapers.com/image/39798289.

The Memphis Daily Appeal, (Memphis, Tennessee), 9 Apr 1862, retrieved from https://newspapers.com/image/39798335.

National Park Service. U.S. Civil War Soldiers, 1861-1865 [database on-line]. Provo, UT, USA: Ancestry.com Operations Inc, 2007, film M231, Roll 18, retrieved from https://www.fold3. com/image/67172710.

The Memphis Daily Appeal, (Memphis, Tennessee), 15 Sept 1862, retrieved from https://newspapers.com/image/39802599.

Hernando Press, (Hernando, Mississippi), 5 Sep 1867. Author's photograph of the original, which is on file in the DeSoto County Courthouse.

Agreed Rate of Medical Charges, 1848, Historical Collections and Services, The Claude Moore Health Sciences Library, University of Virginia, retrieved from http://blog.hsl.virginia. edu/feebill/wp-content/uploads/sites/12/2011/05/Fee-Bill1. jpg.

Hernando Press, (Hernando, Mississippi), 2 Jan 1868. Author's photograph of the original, which is on file in the DeSoto County Courthouse.

Hernando Press, (Hernando, Mississippi), 10 Sep 1868. Author's photograph of the original, which is on file in the DeSoto County Courthouse.

Hernando Press, (Hernando, Mississippi), citation of 1868 newspaper advertisement from Bell, J.B., Hernando Historic Windows, 1986, (no publisher identified), courtesy of the Hernando Public Library.

Public Ledger, (Memphis, Tennessee), 24 Mar 1870, retrieved from https://newspapers.com/image/215145793.

Hernando Press, (Hernando, Mississippi), 9 Jun 1870. Author's photograph of the original, which is on file in the DeSoto County Courthouse.

Hernando Press, (Hernando, Mississippi), 18 August 1870. Author's photograph of the original, which is on file in the DeSoto County Courthouse.

The Weekly Panola Star, (Sardis, Mississippi), 8 Oct 1870, retrieved from https://newspapers.com/image/328857107.

Hernando Press, (Hernando, Mississippi), 16 May 1872. Author's photograph of the original, which is on file in the DeSoto County Courthouse.

The Weekly Panola Star, (Sardis, Mississippi), 23 Nov 1872, retrieved from https://newspapers.com/image/328841872.

The Memphis Daily Appeal, (Memphis, Tennessee), 14 Sep 1873, retrieved from https://newspapers.com/image/39803852.

Public Ledger, (Memphis, Tennessee), 3 Oct 1873, retrieved from https://newspapers.com/image/145510372.

Public Ledger, (Memphis, Tennessee), 14 Oct 1873, retrieved from https://newspapers.com/image/145510741.

The Memphis Daily Appeal, (Memphis, Tennessee), 14 Oct 1873, retrieved from https://newspapers.com/image/164526462.

The Memphis Daily Appeal, (Memphis, Tennessee), 15 Oct 1873, retrieved from https://newspapers.com/image/164526711.

The Memphis Daily Appeal, (Memphis, Tennessee), 17 Jan 1874, retrieved from https://www.newspapers.com/image/39783376.

The Memphis Daily Appeal, (Memphis, Tennessee), 2 Apr 1876, retrieved from https://www.newspapers.com/image/78661609.

Tenth Census of the United States, 1880. (NARA microfilm publication T9, 1,454 rolls). Records of the Bureau of the Census, Record Group 29. National Archives, Washington, D.C.; Census Place: Hamburg, Franklin, Mississippi; Roll: 647; Page: 36C; Enumeration District: 144.

The Natchez Democrat, (Natchez, Mississippi), 26 Mar 1882, retrieved from https://www.newspapers.com/image/235211227.

The Carroll Conservative, (Carrollton, Mississippi), 20 Feb 1886, retrieved from https://www.newspapers.com/image/317499475.

The Clarion-Ledger, (Jackson, Mississippi), 18 Mar 1886, retrieved from https://www.newspapers.com/image/264410065.

The Vicksburg Herald, (Vicksburg, Mississippi), 19 March 1886, retrieved from https://www.newspapers.com/image/36762174.

The Clarion, (Jackson, Mississippi), 24 March 1886, retrieved from https://www.newspapers.com/image/10235029.

Certified copy of Marriage Bond, Author's copy provided by the Clerk of court, Harrison County, Mississippi.

Carroll County Marriage Bond, transcription from author's photograph of the original, which is on file in the Carroll County, Mississippi, Courthouse.

Vicksburg Eve Post (Vicksburg, Mississippi), 1 November 1895, retrieved from https://www.newspapers.com/image/213281496.

The Free Press, (Poplarville, Miss), 9 Apr 1896, retrieved from microfilm at the Mississippi Department of Archives and History, Jackson, Mississippi.

Greenville Times, (Greenville, Mississippi), 25 Nov 1896, retrieved from https://www.newspapers.com/image/267315537.

Land Deed, DeSoto County, Mississippi, Tax Records, transcriptions of copies passed to the author, original on file in archives of DeSoto County Genealogical Society, Hernando, Mississippi.

Land Deed, DeSoto County, Mississippi, Tax Records, transcriptions of copies passed to the author, original on file in archives of DeSoto County Genealogical Society, Hernando, Mississippi.

The Conservative, (Carrollton, Mississippi), 2 Feb 1934, retrieved from microfilm at the Mississippi Department of Archives and History, Jackson, Mississippi. Used with permission of the publisher.

Certified copy of Marriage Affidavit, Author's copy provided by the Clerk of court, Harrison County, Mississippi.

The Weekly Democrat, (Poplarville, Mississippi), 1 April 1948, retrieved from microfilm at the Mississippi Department of Archives and History, Jackson, Mississippi. Used with permission of the publisher.

The Conservative, (Carrollton, Mississippi), 22 Oct 1992, retrieved from https://www.newspapers.com/image/268610656. Used with permission of the publisher.

❖ Acknowledgments

It was before eight o'clock in the morning in mid-August of 2018 when I turned my blue pick-up truck off Mississippi Highway Fifty-One north, following the sign pointing to the tiny town of Oakland, in western Yalobusha County. I was on my second or third research trip, headed to Hernando to read the newspapers in the courthouse, but I wanted to at least drive through Oakland to get a vision of the place where Robert Lee Haley had spent several years in his youth as a ward of Mr. A. J. Black. The middle of the tiny town had a view up to a big house on the hill in a pasture overlooking the spot where the road crossed the train tracks on its way toward a small set of long-abandoned store fronts. Nothing stirred.

A lone car sat in front of the trailer that bore a sign identifying it as the Oakland Health clinic, and I pulled in and parked next to it to have a look around. The clinic had just opened at eight o'clock, so I went up the stairs and pulled on the door. A little bell sounded my entrance, but there was no one in the waiting room at this hour. The nurse seated at the desk behind a window slid the glass to the side and greeted me. Her nametag said "Hope."

"The nurse practitioner won't be in until nine," she said.

"That's ok." I introduced myself and started in on my spiel. For the next several minutes I told her all about my research, how my "one of wife's people" had started out here in the 1870s and the interesting story that I was chasing. "Is there somebody around who knows about the town's history, and can tell me about some of the folks who still live around here?" I asked.

"Sure," she said. "Come on back here."

She got up and opened the hallway door, then led me past a few empty exam rooms to the back door of the clinic, which she went through to stand on the back porch.

"See that house over there?" She pointed across a small yard, through some old oaks, and across the railroad track toward a wooden structure dating to the early 1900s—a large white house with a dormer on the roof and a broad front porch. "Mrs. Margaret Ross lives there. She knows everybody and everything. You ought to go talk to her."

"Do you think you could call her and ask for me?" I figured an introduction from a friend might help. "She might not like a total stranger knocking on her door in the morning unannounced."

"Sure," said Hope. "Come on."

We returned to the front of the building where she picked up the phone and dialed the number from memory. Mrs. Ross must have answered on the first ring. I heard Hope retell an abbreviated version of my tale; then she hung up.

"She said for you to come on over."

Surprised, I thanked Hope, and made my exit, pulling the truck out of the small lot, crossing the tracks, and turning right onto the aptly named Oak Street. In under a minute, I pulled up in front of Mrs. Ross' home, where she was watching for me. She pushed open the screen door and stepped out onto the front porch in her slippers and housecoat. She was tiny, bespectacled, and grey-haired with a warm, pleasant smile. Getting out of the truck, I introduced myself from thirty feet away, down on the gravel drive, aware that I was almost certainly an imposition, and not wanting to allow my height to somehow be threatening.

"Good morning, Ma'am. My name is Bill Thomas. I was wondering about this town. Hope, over at the clinic, she said that you know the local history. Would it be OK if I called you sometime to ask some questions?" I went on some more about my project and what brought me out this far, as she listened intently.

"Won't you please come in?" she said. "I do have some things I can show you." She turned back to the screen door and pulled it open. "Would you like some breakfast?"

I paused, suddenly uncomfortable with my obtuse and untimely interruption. Nevertheless, I was tickled and humbled— grateful to find that genuine Southern hospitality still existed. "Well, yes, Ma'am. If it's not too much trouble."

"No trouble. Already made." She held the screen door open behind her as I came up the stairs to the wooden porch. I could smell the bacon.

For the next two hours we sat at her kitchen table while she shared with me her memories and old photographs of the Oakland that used to be, along with bacon, homegrown tomatoes, biscuits, and strong coffee. When her daughter Carol joined us, we found that we had overlapped a year at Ole Miss in 1983 and talked about the women's basketball program that she had been involved with.

As I left with directions to the cemetery, headed to find the graves of A. J. Black and Mr. Ladd, I asked the eighty-five-year-old Mrs. Ross if she was a native of Oakland—I assumed that she was.

"Oh no," she replied. "I was born up in Quitman County. My parents moved here with me when I was three months old."

~

I am very thankful for the support and encouragement of my family and friends, especially my wife Paula and my mother-in-law Josephine Haley Neill Browning. I also appreciate the input from the new friends and distant relatives that I have met while working on this project.

The following provided valuable information and anecdotes: Tom Smith, June Trehern, and Cathy Smith Coffman (some of Fannie's descendants); Yancy DeLapp, Brenda Haley Davis, Bruce Moore, Cindy Rasberry Childs, and Terry Rasberry Jones (some of Robert's descendants); Judy Grimes (one of Katherine's descendants); Brian Rena (one of Thomas's descendants); and Arthur Broady and Marcia Kidder. I must also thank the staff at the Carroll County Courthouse, the staff at the DeSoto County Courthouse, and the DeSoto County Genealogical Society, whose assistance was invaluable.

Thank you, also, to my manuscript readers whose input, suggestions, and encouragement were extremely important: Cynthia Bennett, Allen Edmunds, Keenan Templeton, Megan Arrington, Melynda Poss, Lee Baker, Karen Stokes, and Sarah Frances Munzenrider.

Most importantly, I must acknowledge Mr. William Greenleaf, whose critique, coaching, and editing have taught me a great deal and have helped to improve this work tremendously.

In the scenes from the Civil War, I included several characters that are taken from Shelby Foote's 1952 novel, *Shiloh*, although I didn't use the names that he'd given them. The Union officer killed in his camp by cannon fire while writing a letter to his fiancée; the boy who suffered a bayonet wound and wore a checkered shirt made of homespun cloth, and the lieutenant he talks with on their way back to Corinth; the lieutenant who led Colonel Nathan Bedford Forrest and the reconnaissance party in disguise—all originated in Mr. Foote's novel.

About The Author

WILLIAM THOMAS became interested in genealogy in 2015. He had several source documents for Michael Haley and his children, but they only led to dead ends and left many unanswered questions. When he came across the letter that Monroe Smith sent to Ruby Haley Lott in 1958, he was compelled to write something to fill in the gaps of the amazing story.

After graduating from Ole Miss in 1987 and then the University of Mississippi School Of Medicine in 1991, Dr. Thomas completed a career in the U. S. Air Force as an Internal Medicine Physician, Flight Surgeon and Commander. He is married to Paula Ann Haley, a great-granddaughter of Robert Lee Haley. They live in Augusta, Georgia and have two sons. This is his first novel.

SOUTHERN LITERATURE is the glory of American culture. Faulkner, O'Connor, Warren, Lytle, Davidson, Gordon, Percy, Chappell, Berry will be known as long as Western civilization survives and long after today's politicians, "experts," and celebrity writers are forgotten. Another of the greats, George Garrett, wrote that "all signs indicate that Southern literature, far from being on its last legs and far from representing a falling off from earlier and better days, seems very much alive." Shotwell Publishing supports Garrett's witness by launching the imprint Green Altar Books—a collection of Southern Literature.

GREEN ALTAR BOOKS
SHOTWELL PUBLISHING

Made in the USA
Monee, IL
31 August 2020

40623871R00213